AMERICAN PIED PIPER

AMERICAN PIED PIPER

~ The ~
AMERICAN TRILOGY
BOOK 3

A NOVEL

SAM FOSTER

Research materials which have been used to direct the narrative include: *History of Cass County, Illinois*, edited by William Henry Perring; *History of Cass County 1915*, by Charles A. Martin; *Historical Encyclopedia of Illinois* and *History of Cass County*, by Bateman; "Beardstown Yesterday and Today 1829–1979," by *Beardstown Gazette*; the Great Courses; *Los Angeles*, by Benedikt Taschen; *Caught in the Middle*, by Richard C. Longworth; *The Boys in the Boat*, by Daniel James Brown; *The Beardstown Ladies' Common-Sense Investment Guide*. Also, newspapers including *Chicago Tribune*, *New York Times*, Bloomberg, and various issues of newspapers from Beardstown and Cass County, Illinois, from 1834–1999, including: *Beardstown Chronicle and Illinois Military Bounty*; *Beardstown Gazette*; *Beardstown and Petersburg Gazette*; *Central Illinoian*; *Beardstown Democrat*; *Cass County Messenger*; *Beardstown Enterprise*; *Beardstown Star West*; *Illinoian-Star* and *Cass County Star-Gazette*, and finally, Google. With very special thanks to the research staff and librarians of the Abraham Lincoln Presidential Library.

Published by Agave Americana Books™, Redondo Beach, California
samfosterbooks.com

Cover design: Rachel Marek
Project management: Emilie Sandoz-Voyer
Developmental editing: Dan Crissman
Cover image credits: © Rita Asia Chow (illustration)
and © W. Phokin/Shutterstock (texture)

ISBN (hardcover): 979-8-9884064-1-9
ISBN (paperback): 979-8-9884064-0-2
ISBN (ebook): 979-8-9884064-2-6

Library of Congress Control Number: 2023913345

PRAISE FOR *AMERICAN PIED PIPER,*
BOOK 3 OF THE AMERICAN TRILOGY

"A highly readable and engaging narrative. . . . This book skillfully explores themes of individuality and collective identity, offering readers multiple perspectives on how best to make a community thrive. A solid final volume."

—Kirkus Reviews

"An engrossing historical trilogy. . . . Sam Foster has crafted a compelling exploration of a town's transformation over a century . . . [with] winding turns and captivating plotlines. Foster's storytelling perfectly captures the essence of a changing era and the moral dilemmas faced by its characters."

—Readers' Favorite

"Sweeping across four generations, Foster's take on the American Adamic myth is sure to spark lively debate. . . . I'm sure you'll enjoy the trip."

—Mike Zarro, forty-year member of
the State Bar of California

PRAISE FOR *BEARDSTOWN,*
BOOK 2 OF THE AMERICAN TRILOGY

"Informative and engaging, with solid pacing and engaging dialogue that keep the plot moving steadily over its half-century timeline. Foster has a deep knowledge of the history of both the region and the era, and his well-developed characters transform a timeline of events into a captivating tale. An epic novel."

—Kirkus Reviews

"At times tragic and at times triumphant, *Beardstown* serves as both cautionary tale and blueprint for any would-be city builder. In this literary tour de force and part two of an American trilogy about western frontier expansion, Foster pens a novel so wrought with ambition, grief, exultation, and relief that the sheer weight of emotion overwhelms the reader while reminding us that the grueling work of placemaking is never done. Foster brings all of this to life in rich detail, with just the right amounts of detachment and sympathy. He's a master at his craft and one who's fun to read. I can't wait for part three."
　　—Ron Starner, executive vice president of Conway Data, Inc.

"Sam Foster's tale of life on the midwestern frontier relates very well with current issues facing industrial development. . . . [an] amazingly entertaining story."
—Ron L. Frierson, director of economic
policy, City of Los Angeles

"Once again Sam Foster has delivered an incredibly delightful novel. As a man setting out to build a modern American city two hundred years after Tom Beard showed up on the banks of the Illinois River, I really identified with the characters. Especially Tom Beard, who is asked, 'Who will build the churches and schools?' by his business partner. 'We will,' he says, 'because we are empire builders; the others are just in it for the money.'"
—Randy Kendrick, developer of Hayden,
Texas, America's city of the future

"A wonderfully done historical novel on the battle for the Midwest. I can't wait to read the third book in the American Trilogy series . . . and anything else Sam Foster writes."
—Catraphoenix, book blogger

weaves together historical facts with a fertile imagination. The result is a thought-provoking novel that is a must-read not only for history enthusiasts but for readers of all ages."

—Readers' Favorite

*This book is dedicated to my grandfather, who first
introduced me to many of the places and stories
included here. But more than that, he taught me
enough about human character to begin to understand
that a man's choices make him what he is.*

PART I

THE CALL

In Italy, for thirty years under the Borgias, they had warfare, terror, murder, and bloodshed, but they produced Michelangelo, Leonardo da Vinci, and the Renaissance. In Switzerland, they had brotherly love, they had five hundred years of democracy and peace—and what did they produce? The cuckoo clock.

—Orson Welles as Harry Lime
in *The Third Man* (1949)

CHAPTER 1

October 25, 1906
Mokane, Missouri

The huge birds rose in a slow upward spiral, their long black necks and heads extended stiff as tree branches before their fat grey-brown bodies; the brilliant white triangle, formed from the back of their heads to the bottom of their necks, evoked the image of the chin strap below a palace guard's black beaver hat. But what it really was, was a perfect target.

C.C. Cunningham had fired both barrels as soon as the flock of Canada geese rose from the quiet eddy downstream. He had missed both times. Sam Clark rose slowly from the blind, all six feet of him standing tall and all two hundred pounds poised, a granite statue, holding the big 10 gauge pointed straight up into the sky.

As the lead bird leveled out, the others rose to it, forming their flying "V" to head upriver.

"Sam, even you will never reach them now."

Without moving, the statue answered, "Bet you twenty-five cents, Mr. Cunningham."

"You're on, son."

Over the steady honking of the flock came the tremendous roar of the big long-barreled shotgun. A second later they watched as the lead bird's head snapped up into an impossible angle and then the bird tumbled, no glide at all, the body rolling over the head again and again, its fall ending in a large splash into the Missouri River.

The rust-brown dog, with curls waving down the length of his back, sat at the front of the blind, a statue just as his master had been save that the tip of his pink tongue jerked in and out of his mouth, steadily drooling saliva. Clark said not a word but leaned down low enough for the motion of his hand to show in his dog's peripheral vision, palm flat and fingers held rigidly together as he swung his arm in an arch from his hips to his waist. The dog bolted from a sitting position into the air, a vision of leaping perfection, hind legs extended behind, front legs tight up against his chest, only his paws hanging down and his head extended as far forward from his body as his neck would allow. The leap pulled him two feet off the ground and landed him five feet into the river with a splash. He didn't head to the floating body of the goose but swam as directly out into the current as he was able until he was as far from the shore as the goose. Only then did he turn his head upstream and dog-paddle easily until the drifting trophy floated into his mouth. He turned and headed to shore, the current pushing him downstream as he went.

"I believe you owe me twenty-five cents, Mr. Cunningham," Sam said.

Cunningham had long since risen from his camp stool to admire everything he had just seen—the majesty of the bird, the not-to-be-believed skill of the shot, and the perfection of the training of the retriever.

"Nobody can shoot flyers that high. I wouldn't have thought even you could do it, Sam," Cunningham said, looking into the light-brown eyes of Sam Clark. He saw a man of no more than twenty, but a man nonetheless. There was no boy in his face anymore. His mass of light-brown hair was almost as wavy as his dog's. The face was wide and the jaw square. The rounded ears lay quietly against the side of his face. Only his nose, which was long and straight but a bit too thick, saved him from being handsome. His lips were neither thick nor thin, but something about them and the flare of his nostrils, even in this small moment of glory and in his role as guide to his father's boss and manager of this entire line of the Missouri, Kansas and Eastern Railroad, showed a hint of cruelty, or perhaps just arrogance.

C.C. Cunningham reached in his pocket, took out a quarter, and flipped it into the air. Sam looked once, extended his hand palm up, and allowed the falling coin to drop into it.

"How do you do it?"

Sam smiled now. It was a smile that softened his face and made him look a touch humble. "I've been doing it as long as I can remember. Shotgun shells are not cheap, and what hard money I ever got was from running a trapline. This time of year, furs aren't worth much yet, so even if I bother to set the trapline, I don't earn as much. Not enough to buy a lot of extra ammunition for certain. So best not to miss; always has been really. Also, I'm prepared a bit differently than you or others." He held the shotgun before him and snapped open the breach. A huge shell popped out. "It's a 10 gauge, so a bit more giddyup than your 12. And I had in double-oh shot. Pretty small pattern, but it will reach a long way."

"Why did you let them get so high? You could have reached them as they circled downriver before they leveled out, but you didn't. Why?" Cunningham smiled now. "You just showing off, or egging me into betting that quarter?"

There was a crunching sound in the brush on the downriver side of the blind. The Chesapeake Bay retriever came crashing through, the goose in his mouth seeming almost as big as he, its head dragging on the ground on one side of the dog's mouth, its feet on the other. He sat down on Sam's left side.

Sam bent down until his hand was under the goose, under but not touching. "Give, Teddy," he commanded softly.

The beast dropped the goose into Sam's hand and then stood and shook, violently throwing water everywhere.

Sam used his other hand to scratch behind the dog's ears. "Good dog." Sam straightened up, shifting the goose so he held it by the neck just below its mangled head, the black tip of the tail still touching the ground. Sam finally answered the question. "Mr. Cunningham, I'm pleased to take your money, and it pleases me to be better with highflyers than most, but that wasn't the reason I let it go so long, sir. It was for your pleasure."

Cunningham cocked his head to one side, looking up at Sam, a quizzical, almost skeptical, expression on his face.

"In the eight years we've known each other, you and I have never hunted birds on the Missouri before. So you didn't know that the problem isn't finding birds. The problem is retrieving them from that current." He pointed to the river. "Teddy is the first Chessie I've ever owned. He's unbelievably strong, and that curly coat of his keeps him warm long after labs have given up. Aside from the fact he likes to fight a bit too much, he's the best dog I've ever owned. But even Teddy can't swim against the current of the Missouri. Only way he was going to retrieve your dinner was if I shot it upstream so he could let it float back to him. As it was, he was pushed a quarter mile downstream before he could get back to shore.

"So, it was for your dinner, sir." Sam held the goose up between them. "That's why I had to wait."

Cunningham beamed a big smile. The two men and the dog walked away from the river into the tree cover above the bank. The leaves were turning golden. The morning sun even revealed a few flashes of red in the canopy above. Enough of the leaves had fallen to make a soft crunching sound underfoot. The big palomino stallion and the smaller black mare stood where they had left them, tied to two small hickory trees. By the time Sam tied the goose behind his saddle, Cunningham was already up on the palomino. The big stallion nickered and nudged Sam's butt as he mounted. Sam, halfway up, stood in one stirrup, reached behind him, and scratched the white blaze down the middle of an otherwise golden face.

"I see the big guy likes you," Cunningham observed.

"I often ride him. But the stable belongs to your railroad. I figure he's yours. You should have him when you're here."

The two walked their horses slowly through the woods to the dirt road that ran along the bluff between Mokane and the bridge across the river at Jefferson City.

"Sam, you've been out of school for a couple of years now. Ever think about going to work for the railroad?" Cunningham inquired.

Sam gave a small laugh. "I already do, sir. I was born and raised in the only town named for a railroad—Missouri, MO, Kansas, KAN, and Eastern, E. MOKANE. My father has cooked in the railroad hotel my whole life. Everyone here works for the railroad. But I would like to drive for one."

Now it was Cunningham's turn to laugh. "Everyone wants to drive a locomotive. Those jobs are damn hard to come by. Seldom come along. How about working in the shop? I could get you a job there easily. Teach you pipe fitting and toolmaking and maybe even boiler making. Good money there."

"It's not that I'm not grateful, Mr. Cunningham. I am. It's kind of you to think of me. But that's just not me. I'm an outdoor guy. Being the engineer; driving a train; watching the world go by; seeing places. That would suit me just fine."

Cunningham pulled back on his reins and stopped the palomino. Sam followed his lead. The two sat facing one another in the shade of the tree-canopied lane.

"I'd like to help you, Sam. Like to have you with us. But an engineer's job just isn't in the cards even if I wanted to. We don't need any and don't know when we will."

Sam nodded and started back down the lane. When the stable was in sight, the two men rode in. Cunningham dismounted and handed Sam the reins of his horse. "Think about it, Sam. I'll be here all day and tonight. I leave in the morning on the 10:12 to Jeff City. Let me know if you change your mind."

* * * *

Sam used his left hand to push open the swinging doors separating the kitchen from the dining room. He held the serving tray high over his shoulder as he walked to the middle of the empty room. C.C. Cunningham sat alone at a round table, the picture of contemporary refinement. He was dressed in a three-piece sack suit, the white of his shirt showing only at the cuffs and the collar, his wide silk necktie covering up almost all the shirt not covered by his five-button vest. The gold watch chain looped between his vest pockets, shimmering even in the low light.

Cunningham saw him looking at it and pulled the large gold watch from one of his vest pockets and held it up by the chain. It became a swinging gold pendulum. "Ball Standard. Only kind a railroad man will have."

Sam lifted the cover off the soup bowl on the serving tray and placed the bowl in front of Cunningham as the railroad baron put the watch back into his vest pocket. "You always seem to like turtle soup, so I got one and had Dad simmer it all day. Hope you enjoy it. Goose will be ready in ten minutes."

Cunningham nodded. Sam collected the tray from the serving table, again hoisted it above his shoulder, and returned to the kitchen just in time to see his father take the goose from the oven and start cutting the delicious-smelling entrée.

"Sam, just five minutes to finish the vegetables and butter the potato and it will be ready for you."

Sam looked across the kitchen at his father working so rapidly to pull it all together. He looked small and old. *Why has he accepted this as his lot?* Sam stood by the half-high swinging doors and watched the back of Cunningham's head as he slowly spooned his soup.

Just then, the front door burst open and allowed in a blast of cold air as well as a stranger. The stranger looked bedraggled, cold, and very thin. It was a thinness not of athleticism or asceticism but starvation. His face was hidden behind a leather hat that looked as worn as he. The stranger shut the door and removed his hat, almost reverentially. It revealed a face gaunt enough to match the body. The cheekbones looked skeletally pronounced. The eyes were sunk so deep that Sam could not make out the color, but even from where he was, he could see they penetrated all they touched with a hellish flame. The man, the beast, whatever it was, walked with a measured pace, unbuttoning his threadbare coat as he came. When the last button parted, the coat fell open to reveal Levi's as worn as the coat and a pistol as powerful as his eyes. The holster hung low from his hip. The gun barrel was so long, it extended out the bottom of the holster. He walked steadily toward Cunningham, who sat watching him come.

When he reached Cunningham, the stranger carefully laid his hat on the table and said, "You're C.C. Cunningham." It was a statement, not a question.

Cunningham appraised the apparition before him carefully. "I am. I don't believe we've met."

"Oh, I know you, Mr. Cunningham, but no reason you'd remember me. I was twelve years old and part of a crowd. You were the station chief for Central Pacific in Fresno."

Cunningham's words came out with forced joviality. "I was

a very young man. Probably twenty-five. My first major assignment with any railroad."

"My parents bought eighty acres from the Central Pacific in 1876. Bought it cheap because there was nothing there and, until the railroad, no way to get crops to market even if there was. But the Central Pacific helped them get a mortgage and promised the new rail would make them prosper. And they did; everyone did, as you remember, Mr. Cunningham. Everyone did until you jacked up the rail rates so high, there was no profit left."

Cunningham started to rise.

The long Colt Peacemaker came out of the holster and leveled at his chest. "The day I saw you, Mr. Cunningham, was in 1882. You were on the courthouse steps. The bank had foreclosed on the mortgage, and the farm my parents worked themselves to the grave to make prosperous was being sold. We went to buy it back, knowing none of the neighbors would bid against us. But you did. You were surrounded by a pack of gunslingers to protect you from my parents and the other farmers. You bought our farm for past taxes and mortgage arrears. Daddy died the year after and Momma a couple later. I was fifteen when she died. That was twenty years ago. I been lookin' for you ever since."

Sam stepped back from the kitchen door, grabbed a serving tray, and threw the plate of goose on it.

"Sam, stop. It's not ready," his father called after him as Sam hoisted the tray to his shoulder and boldly threw open the door to the dining room.

The Colt muzzle came around until it was pointed at his chest. The bore got ever bigger as Sam got ever closer.

"No place for you here, son." The eyes said more than the words.

Sam kept coming. "Mister, I see you have business with Mr. Cunningham. That's between you and him. I have business with Mr. Cunningham as well, and I intend to do mine just as you intend to do yours." He set the tray down on the serving table and slid the plate of steaming goose in front of his guest. "I hope you'll find it as you like it, Mr. Cunningham."

Sam reached back to the serving tray, picked it up, and made a motion as if to hoist it to his shoulder. The edge of the tray slammed into the stranger's Adam's apple with a viciousness that drove him backward even as he dropped. Sam took one step toward the fallen man and kicked him between the legs. The only sound was the crunch of bone as the man, unable to scream through his crushed throat, grabbed at his groin. Sam picked up the fallen pistol, tucked it into his belt, grabbed one of the fallen man's wrists, and dragged him across the floor and out the front door.

He was back inside in less than two minutes, the gun belt thrown over his shoulder. "I've tied him to one of the posts on the porch. I'll let you decide what to do with him." Sam stopped and gave an amused smile. "I'm sorry about your goose. Pa wanted me to wait to bring it until he had the vegetables ready, but I thought you'd prefer it now."

A still-stunned C.C. Cunningham sat arms and legs akimbo and just nodded.

Five minutes later Sam came back from the kitchen, this time with the vegetables, a hot cup of coffee, a bottle of brandy, and a leaded crystal tumbler. "Thought you might want this, Mr. Cunningham," Sam offered.

Cunningham smiled, his face showing its usual composure. "Sam, do two things for me?"

"Of course, sir."

"Take that fellow to the sheriff and tell him what happened. Also tell him I don't want him to do anything just now. I'll be in in the morning to discuss it."

"And the other?"

"Train's at 10:12. Tell the sheriff I'll be in about nine thirty. Have the surrey ready and out front at eight thirty."

"Mr. Cunningham, it will only take you fifteen minutes to get there."

"Sam, I want you to drive me. We have some things to talk about."

* * * *

Sam sat in the surrey, watching Cunningham walk out of the Mokane, Missouri, Railroad Hotel. Cunningham, as usual, was dressed nattily—tweed three-piece sack suit, with well-polished lace-up boots, the derby he perpetually wore covering a receding hairline. Cunningham was a small man with a small frame, but his waist was beginning to bulge. The wire-rimmed glasses he wore gave him a scholarly look, which the fierceness in his black eyes betrayed. It may have been a small man's complex, but C.C. Cunningham was a very hard man who wanted it to show.

He walked around the surrey and got in beside Sam. "Turn around and drive down by the river. We have time and I want to talk."

Sam did as instructed and drove out of the little town of Mokane. Within five minutes they were back along the dirt track that wound through the fall woods.

"Sam, do you know who Andrew Carnegie is?"

Sam thought for a moment. "Steel guy? Right?"

"That's right. Do you know who J.P. Morgan is?"

Sam thought again. "Can't say I do. He from around here?"

"No, Sam. He's from New York. He's a banker. Or a financier, as he would call himself."

"Why do you ask, Mr. Cunningham?"

"Ever heard of Gary, Indiana?"

"Can't say I have," Sam responded.

"No reason you should. It's brand new. Carnegie and Morgan are building it."

"Where?"

"Right at the bottom tip of Lake Michigan, Sam. Just across the line from Illinois."

"Odd name for a new town," Sam offered.

Cunningham gave a snort. "It is indeed. Elbert Gary is Morgan's attorney and one of his business partners. They've named it for him."

"Why are you telling me all this, Mr. Cunningham?"

"Morgan, Carnegie, and Gary are building the largest steel mill in the country and putting it in this new place. They say they'll have four blast furnaces and employ five thousand people. You know what it takes to make steel, Sam?"

"No, sir."

"It takes two things. It takes iron ore and coal. Lots of iron ore and lots of coal. And you know what those two have in common?"

· "No, sir."

"They are heavy as hell and really expensive to move. And you know what they don't have in common?"

"No, sir."

"Nowhere in America are iron ore mines and coal mines close together. So, to make steel, one or both really expensive and hard-to-move things have to be moved. Know where there's lots of iron ore, Sam?"

This time Sam just shook his head.

"Bunch of low mountains called the Gogebic Range right where Michigan and Wisconsin and Minnesota all come together at the far west end of Lake Superior. Know where there's lots of coal, Sam?"

Sam's broad face opened into a tooth-displaying smile as he looked over at his companion. "That one I got. Southern Illinois and Northern Kentucky got more coal than they know what to do with."

"Bingo," Cunningham responded. "And can you guess how they get them together?"

Sam's smile became small and self-satisfied. "They run boats full of the iron as close as they can get it to the coal, say the bottom end of Lake Michigan, and then they run railcars of coal up from Southern Illinois to the same place. This Gary, Indiana, place."

"You are clever, Sam. Now let's keep going. Do you know the rail carrier that is dominant from Northern to Southern Illinois?"

"Not sure, but I'd guess the Chicago, Burlington and Quincy."

"Bingo, again. Now, Sam, you grew up with rail, so this next part is going to be easy. Will they drive those engines the length of the state and then return them with empty cars?"

"Nope. Too far for the crews. They'll uncouple the cars from the engine somewhere halfway, hook them to a new engine with a new crew, and let them take it to the terminus. That crew may even bring the empties back with it and allow the crew members returning south to take the empties with them for refill."

Cunningham looked over at the young driver, a real smile of satisfaction on his face. "You've learned more about running a railroad than just hotels, young man. When the CB&Q bought the Rockford, Rock Island and St. Louis, they inherited a small roundhouse and shop at a town in the middle of the state called Beardstown. US Steel—that's what Carnegie and Morgan are naming this venture—will open the first furnace in two years. CB&Q has that long to expand that Beardstown operation. Part of that expansion is new equipment and crews." Cunningham stopped his speech and turned to look closely at young Clark. He wanted to see his response when he said what he'd been leading up to. "It's your chance to become an engineer, to drive a train, if that's what you really want to do, Sam."

Sam Clark kept his eyes fixed on the road as he brought the surrey to a complete stop. Only then did he turn toward

Cunningham and let his joy show in his expression. "You tell me what to do, Mr. Cunningham, and I'll do it. And be forever grateful."

Cunningham's smile was genuine. "First, turn this thing around. I've got a nine-thirty appointment with the sheriff, and you need to get me there on time. I'll tell you what to do as we ride."

Sam swung the horse around and slapped the leather of the reins along its back and gave an enthusiastic "Click, click," a sound made with his tongue fixed firmly on the roof of his mouth. The horse understood and broke into a trot.

"I have three letters for you, Sam. I'll get them out of my valise when you drop me. The first is to a man named George Grainger. You'll find him at CB&Q's offices in Beardstown. It is a letter recommending he hire you and get you trained as an engineer. The letter is sealed, Sam. Don't open it. It's for Grainger, not you."

"Yes, sir."

"George and I have been friendly competitors for years. I respect him, and I flatter myself the feeling is mutual. I can't guarantee he'll hire you, but I'm hopeful. I'll wire him you're coming.

"Second letter is to a tailor in Beardstown named Lorenz Adler. He used to be in Jacksonville. He's made me suits and is very good. He's German, so it's pronounced like there's a *t* in front of the *z*. Comes out very much like Lawrence. I called him Larry once, and I recommend you don't. See him and get a suit before you go to Grainger's office."

"Mr. Cunningham, I don't have money for a suit."

"The letter takes care of that, Sam. I'm buying you the suit."

"Can't let you do that, Mr. Cunningham. I'll never be able to pay you back."

Cunningham laughed from his belly. "Oh, yes you will. I forgot to tell you, but this Beardstown place is just below a thing called the Sangamon Slough. It forms where the Sangamon River flows into the Illinois. Forms the slough and the Mascouten Bay. They make the best duck and goose hunting on the Mississippi flyway. You owe me free guide services the rest of your life.

"But truth is, Sam, I'm the one who owes you a debt, and I will do my very best to repay it. Starting with that palomino. Take him. He's yours."

CHAPTER 2

November 12, 1906
Beardstown, Illinois

The big golden stallion burst out a frightened whinny as his right rear leg slid forward and under his belly, dropping him downward toward the brick pavement. Sam threw his weight forward, enabling the palomino to get the hoof back under his hip and rise. The large brown dog with an ever-deepening winter coat formed from luxurious waves looked at both as though embarrassed for his companions.

"Easy, big boy. We're almost there. You'll get used to bricks covered with ice, I suppose, but for now, I'll get off and we'll walk together." And he did.

Teddy just stood, tongue lolling, streams of vapor issuing from his open mouth into the cold and darkening November evening.

Sam had never seen streets paved in brick before and could not help but wonder what this had cost. This and other things he saw here. The gas lampposts standing on all four corners of every intersection, glowing warmth as well as light into the evening sky as lighters came down from their tall ladders. Aside from the lamplighters, Sam and his dog and horse seemed the only living things on the street.

Sam walked along with a sense of comfort despite the cold. Another lamp came on and illuminated the sign on the door behind it: "Beardstown Telephone Exchange." And then another lamp, illuminating yet another door-front sign: "Lorenz Adler, Tailor for Gentlemen and Ladies." *Tomorrow, Larry. Tomorrow.*

Another new brick building in neoclassical style. Broad stairs leading up from the street to an entry supported by four Ionic columns. The sign before read, "Beardstown Public Library." There was smaller print below, which Sam walked across the sidewalk to read: "Books courtesy of the estate of Elizabeth Emmons." Beardstown was not the sort of backwoods hovel Sam was used to. This was a real town.

Sam continued down the main street toward the river, and then there it was. The most majestic thing he could imagine, a steel bridge spanning the river. The only other steel bridge Sam had ever seen stretched across the Missouri at Jefferson City.

And then the sign he was looking for: "Beard Hotel, Rooms and Livery."

* * * *

There was still some warmth in the November sun even at eight o'clock in the morning. Sam momentarily removed his broad-brimmed felt hat to feel the warmth as he walked. When he reached the door lettered in gold, "Lorenz Adler, Tailor for Gentlemen and Ladies," he stopped. The window contained two mannequins. The male was dressed like something that must have come out of C.C. Cunningham's closet. The female was bedecked in a deep-purple gown, crowned with a high-necked, lace-ruffled collar, tightly cinched at the waist, and flowing down to satin shoes peeping from under the hem. Sam sensed that when he opened this door, it would lead him into a whole new world.

He opened his hand, palm and fingers stiff. "Teddy, stay," he commanded and walked in.

The tinkle of the bell momentarily produced a small man from the back room. He was precise and neat with a pencil-thin mustache. His most noticeable feature was the halo of rich dark hair surrounding his smoothly bald head. A yellow tape was draped around his neck. He looked at Sam; his expression held just a hint of distain.

"May I help you?" The accent was distinctly German.

"Are you Mr. Adler?"

The expression seemed to ease a bit. "I am. To whom do I have the privilege of speaking?"

"My name is Sam Clark," Sam said, removing his hat. "I have a letter of introduction."

The expression became almost hospitable as Sam pulled the letter from his coat and handed it to the little man.

Adler examined the envelope, letting his eyes and fingers enjoy the high-cloth content of the paper. "Dora," he snapped, turning his head to the curtained doorway through which he himself had entered.

The curtains parted, and a girl of no more than eighteen appeared. Her hair was jet black, with a long braid curled several times around the crown of her head. Her skin was pale, almost white. Her lips were sensuously wide but pulled together, pouting slightly. She had a button nose, but it was her eyes that held him. They were a light brown, and while not improperly forward, they took in all they saw, him included.

As she crossed the shop toward them, Sam did not take his eyes off her until her father said, "I don't read English so good. My daughter does." He handed the letter to her, saying only, "Dora."

It was a command, but she was slow to respond. While

she held her hand toward her father to receive the letter, her eyes stayed on Sam's. She finally looked down at the letter, now in her hand, and once she did, became efficient. She used her thumbnail to rip open the envelope, unfolded the contents, and began to read.

"Papa, you remember Mr. Cunningham. C.C. Cunningham. He was the railroad executive from St. Louis who used to come into our shop in Jacksonville."

Lorenz Adler nodded.

"It seems, Papa, that this gentleman . . ." She looked up at him. "Is it Clark? Sam Clark, is that correct?"

"Yes, ma'am." Sam could not help but smile when he spoke to her.

"Mr. Cunningham has referred Mr. Clark to us and asked that we make him a suit, something appropriate for an interview with Mr. Grainger." She lowered the letter, looked over the top of it, and arched an eyebrow toward Sam as though to say, "Very impressive." "Mr. Cunningham also asks that you complete the suit within two days."

By now Adler's demeanor toward Sam had changed from skeptical to one reserved for his well-heeled clients. "What price range did you have in mind, Mr. Clark?"

"Oh, Papa," Dora interjected, "Mr. Cunningham says the suit should be of a quality you'd prepare for him. And he gives his address in St. Louis and asks that we send the bill there."

Adler looked at Sam, his smile now warm. "We can have it in two days but only if you have time for an initial fitting today and a final fitting tomorrow morning."

Sam seemed not to be paying much attention to the tailor.

"Mr. Clark?" Adler queried. "Will that schedule be acceptable to you?"

"Oh, yes. Yes." Sam seemed to recover.

"Step over to the mirror, please." Adler pointed to the corner of the shop.

Lorenz Adler took the tape from around his neck and walked behind Sam toward the mirror. Dora trailed along.

As they reached the mirror, Dora caught her father and took the tape from his hands. "Papa, I do this better than you. I'll measure. You record."

Adler reached toward a stool beside the mirror and picked up a notebook. "Chest," he commanded.

Dora, still standing behind Sam, stretched her arms around his chest, warping the tape as she went. "Forty-two," she answered.

"Waist?"

This time her arms were long enough to reach around easily. "Thirty-three."

"Hips."

She put the tape around him and held it together at the back of the buttocks.

Sam could feel her fingers pinching the tape together.

"Inseam."

"Turn around, please, Mr. Clark. I need you to face me to do this."

As she kneeled before him, Sam found himself looking directly at the tailor. He didn't know if he was more fearful her measurement would extend all the way up his groin or that it would not. He knew the thing he feared most was her father knowing what he was thinking.

When the measurements were completed, Lorenz Adler spoke. "If you will allow me, Mr. Clark, I will pick a cloth suitable for the season and the occasion."

"Yes, yes." Sam felt as though he were stammering.

"May we see you back at ten o'clock tomorrow, Mr. Clark?" the old man asked.

"Ten will be fine." Sam turned and walked to the door.

"Mr. Clark." It was Dora's voice beckoning. "We are delighted to have you visit our shop and hope you are pleased with our work."

Sam just nodded sheepishly as he walked out the door.

Teddy sat patiently outside the doorway.

Sam's voice was full of joy. "Come on, dog. Let's go for a walk."

* * * *

Two days later, Sam tied the stallion to the light pole and rushed into Adler's shop. His new tweed suit fit perfectly, and even he had to admit it made him look far more than a working stiff who was good with a shotgun. He didn't really feel comfortable in it despite knowing it made him look good. But at this moment he was frustrated, even a bit frazzled. His appointment with George Grainger was in just forty-five minutes, and he couldn't get the damn necktie right. It had seemed like a simple enough knot when she'd showed him, but maybe he had been paying more attention to those twinkling brown eyes with the green halos than the knot. Try as he might, he couldn't get it right in the mirror in his room. He'd tried so many times, his collar was getting rumpled, and he still couldn't seem to get it.

The bell tinkled as he came in. The curtain slid to one side, and Dora, Miss Adler, came out. The moment she saw him, the green halo around her brown eyes started to twinkle. "Why, Mr. Clark, what an unexpected surprise." Then she let a look of mock horror spread over her smiling lips. "But you do look exasperated. How may I help?"

"Tie this damn thing. . . . I'm sorry. You're right. I am." By now he was recovering himself, and even in his rush he could not help but smile in her presence. "I am exasperated. Was that your word?"

Dora merely nodded.

"My interview with Mr. Grainger is in about forty minutes, and I can't remember how to tie this. Would you do it for me again? Please?"

Without speaking, she walked almost up against him. She looked up from under his throat, pulled apart the ends of the mess that was his tie, and then stroked them flat against his vest. Her fingers felt like warm flannel on his chest. He was no longer in a hurry.

She picked up the ends and adjusted the length so one was six inches longer than the other and then slowly tied the silk pennant and slid the knot snuggly against his throat. The narrow ribbon of the tie lay half an inch short of the wider ribbon. Then without a word, she unbuttoned every button on his vest and stroked the tie flat against his shirt and even more slowly buttoned the vest back up.

"There, Mr. Clark. You look like the perfect young businessman." Without stepping back, she looked straight up into his eyes. "You'll get the job, Mr. Clark." Then she patted his vest one last time. "Now go, and don't be late."

"Thank you, Miss Adler." Sam swallowed hard and turned to go.

As he put his hand on the door, she spoke again. "Mr. Clark, after you get this job, you should thank God for it. Perhaps St. John's Lutheran Church Sunday morning at ten o'clock?"

He turned and stared one last time into those sparkling brown eyes and then, without a word, opened the door and departed. She stood in front of the shop, watching him go.

* * * *

George Grainger was like most railroad executives. He was a hard man. He sat behind his large desk, holding the unopened letter in his hand as he appraised the young man before him. He'd not risen as he'd watched this applicant cross the room. That was his habit. He wanted them to know who was in charge, always. And he wanted to see what happened to their posture. He liked hard men around him, hard but knowing who was boss.

If their posture slumped, if they became servile in any way, it was over before the applicant even opened his mouth. Sam walked like he knew he was being appraised. His pelvis was tilted slightly forward, his shoulders back, his chin down, his eyes straight forward on Grainger. Sam had smiled, but it was not a smile that reflected anxiety. He'd extended his hand and introduced himself. Grainger had accepted the hand but made no attempt to rise. He'd motioned Sam to the chair, and he took it.

"Mr. Grainger, I have been sent to you by C.C. Cunningham. He said he'd wire you I was coming, and Mr. Cunningham is a man who does what he says he'll do, so I suspect he has." Then Sam shut up until Grainger nodded agreement. "And he gave me this to give to you." Sam handed him the letter.

Now Grainger held it and studied the young man's face. Could he hold that indifferent but not challenging expression on his face? Could he maintain eye contact? When Sam had passed that test, Grainger ripped the edge off one end of the envelope and slipped the letter out. He read slowly and then reread a bit before he looked up. "Seems as though you and Cunningham are friends."

"My father has worked for him as long as I can remember, but that's never made us friends."

Grainger grunted. "Says you want to be an engineer. He goes so far as to recommend I hire you."

"Yes, sir. That's what I want. To drive one of those trains." Sam pointed out the window at the worm squiggles of tracks threading the roundhouse and shops below.

"Well, you're sure as hell not dressed for the job. You'll need a set of coveralls, a work shirt, some good boots, not that fancy shit you've got on. And you'll need a Ball Standard watch. Go to Pasco's Jewelers and get one. If you haven't got the money, they'll put it on the railroad account. We'll get it back from your first few checks. Report to Wheeler at the roundhouse before first whistle in the morning."

Sam sat momentarily. He was stunned but knew better than to let it show. He rose and extended his hand. This time Grainger rose to take it.

"Thank you, sir," was all he said. Any more would have seemed like gushing, and he knew it. If abrupt was the way things were here, it was the way he would be. He stepped away from his chair and walked the two paces toward the door.

"Clark." It was a bark.

Sam stopped and turned slowly back toward the voice. It was the first time he'd been able to take in all of Grainger. He was a big man, very big. At least two inches taller than Sam and forty pounds heavier. His forearms were like hams and his chest like a small oak. The most pronounced part of his face was his forehead, broad and sloped down like a riverbank ending at his eyebrows, which were as bushy as his rolled-up sleeves revealed his forearms to be.

"Yes, sir."

"I forgot one thing. Bring a good padlock with you. You'll need it for your locker."

Sam's surprise showed. "Railroad men not honest?"

"Oh, they're honest, Clark. And locks keep honest men honest. Clark, C.C. says you're a good shot." For the first time, Grainger's face allowed a small smile.

"No better than anyone else with a pistol or a rifle, but I can hit more than most with a shotgun."

"I'm the other way around. Most of my career has been on the prairie and in the mountains. That's all rifle hunting. Lowland birds are the thing here. Ducks and geese. I've not learned. You're going to teach me."

Now it was Sam who smiled. "We need to start before the water freezes. Pick a day in the next week; keep me off the schedule and we'll get started."

CHAPTER 3

November 28, 1906
Beardstown, Illinois

Sam sat toward the back of the church. It was intentional. He wanted to be certain to get past the minister and be out in front of the church when the Adlers came out. He could see Adler's balding head when the congregation was seated. He sat tall for a small man, but when they rose to sing, he was lost in a forest of taller men in the fifteen rows between them. He'd not been able to see Dora's face, but there were three women in black bonnets sitting beside Adler, the last in line with a tall man sitting beside her. Sam had spent most of the service hoping that one wasn't Dora. Every time heads moved between him and them, he'd tried to glimpse a profile to see, but none of the three women had ever so much as turned a cheek toward the rear of the room.

The minister finally finished. *Finally.* And then the organist broke into a tune he knew, "A Mighty Fortress Is Our God." Sam liked to sing, and he especially enjoyed it when no one he knew could hear him. So he bellowed out the hymn as loud as he could. He'd never heard an organ before, but this had to be one. It didn't sound like a piano, and it had a lot of pipes sticking up above it.

The minister walked down the aisle as they sang and, when the music stopped, gave a benediction to his congregation from the rear of the church. And then they started to file out past him. The minister kept conversations and congratulations from his parishioners thankfully brief, until he got to Sam.

"You're new with us." The minister gave a sober smile.

"Yes, sir . . . Reverend. My first time with you. Just moved here."

"We're glad to have you. What brings you here?"

"The CB&Q, Reverend."

"You're one of their new executives, I'm guessing."

"Then I fear, Reverend, you guess wrong. I'm an engineer. An engineer in training."

The minister took a step back and looked him slowly up and down. "Then you're the best-dressed engineer I've seen." There was a skeptical smile on his face.

"You can thank Mr. Adler for that, sir . . . Reverend. He made the suit, and the recommendation of your church."

"We're glad to have you, son. What's your name?"

"Clark, Sam Clark."

"I'm Reverend Berlin. See you next Sunday, Mr. Clark."

"If I'm not working, Reverend Berlin." He stepped outside into the soft sunlight. Waiting for her, and hoping it was not Dora with the man beside her, made him nervous. She seemed to do that to him.

He walked to his horse to give himself something to do and someplace to hide. He stood on the side of the beast away from the door and fooled with tack that was fine just the way it was, the whole time looking over the saddle to the church entrance.

They walked out the church door, Lorenz Adler in the lead,

followed by a very short and stout woman in a well-made but styleless black dress and bonnet. Then appearing through the dark of the church door came Dora and immediately behind her a tall and very thin man of just a few years more in age than Sam. The man dropped his head and pulled a wide, dark hat on over it. Sam could not make out his face below the hat, but what he looked like didn't matter. He was with Dora. Sam's heart sank. He didn't bother to look at the young woman who came out behind him, the last of the party. Sam hung his head low, walked around to the left side of his horse, and put a foot into the stirrup.

"Mr. Clark."

He recognized the soft voice of Dora Adler without turning. He swung his leg over the saddle before he turned to look at her. "Ma'am." He touched the brim of his hat.

"Mr. Clark, you weren't going to go without doing your courtesies, were you?" Her eyes twinkled up at him.

He held himself rigid. "Sorry, I didn't know you were here," Sam lied.

Her eyes squinted up into the sun. "We are indeed here, Mr. Clark. Now please come and let me introduce you to my family."

He was trapped. He stepped back down, tied the horse again, and followed her across the yard to fulfill social obligations he would have preferred to avoid.

By the time he and Dora reached the Adler family, they were gathered with another couple.

"Mr. Clark, you remember my father."

"Of course, I do." Sam extended his hand.

"Fine-looking suit, young man." There was a twinkle in the little tailor's eyes.

Sam's gloom momentarily disappeared. "Not only fine looking, but it serviced a fine purpose as well, Mr. Adler. Thanks in part to you, I am now the youngest engineer at the CB&Q."

There was a chorus of congratulation even from those in the group he didn't know.

"Mr. Clark, let me introduce my wife, Fredericka." Adler pointed to the short, stout woman whom Sam had seen coming out of the church behind him.

She gave a small curtsy, her eyes twinkling great merriment. "Pleased to meet you, Mr. Clark." Now he knew where Dora got it.

"And this, Mr. Clark, is James McHugh." Adler pointed to an elderly gentleman of medium height, thin build, and a profoundly sober expression standing beside him. His eyebrows and temples were grey, the rest of his hair covered by a bowler hat. "Mr. McHugh is our state's attorney, a very important man in our city."

"Lorenz, do not make overmuch of a country lawyer." His voice held charm despite its nasal quality. He extended his hand and gave Sam a loose handshake, which later in life Sam would come to find common among every politician he would ever meet. McHugh then turned to the woman beside him. She was at least ten years his junior, perhaps fifteen, and despite her age, the most handsome woman Sam had ever seen. "Mr. Clark, this is my wife, Louise McHugh."

Sam was hard-pressed to speak. Though she was a few years over sixty, he had never seen any woman like her. She was her husband's height. Her hair, dark brown and almost entirely unblemished by grey, was rich with luster. She had it parted in the middle and pulled tight around the sides of her head and then braided together, the braid pulled up into a bundle at the nape of her neck. It was something other older women would not dare. Something only one with a still-beautiful face unravished by time would. The color of her eyes matched her hair. Her skin was a shade of light olive, not common in women who thought the paler the skin, the more beautiful. This one seemed to glory in the soft, almost amber tone of hers. She had a straight, thin nose and a jawline to match. Her smile displayed teeth that still appeared perfect and white.

Sam finally stammered, "My pleasure to meet you, ma'am."

"And this, Mr. Clark," Adler added, "is my other daughter, Rosa, and her husband, Patrick Butler." Adler nodded to the other woman in the black bonnet standing by the tall, thin man with the wide-brimmed hat.

"Pleased to meet you, Mr. But . . ." And then the realization of what had just been said struck him. Sam looked into Dora's twinkling eyes and quickly back to Patrick Butler. "Mr. Butler. Very, very pleased to meet you." It was the largest smile Sam's face could accommodate.

After ten minutes of conversation and introductions to others who stopped to say hello, Mrs. Adler spoke. "Lorenz, if you don't get me home, I fear the roast will be drier than you like."

"Of course, Momma. Shall we?" He offered her his arm. "To the surrey."

"May I escort you to your surrey, Miss Adler?" Sam proudly offered his arm, and she took it.

When they reached the surrey, Sam put his hands around her waist and lifted her easily up into the surrey. She smiled down at him with a look that forgave any impropriety.

Sam waited for Mr. Adler to walk Mrs. Adler around and help her up and then back around to the driver's side. Sam extended his hand. "It was my pleasure to be introduced to your family, sir."

Adler shook hands without comment and stepped up and took the reins.

Sam looked up at him. "Mr. Adler."

The tailor looked back down.

"May I have the honor of calling on you and your family soon?"

Adler said nothing for a moment. Mrs. Adler's elbow

seemed to move against his ribs. "We will be pleased to receive you, Mr. Clark." He tapped the reins on the horse's back.

As the surrey moved away, Dora looked back over her shoulder, her eyes twinkling.

CHAPTER 4

December 4, 1906
Sangamon Slough, Illinois

The two big men rose in unison, brought shotguns to their shoulders, and fired. The ducks, gliding into the slough for the evening, awkwardly and instantly changed their direction of flight, the flock losing all cohesion as the birds scattered in all directions. All save two. Those two lay on the water, one still as death, the other flapping one wing and trying to rise. Sam made the silent motion of "retrieve" to his big-chested Chessie. The response was instant, the beautiful beast perfectly postured to dive into the icy water. Sam had pointed him to the cripple. Teddy laid it in his mouth as softly as though he were cradling a baby rather than capturing a half-dead dinner. He stepped into the blind and stood before his master who, without comment, held his hand palm up to receive the trophy. The dog dropped it and looked up as a dutiful student with a correct answer might. Sam gave him one pat, turned slightly to face the dead duck still floating, and made the gesture again. His signal was again followed instantly with the same graceful entry.

Sam handed the almost dead duck to George Grainger, who put one hand on the body and the other on the head and twisted the neck. "How does that dog of yours work in this cold, Sam? There's already ice on that water."

"They're bred that way, George. Work all day in the Atlantic surf off the Chesapeake Bay. They are tough. It's the double coat and the huge chest. Sometime when he's dry, rub your hands along his back. Under those long curls, you'll feel a short, and very thick, undercoat."

He turned to watch the dog returning, bird in mouth. "Along with tough comes stubborn. He was harder to train than a lab or a poodle. And he does like to fight." Sam smiled up at the bigger man, who returned his appreciative grin. "But I don't think I'll ever hunt with anything else."

Grainger stuffed his bird into the open panel at the back of his shooting vest and looked up appraisingly at the western sky. "Dark soon. I think those are our last birds for the day."

Teddy again entered the blind and dropped his offering into Sam's outstretched hand. Sam, like Grainger, stuffed the dead bird in the pouch at the back of his shooting vest and followed the bigger man out of the blind and toward the horses. As they rode back along the edge of the slough, Sam pointed to the large three-story brick house a quarter of a mile down a tree-lined lane. "George, who owns that huge house?"

"You called it just right." Grainger laughed as he said it.

Sam looked befuddled. "I called it a house."

Grainger looked at him, no longer laughing but a smile still on his face. "It's a house, Sam. A whorehouse."

Sam stared over in disbelief. When his gaze returned, he said, "That legal in Illinois?"

"What? They don't have whorehouses in Missouri?"

"Oh, we got 'em, but they aren't in big mansions and sorta in your face. In Missouri they are all little and dark and down alleys."

Grainger smiled. "Ours are a little different, I suppose, but to use the expression, 'same church, different pew.'"

"And people here don't object?" Sam asked.

"Oh, I suppose most places in Illinois they might. You'd never find something like that in any of the farm towns around here. Hell, not even Springfield. But you'll find Beardstown is a pretty free place, Sam. Mostly we let people do what they want. You'll find a card game at the back of every saloon and social club in town. I even saw one of them new 'slot machines' in the back of Jensen's Pharmacy. That's not to say old Sheriff Hitchcock and his deputies don't bust a few heads and put a few of our boys in a cell on payday nights. But as long as people around here stay out of each other's way, it's pretty much live and let live."

Sam sat taking it all in, but he was confused and it showed. "George, I went to church Sunday. Place was packed. And as I rode home, I must have seen ten other churches, two of them Lutheran. And all of the yards and lots packed with people and buggies. And all with preachers shouting fire and brimstone. Those people don't care about"—he turned to point at the building now fading behind them—"THAT!"

Grainger pulled off his hat and scratched the top of his balding head. "Oh, I suppose they do. It is a bit ostentatious, I believe is the word. But that particular house has protection."

"What kind of protection?"

"Owned by a woman named Vivienne de Villiere. She's very smart. Built that over thirty years ago. Donates to politicians and civic organizations. Does it quietly, but everyone in town who counts knows it's her. So, she has friends."

It was darkening as they approached town. "Sam, give me the ducks in your vest."

Sam frowned. "Thought I'd take a few over to the Adlers' tomorrow evening."

"Wouldn't you rather take them plucked and cleaned? I'll

get one of the cooks to do it and give them back to you tomorrow. You'll have them in time for Sunday dinner."

* * * *

The following evening at the Adlers', the men sat in the living room as the women cleaned up in the kitchen. The entire house still smelled of the sweet fat of duck that Fredericka and her daughters had roasted. The roasting pan was just big enough for the three ducks along with a few potatoes and carrots made sweet by fat dripping out of the beasts.

"Sam, we are getting used to Sunday dinners of duck or goose, thanks to you," Lorenz Adler said.

"I fear, Mr. Adler, that's the end of it until next season. Teddy and I may find a late flyer or two, but mostly everything that is going to fly south already has."

"Then, I fear," Patrick Butler spoke in his usual soft, rumbling base, a voice completely at odds with the razor thinness of his body, "that we'll have to go back to pork. Something this town never seems to run low on."

Patrick Butler was a thin man with a thin face and a thin contribution to conversation. Laconic was an understatement, Sam thought.

"Oh, I can smell the cinnamon and the apples in that pie. Momma will have dessert to us soon. But for now, I can sit and enjoy the company of men," the little tailor said as he calmly exhaled the blue smoke of his pipe toward the ceiling. He held the pipe in his left hand. With the right, he was making the same gesture Sam observed him making almost constantly, certainly without knowing he was doing it. He was moving the large ring he wore on the fourth finger of his right hand around in circles.

Sam had come to believe the tailor was so used to his fingers moving, he could not be at peace unless they were. "Mr. Adler, may I know what that large ring you wear is?"

Adler took his pipe out of his mouth and stared down at his right hand, focused on the ring. Finally, he set the pipe in the ashtray at his side, slipped the ring off, reached forward in his chair, extending his arm toward the sofa where Sam sat, and offered him the ring. The front of the ring displayed a large and odd bird, two birds really. At least there were two heads, one pointed in each direction.

"It is the ring of a Mason, a Master Mason."

"And what is that? What is a Mason?" Sam asked.

Adler smiled. It was the smile of a man who is pleased at the interest of another. "The Masonic Order is a society whose history runs back over four thousand years, to the time when the Pharaohs built the pyramids. Masons built those wonders. You will notice on the side of the ring a triangle and a square. With only those tools to guide them, the Masons constructed what has lasted longer than any other thing man has ever built on this earth."

"You say the ring is that of a Master Mason. What is that, Mr. Adler?"

"A Master Mason is one who has learned the wisdom the order has to teach."

"And that wisdom is what exactly?" Sam asked.

Patrick's voice seemed to bounce heavily through the air. "On that subject, Sam, my father-in-law will be more laconic than I."

Lorenz Adler smiled and smoothed his thick black hair back along his temples. "You can ask me many things and I will answer. But on that subject, Patrick is correct. I will not speak. Those are secrets not to be revealed."

Sam laughed a short polite laugh. "Then let me try another subject."

Adler puffed his pipe and nodded.

"I have been here less than two months. In that short time, I've managed to get a wonderful job, make wonderful friends"— he made a sweeping gesture as though to encompass the whole house—"and learned many new things. But there is one thing I've just not been able to figure out."

"What is that, Sam?" The question was spoken as precisely as the pencil-thin mustache on the speaker's face was trimmed.

"This town. Beardstown."

"What about it?"

"Let's see how to phrase this. It seems to be several things at the same time."

"Is that unusual?" Adler asked.

"No. Well, yes, in one particular way. The two things it seems to be . . . well, it can't be both. At least not at the same time."

For the first time since he'd met the man when he first walked into his shop, Sam realized he had Lorenz Adler's full attention. "Tell me what it is you see."

"This all started with a conversation I had with my boss, George Grainger, while we were hunting. Here's the paradox. I meet you at St. John's on Sunday morning. The place is full of God-fearing folks listening to the word of God. And this town is full of churches where the same thing happens. Beardstown is full of God-fearing men and women, and they act like it. They are kind and pleasant. You have schools, public schools, private ones like the one at St. John's and others I've seen. You have a library. The town is far more civil than the rough railroad stop where I grew up."

Adler nodded agreement. Patrick Butler was leaning forward, his elbows on his knees, his chin propped in his hands.

"But there is so much . . . well . . . vice. Bars everywhere, and all have gambling. There are slot machines in stores. There appear to be all manner of illegal things here. And no one seems to care. The God-fearing appear not to be at war with the sinful."

"Often, Sam, the God-fearing are the sinful," Adler said slowly, the blue tobacco smoke coming out of his mouth in puffs as his tongue and breath formed the words. "Sam, let me ask a question. What else do you see here?"

Sam thought for a moment. "This town has everything I would expect to see in Philadelphia or Boston. Perhaps such cities have more, but I don't know what that would be. And everyone here seems to have money—houses, surreys, horses, and clothes, very fine clothes, Mr. Adler." He smiled at the old man, knowing he was complimenting him.

"Sam, I was twenty years old when I came to America. I came from a place of great culture. But also, a place of great rules. Germany is run by men who believe in science, and they believe that science is the answer to all things. So, the leaders allow professionals, the scientists, the trained, to make the rules. All the rules. And they believe they can make Germany perfect. We Germans fight wars among ourselves over whose rules can make society most perfect. I don't think much of Frenchmen usually, but while I was still in Germany, I read a book from one titled *Democracy in America*. He'd traveled here and observed the oddest thing. He said Americans were religious and most believed in the teachings of whatever church they went to. But they'd also decided that their morals were between them and God. There was no place for the state in that. They were willing to let others have their own understanding with God. And he said Americans didn't need, want, or ask much more from their government. They were not only willing but preferred to make their lives and their wealth and their families on their own. So I said, 'That's the place for me,' and I came."

"Gentlemen, dessert is on the table." It was Fredericka's cheery voice calling them.

"Sam." It was Mr. Adler's voice that stayed his movement. "Freedom makes a man find his own path, and that creates wealth and happiness. And if it does not and he fails, at least it has been his failure, not one put upon him."

CHAPTER 5

October 10, 1908
Beardstown, Illinois

"If any man here knows any reason this couple should not be joined in holy matrimony, speak now or forever hold your peace," the booming baritone commanded. The minister's eyes drifted slowly around the church, offering opportunity for response. The eyes came at last to rest on the couple before him. They twinkled merrily as he proclaimed, "Finding none, I now pronounce you man and wife. Mr. Clark, you may kiss your bride."

Sam had a choice. He could crane his long frame down over her short one or elevate her to him. He chose the latter. His arm, wrapped firmly around the small of her back, lifted Dora to his height, and he kissed her lips.

The church bellowed hoots and hollers of good wishes as the happy couple turned and walked purposefully down the aisle into the great sunshine and warmth of the future.

* * * *

One end of the Masonic Lodge's hall had been set in long tables. The band had been given the slightly elevated platform in the front. The space between the platform and dining tables was left for dancing. The ladies had congregated, standing near the dining tables. The gentlemen drifted to the bar.

When all seemed to have gathered and the noises of laughter and goodwill filled the hall, Lorenz Adler stepped up onto the stage, tugged at his vest to straighten it, ran his hand across his balding head, and allowed his tenor to fill the entire hall. "Gentlemen!" it boomed. The noise abated but only somewhat, so he bellowed again, "Gentlemen!" as he banged the dull edge of a dinner knife against his glass.

The sounds of laughter slowed and then halted as every eye in the room turned to him.

"Gentlemen, get one last drink, and then collect your ladies and find a place at the tables. Dinner will be coming out of the kitchen as soon as you do. And be certain to leave those two seats at the head of the table for the happy couple."

Instantly the laughter started again, but all were doing as instructed, couples slowly forming together at their seats. Adler looked at the bandmaster and said, "Softly during dinner." The bandmaster nodded, turned to his players, and lifted his baton. Upon his command, the musicians struck up a Scott Joplin tune with as much enthusiasm as the command "softly" would allow.

Adler walked to the head table, where Sam and Dora sat beside Fredericka, who was holding a chair for him. Big George Grainger sat beside Sam. Reverend Berlin had a place of honor at the head table with them, as did white-haired James McHugh and his dark-haired wife. Every member of St. John's congregation and the lodge had been invited as well as dozens of neighbors and dignitaries who were not members.

Sam leaned in front of his bride toward his father-in-law. "Lorenz, do you know everybody in this town?"

"A lot, Sam. A lot. Between clients and congregation and this Masonic Lodge, I am blessed with many friends."

"Indeed, you are, Lorenz. But I fear feeding them all, not to mention the bar bill, will make this ceremony very expensive. I thank you for it."

"Life is very kind to me, and my shop is prosperous, so do not worry. Besides, it is a father's privilege to celebrate his daughter's marriage to a good man."

"Thank you, Lorenz. From you I take that as a high compliment." Sam leaned back into this own chair just as the waiter placed a huge slab of roast beef before him.

As he cut into it, Grainger turned to him and spoke in what, for him, was a very soft voice. "Sam, this is for you and Dora," and handed him an envelope. "You'll need it to furnish that house I hear Lorenz has given you two."

"Thank you, George. You know we are both grateful," Sam said as he slid the envelope into this vest pocket.

"I have something else for you, which you may enjoy even more."

Sam looked into Grainger's eyes. They held an oddly conspiratorial glint.

"It is news but news not to be announced until later next week. You must tell no one. No one."

Sam nodded soberly.

Grainger continued. "You know the old Missouri, Kansas and Eastern was purchased by the Union Pacific. There was no place in their organization for your old friend. So he's been hired by us, and as of the first of this month, C.C. Cunningham will be running this line. You and I will both have him as our boss."

Sam Clark was stunned, and his face showed it. He finally spoke. "It won't make a bit of difference to me day to day, but I'm glad life is working out for Mr. Cunningham. But are you OK with it, George?"

"My life is very good, Sam. Just take me hunting next week and it will be perfect."

"Sam, honey." It came from Dora beside him.

He turned toward his new bride.

"You eat some dinner, my husband. Pretty soon Papa is going to have the band play a waltz for us. I don't want you short on strength." She had an almost naughty smile. "For the dance," she added as the smile grew.

"As long as you keep the train on that dress behind you so I don't step on it, we'll be fine."

Thirty minutes later, Lorenz Adler did as his daughter had predicted. He rose and again used the dull edge of his knife to tap on his glass. The room gave him its attention. "Ladies, gentlemen, I hope you have enjoyed your dinner. But it is now time to start the festivities. If the band will give my daughter and her husband a moment to reach the floor and then offer them a waltz, we will honor their marriage by allowing them the first dance." He looked at the glowing couple beside him and said softly, "Sam, Dora, are you ready?"

They each nodded.

"Ladies and gentlemen, I give you Mr. and Mrs. Sam Clark."

James and Louise McHugh watched, as did the rest of the room. Sam rose, offered his hand to his wife, and as she rose, slowly pulled back her chair. Dora threw her train clear; the couple stepped from behind the table and strolled slowly to the middle of the dance floor. The band offered the opening cord of a Strauss waltz. Sam took Dora's hand in his, put his other hand firmly on the small of her back, and with a command that never hinted this was his first public waltz, stepped off and led her in a graceful arc around the floor.

A small tear ran down Louise McHugh's face.

"My dear, whatever is wrong?" a concerned James McHugh whispered into her ear.

She dabbed the corner of her eye with a lace handkerchief. "Why nothing, darling. In fact, everything is perfect."

"Then why are you crying?"

"The beauty in her perfection has made me emotional."

He looked blankly at his wife, his expression the one men wear when they are truly convinced that women are creatures beyond their understanding.

She smiled sweetly at him. It was the smile an adult might give to an uncomprehending child or a woman to an uncomprehending man. "James, her father is not a tailor; he is an artist. Look at her. Her father has made her art. The white of satin scooped off her shoulders and down below her collarbones; the lace of the widening sleeves off her shoulder; the gown fitted at her waist and flowing down to the floor and widening as it goes so there is enough train to float behind her as he turns her. She looks a fairy queen dancing across water lilies on a pond, the rising sun flashing on her wings.

"When I was a girl, James, I looked like that. We all looked like that. We thought it would never end. And it did so suddenly and abruptly. She makes me believe there is hope for her and the world. That's the wonder of her; that the beauty she creates this moment will go on forever."

CHAPTER 6

January 26, 1915
Beardstown, Illinois

Sam sat in the front room trying to appear calm. The sun had been up six hours, and there was no sound coming out of the bedroom. From time to time, Fredericka would scurry into the kitchen to put on water or stick her head out the bedroom door and shout down the hall for Sam to bring another towel. He hadn't seen Doc Jones since four in the morning, when Sam had escorted him into the bedroom, only to be unceremoniously thrown out by Fredericka. No one seemed excited, not even Lorenz, who sat reading one old newspaper after another. No one except Sam. All he could do was chew on his nails and worry about Dora. He wasn't worried about the baby. He'd never been worried about the baby. It wasn't real to him. Even when Dora got big, he couldn't conceptualize a person in there.

"Sam, something I've wanted to talk to you about for a long time," Lorenz said as he folded the paper. "Now is perhaps not the best time, but if I don't talk to you about something, I fear you will eat the ends of your fingers off." Lorenz gave a teasing smile. "I've never seen you chew your fingernails. By your age, most men have stopped."

"I've never chewed them before. What is it you want to talk about?"

"I'd like you to join the Masonic Lodge."

"What? Why?"

"You'll be a father soon. Very soon. First you had just your-self to care for, and best I can tell, you did a fine job of it. You've done a fine job of caring for my daughter as well. Once you're a father, there becomes more to it. More responsibility. More burden to carry."

"What's that got to do with the Masons?"

"A lot."

Sam pulled his nail out of his mouth and sat forward in the overstuffed armchair.

Lorenz could tell he had his attention now. If nothing else, he'd gotten the man's mind working instead of worrying. "Sam, there is an old saying, 'If you want to travel fast, travel alone; if you want to travel far, travel in a group.'"

"Yeah, I've heard it."

"You've been young, Sam. You've traveled fast. Now it is time to slow down and plan to travel far."

Sam looked perplexed. "I don't understand. How does that relate?"

"Do you remember the first time you came to church? The time you asked me if you could call?"

Sam nodded.

"Do you happen to remember who I was standing with in the churchyard when Dora brought you over?"

"Yes, your wife and the Butlers."

"Who else, Sam?"

"The McHughs, James and Louise."

"Did you ever stop to wonder what one of the most powerful

men in town was doing socializing with a simple tailor and his family?"

Sam's eyes narrowed, and his lips pulled tight as he cocked his head to a slight angle.

"He and I, Sam, are Master Masons. I ran the lodge when it opened, and he followed. We are more than friends. We are brothers. There are half a dozen tailors in town. How do you suppose it is that I have the most expensive such shop with the best clientele?"

"Because you are very good. Very, very good."

"I appreciate the compliment, Sam. But in any business, skill is merely the baseline for success."

Sam looked quizzical.

"Let me try this. Were you the best candidate for your job?"

"Probably not."

"How'd you get it?"

"A recommendation."

Adler nodded agreement and understanding. "Are you the best engineer out of Beardstown?"

Sam thought for a moment. "I'm good, but some guys have way more experience. Why?"

"If not, why is it that every fall you get the best schedule?"

Sam smiled a guilty smile. "Because Grainger likes to go duck hunting with me."

The bedroom door burst open, and Dr. Jones stepped into the front room. He wore a tired but pleased smile. "Mr. Clark, would you care to come meet your son?"

Sam burst to his feet and virtually ran across the room and through the door. A very tired-looking Dora lay propped up on pillows, holding a small, tightly wrapped bundle to her breast. Sam kneeled down beside her, kissing her cheek and stroking her disheveled hair.

"You have a boy, Sam. Care to hold him?"

Sam accepted the offered bundle, making certain he had

both hands firmly around it before taking it from her. He did not pull it to him but looked into the red and wrinkled face that peered back with dark-grey eyes staring at him as intently as he stared at it. Both pondering what this could possibly mean. Sam turned and saw Lorenz standing behind him. "I know Rosa has given you a granddaughter, but would you care to see your first grandson?"

The old tailor held out his steady hands to accept the offer. As he pulled the child to him, his face broadened into a glow of warmth and affection.

"Papa," came the quiet voice from the bed. "Sam and I decided if it was a boy, we'd name him for you. Say hello to young Lorenz."

"But I'm gonna call him Larry, whether you like it or not," Sam said.

Lorenz Adler held the warm bundle close to his heart and said nothing.

"And I'll join the lodge whenever you want."

CHAPTER 7

May 31, 1917
Beardstown, Illinois

Sam took the stairs two at a time, running up to Grainger's office. He was still wearing his coveralls and the long-billed blue-and-white-striped cap that was the work uniform of engineers. He stopped momentarily before the door to remove the cap and pull his goggles over the top of his head before he knocked.

"Come," growled the deep voice on the other side of the door.

Sam threw it open and strode a brisk three steps to the front of Grainger's desk.

"Jesus, Sam, you look like a fucking raccoon with that soot all over your face. Didn't you even stop to wash up?"

"As soon as I stopped, the station master was beside the engine. Said you wanted to see me immediately."

"Not me," Grainger grumbled and pointed to the big wing-back chair overlooking the rail yard. "Him."

Sam turned on his heel and looked into the light pouring through the double windows. Backlit as he was, and as long as it had been since he'd seen him, Sam instantly recognized the natty, if slightly rounder, figure of C.C. Cunningham smiling up at him from the leather-covered wingback chair.

"Long time no see, Sam," the small man said as he rose.

Startled and pleased as he was to see him, Sam's antenna immediately rose. *What's he doing here, and what does he want with me?* But a smile covered the thought as he strode to the man largely responsible for making his life what it was. "A very long time, Mr. Cunningham." Sam extended his hand as he walked across the room.

Cunningham accepted the hand. "I see you made the most of the introduction, Sam. Good for you. And you seem to have gotten what you wanted. Even better for you."

"Thanks in large part to you, Mr. Cunningham. I wouldn't want to have disappointed you or been unworthy of the introduction to Geor . . . Mr. Grainger. He's been very good to me."

Cunningham nodded and let go of his hand. "Sam, have a seat." He pointed to the cane-back chairs beside him. "George and I have something we want to talk to you about."

Grainger walked across the room to join them. He grabbed one of the chairs and set it in front of Cunningham's larger one. He pointed for Sam to sit. He pulled the other beside it and sat.

Sam turned his cap in his hands, his mind running in wonder.

"You start, George," Cunningham directed.

"I'll be too abrupt," the big man grumbled.

Cunningham just nodded a command to do it.

"Sam, you're going to California."

"Whaaa?"

Cunningham rocked forward and looked at his manager. "You're right. You were too abrupt." But there was a small smile behind the words. "Sam, you know Wilson has gone and gotten us into this European war."

"Germans sinking the *Lusitania* mighta had something to do with it," Grainger growled.

Cunningham gave him a bemused smile. "They ever get that boat off the bottom of the Atlantic, we may just find the Germans were right. There may well be guns in that hold."

Grainger started to speak again, but Cunningham held up his hand, palm out, to stop him. "Anyhow we're at war." He looked back at Sam. "You know that, Sam, but what you don't know is the US is going to nationalize the railroads for the duration of the war. Create a thing called the US Railroad Administration, and me and all the guys like me will report to its director general."

"Nationalize? What . . ." The words burst out of Sam's mouth.

Again, Cunningham held up his hand, palm out, this time toward Sam. "There's more. America will be building ships. A lot of ships, both military and cargo. And they need some help from us to do it."

Sam looked even more confused. "Ships? What's that got to do with . . ."

"Let me explain," Cunningham continued. "Shipyards make those huge things a section at a time. Sometimes the materials come to the section being built, but sometimes the partially finished ships have to be moved around the yard. You know how they move something that big, Sam?"

Sam just shook his head.

"The whole damn frame of the ship," Cunningham explained, "is on a platform resting on railcars. Shipyards are covered with rail lines. And when the partially finished ship has to be moved, it moves on rails. And you know what pulls it around?"

"Big-ass engine," Sam answered.

"Yep. That's where we come in. Navy has asked for our help. They want some of our engineers to pull their partially finished ships around the yard."

"And one of those yards is in California?" Sam guessed.

"Yep. Several. The one we're sending you to is in Long Beach, outside of Los Angeles."

Sam rocked back in his chair, at ease now that he understood. At ease but uninterested. "Sounds like a real adventure for a young man, Mr. Cunningham. Maybe Mr. Grainger hasn't told you, but I got married and not only that but have a boy a little over a year old. My days of adventure are past. Now if I were still single, I'd be—"

Grainger barked into the middle of Sam's sentence, "If your aunt had balls, she'd be your uncle. No ifs here, Sam."

Cunningham held up his hand toward Grainger, looked back at Sam, and continued. "There's a bit more to this, Sam. Wilson's call for volunteers to go get killed in Europe ain't workin'. He got maybe fifty thousand of the more than ten times that he wants and needs. It's not public yet, but next month the country will start the first draft since the Civil War. You know who they are going to draft, Sam?"

Sam said nothing.

"They are going to call every man eighteen to forty-five, and they don't care if you're married or a daddy. They don't care what you do; they'll call. We're thinking, George and me, that you and your wife and little . . . Larry, is that what I hear his name is?" Cunningham smiled. "See, I do keep up with you . . . Anyhow we're thinking you'll be safer and your family happier with you in a shipyard in the sunniest place in America than in some muddy trench in France."

The room was silent, an almost oppressive silence, Sam thought, but he wasn't going to be the one to break it.

"Sam, remember when I told you I would buy your suit?"

Sam looked up, startled by the sudden change in direction. "Yes." He nodded.

"Do you remember you didn't want it? Said you'd never be able to pay me back."

Sam nodded again.

"Then you'll remember I told you how you were going to pay me back."

Sam smiled now. "Yes, sir."

"Well, I know they're out of season and most of them are already well north of here, but pick me up before dawn at the Park Hotel and make your first installment on paying me back."

"I'd enjoy that, but I'm driving the 6:00 a.m. southbound."

Cunningham looked at Grainger, who said, "I'll have Blondie or Talbot take the 6:00 a.m. for Sam."

"Pick me up, just before dawn, Sam. Between now and then, talk with your wife about it and give me your answer once we're in a duck blind."

CHAPTER 8

December 26, 1917
Long Beach, California

Dora stooped to hold both of the baby's hands for balance as he took tentative steps, walking his father out of the front door and down the driveway of their bungalow six blocks from the beach. The smell of the ocean overwhelmed her, as it seemed to every morning since they had arrived.

"Everything in California seems strange. Strange and wonderful," she said as she smiled. "It's the day after Christmas, and it's as warm as Beardstown is in the spring. I'm liking this place enough to hope the war lasts awhile."

Sam opened the door of the Buick and threw his lunch pail in. "Where do you want to go this weekend?" he asked. "We've not seen the canals in Venice, the car races in Santa Monica, those old tar pits with all the animal bones. What's going to be your pick?"

"I think the thing I want to see most is you home this evening," she teased.

"And Saturday?"

"I want to take the Red Car up to Hollywood."

"Anything special? Want me to see if the navy can get us a couple of tickets in the visitor's observatory at the Universal Studios lot? I heard they're shooting a Harry Carey Western."

"No tickets. Maybe we can take Larry out to the racetracks in Pasadena? But what I really want to see is that set of Babylon Court gates that D.W. Griffith had built. Maggie next door said it's over one hundred feet tall with statues of elephants holding it up."

"OK, if that's what you want."

"Maggie says you'll like it, too, Sam."

"How's that?"

"She said there are statues of naked women riding the elephants." She giggled.

He kissed her, got in the Buick, and backed out the drive.

* * * *

On New Year's Day, Larry bounced up and down on his father's shoulders, laughing with glee at his father's excited jumping.

"Come on, you nags. All you have left to go is the homestretch." Sam's shout was drowned out by twenty thousand other voices as the ground began to move with the thundering hooves pounding toward them.

The chariot behind was coming faster, but getting around four horses harnessed in width would be a long arch. While the horses on the inside chariot seemed not to have another gear left, neither were they slowing. Sam's money and heart were with the foursome charging around in the arch, but he wasn't certain there was enough of the stretch left for the horses to get by.

Larry had all of his chubby fingers woven into his father's wavy locks and was hanging on for dear life, squealing with the joy only a three-year-old can capture.

"Use the whip," he heard from the shrill voice of his mother. She was jumping up and down, her hands on the rail boosting her leaps.

The two teams roared past, the inside chariot team hanging on to reach the white pole first, to the screaming approval of half the crowd.

Sam dug into his pocket, withdrew his betting slip, and slowly tore it in half. "Well, it was only $2.00. How on earth is a guy supposed to handicap a chariot race?"

"Same way Lew Wallace did." Dora beamed up at him, the glory of the day glowing from her.

"Huh?" Sam grunted.

"You should read more, my love," she teased him, and stood up on her tippy-toes to be kissed.

Sam bent down and gave her one. "Best consolation prize any man ever received." He reached up to the top of his head and unwound Larry's fingers from his hair. "Daddy is no longer your horsey, young man." He slid his hands under the little guy's armpits, pulled him up and over his head, and lowered him slowly to the dirt along the track.

He stood up straight again, holding Larry's little hand firmly, and looked lovingly at his wife's smile.

"Sam, can we live here forever? Can you make this never end?"

CHAPTER 9

October 3, 1918
Beardstown, Illinois

Lorenz Adler whistled as he walked down the evening sidewalk. The Masonic Lodge meeting had not lasted long. Actually, there had been no meeting at all, just a dinner of camaraderie among the members. The fall air was cool, breezy. Lorenz had pulled the collar of his black wool greatcoat up around his neck in protection. He turned at the corner to cross the street. It was not until he reached the middle of the street that he saw the car approaching on his right. He had never gotten used to how much faster autos traveled than carriages. They just seemed to appear out of the dark. He stepped back one pace to allow the oncoming car a bit more room to pass in front of him.

"John, the man!" The scream came from his passenger.

John Bunties slammed on his brake, throwing the car to a stop two feet too late. Adler was thrown forward some five feet by the bumper that struck him. The driver and three other men jumped out of all four doors.

The passenger in the front seat was the first to reach him.

"Jesus Christ, it's Lorenz Adler! Lorenz, you OK?" he said in a softer tone.

The four men all came forward to help Adler to his feet and brush him off. "Lorenz, you should have let us give you a ride."

"I'm a bit stunned, but I think I'm OK, John. I bumped my head. I'll let you take me home now." Adler said it with a weak smile.

The men helped him into the car and then out again when they reached his house. All four of them walked with him to the front door and rang the bell. Fredericka opened the door to see her dazed husband being propped up by his fellow lodge members.

"Fredericka, I fear I've damaged Lorenz," an ashen Bunties said. "I've hit him with the car. I didn't see him until I was on top of him. The black coat, I suppose."

She held the door open and said in a controlled tone, "Bring him in and set him on the sofa here."

The party did as she instructed.

As they helped him to his seat, Adler objected, "I'm fine, truly. Just dazed." He looked up at his wife. "Not John's doing, Momma. I stepped back to avoid a car coming the other way and appeared to have stepped right in front of him. I never will learn how quickly the auto-buggies come."

"Shall I get a doctor, Mr. Adler?"

"No, no, no," Lorenz insisted. "I'll be fine. Just let Momma put me to bed. I'll be fine in the morning."

All stood in silence.

"Momma, make them go. I'm embarrassed."

Fredericka politely escorted all out and returned to her husband.

"Put me in bed, Momma."

She let him prop himself on her shoulder as they walked down the hall. Once she had seated him on the bed, she removed his coat, pulled off his shoes, socks, and pants, and then unbuttoned his shirt and removed it. She pulled the long nightgown over his head and covered his body and legs and then laid him against the pillow and pulled the covers up under his chin. She stood up and turned out the light.

"Momma, it's those damned automobiles. One of these days one of them is going to kill someone."

Lorenz Adler never woke.

CHAPTER 10

October 7, 1918
Beardstown, Illinois

Dora Clark stepped out of the train car and onto the platform, one hand holding a valise and the other that of her son. Rosa Butler rushed forward in quick, scurrying steps and threw her arms around her younger sister. Dora dropped both the valise and her son's hand. The two women, the image of a black statue of human pain, stood weeping, the support of each keeping the other from falling.

The little boy stood, his curls and his face each a mass of confusion.

Patrick Butler, coming quickly behind, released the hand of five-year-old Dixie Butler and whispered, "Go take your cousin Larry's hand." Dixie hesitated, her confusion as clear as that of the other child, and looked up at her father, who merely pointed with his chin to her younger cousin and said, "Go on now. He's little and he needs you."

Not knowing just what or why, Dixie did as she was told

and went to the little boy. The two stood holding hands, watching their mothers cry.

Patrick took a step forward, collected the dropped valise, and stood waiting.

"Am I here in time?" Dora finally asked, wiping tears from her eyes and then using the same hankie to cover her mouth as she coughed.

"Yes," Rosa responded. "You can still see him. Many came to the viewing last night, but we've left the coffin open, knowing you'd be here this morning. We'll bury him as the sun sets."

"I'll get the bags and keep the children. Rosa, you take Dora to the car," Patrick instructed.

Rosa nodded, slipped her hand under the younger woman's elbow, and escorted her down the platform.

"How's Momma?" Dora asked.

"She's taking it very hard. She's spent the last two days mostly crying in her bedroom. When she comes out, she's very weak. She didn't even step out for the viewing last night." Rosa stopped and turned to Dora. "You don't look so strong yourself. The trip must have been very hard."

Dora gave a very weak smile in response. "Little Lorenz and I had a sleeping car until Kansas City, but I haven't slept much in the last two days. I'll be all right today, but I will look forward to sleeping in my own bed."

Rosa shook her head. "No, you'll stay with us. I know all thought Patrick and I were extravagant when we built a four-bedroom house, but this is just why. We've already moved Momma in with us. We'll move all her things, even the piano, over very soon. But even with her in the house, there is a bedroom for you. We will not hear of your taking care of yourself. Lorenz can sleep in Dixie's room. We have a cot we've rolled in."

* * * *

The view from the cemetery was the most peaceful in the whole of the Illinois River valley. It sat high on the hill with the entire city below, the river behind it and the wide plain on the Schuyler County side fading from view as the sun sank, disappearing into the river to the southwest. Reverend Berlin had words that were personal and kind for his long-term parishioner and friend. But Dora didn't hear them. She was so weak, she was certain she would have lost her footing and fallen had it not been for Rosa's support. She had stopped coughing but still kept her lace handkerchief out to wipe the sweat from her brow. As the sun sank below the earth, the remains of her father sank into it. She felt herself sinking with them.

* * * *

Dr. Jones closed the door to the bedroom behind him. He could feel his tall, lean frame threatening to collapse, starting with his shoulders, down then to his waist and even his knees. He didn't know if his exhaustion was physical or mental, but he knew he was feeling the weight of far more than his sixty years. His head was down as he reached the end of the hall and walked into the light of the front room. The only ones to greet him there were Patrick and Rosa Butler. They had put the children to bed. They both rose anxiously upon his arrival. Neither said a word. They just stared at him, trying to read from his expression and posture exactly how grim the circumstances were.

It was Rosa who spoke. "You look very tired, Dr. Jones. May I get you something? Tea perhaps?"

He stepped to the large overstuffed chair beside the sofa where they'd sat holding hands and dropped his weight into it. "Thank you, Mrs. Butler. I could use that."

"It will just take a minute. The water is on. Could I ask that you wait until I return to give their prognoses?"

He nodded. She turned to walk into the kitchen.

Patrick Butler stood, walked to the carved black-walnut credenza across the room, picked up a bottle of bourbon sitting on a silver platter as well as a shot glass beside it. He carried them both back across the room, set the glass on the table beside the doctor's chair, and poured it full. "I think you need this more than tea."

"Thank you, Patrick. I fear you are right." He drank the shot in one swallow.

Butler started to pour another.

"No, Patrick, no more. My day is not finished."

Rosa Butler walked back into the room carrying a tray with a full tea service that she set on the same end table, sliding the bourbon bottle to one side. "Cream or sugar, Doctor?"

"No, ma'am. Just as it comes out of the pot."

She poured, handed him the cup of steaming amber warmth, and sat down and waited for the doctor to speak.

A very weary Dr. Jones lifted eyes filled with sadness to her. "Your sister has the Spanish influenza."

Rosa gasped.

"I have done what I can. The rest is up to Dora and God."

The silence was heavy like summer humidity in the room.

"When will we know?" It was Patrick who asked.

"Very soon, Patrick. This Spanish flu is killing millions around the world because it moves so fast. If she does not pass tonight, she may well wake up thirsty and perhaps even hungry tomorrow. You'll know then.

"There is still some danger to all of you. The children especially. Keep them out of her room. Keep Dora comfortable. Cold compresses will keep her temperature down. Try to make her drink, though she may resist you. Try at least."

The silence returned.

"And Momma? What of her?"

The sadness remained in his eyes. "She is heartbroken,

Rosa. There is nothing wrong with her save that it appears she has no desire to live. Perhaps the children will cheer her. Or you. Or a favorite book." He pointed across the room to the piano shoved awkwardly against one wall. "I see you've brought her piano over. Play for her. Anything she enjoys may work. Give her a reason. Try to give her joy."

"And if Dora dies?" Again, it was Patrick who spoke what was in their heavy hearts.

"They may go together."

CHAPTER 11

October 9, 1918
Long Beach, California

"Clark!"

Sam, who had just stepped down from the engine, looked toward the sound of his name being shouted by some unknown clerk running across the yard.

"Yeah, what?"

"Get your ass to the office. Now!"

"About what?"

"Don't have a clue. Boss just said to get you fast so the phone bill doesn't run up. Long distance."

As Sam burst through the office door, the room went from a noisy hum to dead silence, as though everybody in the room had been struck dumb by his appearance. All eyes fixed on him, but no one said a word and no one maintained eye contact when he looked back. A yeoman in his white uniform held the receiver toward him.

"Clark here," he said as he put the receiver to his ear.

"Sam, George here. George Grainger. You sitting, Sam?"

"No, I'm standing in the office, holding the fucking phone to my face, talking to you."

"Sit down, Sam." It was the softest he'd ever heard that voice. And it was gentle. Unbelievably gentle. Neither a tone nor emotion that he knew Grainger possessed. And it commanded him. He gave the phone back to the yeoman, walked around the counter, and sat in the chair the navy clerk had stood to offer.

"OK, George. I'm sitting." The rushed exasperation was gone from his tone.

"Sam, you have to come home."

"What? Why, George? Why am I coming home?" Fear struck him. None of this was normal. His backbone went limp, and he melted into the chair.

There was long silence on the other end. "It's Dora, Sam." The voice said no more.

Sam's backbone would no longer support him, and he folded forward, his elbows on the desk and his face down. "What about her, George?"

The silence was even longer this time. "Sam, Dora died last night."

Everything went numb. Nothing worked. There was no time. There was nothing. After a moment, he forced himself upright, but his heart seemed not in his body. His mind seemed not to work. His throat was full and he swallowed. "What do you mean she's dead?" Sam heard himself saying.

"Everybody thought it was grief after her father died. She collapsed at the gravesite. They took her home and called Doc Jones. It wasn't grief. It was the Spanish flu. She died in her sleep."

Sam collapsed his face onto the desk, on top of the papers stacked there. His left arm simply lay before him, the right holding the phone to his face.

"Sam. Sam," the voice said softly, "can you hear me?"

"I hear," he mumbled.

"Larry seems to be fine. The Butlers have him. Mrs. Adler is not. She seems in a coma of some kind. But you need to come home, Sam."

* * * *

Two weeks later, Sam Clark sat alone, save the company of his bottle on the bar before him. There was the usual laughter of camaraderie at the almost-perpetual nickel-ante Masonic Lodge poker game behind him. He'd been invited to join when he came in, but he just hadn't felt like camaraderie since he got home. He knew they would tolerate him, even glum as he was. He was invited every time he stepped in the door. Before he'd left for California, he'd been reasonably good at it and most evenings left with a couple of bucks more in his pocket than he'd come in with. But unless he was attending a lodge meeting, all he came here for now was to drink.

Sam wasn't an angry drunk. He was cordial and even returned smiles. But he stayed inside himself and medicated his pain with whiskey. A man was welcome to do that here.

"Sam, you don't know me, but I'm going to sit and talk with you."

Sam unhunched his shoulders, turned his head to the sound of the calm tenor voice, and looked up. The man beside him appeared just a bit younger than he. He had a head full of brown hair that seemed to hang off his forehead and almost into his eyes. Sam guessed that the hair and the pale skin that was still dotted with a few freckles made the stranger look perhaps younger than he actually was. His eyes were a brilliant blue and set inside eye sockets so deep as to make them appear wise or at least smart. His eyelashes were long enough to soften a face whose long jaw and pointed chin would have made it look sharp without them.

"Pull up a stool and share my bottle," Sam said. No smile accompanied the offer.

"If I'm going to drink your whiskey, let me introduce myself first." He extended his hand at an angle that forced Sam to turn toward him and straighten his shoulders. "I'm Lloyd McHugh. They let me in here last year. It was after you'd gone to the West Coast."

Sam shook the hand and then patted the top of the stool beside him. As McHugh sat down, Sam rose above his stool, reached over the bar, and fumbled for a clean glass from below the counter. He found one, set it before McHugh, and poured. "You related to James?"

"My grandfather." He picked up the newly filled glass and held it up toward Clark. "To lodge brothers and new friendships."

The glasses gave off a clear, crisp tone as they touched.

"Your grandfather was one of the first men I met in Beardstown. How is it I've not met you?" Before McHugh could answer him, Sam added, "Come to think of it, I've never met your father either. You both wanderers?"

"He is, not me. Dad never much liked this place. You said it just right. After my mother died, he just wandered off when I was pretty young. Grandfather and Louise raised me." He smiled a smile of reverie. "She never wanted to be called 'Mom.' Always insisted on 'Louise.' I guess all her students called her Mrs. McHugh, well, Miss Gartland at first. She wanted something different from me, and she didn't want to be 'Grandma.' I suppose 'Louise' was merely the default."

Sam nodded, somewhat surprised he was getting all this autobiography but glad for company who didn't expect him to talk, didn't want to ask him how he felt. "So, why have we never met?"

"I left fourteen years ago. I think that's just before you arrived. Went away to college and then law school in Iowa. For the last five years, I've been clerking for a judge in Chicago. When Granddad got sick last year, it was time for me to come home. I was here for him the last few months before he died."

Sam said nothing and stared back down at the bar. So much death. Dora, old Lorenz and Fredericka, almost all together, and old James McHugh as well. Death seemed to stalk this town.

"He thought very highly of you, Sam. Do you know that?"

"Who?"

"My grandfather."

There was silence between them.

"I've made you think of your sorrows, Sam. I didn't intend that. I'm sorry for your Dora. She and I were kids together. She was a wonderful girl. So full of life. I can't imagine your pain. But pain is one of the things we have in common."

"What else do we have in common?" Sam asked.

Lloyd smiled. The first big smile Sam had seen on that face. "Sons. My Milton is four. Same age as yours, I believe."

Sam nodded and smiled. "Larry will be four in about three months."

"They'll grow up together, Sam."

Sam's heart was lifting for the first time in weeks. "Now that you are home, what are you going to do? Open a law practice?"

"I plan to take over Granddad's old practice," Lloyd said, smiling.

Sam paused, his lips pursed in thought. "He was the state's attorney, right?"

"Damn near his whole life," Lloyd responded.

"When he died, what happened to his job?" Sam was clearly perplexed.

"Governor appointed an attorney to fill out his term. Guy named, Carson. Jed Carson."

"So how you gonna take over the job?"

"Granddad's term was to end January first. His replacement only lasts until then. It's an elected office. I'll run for it."

Sam looked even more confused. "Election is next Tuesday. Right?"

"Yep. I'm on the ballot."

"It's that simple?" Sam asked.

Lloyd McHugh chuckled. "Pretty much. Jed Carson is from Robinson. Up against the Indiana line a lot of miles east and south of here. Not a soul in Beardstown knows him. Me they know. I'm a McHugh. It's a name they trust. I'll win."

Sam marveled at Lloyd's confidence but couldn't muster any words. He turned to his glass and took a drink.

"I forgot. There is a third thing we have in common as well." Lloyd McHugh was still smiling.

"What's that?" Sam said, turning back to his new friend.

"We love to hunt. I hear you're a very good shot. Better than anyone around at highflyers. I also hear you've got a very good dog."

Modesty caused Sam not to speak.

"You working tomorrow, Sam?"

"No. Don't have a run until Monday. Why?"

"How about I pick you up a bit before dawn and we go hunt some dinner for our families?"

It was the first time Sam had really felt joy in what seemed like forever. "You're on."

* * * *

Sam was two houses from home when he heard the piano. In a few steps he knew it was coming from the living room, the Butlers' living room. And it was ragtime. *Odd music for a house in mourning.*

The piano was still pushed against the far wall of the living room. Rosa sat on one end of the bench. Beside her sat a boy of about ten with bright-red hair, pounding away at the keyboard with surprising agility and ease for one so young. To one side of the piano another redhead, a girl of maybe twelve or thirteen, sat watching what Sam guessed were her younger brother's fingers flying across the keyboard.

Sam stood inside the door, mesmerized. Only when the boy came to an end did Sam make himself known with a small round of applause. Rosa and the girl and boy all looked up.

Rosa glanced over her shoulder at him, her face slowly brightening. "Nice to see you smile, Sam."

He said nothing but merely shoved the door until the metallic click sounded.

Rosa stood up. "Sam, these are my first students. Children, say hello to Mr. Clark. Sam, these are Portia and Kenneth Norville."

The young girl stood up from her chair as the boy slid off the bench and stood beside her. "Pleased to meet you, Mr. Clark," they said almost in unison.

"My pleasure as well," Sam offered and then, looking at the boy, added, "Thanks for making me smile. I needed one."

"All right, children, time for you to go. Let me help you bundle up and get you on your way home," Rosa commanded as Sam stepped through the living room and into the kitchen.

He was drinking a glass of milk at the kitchen table when she came back in.

"Who is that kid?" Sam asked.

"That kid is a difficult student, is who that kid is. His sister is almost a model student. Does her scales and practices her timing and technique. All that boy wants to do is bang out ragtime. Poorly."

"Being a bit of a perfectionist, aren't you?"

"The only way one learns to be good at something is doing it by the rules as the master teaches the rules, over and over and over."

"How long's he been playing?"

"Since the piano's been here. Just a few weeks. His mom tried to teach him a bit before that, I believe."

"Well, he already plays good enough to make a sad man smile."

"He'll make me smile if he follows the rules. That's when he'll get better." She came over and gave him a little kiss on the cheek. "Don't forget to turn off the kitchen light when you go to bed." She turned and walked away.

"Rosa," he said softly.

She turned to him.

"People who break the rules are the ones who bring new things into this world; they make the world richer."

CHAPTER 12

February 14, 1919
Beardstown, Illinois

The automobile lights flashed off and on in front of the house. Sam stepped out the back door and whistled as he closed it. Teddy came bounding from the shed as he walked around the corner of the house and toward the big four-door enclosed sedan parked at the curb.

"Lloyd, this new Dodge is too fancy for Teddy to ride in the back. We can park this and take my old Buick."

"Nope, I'll wipe the leather down before Beulah sees it. Get the beast in the back and hop in."

Dawn found them sitting on camp stools inside the blind, waiting for the ducks to fly. Many had already made their way south, but they both knew there would be plenty enough left to bring home dinner. The sky moved from black to grey, soon becoming golden through the trees upriver. But the water before the blind was open, the ducks yet to rise. They would soon, and the two men knew they'd be home in time for a late breakfast.

There were a few quacks from early risers, and then the

first flyer splashed loudly, kicking with webbed feet and driving the tips of short wings into the water as he rose.

"He's yours, Lloyd," Sam offered.

Lloyd waited until the bird was high enough to be clearly outlined against the lightening sky, rose, pulled the gun tight into his shoulder, and squeezed the trigger. The bird dropped straight down.

The dog, though eager, remained seated quietly on his haunches, awaiting the instruction. Sam's hand made the anticipated motion. Teddy bolted straight up, front paws held tightly against his chest, landed with a splash, and swam straight and sure toward the floating bird. Once he had it, the dog did not turn back to the blind but swam straight forward to the nearest clump of grass rising above the slough.

Sam rose and whistled sharply, but the dog paid no attention. Sam whistled again and then shouted. The dog merely walked up onto the patch of grass, shook himself dry, and then sat down to enjoy a leisurely breakfast. "God damn it, dog. Get your ass back here now."

Lloyd started to laugh. It was a chuckle at first and then became a full-throated roar. "You forget to feed him breakfast, Sam?"

Muttering to himself, Sam laid his shotgun across his camp stool and stood cursing, hands on hips. He turned to look at his roaring companion and admitted, "I did, Lloyd. Indeed, I did. I've always said Chesapeakes are the best water dogs but a touch stubborn. And when I don't feed this one, he feeds himself."

Both men stood laughing in the morning dawn as a happy Chesapeake, his stomach now full, swam back to the blind, which he entered, throwing water all over the hunters.

Within forty-five minutes, they had the backs of their hunting coats full with more birds than they wanted to clean, each dutifully retrieved by Teddy. They walked, not talking, absorbing the beauty of a cool fall morning. When they reached the Dodge, they threw the shooting coats and guns in the trunk, rubbed the dog halfway dry, and started the drive home.

"May I ask a personal question, Sam?"

"Fire away, but I get one first. Why did the governor appoint a short-term fill-in that nobody around here knows?"

"So I'd win."

"That simple?" Sam asked.

"Yep. That simple. Now my question."

"OK, ask."

"You gonna spend your life driving a train?"

"It's a pretty good job, Lloyd. Only thing I'd rather do is this." He pointed at the dog in the back. "Before I came here, it's what I did. Guide rich men hunting. Good work, but it doesn't pay real well."

"And if you could make it pay well?"

"Even then bird hunting is seasonal. Just the fall and early winter."

"What if you could do both?" Lloyd asked.

"Huh. I don't understand."

"What if you could get time off from the railroad every year during hunting season?"

"That, Lloyd, would be perfect. But I don't think it's gonna happen."

Lloyd drove in silence for a few moments. "Sam, you know what Beardstown needs that it hasn't got?"

"What?"

"A business where people come from all over to leave money and then go home."

"What city wouldn't want that? But I don't think people just come anywhere and leave money. They always want something."

Lloyd nodded. "Think with me, Sam. Can you imagine a

business where people, maybe wealthy people, ride the train into town, take a hack to a hotel, stay in the hotel, buy meals and drinks, pay for all that, and then go home and don't take anything with them?"

Sam began to grin. "Don't take anything with them save some dead ducks that the good Lord provided and maybe a memory or two. Maybe even a photograph?"

"Now you're getting it."

"But you're not talking about just coming in, in ones or twos. You're thinking about lots of them. Right?" Sam asked.

Lloyd didn't respond except with a nod. He sat silently as he drove until the light of the still-low sun behind them began to reveal the red vision of a tall brick building through the trees. Lloyd pointed out the window. "Do you know that house up there? Le Salon?"

"I've heard it is a very elegant whorehouse, but I've never been there."

"About right, Sam, but you have the verb tense wrong. It hasn't been that for a long time. Old Vivienne de Villiere is about eighty by now. She brought all her women up from the South with her at the end of the Civil War. They were cultured and sophisticated. That"—he pointed out the window again to the building receding behind them—"was not really a whorehouse so much as a center of culture and refinement where, on occasion, a man might get the opportunity to spend a night with the sort of women seldom found on the frontier. You know what it's like in there?"

"No."

"It has a library, a billiards room, card tables, a kitchen to feed dozens of meals, a large stable, six large bedrooms on the second floor, and sleeping quarters for the help on the third floor."

"You sound like you know it well." Sam seemed surprised.

Lloyd laughed loudly. "In ways you'd never imagine, Sam.

Imagine it not as a whorehouse," Lloyd continued. "Imagine it a hunting lodge full of very rich men looking for an experience of hunting of a quality not really found anymore in America. Now, Sam, imagine one more thing. Imagine what it would take for you, you, Sam, to make that imagining a reality."

Lloyd said no more. He just waited as they drove along the brick paving of the city.

Finally, Sam spoke. "It would take three things, none of which I have or could get."

"Those are?" Lloyd asked.

"One, money. Two, that house. Three, an annual leave of about six months from the CB&Q."

Neither man spoke further until Lloyd pulled up in front of the Butlers'. "Sam, come to dinner on Sunday. Bring little Larry with you. There's someone I want you both to meet."

* * * *

When they arrived at the McHughs' that Sunday evening, Sam grabbed Larry's hand and ran up the walk, bounded up the front steps as fast as his son's short legs would allow, and knocked sharply on the front door. The door opened immediately, releasing a blast of warm air carrying the sweet smell of duck fat along with it.

"Come on in where it's warm," Lloyd welcomed. A boy about Larry's size, with a mop of unruly brown hair, had his arms wrapped around Lloyd's legs, half his head and one eye peeking out from behind.

Sam quickly stepped through the door, still clutching Larry's hand. As soon as the door was shut behind him, he said, "Larry, this is our friend Mr. McHugh."

Lloyd looked down at the boy standing beside his father. That he was his father's child was certain. Same wide face, square jaw, and light-brown eyes. His mother only showed in two ways. The hair was wavy like his father's but dark, almost black, like Dora's, and that the nose would become rounded in adulthood showed even in the child's face.

"Pleased to meet you, Larry," Lloyd McHugh offered with mock solemnity.

Four-year-old Larry stood, feet wide apart with his head somewhat bowed in shyness, but he held up his hand, his left hand, turned awkwardly so the palm would lie against the palm of the much larger one extended in greeting.

McHugh, offering no look of condescension or amusement at the youngster's gesture, wrapped his hand gently around Larry's and said, "My pleasure to meet you, Larry." Then, looking directly down his leg toward his son, instructed, "Milton, say hello to Mr. Clark."

The shy little boy kept his eyes firmly fixed on the floor and said, "Hello."

Sam squatted down to eye height with young McHugh and said, "It is my pleasure to meet you, Milton. Would you do something for me?"

The boy looked up but only momentarily.

"Milton, would you keep my son company?"

He looked out from around the leg behind which he had been sheltering and nodded. Then he turned and ran off.

It was McHugh who spoke. "Go on, Larry. Follow him."

Sam gave his son a nudge, and the boy went running off, following the other.

The two men laughed.

"Come on, Sam. Let me take you to the kitchen and introduce you to the women of my family."

Sam followed Milton toward the rich smell wafting from the kitchen. "Ladies, let me introduce Sam Clark. I'm not certain any of you know him. Sam, let me start with my beautiful wife, Beulah."

A woman with a pale face and white-blond hair, which

she'd tried without entirely succeeding to keep off her face by pulling it into a bun on top of her head, looked across the room with genuine warmth showing on her face. She was a thin woman, of medium height with breasts that seemed unusually large for her stature. "It is truly my joy to meet you, Mr. Clark. My husband genuinely enjoys your company, and if he does, I'm sure I will as well." She gave her husband a look that held love as well as scolding. "But if my husband had given me ten minutes more, I could have met you not looking like a disheveled cook and more like a well-groomed hostess," she said, using her hand to push a wisp of thin blond hair away from her face.

"Mrs. McHugh, you are lovely as you are. Any man would be in a haste to introduce you to his friends."

She looked directly toward her husband. "You did not tell me he was charming as well, Lloyd."

The McHughs shared a chuckle.

"And this, Sam"—McHugh pointed to a woman a few years older than his wife but clearly related—"is my sister-in-law, Lillian Wright. When I was clerking, I fished Beulah out of Morgan County, where Lillian still lives. She's just with us visiting for the holiday season."

"It is my pleasure to meet you as well, Miss Wright," Sam said with a neighborly smile.

"And I you, Mr. Clark. I believe it was your son I saw running through here just a moment ago, chasing after young Milton, but he didn't slow down enough for me to introduce myself."

They all shared another chuckle.

"Perhaps, over dinner, I can slow him down enough to make a proper introduction, Miss Wright." Sam then turned to the corner of the kitchen where Louise McHugh had been sitting and watching since the moment he walked in. He stepped toward her, the warmth of feeling showing in his smile. "And this beautiful woman is nearly the first person I met when I came to this town. She made me feel welcomed." He stooped low, almost in a bow, to extend his hand. "Hello, Mrs. McHugh. I've not seen you since your husband's death. I am so very sorry you lost him." No matter how often he saw her, he could never help but be taken by the beauty of this woman who, by now, had to be seventy-five but still her face was virtually unlined, the skin on her long jaw clinging firmly to the bone with almost no sag. Nor was there any truly noticeable bagging of the skin below her eyes. Her nose was still slim, her brown eyes glimmering with vitality. The only change seemed her hair, which while remaining rich and thick, had become a beautiful silver.

"Hello, Sam." She smiled up. "Let me share the same for your loss. The last time I had cried before James died was at your wedding. Dora was so beautiful waltzing with you in that creation with which her father crowned her."

Sam, still bending low, halted where he was. She could see him struggling. Only when he gained control of himself and his voice did he respond. It was slow and very controlled. "Thank you, Mrs. McHugh. That was a very special day. Thank you for bringing the memory back to me."

The room was entirely silent.

Two small figures came racing through, screaming.

"Sam, let's get out of here and let these ladies finish their work."

The two men sat at the table as the ladies decorated the long lace tablecloth with platters and bowls of steaming perfection. When they had gathered, Lloyd McHugh offered a blessing. Immediately upon his "Amen," Lloyd said, "This is one of the ducks that Sam's Chessie didn't eat."

The meal was one of much laughter and joy all around. Civilization was not only saved from freezing weather but brought to a perfection of food, drink, beauty, and camaraderie. And after the rich chocolate cake, the only ones at the table who were anxious were two little boys who wanted desperately to be given permission to go outside and frolic in the falling snow. Permission received, they bounded off, each followed by a woman determined to get him into winter clothes, scarves, and mittens whether the boys wanted them or not.

Louise McHugh offered, "You men go on to the front room. I'll bring you each a brandy and then start clearing."

"Louise," Lloyd said, "I like part of that, but not all of it."

"Which part do you like?" She smiled.

"I liked the bringing brandy to the front room, but not you clearing. There is a conversation I want to have with Sam, and you are part of it."

Louise nodded a perfect understanding. "Then you two step into the front room and let me bring a bottle and three glasses."

Lloyd rose and led the way to a sofa in the front room, where he pointed Sam to one end. He took the other. Louise followed quickly, carrying a silver tray with a crystal bottle and three matching glasses. She laid the tray on the table before the sofa and poured generously into the three glasses. She handed one to each of the men, took one in her own hand, and seated herself in the chair facing them.

"Sam, I've told Louise that I think you should modify your career and how doing so would not only make life better for you but also for the city. I've also told her of my grand plan to make that happen and the dilemmas you see along its path, the first of which being that the only place in Beardstown that will work for a lodge is Vivienne de Villiere's old Le Salon on Chandlerville Road."

Sam was astonished at the directness of this and even more surprised that Louise McHugh would be included in the discussion, and it showed all over his face. He took a sip of brandy to collect himself.

Lloyd continued. "I thought Louise might be able to help

with one of the issues you saw. So I've taken the liberty of shar-
ing our conversation. And she agrees she may be able to help
and is at least willing to try."

Sam now added confusion to his astonishment.

"Louise, may I ask you to continue from here?"

The refined and elegant woman set her snifter down.
"Where do you want me to start, Lloyd?"

"At the beginning."

Louise leaned slightly forward. "I think you know some of
my background, Sam. You knew I was James's wife and had
married him after Lloyd's mother died. And I believe you also
know that I had been the schoolteacher at St. John's School.
You knew those things, correct?"

"Yes, ma'am."

"Did you also know that James gave me that job? The job
teaching at St. John's School."

"That I did not know."

"Then neither do you know that I was introduced to James
McHugh by Vivienne de Villiere." A small, almost coquettish smile formed at the corners of her lips as she revealed this
secret.

Sam set his glass down abruptly, not even attempting to
hide the startled look on his face.

"Vivienne not only made the introduction but made the
contribution to St. John's that made the school possible."

"She did!" This time it was Lloyd McHugh's turn to be
startled.

"She did, Lloyd. It's true. I'd never have known that had I
not married your grandfather. He was the only one who knew.
Vivienne thought the church might reject the donation if they
knew it came from her. She channeled the money through
James and asked him to keep the donation anonymous. Her
contribution was a complete secret." Louise moved her eyes
back to Sam. "Sam, Vivienne and I were girls together. She was

a few years older than I, but our families knew one another. I'd always looked up to her as one of the older girls." Louise's face again took on the coquettish smile of a secret being revealed. "Truth is I was always a bit envious of her. She was the queen, the belle of the ball, in our social set.

"Our social set, Sam, was the Old South. We were among the Mississippi plantation elite. And then came the war. Sam, do you know anything about the battle of Vicksburg?"

"I know it was a long one. A siege, I believe."

"That's right, Sam, a siege. And the Yankees held the river. Porter and his gunboats sat in the river and cannonaded Vicksburg for weeks. There was not a building left standing. We all dug caves and lived in them to keep from being killed by Porter's guns. Almost as soon as Vicksburg surrendered, Vivienne got out. Not sure how, but she had money and she had guile. She picked Beardstown as her safe place to run. She wanted to live out her life in the manner she'd become accustomed, so she did what she had to do. That's how Le Salon came to be. After she got here and got set up, she sent back for us. I owe Vivienne de Villiere much, almost everything, really."

Louise took a sip of brandy. Both Lloyd and Sam just stared at her, unable to speak.

"Le Salon would be the perfect place for your hunting lodge," Louise finally said. "I have no idea if Vivienne will sell it, and I will do nothing to persuade her in any way if she doesn't. But if you want to meet and talk with her, I can certainly effect a proper introduction. The rest will be up to you."

Sam exhaled and sat back deeply into the comfort of the sofa, pondering and wondering at all he had just heard. After a moment he sat forward again, his eyes focused on Louise McHugh. "Mrs. McHugh, I'm not certain I can thank you enough for your offer, and I'm even less certain I'm worthy of it."

Louise McHugh started to speak.

Sam held up his hand, palm out, to stop her. "Mrs. McHugh, I haven't money to offer Miss de Villiere. If I can figure out how to get enough to approach her, I would very much enjoy meeting and talking with her. But not now. Now I have nothing to offer."

"Sam." It was Lloyd's voice beckoning him. Sam turned his head toward his friend at the end of the couch. "Do you know where one goes to get money?"

Sam was befuddled by the question and said nothing.

"To the bank, Sam. Let's go see what we can do now about getting you some money."

* * * *

For a man as old as he was, Anthony Hoskins had an incredibly modern style. He wore a thin worsted herringbone suit, blue-striped shirt with a white collar, and a silk necktie with a matching pocket square. It all seemed just a little too stylish for an old conservative banker, Sam thought.

After Lloyd's introduction, the very tall and almost skeletally thin old banker extended a hand, the skin of which seemed nearly translucent and showed the blue of every vein.

"My pleasure to meet you, Mr. Clark. Any friend of the McHugh family is a friend of mine, and I hope that of the Beardstown State Bank as well."

There was a precision to his speech, almost a clipped crispness that Sam found oddly out of place with the mumbled slurring of English he was used to. "My pleasure to meet you as well, Mr. Hoskins. I'm grateful you would offer me your time."

The light-brown eyes, showing no sign of clouding, twinkled down at him. "Most people who come to see me, Mr. Clark, seem to want me to offer more than my time."

Lloyd laughed out loud. "Anthony, you are direct."

Sam thought it odd that one as young as Lloyd would be

so comfortable with the aging banker as to make a joke of his approach and so familiar as to call him by his first name.

The banker ran the thin fingers of one hand through his hair, which was something between blond and silver, to push it smooth across his head. "Then allow me to be more proper and congratulate you on your victory and welcome you as Cass County's new state's attorney. I'm certain you will do the memory of your father proud." It was all said with a friendly, if paternal, smile on his face.

"As you have done yours my entire life, Anthony."

Sam, having no idea what they were talking about, resorted to the refuge of silence.

"Mr. Clark, young Lloyd and I run ahead of you, I fear." The banker's tone continued with its fascinating crispness. "My father was the first president of this bank. And while I am, in every fiber of me, a frontiersman, he was to his core a London banker. He used his skills to be the engine of this city's growth. Lloyd does me a great compliment in the comparison. And before we go further, let's stop the formality and call one another by our Christian names. Mine is Anthony, as you have heard."

"I'd be honored. I'm Sam."

"Good. Now that's past, sit down, please, and tell me how I can help."

Sam and Lloyd sat themselves in the two small wingback chairs before Hoskins's large walnut desk as he lowered himself into the huge Chippendale behind it.

"Let me start, Anthony," Lloyd said. "Sam is an engineer for the CB&Q. But that's just what pays the bills. What he's famous for are his hunting skills—bird hunting. Sam can knock the head off a Canada goose and not put one pellet in the body and do it to one so high in the air, your old eyes wouldn't see it until it started to fall. The honest truth is that's how he got the job at CB&Q. Do you know C.C. Cunningham, Anthony?"

"Only by reputation. Never met the man. Why?"

"He's the one who found Sam. He didn't have a job for him but knew Grainger did and sent him here with a very high recommendation. Grainger hired him and thinks enough of him that he protected him from the draft during the war. But I want more out of him than that. I want Sam to bring money into our city."

Anthony leaned forward. Money always got his attention.

"Anthony, imagine if Beardstown had a hunting lodge run by a man with enough reputation that men came from all over to hunt. We lack for tourist dollars in Beardstown. I think Sam can turn on that tap."

Hoskins wheeled his head, his eyes pinning Sam Clark. "Just how are you going to do this?"

Sam sat quietly for a moment. He didn't want his excitement to show. He wanted to be the picture of self-assured calm. "I'm going to buy Le Salon. I'm going to put up hunters in style. They will get much of what they got in the old place before it closed. Much, but not all. I'm not a pimp. I'm a hunter. They will get a great hunting experience on the richest flyway along the entire Mississippi drainage, and they will get it with a great room, meal, and whiskey."

"What does your proforma look like, Sam?"

"Proforma?" Sam was stumped.

Hoskins chuckled. "Fancy banker word for books. What's all this going to cost you, and how much will it bring in?"

Lloyd hopped in. "Anthony, what we wanted was to see if the idea interests you. If it does, we'll put the books together. But it will make money. Enough for the bank to make some money and get paid back. And all those hack rides, meals, drinks, guns, and hunting gear that will be sold in shops all over the city will be good for us all."

"Gentlemen, you have my attention. My father loaned Miss de Villiere the money to build that place. Come back when you have numbers and we'll talk turkey." The banker paused and then smiled. "No, we'll talk geese and ducks, won't we?"

They all chuckled.

"But I do have one question," the banker continued. "Will Vivienne de Villiere sell?"

"We'll go find out, Anthony," Lloyd said as he stood up. "We'll go find out right now."

* * * *

The Dodge rolled slowly up the gravel-covered path through the park bereft of flowers, leaves, and warmth. Lloyd pulled to a stop at the wide circulation near the front door. He stepped out and opened the rear door, offering his hand to Louise. She stepped into the weak sunshine, her broad-brimmed black silk hat providing shade from even these palest of rays. The top of her outfit was a double-breasted garment hanging to her hips and serving as both dress and coat. The black pleated skirt coming out below the hem hung to the middle of her calves.

Lloyd's black topcoat covered all traces of what he wore below save the dark, sharply creased gabardine trousers and cordovan brogans showing below. Sam stepped out of the passenger-side front seat. He was dressed in his best suit, the one Lorenz Adler had made for him a dozen years before. The three slowly walked the flagstones to the steps rising up to the large double doors.

The woman who answered their knock was in her midsixties. Her hair, which appeared once to have been blond streaked with grey, now appeared to be grey streaked with blond. She had cut it smartly short. Her dress featured a long collar leaving her pearl-bedecked neck open. Like Louise's, the garment hung to the bottom of her calves, her white hose matching the rings of white orbiting her dress from waist to hem.

It was Louise who spoke. "I'm Louise McHugh. Miss de Villiere's note said she would receive us this afternoon."

"Yes, you're expected. Please do come in." She stopped momentarily in the cloakroom to allow Lloyd to hang his topcoat and then proceeded through the large front room and to the library in the far corner of the ground floor. The tall curtains had all been swept back to allow the winter light to illuminate the room. "Please, make yourselves comfortable. I'll bring you some tea. Miss de Villiere will be in shortly."

Louise made herself comfortable in the seating group by the far window where she could enjoy the vision of stark beauty offered by the winter's day. Sam stepped to the billiard table and rolled a cue across its green felt, amazed that the stick did not show any bounce as it rolled. Lloyd stepped from book to book on the library shelves, caressing the spines with the same tenderness one might use to stroke the hair on a beloved child's head. All found contentment here.

Their greeter stepped back into the room, carrying a large silver tray before her; a porcelain teapot and four matching cups and saucers twinkled in the glow of the silver. Without a word she laid the tray on the table before Louise, turned, and walked away. Louise stroked the rim of one of the cups with almost the same love Lloyd had offered the books. She lifted it and held it to the light of the window, the porcelain so thin that not only the light showed through but the shadow of the curtain as well.

"Do you think it is Chinese or bone, Louise?" The question came from the entry door in a voice held together with honey.

Louise McHugh didn't look up. "It is Staffordshire, Vivienne. Even the finest Chinese porcelain isn't this translucent." So saying, she rose, stepped around the table, and strode across the room with movement that made it seem she was floating.

The two women met midway across the floor and holding one another by the shoulders, exchanged kisses on the cheek.

"Gentlemen," Louise commanded, "allow me to introduce the friend I have held in my heart longer than any other, Vivienne de Villiere."

Sam and Lloyd had both turned, entranced to watch the embrace of the two elegant figures. Transfixed, neither man had taken a step. Simultaneously each seemed released from the spell and stepped forward to see a woman who, even now, showed she had been a great beauty, but now, in her declining years, her black hair was salt-and-pepper; the skin on her face was still pale white but now hung low below her eyes, filling in what once must have been the profound ridge of her cheekbones. It also hung below the line of her jaw, robbing her entire face of the firm lines that once defined its beauty. Her eyes seemed to penetrate Sam's every thought yet leave complete mystery as to hers.

"Vivienne, allow me to introduce my escorts. First, my step-grandson, Lloyd McHugh."

Lloyd took a step forward. "It is my great pleasure to meet you. Both my grandfather and Louise have sung your praises to me my entire life."

Vivienne held her hand out to him. Lloyd accepted it and, bending forward, made the antique gesture he knew she expected and kissed the white skin tracked with blue veins.

"You favor your grandfather, Lloyd, and that fact alone is enough to give me joy in your presence."

"Vivienne, allow me to also introduce Sam Clark," Louise said. "He is both friend and business associate to Lloyd."

Vivienne turned to the tall, handsome young man with the wavy mass of light-brown hair. She studied him and made no pretense that she was not.

Sam waited, uncertain if it was courtesy or fear that stayed his tongue.

Vivienne eased her studied look and replaced it with a smile so full of honey that it matched her voice. "Mr. Clark, it is my pleasure to meet you, and know that any friend of the McHughs is welcome in my home. Now enough of the formalities. Please let's all sit together and chat. Nancy will be in momentarily with scones and cream and perhaps a finger sandwich or two."

Almost immediately upon their seating, the door opened, and Nancy, as though on cue, appeared with another tray, this one a bit smaller and carrying a basket of sweet breads, a cup of clotted cream, and a separate tray of small sandwiches.

Sam had never seen anything like them. They were bite-sized, and the bread crusts had been trimmed. Dainty but useless.

Vivienne poured for all and offered the small snacks around before she spoke of anything other than polite platitudes. When her guests had all been made welcome and comfortable, she opened the conversation. "Louise, it has been so seldom we've seen one another. But you have been working and then raising Lloyd and caring for James. And I, until just a few years ago, have been busy with Le Salon." She raised her right hand; her index finger pointing upward moved in a small arch. "But we have known one another since we were girls. I do hope this meeting may be a new beginning for us." She let the phrase drop in a way that said she wasn't yet finished. "Unless, of course, that would be difficult for you in any way." There was no guile in her tone.

Lloyd was taken aback. He felt as though he'd just heard a plea of the heart.

Louise held her cup delicately, the pinkie extended. She did not set it down but looked over it, her face as unguarded as Vivienne's. "How very strange our lives have been, yours and mine. Ours. There is no one in this room, no one in this town, perhaps no one in this world save you and me who would understand. Our paths were the same, and then they diverged. But they didn't go in opposite directions, did they? Our paths ran parallel through the forest of the danger of our young adulthood. Now that both paths have come safely to shelter, I think it would be wonderful if they came back together."

Vivienne's steel-grey eyes had been held unblinking and remained so as one small tear rolled out of the corner of one eye. She let gravity pull it downward for a moment before dabbing it with her napkin. "Then we will make them do just that." She seemed to have recovered herself. "Louise, we will have much time to reminisce, but you did not bring these two beautiful young men with you today to watch an old woman cry. So, at the risk of being abrupt, may I ask what is on your mind? Your note did not say."

"Well, my purpose was to introduce them to you, but Lloyd asked for the introduction for a particular reason, so perhaps it's best if I let him explain." She turned her eyes to her step-grandson as though to say, "You're on."

"First, Miss de Villiere, let me thank you for receiving us into your home. I admit I have wondered about you forever. You who appeared in our frontier town, when it was a frontier town, as though by magic ascended from a cloud, or perhaps just a river queen instead of a cloud. But you appeared. Just appeared and created here what was a sanctuary of culture and refinement. We owe you much."

Vivienne watched with interest. Not taken with his flattery, just interested in how this very articulate young man was going to weave his web. It was the appreciation one seller of dreams offers to another.

"What you created here seems to no longer interest you but still has value, real value, to our little city. Sam Clark"—he nodded his head toward Sam—"is a man of many talents, some of them hidden, but they are talents I think could bring much to our city, both in terms of dollars and culture, and bring life back to what you have created. And I think it best if he tells you of his dream rather than I." And he stopped talking.

Sam was unprepared for this. He was not the smooth, articulate spinner of dreams his friend was, but Lloyd was right. It was his dream. Lloyd had only managed to form something solid out of the clouds of his imagination. But the imagination was his.

The teacup was far too small for his hand. He set it down. When he looked back up, the grey eyes were giving him their undivided attention. "Miss de Villiere, I'm not like you or your friends. I'm not educated. I'm a frontiersman still. A man who grew up a boy with dogs and traplines and shotguns. I managed to get a job as an engineer on the CB&Q and came east for it. It's a good job. I like it. It feeds and houses me and my son comfortably."

"Son?" she asked. "You don't mention your wife."

Sam swallowed. "Only because I don't wish to make a fool of myself showing emotion. We lost her just over a month ago to the flu. Truth is, I think Lloyd stirred up this pot in me to get me out of a deep ravine of sadness."

"I'm so sorry. Forgive me."

Sam smiled a weak smile. "It's all right, Miss de Villiere. I've heard a bit about you, and I believe you were about my age when you lost your family as well. If I could live my life any way I wanted, Miss de Villiere, it would be hunting."

"He is stunningly good at it, Vivienne, from what I hear. At least I know I, and all Sam's friends, seem to have goose on our tables long after other houses don't." It was Louise who spoke.

Sam continued. "Lloyd thinks I can not only do that but prosper at it if I don't guide just one hunter at a time but open a hunting lodge."

"A very fancy hunting lodge," Lloyd McHugh interjected.

"And that's where I come in." It was a statement from Vivienne de Villiere.

"Yes, ma'am," Sam responded. "Would you sell this to me?"

Vivienne reached forward, picked up the teapot, and poured around to each of her guests. When all cups were filled, she set the pot back on the silver tray and looked at Lloyd.

"Lloyd." She paused. "May I call you Lloyd? I know it is familiar, but I've known your step-grandmother all my life and was on a first-name basis with your grandfather, who represented me and my interests for years."

"It would give me pleasure if you would, Miss de Villiere."

She nodded. "Lloyd, I read the papers. I have much time to do so these last few years. I believe congratulations are in order to you."

"Congratulations? Why?"

"Did you not win election to fill your grandfather's long-term role as state's attorney for Cass County?"

Lloyd smiled. "I did, and thank you."

Vivienne's nod said her congratulations were a matter of little significance. "But you are now a county official?"

"Yes."

"And as such you have access to county records?"

Again, Lloyd said, "Yes," but suddenly his eyes were wary.

"So, you would know who in the county is in arrears in their property tax payments?"

His eyes held hers as he nodded.

"Do you, Lloyd, happen to know that I and Le Salon are three years in arrears on property tax payments?"

Lloyd tried to avoid the sheepish look of a small boy caught looking at someone else's exam paper for a proper answer. "Yes, I do."

Sam and Louise both looked toward Lloyd, but neither spoke.

Vivienne sipped her tea, set the cup down, picked up a scone, covered it with clotted cream, and took a small bite. No one seemed to breathe as she indulged her whimsy. "Since Le Salon has ceased to be of sufficient interest to me to continue its management, my income has declined to almost nothing. My tastes, I fear, have remained expensive. Property taxes have been beyond my reach. Lloyd." She looked back at him. "How many years must property taxes be in arrears before the property is sold by the county?"

"Five."

"Short of selling off possessions, nothing will change in my circumstances in the next two years. And that I don't wish to do. So, I will be gone from this"—she made an exaggerated gesture taking in the entirety of the premises—"in two years whether I sell it or not."

She looked around the group, but no one spoke.

"Here is what I want. I want a place for Nancy and me to live. She was eleven when I hired her as a maid and has been with me since. She will be with me when I die. The place will need to be at least two bedrooms. I don't wish to leave Beardstown. And, Louise"—she looked directly at her old friend—"if you meant what you said, I would like the place to be close enough to you that two old ladies can easily walk to one another for afternoon tea and gossip."

Louise said nothing; her face was warmed to appearing deeply sentimental.

"I will need something to live on. I think the $5,000 that I paid for this"—she looked back at Louise—"which is what Daddy sold the 'Leaping Kitty' for, will do. So, Mr. Clark"—her gaze turned to Sam—"Le Salon will cost you one house, $5,000, and back taxes."

* * * *

Anthony Hoskins's still-tall frame but failing eyes caused him to crane down over his desk when he read figures, which was what he was doing now. He'd been studying the page for ten minutes as Sam Clark and Lloyd McHugh sat with apparent patience but great internal anxiety as the old banker reached his conclusion.

Hoskins raised his head to the length of his spine and pointed his chin upward to straighten the kinks out of his neck. "You wouldn't think banking an arduous task, but the older I get, the more my body objects. Don't suppose there is one damn thing to be done about that.

"Well, let me summarize what it is I see. Sam grants his house to Vivienne de Villiere; the Beardstown State Bank puts in $8,000. That's $1,000 to pay off taxes in arrears, $5,000 to Miss de Villiere, and $2,000 to clean up the old place and stock the bar and kitchen. The bank gets a first trust deed, again"—the old man's face became a most amused, if crinkled, smile—"and this new business makes regular payments to eventually clear the loan, at which point Mr. Clark owns the property free and clear. Have I summarized correctly?"

Sam and Lloyd looked at one another and both nodded.

"There is only one issue the bank has with this deal."

Both men sat forward.

"Sam, would you agree the value of your house is $2,000?"

"Yes."

"All in, that means there's $10,000 in the deal. The bank has got in $8,000 and you've got in $2,000. That's eighty percent contribution from me and twenty percent from you. Right?"

"That's right?"

The old banker took off his glasses, took the silk pocket square out and rubbed them clean, and put them back on. He offered a hard and penetrating look to Sam. "Not enough from you, Sam. I need twenty-five percent from you. That is, the most the bank will put in is $7,500. You have to come up with another $500."

Sam tried to keep the anxiety off his face. "I haven't got it. I've got about $75."

There was a long silence in the room.

Finally, Lloyd spoke. "I'll put in the $500, Sam," he said as he turned toward him. "That means between us we've got in $2,500 of which $500, so twenty percent, is mine. That gives me a twenty percent interest in the business. That make it work?"

Sam sat numb, not knowing what to say or do. This was all very quick.

"Thanks, Lloyd. I'd agree to that, but there is one other thing that really bothers me. The longer I think, the more it does."

"And that is?" Hoskins asked.

"The house isn't mine."

Both men turned sharply to him and stared.

"Lorenz Adler did not give that house to Dora and me for a wedding present. He gave it to Dora. And when she died, her will didn't give it to me. She gave it to Larry. I'm the trustee. Control goes to him when he turns twenty-one."

"That's all, Sam? That's the problem?" It was Anthony Hoskins asking.

"Yes, that's the problem."

"Then it's not a problem, Sam," Hoskins responded. "You have perfect legal authority as trustee to handle the asset, invest, as you see the interest of the trust to be."

"And as a father?" Sam peered forward.

There was momentary silence before Hoskins spoke again. Before he did, he peered up at the ceiling briefly. When his eyes came down, they were focused on Sam again. "This is something only you can decide. Do you take some modest risk with your four-year-old's estate, and may I add you personally are risking your life to make this work—your risk is far greater than his, and if this works as we all think it will, you will create far more wealth for the boy than merely a small house in seventeen years. Do you take that risk to create something beautiful and of value? Or do you merely drive trains the rest of your life?"

* * * *

Sam and Lloyd walked out the front door of the bank, turning up their coat collars and tucking their hands into their coat pockets.

Sam's lips were pursed tight. "We have one remaining problem. I still don't have a clue how I'm going to get the CB&Q to agree to give me six months off every year."

"You may just have to ask!"

CHAPTER 13

January 1919
Beardstown, Illinois

The wind coming off the river made it feel even colder than the thermometer may have suggested. The men pulled up their collars, and Cunningham pulled leather gloves from his pockets to warm his hands. They walked in silence from the Princess Theatre toward the Park Hotel. Cunningham stopped to light another cigar.

"That's $5 you owe me, George." Cunningham looked up with a most satisfied smile at his much larger companion. "But how about we settle up with you buying the drinks?" Cunningham's grin got bigger as he took the cigar out of his mouth. "Your local boy never had a chance. Jimmie Hanlon didn't come all the way from Denver just to lose a boxing match to an unskilled ox."

George Grainger walked in what Cunningham couldn't tell if it was sullen silence or thoughtfulness. When Grainger finally spoke, Cunningham got his answer. "C.C., I've had a strange request from Sam Clark. Anyone else I'd have said no immediately, but it was Sam, so I said I'd talk to you about it."

Cunningham waved the flame out of the match, exhaling a cloud of smoke both men watched disappear into the night air.

"What did he want?"

"He wants a year off without tendering his resignation. And after that, he'd like to come back but only six months each year."

Cunningham stood expressionless for a moment. "Is he asking to get paid while he's gone?"

"Nope. Just wants time."

"What for?"

"He wants to start a hunting club." Grainger looked steadily at his boss, who looked back in silence, so he continued. "He's thought it out, C.C. Old Vivienne de Villiere has agreed to sell him her place, Le Salon. Hoskins and his Beardstown State Bank have agreed to bank him. City seems behind it as well. Thinks it will increase passenger traffic into the city. Kind of hunters who would come and put up at that old whorehouse are well-heeled outsiders. Perhaps they'd spend some money here other than their bill with Sam."

"Why does he need a year?"

"He says, the first season, he needs to lay out a bunch of blinds and will need to cut a road into the slough with a crawler tractor. He also will need to capture a lot of decoys and get a kennel of dogs trained. And he needs to refurbish de Villiere's old place. Says that will take all year, but once he gets it up, he will only need six months a year—October through January for hunting season, plus a month before to open up and a month after to close down."

"What do you think, George?" Cunningham was still expressionless, just calmly smoking.

"I like Sam and I like hunting with him and I'd like to see him succeed at this, but I hate playing favorites, and from the railroad's perspective, I'm going to need all the experienced engineers I've got."

"Why do you think that, George?"

"Congress is going to pass the Jones Act, isn't it?"

Cunningham nodded agreement.

"And Wilson will sign it, won't he?"

"He will. And after he does, every commercial vessel, including barge traffic, especially barge traffic really, that runs between two American ports will have to be built, owned, captained, and crewed by Americans, the idea being to cut out foreign competition on American waterways. Wilson's intentions are good," Cunningham said.

Grainger smiled down, and when he spoke it was so forceful, his breath blew steam into the night air. "The road to hell is paved with good intentions. He thinks this will be good for American riverboat owners, but it won't. And it sure as hell won't be good for farmers, growers of grain. Who it will be good for is us, the railroads.

"Wilson seems to have no idea how many barges are foreign built or owned. Barge carriers will be cut in half. Prices for river transport will rise so high, it may kill it, and it may kill river ports like this along with it. But one way or another, it will sure be good for the railroads. We may actually become the best-priced alternative for moving grain." George Grainger's grin was so wide, it filled his large face.

Cunningham didn't respond save to exhale more smoke into the night air. His expression became thoughtful. "You may be right about that, George. In fact, I suspect you are. But you're still wrong about needing all your experienced engineers."

Grainger looked startled. "Why?"

"There are a lot of other issues going on that will outweigh the positive effect of the Jones Act for the railroads, for the CB&Q. Let me mention a few. First, this line through Beardstown really serves almost no customers. Right?"

"Yes," Grainger dutifully responded. "We haul coal for US Steel's Gary works."

"And you know what's going on in Gary. Labor action there is not going to slow. There will be a strike, a big one, I think. Rumor comes to me that Indiana's governor, Goodrich, has contingency plans for inviting federal troops in to quell it when it happens.

"That's just one. Even if US Steel can settle with its laborers, I'm not sure they'll be able to stay open. To run those blast furnaces, they need all the coal we can get to them. And the miners are even more adamant than the steelworkers. There's a guy named John Lewis, John L. Lewis—biggest damn bushy eyebrows you've ever seen—who is trying to organize them. Even if the Gary works can keep their steelworkers happy, I'm not sure they'll be able to keep the coal miners happy."

The two men stood in the soft light of the gas lamp, blowing steam and smoke into the air.

"C.C., I hadn't meant this conversation to go this way," Grainger said, "but as long as we are here, this is as good a time as any to tell you."

"Tell me what?" Cunningham was scowling now.

"Beardstown will have municipal elections in April. Our union guys are running a slate for every seat. It looks like they will win," Grainger said.

Cunningham nodded understanding. "So, our labor troubles may not just be national or with our main client. They may become local as well."

Both men stood silent, Cunningham thinking and Grainger waiting.

"OK, George, give Sam his year starting when the ground thaws. I've become used to my masters at the Railroad Administration running this company. I'll know how to paper it by spring. This may get very ugly locally. Men will have to choose. Those who side with us will lose friends and family to those who don't. It may even get violent if we have to bring in contract laborers, scabs the union guys call them, to run this place. Maybe getting him out of the way will save Sam from some of that. Meantime, I've been told to lay some contingency plans for moving the shop and roundhouse to a less union-strident place. Maybe Galesburg."

CHAPTER 14

January 23, 1920
Beardstown, Illinois

Lloyd McHugh sat hunched over the accounting ledger, squinting at the numbers precisely penciled into the columns in Sam Clark's neat hand. Clark sat across from him, sipping at the tumbler of bourbon.

A chubby five-year-old mass of black curly hair came running into the study screaming, "Daddy!" and jumped into Sam's lap, splashing his father's whiskey across the chair, the rug, Sam's clothes, and the edge of Lloyd's desk, barely missing the ledger.

Sam picked the little boy up high over his head and let him fall back into his lap. The boy climbed up the front of his father's vest, threw his arms around his neck, and held on tight. Sam pried the thick little fingers from around his neck, pulled the boy back, and gave him a kiss on the cheek. Then in a tone of severity said, "Larry, you need to be more cautious when you jump. You not only spilled my whiskey; you spilled it all over my clothes and Mr. McHugh's furniture."

The little boy looked very solemn. He dropped his head low in contrition and said, "I'm sorry, Daddy."

"Honey, it's really Mr. McHugh you need to apologize to."

The little bundle turned in his father's lap and looked across the desk. "I'm sorry, Mr. McHugh. If I promise to be better, may I still come over to play with Milton?"

McHugh's face transformed instantly from a frown to a smile. "Larry, there is nothing you could do to make yourself unwelcome here. But I would be grateful if you'd go back to playing with Milton until your father and I finish."

"Yes, sir," came the still-solemn response. Then a turn and a quick kiss for his father, and he bounded off Sam's lap and away with the energy and enthusiasm that only a small boy could muster.

Both men looked after the little boy running out of the room, off to a new adventure.

"It really is good of you and Beulah to give him the run of the place," Sam said.

"Sam, he's here more than you are. Milton wouldn't know what to do without 'my best friend.' And," Lloyd added with a smile that said more than his words, "since Lilly moved in, she's really learned to love that boy. She seems to enjoy looking after the both of them."

Sam's expression offered no understanding of any double meaning intended.

Lloyd looked back at the books for just a second and then quickly back up. "It's a good first year, Sam. Very good. We did a bit better than break even on the lodge, which is far better than the first year of most businesses."

"Yes, we did, but I'm still worried."

"About what, Sam?"

Sam held up his now-empty glass and twisted it in his hand.

"Oh, sorry." Lloyd reached for the bottle behind him and then poured into Sam's glass.

Sam held it in place. "Thanks, but I wasn't intending to ask for more. I was making the point that my worry is whiskey. Specifically, the sale of the stuff. It was just like in our original pro forma projections." Sam smiled a self-deprecating smile. "Look at me using Anthony Hoskins's big word. But that big word predicted the sale of whiskey would make up a large percentage of the lodge's profit. And it did. What will we do next year without it?"

Lloyd held up his glass. "Yep, this may be the last. We're one week into Prohibition. No longer legal to make, sell, or transport any alcohol in America. Once we drink this up, it's the last. In theory."

"Why, 'in theory'?"

"Sam, a new business is about to blossom in America. A tax-free business. Stills and breweries will spring up in every city and town in America. There will be plenty of booze."

"And we will sell that at the lodge?"

Lloyd McHugh sat placidly for a moment, but finally a small grin appeared at the corners of his mouth. "Sam, let me give you a long answer. First thing is you will go back to the lodge and, except for a few bottles of whatever you have around for yourself, you'll smash every bottle you've got in the place."

"Every bottle?" Sam gulped.

"I'm the state's attorney, and I'm also your partner. I cannot be caught breaking the law. So yes, every bottle. Daniel Roper is the guy who heads the Bureau of Internal Revenue. He's a proud teetotaler and has publicly announced that every spare agent he has will be assigned to root out the sin of production or sale of alcohol. Don't know if you've heard yet, but just this week, he sent a couple of feds over from Springfield. They busted two guys in an old Buick, something about Buick drivers"—he gave a wicked smile—"who were transporting twenty-five cases of Old Crow whiskey. Feds are like flies on shit on the issue. And they will be . . . for a while. But it's like everything else. It will cool after this first burst of zeal. When it does cool, the feds will focus on a few big fish. Maybe that time will come by next year's duck season. Maybe it won't. If it doesn't, we'll just have to find some other source of revenue for our business. But that is tomorrow's problem."

Lloyd broke into a smile big enough to show a row of smooth white teeth. "Today's problem is my wife said the goose would be out of the oven by five o'clock and it's five fifteen now. Time to go join the women and boys before I get yelled at."

Sam smiled back, drained the last of his glass, and stood up. Lloyd was ahead of him, walking toward the office door. He stopped so suddenly, Sam almost ran into the back of him.

"A thought just came to me. If, by opening next year, we still haven't figured a way to increase revenue, I know a way we could decrease expenses." His smile was almost overbearingly large.

"How?" Sam responded, his tone made skeptical by the look on his friend's face.

"You could always fire your chief cook and housekeeper. I'm pretty sure I know someone who would do the job for free if the circumstances were right. Might even get your son back into your house at the same time."

Sam frowned and lowered his head. "Come on. Let's go to dinner."

* * * *

Sam took the key from his pocket, unlocked the padlock, and opened the door. He smiled, looking at the bib overalls and goggles hanging from pegs, the boots on the floor, and the duck-billed, pin-striped hat sitting on the top shelf of the locker. He'd not seen them in almost a year. He not only took pleasure at the sight but was flooded with a wave of nostalgia by it.

"You've been away for a long time, Sam." There was no warmth in the voice.

He turned to see the short, powerful man behind him. Sam's face flooded with delight as he extended his hand to Talbot, a fellow engineer he'd not seen all year. "Talbot, I've missed you, you rowdy."

"Have you, Clark?" Talbot's tone was flat. He did not extend his frying-pan-sized hand to Sam but curled the fingers of both hands into balls and planted them firmly on his hips. His frown plowed the lines of his forehead into deep furrows.

Sam withdrew his hand. "What's eatin' you, Talbot?"

"A lot's happened since you left, and you've not been part of it, Clark. I'm wondering if you just ran."

"Ran from what?"

"The brotherhood, Sam. You still part of it?"

Sam arched his back to its full height so he towered over the fireplug. "If by brotherhood you mean the Brotherhood of Locomotive Engineers, the answer is yes. I'm not only part; I pay my dues every month whether I got a paycheck or not."

"Then where were you when we needed you?"

"Needed me for what?"

"Oh, couple of little things you might have heard of while you were hobnobbing with the big shots—two strikes, one hundred thirty firemen released from payroll, forty engineers demoted to firemen, couple of deaths in strikes in Chicago, and the fucking Walker Hines of the US Railroad Administration refusing to even meet with Warren Sloan, our guy running our brotherhood. And lest I forget, the effort to unionize all the other workers in town—hotels, restaurants, and the like— if news of those events didn't make it to the confines of the Masonic Lodge. Where were you, Sam?"

Sam let his shoulders drop and exhaled all the belligerence that he could. "Talbot, I've liked you since you called me 'New Kid' all those years ago. You have no reason to fight with me. So let me answer your question.

"In the last year I've tried to convert the old whorehouse

into a lodge. That has taken hiring cooks and housekeepers to do it and making payroll for them every week. I've had to train a stable of a dozen retrievers, cut a road into the Sangamon Slough, capture decoys, build a small warming hut and a bunch of duck blinds in a swamp. I've had to get the word out in order to get rich guys to come to this town and hunt with me and spend money in the rest of this town. And, oh yeah, try to raise a five-, no six now, year-old without a mother. That's what I've done for the last year."

Talbot took a step forward until he was close enough to look straight up at Sam. "Clark, I don't mind your peeing on my foot, but don't try to tell me it's raining. What you've been doing is having one hell of a good time thanks to the ass you've kissed at the CB&Q and the dicks you've sucked around here—Grainger's, Cunningham's, and Lord only knows who else's."

"OK, Talbot, that's enough."

Talbot turned to look behind him to see the flowing blond hair on the tall, thin, and still-youthful figure of the engineer nicknamed for his golden hair.

"You're a good union man, Blondie. Don't get on the wrong side of this," Talbot barked.

"You're right, Talbot. I am a good union man" was the response. "And so is Sam. I just heard him say it, and if he says it, I believe it. Don't confuse his desire to prosper with his loyalty to his brothers."

Talbot snorted, pushed his way past Sam, and continued down the concrete floor to his locker at the far end of the room.

Sam and Blondie stood staring at one another, neither seeming to know what to say. It was Blondie who finally smiled and extended his hand. "Good to see you, old friend. Good to see you."

Relief spread across Sam's face. "Thanks, Blondie. I appreciate your breaking that up. Never fought anyone with hands that big. Not sure I'd like to." He said it with a grin.

"Times have been tense. You've missed a lot, Sam."

"I guess I have. I read the papers, but I didn't know it was that bad. From what I read, engineers now get almost $6.00 a day compared to less than $5.00 just a few years ago. I read of the $65 million Congress gave Hines and his commission to run the railroads, that President Wilson's appointed a tribunal to look at wages again, and that today's the day control of this line goes back to the CB&Q management. Didn't seem all that ugly. I guess I just didn't know."

"It's amazing how war and government intervention and wages have torn apart this country and this town. Talbot is the hottest of all of us on these issues. You won't be popular around here, Sam. All the guys know of your palsy relationship with the brass. But as long as you're a good union member, you'll be fine. As long as you never cross a picket line, you'll be fine. But, Sam, never do that. I mean never. You do and there will be hell to pay."

CHAPTER 15

February 12, 1921
Chicago, Illinois

Sam walked slowly up the alley. The sun went low early this time of year. At five o'clock it was already dark. And Sam was weary. He'd gotten up early enough to catch the 6:10 into Chicago, carrying two old but large suitcases. And he'd spent the day walking the alleys in "the Loop," learning where the back entrances, the kitchen entrances, to the better hotels were. It had gone well. One suitcase was completely empty, and the other had only five ducks left, and Sam had $75 in the pocket of his tweed slacks. The Lexington was his last stop. Whether he sold his remaining ducks here or not, it would be his last stop. He had to make the 5:45 back home.

Sam had come up with the plan earlier that month, when he and Lloyd went through the lodge's books. The numbers just weren't adding up anymore without the booze. The only other thing he was good at was shooting, but he couldn't legally sell hunted game out of season. But as a licensed guide, he could sell the decoys. He never used wood decoys; only live ones he trapped. He figured he could drown twenty or so every week, pluck them, clean them, stuff them in a couple of suitcases with a little ice, and take a train ride to Chicago and visit a few chefs at a few of the finer hotels and sell them. At $5 each, he could get $100 bucks a trip. Maybe that would be enough to keep the lodge going. He hoped so, at least.

The alleys in Chicago depressed him. Even when the sun was up, the narrow canyon created by the closely pressed brick walls of the buildings on either side left little room for direct sunlight. And there were trash cans and litter everywhere. And periodically a drunk or a bum sitting with his back to the wall on one of the cans. Earlier in the day, two such had decided he was an easy mark and approached him from the rear. The mere display of the little 32 in his pocket changed both of their minds.

A bread van was pulled up beside one door, the driver just hopping back in. "This the kitchen entrance to the Lexington?" Sam asked.

"Yep," the man answered, not stopping.

"What's the head chef's name?" Sam shouted.

"Torrintino, Giuseppe Torrintino" was the shouted response.

Sam stepped between the truck and the wall and then through the door into the darkened hallway. Light and much noise were coming from the room at the end. That and the smell of meat roasting. Sam stepped into the kitchen. Men in white uniforms were scurrying busily. Not a head turned toward him.

"Which one of you is Torrintino?" Sam shouted over the din.

Several heads looked toward him but turned away without comment. A big man, in a white uniform, a white hat perched straight up from his mass of black hair and then puffed open at the top like a loaf of freshly baked bread, his stomach spreading the gaps between the buttons of his shirt, stepped toward him with a disgusted scowl and growled, "Who you and what you peddling?"

"I'm Clark, Sam Clark, and I've got fresh, and legal, wild duck here." He hefted the suitcase in his right hand.

"No legal duck now. These you shot."

"Nope. Not a shot in 'em. They're my decoys and legal."

The man's scowl disappeared, but no welcome showed behind it. "Throw it up there."

In one smooth motion Sam threw the suitcase onto the indicated counter.

"Open!"

Sam threw the latches and lifted the lid. Five plucked, plump birds appeared.

The chef took two steps forward, picked one up, poked at it with a finger of the other hand, and twirled it, looking for pellet holes or bruises. "Birds are shit. What you want?"

"$5 each."

"Bullshit. Give you $10 for the lot."

Sam stepped to the counter, shut the lid, snapped the latches shut, took hold of the handle, and slid the suitcase off the counter.

"$20," the fat chef offered.

"Mr. Torrintino, I can supply you with the same quality birds all winter. And I'll do it one of two ways. I'll sell you these five for $20 now, but the next time I come back, and you will want me back"—Sam smiled, arching one eyebrow—"they'll be $7 each. No less and that price all winter."

Torrintino, saying not a word, reached in his pocket and took out a $20 gold eagle and a $5 bill, both of which he handed to Sam.

Without a word, Sam turned to go.

"When you be back?"

"Same day next week."

* * * *

Sam came back exactly as promised, but the city was much colder than the week before. He had worn a three-piece suit, a heavy wool topcoat, and a cashmere scarf pulled high against the cold and was damn glad of it. He had turned the overcoat collar up, pulled the scarf up higher around his neck and the fedora down tight, but he was still freezing as he walked in the door.

"Giuseppe in?" Sam asked the first man he saw.

The man grunted and nodded his head to a small desk in the corner of the kitchen. Sam turned and saw the fat cook sitting hunched over some papers.

"Giuseppe, duck man is here to see you!" the voice behind him shouted.

Giuseppe sprang up with extraordinary vigor for a man his size. "Good, you're back!" he shouted to Sam as he started across the kitchen toward him, arms extended as though to offer a hug.

"Giuseppe, don't. You'll get flour all over this navy topcoat, and I'll look like I'm ready to be panfried," Sam warned and extended his hand to stop the exuberant Italian greeting.

Giuseppe's face became business now. Friendly still, but business. "How many ducks you bring me?"

"Only got four left today."

Giuseppe pointed to an uncluttered counter, and Sam threw the suitcase up and opened the latch.

Giuseppe took the four out and laid them beside the suitcase. "All big mallards or canvasbacks. No pintails or wood ducks. Good."

Sam chuckled. "Giuseppe, I don't use any of those for decoys, and I don't shoot them even in season. Too damn much work cleaning them for just a couple of little bites."

Giuseppe nodded. "But only four. Next time you stop here first. I want more."

Sam just smiled an easy smile and nodded.

Giuseppe stepped to his desk, opened the drawer, pulled out a double eagle, and handed the small gold coin to Sam. "Tell me your name again."

"Clark. Sam Clark. Next time I'll stop here first. Thanks, Giuseppe." And Sam turned to go.

"Sam. Mr. Clark," Giuseppe called to turn him back. "Don't go yet. There is someone who wants to see you."

"See me? I don't know anyone here."

"No, you don't know him, but Mr. Nitti wants to meet you."

"Nitti? Who is Mr. Nitti?"

Giuseppe's eyes startled. "You don't know Frank Nitti?"

"Never heard of him."

"He is a very important man, Mr. Clark."

Sam could not help but note the tone of respect, a tone he did not receive, and that he had become "Mr. Clark." "What's he want from me?"

"I don't know. Mr. Nitti does not tell me his business. Mr. Nitti doesn't tell anyone his business."

"Well, Giuseppe, while I don't mean to be impolite, I have a train in an hour. I haven't got time."

"If you miss your train, Mr. Clark, when is the next one?"

"9:00 p.m."

"Then I advise, Mr. Clark, you take the nine o'clock."

"Sorry, Giuseppe. Gotta go." And Sam buttoned his overcoat and started to turn.

"Mr. Clark," Giuseppe said, his voice taking a tone of authority, "Mr. Nitti is not a man other men say no to."

Sam snorted and turned without comment.

"Mr. Clark," Giuseppe said, the tone of authority replaced by a tone of begging, "don't do this."

The tone startled Sam, and he turned again back to Giuseppe.

"Please, Mr. Clark. I beg you. If you don't go for yourself, then go for me."

"You?" Now it was Sam's turn to sound startled. "What have you got to do with this?"

The eyes looking up at Sam showed fear. "Mr. Clark, last week I served one of your ducks to Mr. Nitti. He lives in the hotel, takes the entire fifth floor, and he also takes most of his meals here. He loves duck but doesn't like domestic duck. Claims he can taste the difference. He was surprised I could get wild duck that showed no sign of being shot so far out of season and asked where I got it. I told him what you told me, that you were a licensed guide and allowed to harvest your decoys. He asked when you'd be back. I told him what you'd said, that you'd be here today, and he instructed me to have you see him when you came in. Mr. Nitti is not a man whose commands I can disobey."

"Who is this guy?" Sam almost shouted.

"He is a man who will have me fired if I disobey him. This is a job I need. Please see him and take the late train. Do it for me. And knowing Mr. Nitti, there may be great profit in it for you as well. Fifth floor."

Sam set both his suitcases by Giuseppe's desk, removed his topcoat and laid it over them, added his scarf and hat to the top of the stack, and turned out the main entrance to the kitchen and across the lobby to the elevator.

* * * *

Frank Nitti was a small man with an olive complexion, dark hair parted on the right and slicked back with oil. He had a very wide forehead, thick nose, and even thicker lips, sensuous almost. But it was his eyes that were most interesting.

He sat at his desk, bent over a ledger as two very large men escorted Sam into the room. Sam stood in front of the desk, waiting for Nitti to invite him to sit. The two large escorts stood on either side of Sam, no more than a step behind. They seemed like palace guards.

After a moment Nitti looked up, his lips offering a smile wide enough that white but crooked teeth showed through. But the eyes held no smile. They were hard eyes, very hard, and they bored into him.

Nitti shoved his chair back slightly and stood but only enough to be able to reach across the desk and offer his hand to Sam.

Sam took in the incredibly fine weave of the pin-striped navy suit, the perfectly tied and positioned paisley tie, the white Sea Island cotton shirt with a gold collar pin, and the white silk pocket square. The extended hand revealed a shirt cuff held together with what appeared to be a two-carat ruby cufflink.

"Please have a seat, Mr. Clark. There are two reasons I wanted to talk to you, but the first is to thank you for supplying Giuseppe with your wonderful ducks. Please continue to do so."

"I'm glad to, Mr. Nitti. I run a hunting lodge, and after the season is over, business is very slow. Having decoys to harvest helps pay the bills."

"So business is bad for your lodge."

"Well, we still have plenty of hunters. It's a six-room lodge, and we are almost entirely booked during the season. But we counted on liquor sales to make our profit. I'm covering that loss with the sale of decoys."

Nitti cast his eyes up to one of the men standing behind Sam. It was a knowing glance.

"Tell me a bit about your lodge, Mr. Clark."

Sam started his tale at the beginning. He started with Vivienne de Villiere's arrival in Beardstown and finished with his changes to make Le Salon into a lodge. Nitti smiled as he spoke.

"When I was young"—it was Nitti who spoke now—"I was considered a very good shot. I was poor in Salerno. Ammunition was expensive. I shot well or my family didn't eat some days."

Sam laughed loudly. Nitti's eyes went hard.

"No insult intended, Mr. Nitti. It's that you just told my story. That is exactly the same reason I became good."

Nitti now joined the laugh. The two men behind remained silent.

"I miss hunting, Sam. May I call you Sam?"

"Then I'll call you Frank."

Again, Nitti's eyes went hard. But only for a moment. Then they softened. "Frank and Sam it is." Nitti paused a moment. "Sam, you ever shoot a Beretta over and under?"

"Once, Frank. One of my better-heeled guests let me try his. So well-balanced."

"Aren't they? In Italy I could not afford one. But in Chicago I made money. One of the first things I did with it was buy a 12-gauge Beretta. I'll let you try it when I come to shoot with you."

It took Sam a moment to realize what had just happened. Nitti would be his guest next season.

"Sam, Giuseppe tells me you have a train to catch"—he thrust his left hand forward, revealing what Sam took to be a Patek Philippe watch—"in about fifteen minutes. So I will let you go."

Sam smiled. "There's no way I can get to the train now. But thanks for the thought."

Nitti gave a small, sure smile. "Oh, Bruno will get you there. And I'll have my secretary escort you. He'll need to make arrangements for us to hunt together." Nitti rose, fully this time, and shook Sam's hand again.

By the time Sam turned to walk out, Nitti's eyes were already down again, focused on the ledger before him.

"Mr. Clark, follow me, please," a small man in an overcoat greeted him as he stepped through Nitti's door.

Without another word the man led him to the elevator, which was open and being held by a uniformed attendant. The two men stepped in. The doors closed behind them. Not a word was spoken until they reached the lobby and the elevator doors opened.

"This way, Mr. Clark." The small man started toward the revolving doors leading to the street.

"No, gotta go to the kitchen to collect my bags, coat, and hat."

"Everything is already in the car, Mr. Clark. Please, we're in a bit of a rush."

As the revolving door opened to the street, the arctic blast that struck them made Sam lower his head.

Again, the small man's voice commanded, "Just here, sir." He pointed to a large black Cadillac limousine parked at the curb, steps from the door.

Another uniformed attendant held the rear door open. Sam saw his overcoat, scarf, and hat lying just inside the door. Cold as it was, Sam paused for just a moment before getting in to look at two police cars, one parked before the limo and one behind. The mounted lights on both roofs were flashing red and blue.

The small man stood immediately behind Sam as though waiting to get in behind him. "I see you've got my coat and hat in the car, but I've got two suitcases in the kitchen as well. We'll need to go back."

"No need, sir. They're in the trunk."

Sam slid in, the small man behind him. The instant the door shut, the limo pulled away from the curb with a police car before and behind. Now their sirens turned on as well as their lights. The small caravan flew south along the lake toward the train station.

"Mr. Clark, I will need your contact information. I'll also need the rates to lease out the entire lodge for two days. And for hunting all your blinds as well."

"If you want the entire lodge, will your hunters need dogs, or will they supply their own? And guides?"

"Mr. Nitti will require you as his guide and one dog. No more will be needed. But do add in breakfast, lunch, and dinner for all six men. Does the lodge serve dinner for non-hunters as well?"

"Sometimes," Sam answered.

"Mr. Nitti will require the entire lodge. You'll not be able to serve others or allow anyone into the lodge except staff while he's there. Please factor that into your quote."

A somewhat overwhelmed Sam Clark gave Nitti's secretary the numbers he requested and was done just as the limo and escort pulled up to the train station. Before Sam could get out, a policeman was at the door.

"Mr. Clark," the secretary said, "when you get out, the police will escort you through and make certain you reach the train in time. You'll also see the trunk is open. Our men will put your bags on the train and get the claim checks to you before the train leaves. When you collect your bags, you'll find one more than your suitcases. It is a gift from Mr. Nitti. He says, if you enjoy the gift and find it helpful to your business, to contact me and more can be made available. Enjoy your trip, Mr. Clark."

Sam pulled on his coat and hat, grabbed the scarf, and slid out the door being held by a uniformed policeman. Baggage claim checks in his pocket, he was sitting in his seat, rolling out of the train station, still unable to clear his mind of the magic and mystery of what had just happened.

CHAPTER 16

April 5, 1921
Beardstown, Illinois

The fire was roaring, throwing heat into the room and light as well. Some atavistic impulse in Lloyd made him feel not just warmed by it but made safe by it as well.

Sam came around the corner of the leather sofa, carrying two tumblers of amber liquid. He handed one to Lloyd and eased himself against the arm at the other end. Sam held his tumbler toward Lloyd and said, "To silent partners."

Lloyd returned the gesture and took a pull at his whiskey. His expression changed as he swallowed. He looked at Sam and then, in silence, took another pull but this time seeming to allow the whiskey to settle on his tongue. Then he swallowed slowly, savoring every second of the process. "What is it, Sam?"

"Laphroaig, twelve-year-old."

"Where did you ever manage to get it?"

"My 'silent partner' does not want to say."

Lloyd let his eyes glimmer understanding as he sipped the last of his glass. "May I have more?"

Sam rose and walked to the bar, returning with a plain round bottle of dark glass with a label on one side. He held the label up to Lloyd to prove his claim of the contents and then poured more into the empty tumbler. "You may not only have more. You may have as much of this as you want. You may also have almost any other scotch you prefer as well as Crown Royal or any other rye whiskey and a large assortment of British gin. Pretty much any foreign label you want.

"If you say it's time, I propose we let locals handle the bulk stuff and offer our guests nothing but the finest of imports and at an appropriate premium price. That is not to say I can't get bourbon or other domestic stuff; I can. But we both know none of the domestic brand names are available, so I'm thinking let's add to the prestige of staying here, and the price."

"Yeah, it's time. Be careful about your shipments, but we can start serving our own clients again. And if you can continue to supply this quality, then I agree. Charge a lot to a few—our select clientele. Nicely done, partner . . . silent partner. But, Sam, if you get caught, I will insist, under oath if necessary, that I knew nothing of it."

Sam merely nodded understanding. "Now that you're happy on that account, Lloyd, I want to make you happy on another as well as asking for some advice," Sam said. "It is time for me to move Larry out here. Well, perhaps not time, but he really wants to come here. I'm feeling guilty as hell keeping him away. Ever watch a little boy cry, asking to live with you? I can't say no anymore."

Lloyd's eyes, reflecting the flicker of the fire, glowed true happiness. "Good for you, Sam. You're right; it's time."

"The problem, of course," Sam continued, "is I need a woman here full time to care for him and not just in duck season. Year round."

"And?" Lloyd helped him to continue.

"And, Lloyd, there are two possible paths as I see it. One

way is to hire a full-time housekeeper and cook. But really a full-time mother to Larry. The other is to marry again."

This time Lloyd kept still but continued his twinkling stare.

"Lloyd, I don't want to marry. Perhaps Dora still has my heart. Perhaps I'm just a bachelor at heart. I don't have a heart to offer. Dora I loved. I shared everything with her. That seems like a marriage to me, what a marriage should be. So if I offer a woman marriage, it would be a marriage of convenience. A marriage without true love." Sam stopped talking, just letting his unfinished thought drift into the flames.

Lloyd let him drift and did not speak.

Sam returned and looked at him, his eyes focused now. "Is that enough to offer a woman?"

Lloyd sipped and rolled the warm, peaty tastes of the scotch on his tongue. "I believe you are asking me if that is enough for Lilly Wright, is it not?"

"Yes, that's what I'm asking."

"Sam, the direct answer is hard. It is that you'll have to ask her. But there is a longer, less direct answer, and I've given it to you before. Lilly likes everything you have to offer. And since she left Morgan County and moved in with us, every time you come to dinner or even come to my office, she is always a bit sad when you leave. Sad that you have not sought her out; sad that you have not engaged her in conversation; sad that you've not gone into the kitchen on some pretext when Beulah is with us and so you know Lilly is there alone. But if you ask her, Sam, you must tell her what you're offering. Or in your case, what you're not offering. I'm not suggesting you be brutal. I'd not bring Dora up. That was long ago. Lilly never knew her. But I think you owe it to her to say your love, at this point in life, belongs to your son. That you cannot promise it to her. But what you can promise her is kindness and a good home. Lilly is not a fool, Sam. She will understand entirely. And whatever decision you get will be an honest one, one she will live with."

* * * *

Three weeks to the day later, Sam stood rigid, but the smile on his face registered contentment. He was dressed in a brand-new navy worsted three-piece suit, a plain grey tie knotted precisely into the neck of a white cotton shirt. His only adornment was a gold watch chain looped low between the pockets of his vest. Lloyd McHugh stood at his right; his smile registered satisfaction. They were both turned slightly away from the altar and looking down the nave, watching Lilly Wright walk slowly toward them.

Lilly's white dress hung off her shoulders, scooped just below her collarbones, the fabric pinched tight below her waist and then opening in a long, narrow front hanging to her ankles. An outer skirt of the same cloth opened from a cloth belt held in place by a fabric camellia buckle. Behind her, the dress fell away into a low shallow train. The sleeves fell down her arms, widening as they went. They were just short enough to show a patch of pale skin between their wide lily-like bells at the cuff and ruff of her white mesh gloves. The toes of her white patent leather shoes danced out before her with each step. The ensemble was crowned with a large white lily made of satin and lace tied into her pulled-back blond hair. Her smile registered joy.

When she reached the altar, Lilly was greeted by her sister, Beulah, who had preceded her down the aisle, and Sam, who offered his arm. Together they turned to face Reverend Berlin, who smiled paternally down at the couple.

The assembled witnesses consisted of an almost eighty-year-old Louise McHugh sitting calmly between two six-year-old boys, each dressed in a first suit, both of which were cut with knee-length pants. Even the little boys seemed controlled by her regal demeanor. The Butlers—tall, thin Patrick, Rosa, and eight-year-old Dixie, very self-satisfied sitting in her favorite dress and, in her mind, more a part of the gathered adults than the children—witnessed as well.

If Reverend Berlin was trying to control his booming baritone to match the intimacy of the setting, he failed. "Sam, Lilly, I have known this day would come, and I am glad of it. Destiny has drawn you two to me and to the care of God. And I am glad to sanctify what he has clearly put together."

The reverend paused and smiled down. "Sam, do you take this woman to be your lawfully wedded wife, to have and to hold, in sickness and in health, for richer or poorer, till death do you part?"

"I do."

"Lilly, do you take this man to be your lawfully wedded husband, to have and to hold, in sickness and in health, for richer or poorer, till death do you part?"

"I do."

"Sam, do you have the ring?"

Sam looked over at Lloyd, who reached into his vest pocket and pulled out a simply mounted diamond of well over a karat and handed it to his friend.

"Put it on her finger, Sam."

Sam did as directed.

"I now pronounce you man and wife. You may kiss your bride, Mr. Clark."

Sam bent down to the radiant face beaming up at him and gave the red lips a slow, gentle kiss.

The small family cheered as Sam offered Lilly his arm and strode down the nave to the warmth of the sunlight beyond.

* * * *

The three cars rolled slowly up the winding gravel path leading through the new green foliage of the park in front of the lodge, Sam and Lilly in the lead, Lloyd, Beulah, and Louise McHugh with the two boys next, and the Butlers with Reverend Berlin following.

Sam jumped out and shouted, "Just leave them here. No reason to park in the rear," as he ran around the front of the car to open Lilly's door. He escorted her slowly, ever cautious of the hem of her dress, along the stone path and up the stairs to the porch where he threw open the door and stood holding it, waiting for Lilly to enter. She didn't move. She just stood, the look on her face giving no indication of her thought. It was a blank slate to him. Sam stood, his face a completed blank as well. He had no idea what she was waiting for.

He could see all the others standing, waiting patiently at the bottom of the steps.

It was laconic Patrick who finally spoke. "Sam, for God's sake . . . Oops, sorry, Reverend. Would you just pick up your bride and carry her over the threshold?"

Now Lilly blushed and looked down. Sam, now understanding, shared her embarrassment but at least now knew what to do. He scooped her up with the ease with which one might collect a bundle of kindling, held her pulled tight to his chest, and stepped through the opening. The adults all cheered.

"Welcome to your new home, Lilly."

She looked into his eyes no more than inches away. "I'll make a good wife to you, Sam. And mother to your boy as well." She kissed him on the cheek.

Sam set her down and kissed her forehead in return. Then clearing the threshold, he shouted behind him. "Come in; come in, all."

And they piled into the warmth and the aroma of roast beef, all laughing as they came.

Sam took Lilly's hand and walked her to the bar, where he again picked her up and set her on a stool, walked around behind the bar, and pulled a bottle from underneath. As he reached for glasses, he paused, glanced back up, and looked straight at Reverend Berlin. "Reverend, if I promise you this has been in the cellar since before Prohibition, will you join us in a drink?"

The grey-haired minister, whom Sam had always known as a humorless man, cocked his head, looked out of the corner of his eye at Sam, and said, "Bearing false witness, my boy, is a sin. Trading in whiskey is merely illegal. I'd prefer some good Canadian rye. About two fingers, neat. If you have it."

The assemblage roared with laughter. The celebration had begun.

As all stood around the fire, laughing and drinking, the sound of billiard balls could be heard from the next room. None seemed to notice but old Mrs. McHugh, who rose from the sofa and, taking a moment to pull her aging spine erect and then smooth her grey hair back off her ears, walked with still-fluid grace into the library, where two small boys were standing on tippy-toes and, unable to get their elbows above the table, were holding cues sideways, banging away at the billiard balls.

"Gentlemen," she announced abruptly.

It was not the word so much as the tone that caused the boys to stop and turn toward her. When they recognized the woman, both boys became instantly sober and attentive.

"I imagine your fathers do not mind that you teach yourselves billiards. It is a gentleman's game, not like that foolish 'pool' thing they play in saloons. But if either of you cause your cue to rip the felt on the top of that table, I will paddle your butts until they are pink no matter what your fathers may think."

Both boys stood heads down and eyes averted to the floor and, in unison, said, "Yes, ma'am."

"Until you are tall enough to reach the table, I will suggest you put those cues back into the rack where you found them and confine yourselves to rolling the balls with your hands."

The frightened boys stood as they were, heads down.

"For now, I recommend you find some other way to amuse yourselves. Perhaps outside in the park until dinner."

The boys nodded and ran off, screaming again before they reached the door. Louise stood, surveying the room.

"I'd forgotten you were a schoolteacher. You're very good at that."

Louise turned to the kitchen door to see an aging Nancy standing, door held open, her dress covered with an apron.

"Hello, Nancy. Has Vivienne loaned you to Sam for the day?"

"She has indeed. Said she wouldn't trust anyone else with Sam's wedding feast. Also said to extend her apologies for not accepting Sam's invitation. She is getting frail as you know."

"We're getting older, she and I. Would you tell her I'll stop over after church tomorrow?"

"I will indeed. And will you tell Mr. Clark that if he'll seat his guests, I'm ready to serve."

* * * *

It was well past dark when Sam and Lilly stood waving good-bye to their guests. Larry waved his little hand to his father as he got into the Butlers' car.

"It was hard for Larry, wasn't it?" Lilly asked.

"He thought he'd be able to move in here as soon as we married. But I thought you'd like a week to get used to the place."

Lilly smiled a knowing smile. "That was good of you, Sam. I would like a little honeymoon with you." She paused. "You know what I'd like for a wedding present, Sam?"

"What?" Sam again had a blank, unknowing expression on his face.

"You to teach me to drive."

"To drive? Why?"

"Larry starts school in September. It will be too far for his little legs to walk. Someone has to take him."

Lloyd was right about her. Sam put his arm around Lilly's waist, pulled her away from the door and closed it, took her by the hand, and led her up the stairs to her new room and her new life.

CHAPTER 17

October 19, 1924
Beardstown, Illinois

Sam's decoys sat calmly paddling no more than fifteen feet in front of the blind. Each had a light cord tied to one leg, the other end of the cord weighted with a brick resting on the bottom of the slough but with sufficient extra cord to allow the ducks to swim and dive easily to the abundant corn salted on the bottom. It was enough to make their lives contented and that state enough to attract other ducks flying over. As a small flock of mallards appeared upriver, Sam brought the duck call to his lips and created a perfect imitation of the sound a satisfied duck might make. It worked. The leader of the flock lowered the backs of his wings to allow him to drop in.

As the rest of the flock mimicked their leader's gesture, the small man beside Sam rose, pulled the Beretta over and under tight into his shoulder, and pulled one trigger. The lead duck dropped straight to the water as the hunter swung the barrel slightly to his right and pulled the other trigger. Another duck dropped but this one struggling with her one good wing to stay aloft. The effort failed, and she landed flapping one wing, struggling to right herself in the water.

Sam stood and gave Teddy the retrieve signal. The dog launched himself from the sitting position straight into the air and headed unerringly in the direction Sam had pointed. The decoys, far more annoyed at the swimming retriever than they had been with either the boom of the 12 gauge or the splash of their dead and injured fellows just beyond them, squawked and paddled away as rapidly as they could and as far as their tethers would allow. One or two even tried to fly, only to have their line pull them up short before they cleared the water.

The Chessie wrapped the thrashing duck in his mouth with the gentleness of a mother cat moving her kitten, turned, and headed straight back to the blind. As soon as the Chessie entered, Sam put his hand below the dog's jaw and commanded, "Give." The dog immediately dropped the bird and started to shake, but Sam, using his other hand, made the retrieve signal, and the dog remounted the water and swam powerfully to the floating but very dead duck.

Sam twisted the neck of the thrashing bird sharply, its struggles ceasing instantly. Sam threw it into the bulging burlap bag behind him just as he heard the soft pop of the Beretta being broken open and both spent shell casings flying out the back and landing with the pile of others gathering beside the hunter.

"You shoot better to your left than your right, Frank."

"Always have. If that hen had been left of the drake instead of to my right, she'd have fallen as dead as he. Any clues to solve it?"

"Yeah. Force yourself to move your eyes with the gun instead of behind it. Sounds simple, I know, but it's harder for all men when swinging toward their dominant hand. You're right-handed, correct?"

Nitti swept the camouflage cap off his head and nodded

acknowledgment as he brushed his black hair back over his head.

"If you were left-handed, you'd have a harder time keeping your eyes down the length of the barrel when you swung left. It's not just you; it's something all hunters have to deal with." Sam pointed to the bulging sack. "You had enough, or you want to keep at it?"

"Your dog's made maybe two dozen trips in the last two hours. He tired?"

Sam snorted. "Teddy, tired? Teddy is a Chesapeake Bay. Those dogs are bred to retrieve in the Atlantic surf. He can do this all day."

"Your wife, Lilly, that her name?"

Sam nodded.

"Lilly's going to get tired plucking and cleaning all these."

This time Sam laughed outright. "Probably would, but she's not the one who has to do it. We got help to do that. And Larry still likes to do it. Takes him forever, and every now and again he gets a finger in that boiling water as he dips them, but he'll help. No, we can clean and dress as many as you want.

"Your boys out there cold?" Sam asked, pointing to the deep grass around the blind. "Sitting, doing nothing makes a man feel cold."

Now it was Nitti's turn to snort. "They're like your help, Sam. They do what they're paid to do. Which is make certain I stay alive. That I don't have no 'hunting accident.' It's a job that pays well. Let's hunt another hour. I want to practice some right throws."

It was almost ten o'clock when Nitti, broken shotgun over his shoulder, and Sam, two burlap bags of ducks over his, and a wet but seemingly content retriever at heel, walked out of the blind and started down the wet path toward the cars. As they walked, six men appeared from other blinds in the tall grass around them and fell into place, two before them, two behind, and one on either flank. They each carried guns as well, but not like Frank Nitti's Beretta. Each of the six carried a Thompson submachine gun.

"Good hunt, Mr. Nitti?"

"Good hunt," Nitti said without looking toward the speaker.

When they reached the car, Sam threw the ducks and Nitti's gun in the trunk. He then opened the rear door and motioned Teddy in, the wet beast bounding up and onto the army surplus blanket covering the seat. Sam turned to the passenger door and held it for Nitti. The six bodyguards entered the other two cars parked beside Sam's Buick. As they headed back to the lodge, one led and one followed.

"Frank, I was worried when your secretary said you'd be coming downriver on the *Chicago Queen*. Some years the river is iced over by now. But looks like you were right; you'll get back to Chicago in style."

Nitti turned his head toward Sam and smiled. "I usually plan well, Sam. It's why I'm successful." He paused momentarily and added, "And alive."

"The *Queen* leaves at five o'clock, Frank. Plenty of time for you to get a warm bath and dressed. Lilly will have lunch for us, and the help will get these ducks on ice for your travel."

"Be a good end to a good trip, Sam. Like your lodge. Don't think I'll tell others about it. Keep it to myself."

"As long as we can look forward to periodic visits from you and regular deliveries from you, that's all I ask. And, Frank"— Sam turned his eyes toward Nitti and away from the road for a moment—"I really do appreciate your deliveries. I have to buy my beer local. I thought they might ask why I'm not buying whiskey from them as well, but they don't."

Nitti smiled a conspiratorial smile. "They won't. I made sure the locals knew I was your supplier."

* * * *

Frank Nitti strode into the main room of the lodge, his usual picture of sartorial splendor.

It was Lilly who greeted him. She was wearing a print dress covered with a kitchen apron festooned with frills along the edges. Her blond hair was pulled to the back of her head in a bun. Her smile of greeting was genuine. "Mr. Nitti, your timing is perfect. Sam is only moments behind you, I'm sure. He always compliments the way you dress. I'm certain he won't appear until he's in his best. Lunch will be served just as soon as he's here. Meantime may I pour you a drink and welcome you to a seat by the fire?"

"How very gracious of you, Mrs. Clark. A grappa would be very warming right now."

Lilly worked her way behind the bar, pulled the one remaining bottle of grappa that had been sent with their last order. Neither she nor Sam had ordered it or even knew what it was at the time, but after one evening with Nitti and his Italians, she knew. She poured a snifter of the pungent liquor and was handing it to Nitti as Sam walked into the room.

"Lilly, Mr. Nitti doesn't know it, but his men have packed the cars and are waiting. The *Queen* leaves in just ninety minutes. Time for a quick bite and then off."

The three cars rolled south rapidly, the lead car taking the right onto State Street and the dock fast enough that the tires squealed all the way around the corner and then making a cloud of dust as it slammed to a stop in the dirt parking lot before the *Chicago Queen*. Sam hopped out and around the front of the car to open Nitti's door, but one of his guards was already there. Amidst the hurrying and rushing of his companions, Frank Nitti was the picture of calm as he and Sam strolled up the gangplank and onto one of the last remaining river palaces working the Illinois River.

Once on deck, Nitti turned to shake Sam's hand, but Sam's eyes were drawn away, and he momentarily left Nitti, his hand extended. He recovered quickly and took the offered hand firmly.

"Forgive me, Frank. I was distracted by the poster on the wall there. The one advertising the boat's entertainment. Who is that kid on the poster? Red Norvo? And what's a xylophone?"

Nitti turned to the picture. "He was the entertainment on the way down. Young, very young. Maybe fifteen or sixteen. I've never heard anything like him. I'd never heard his instrument before either. Guess the xylophone has been around, but at least in the Chicago jazz scene, this kid is the one who's made it."

The two men turned to the poster, Sam looking at the freckled face of a redheaded boy. He seemed familiar. In the picture he was standing over a long table made of short metal plates an inch or two wide. Each hand held two short wooden sticks that looked like nothing so much as elongated lollipops.

"He looks familiar, but I just can't place him," Sam said.

"You may know him, Sam. We heard him play on the way down, and when they introduced him, they said the reason they'd got him to play on the boat was because he was from Beardstown. Wanted to visit home, I guess. You want the poster?" Nitti asked.

Before Sam could answer, Nitti grabbed the poster and ripped it from the wall. "Here." He handed it to him. "Read the fine print."

Sam accepted the poster and did as instructed. "He's Kenneth Norville. My sister-in-law taught him piano!"

"The world is full of strange wonders, Sam. See you next year." And Frank Nitti turned and departed.

* * * *

Sam opened the door to the sound of screaming children. The children were screaming, but Lilly, her sister, Beulah, and Rosa Butler all sat contentedly by the fire, sipping tea.

"Please, do come join us, Sam," Lilly called across the room.

He strode across the room but to the bar rather than the fireplace, poured two fingers of his favorite Laphroaig into a tumbler, and then walked to the warmth of fire and conversation. "What brings you ladies out here today?"

It was Rosa who answered. "The boys were going to play today, and when Dixie heard, the little girl in her seems to have overwhelmed the disdainful young lady who disapproves of roughhousing boys. Look at her now, as sweaty and disheveled as they."

They all joined in laughter.

"What is that you've got, Sam?" Beulah asked.

Sam held up the torn poster, keeping the front to himself. "I just took some guest to the dock."

"We heard," Beulah said teasingly. "Famous and disreputable guests, we hear."

"You forgot rich," Sam teased back.

"And this I collected from the wall of the *Chicago Queen*. I got it for you, Rosa," he said, holding it toward her. "And here you are."

Sam handed her the poster, which she studied. "Just what I said, 'saloon singer.' He won't follow the rules, and he'll never amount to a thing." She threw the poster into the fire and watched it burn.

CHAPTER 18

April 14, 1927
Beardstown, Illinois

Sam paced nervously back and forth across the big room, the floor standing radio against the far wall constantly reporting the news. Lilly sat knitting, attempting to appear calm, but her ear turned to the same sound. Only twelve-year-old Larry was unconcerned. He was excited. To him it was an adventure.

The sky outside was black at midday, the rain falling heavily. Falling, falling, falling as it had for almost three weeks.

Through the static it was clear that even the announcers could not stay calm. "Beardstown streets are, except for a very few blocks in the far east end of town, covered in at least three feet of water. The river has already exceeded the previous record crest of twenty-four feet two inches. Water has flooded the power station, and only those of you with battery backup are hearing my voice. Papers all over the country—*Chicago Dispatch, St. Paul Daily,* dozens of others, are leading with stories of 'the Beardstown Flood.' The governor says he may declare an emergency and order immediate evacuation of the entire city."

Sam jumped straight up, both his feet making a small boom as they landed together. "If the telephone exchange floods, we'll lose contact with them. Then we'll sit here high and dry while they drown. We're going now."

"We?" exclaimed a startled Lilly.

"Larry and I. We're going to go get them all."

Larry jumped straight up. "Give me a minute to put on my weather gear. Hunting gear will do, won't it, Dad?"

Sam nodded and Larry started to run out of the room.

"Larry, stop." It was Lilly. "Sam, you can only get four people in one of the skiffs. If you take Larry along, it means you won't be able to get all the Butlers in the skiff, much less the McHughs. You'll end up making two trips into three."

"We have two skiffs. We'll get one family in each."

"You're going to have Larry pole a skiff in this storm?"

"I pole skiffs all the time, Mom."

"Not in the dark and in flood waters with Lord knows what floating toward you trying to sink you."

"Larry's right, Lilly. He's a river rat. He not only poles skiffs all the time; he can pretty much handle any water craft in any water. And if that dirt levee fails, we won't have time for two trips."

"Sam!" It was a tone of disbelief and admonition.

"Don't argue with me, Lilly. You have two jobs right now. Both Larry and I will need . . . Make two baskets with a coffee thermos and a bottle of whiskey. Pack a few sandwiches in each, and pile as many blankets on top as you can stuff in."

She nodded begrudging acceptance and went off to the kitchen.

A few minutes later Sam and Larry stepped outside the back door, each carrying a hamper in one hand and a large flashlight in the other, splashing the muddy path to the garage.

Both skiffs were sitting on four-wheeled carts stored for their need come September.

"Now listen to me, Larry. We'll push a skiff down the lane to the point where water covers the road, tie it there, and come back and get the second. So, throw your basket in one and cover it with the canvas tarp. Might as well leave your light there. You're going to need both hands to push, muddy as the lane is. You lead and I'll push hard. Let's go."

The boy tried to cover the excitement in his eyes. Tried to mimic his father's "This is just a job" demeanor. But he couldn't.

Once they'd reached the road and floated the skiff, Sam used the bowline to tie it to a tree, and they started back up the path. When they got to the house, Sam motioned Larry up the front stairs and inside the front door.

"Lilly," he called.

She appeared momentarily, rushing from the kitchen, her pale cheeks now flushed pink with excitement.

"Lilly, honey, you know Lloyd is in Springfield trying to get the governor to send five hundred National Guardsmen to raise the levee with sandbags. Your sister is not going to want to leave home without him. There's no way he can get back to her now. Phones are still working. You call her and make her, make her, pack no more than she can carry in her arms and get herself, young Milt, and Louise bundled against the weather. Tell her I'll be there in an hour and they're coming with me to safety. You must make her agree. Lie; tell her the governor has ordered an evacuation if you have to, but if she's not ready to go when I get there, I'll force all of them into rain gear and carry them if I must.

"And then call Patrick and tell the Butlers the same. I'm sending Larry to them so he'll have Patrick's help with the skiff on the way home."

Lilly nodded, her expression one of mortal concern. Sam seemed to see her anguish for the first time. He pulled off his hat, put an arm around her waist, and pulled her close. She tilted her head up, and he kissed her gently on the lips. "Honey, this is me. I'll get this done. And you know it. Now smile for me."

Lilly, in ways only women know, knew he needed her to believe in him. He was the one who needed that. She unburdened her heart and gave him what he needed—a genuine, loving smile and a warm kiss.

Without further word, he turned to walk back out into the rain. As he stepped away, she gave him a small swat on the butt.

The man and the boy each stood feet wide, a ten-foot-long hickory pole in their hands, captains of their ships, their own fate, and the fate of others. Rain poured down upon them, rolling off the wide-brimmed rubberized weather hats each wore. There was no wind. But there was serene beauty in the dark lane of a water-road struck by drops heavy enough to make a discreet "plop" as they entered. Except the tens of thousands did not make discreet sounds but instead a symphony of God's creation.

"Listen to me, Larry," Sam shouted over the sound. "This is no different from poling along the slough except we've never done it in the dark. But we have streets and houses to guide us, so we won't get lost. You follow me all the way to the Butlers'. We'll load them. I slid an extra pole on the bottom so Patrick can help you on the way back. Then I'll go another block to the McHughs'. So, I'll be twenty or thirty minutes behind you coming home. You've got blankets to keep them warm and hot coffee and a bottle of whiskey for Patrick or Rosa."

"Why did you have Mom put in sandwiches?" Larry shouted back.

"There is only one risk to this trip, Larry. That's if the levee breaks. Do you know what happens when they break?"

"Nope," came the chipper reply.

"They don't split from the top. Pressure under twenty feet of water is very high. So, the water drills into weak spots in the bottom of the levee. If the water manages to drill all the way through, water rushes through the little tunnel it just drilled and boils up from underneath. That's what it's called. A boil. So, there's no wall of water rushing toward you. The water rushes forward underneath you, rising very fast. If that happens somewhere behind us, there will be no resisting it. It will sweep us forward all the way to the bluff. That happens, we'll need a few groceries before we can get back."

"What fun," the twelve-year-old cheered back across the water.

The Butlers stood waiting on their covered porch, bundled in rain gear and each carrying one suitcase in their hands. Sam and Larry poled across the lawn and up to the porch. The top step was covered with water, but the porch was wet only from the rain.

As Dixie got in and settled onto one of the plank seats, Larry beamed. "Welcome aboard, my lady."

"Oh, hush," Dixie snapped back.

Rosa smiled at the young captain standing in the rear, holding the skiff in place with his long pole. "If that was meant for me, Captain, I am glad to be rescued by you. And our daughter is as well." She gave her daughter a hard look. "Aren't you, Dixie?"

Rosa got no response as she sat down on the plank beside her daughter.

Patrick, seeing the long hickory lying in the bottom, pulled it from under the seats until he could hold it free. He stepped into the skiff and pushed away from the stairs of his house. "See you half an hour after we get to the lodge," he shouted to the tall figure standing firmly in the other skiff departing in the dark. And then, "Let's get out of here, Larry. I'm looking forward to that warm fire I'm sure Lilly has going for us."

* * * *

Sam poled up to the McHughs' darkened porch, tied the bow-line to the brick support column holding up the porch roof, and stepped onto the concrete porch, splashing with each step toward the door. He pounded hard. An excited twelve-year-old, looking ready to explode into the adventure, threw open the door.

"Hello, Mr. Clark," he fairly gushed.

"Hello, Milton. You the man of the house tonight, I see." Sam cast his eyes over the boy's head to see a very sedate Louise McHugh sitting quietly on the front room sofa. She was dressed in what appeared to be an old-fashioned riding cape that draped down past the tops of her black lace-up boots. Her head was covered with a very wide-brimmed felt hat. She held a pair of long gloves in one hand.

"Hello, Mrs. McHugh. You are a woman dressed fashionably in the worst flood on record. You are amazing."

She smiled up at Sam, her dignity intact even now. "Sam, every woman, even an old woman, has standards she must maintain."

Beulah came rushing into the room, a suitcase in one hand and a long, rubberized slicker in the other. "She will not listen to reason, Sam. Will you talk to her?"

Sam became serious. "Mrs. McHugh, Beulah is correct. We will be perhaps an hour in very heavy rain. I do not mean to be unkind, but you have become 'a woman of a certain age' is the proper phrase, I believe. If you get soaked, you will get sick. And if you get sick, we may lose you. I hate to be abrupt, but I fear it is so."

If any insult was taken, she did not let it show even for a second. Warmth still showed on her face. "Sam, you are, of course, correct, and even gentle with me. I am, to be a bit less circumspect than you, eighty-five years old. And you are perhaps right. But I have firm reliance on this old felt riding cape. I will keep it."

Sam shrugged. "Fair enough. But I will insist—insist, Mrs. McHugh, something I've never thought to do with you—that you not wear the felt hat. Even if it is beaver felt, within thirty minutes, it will be no protection at all. And take the word of a man who has lived his life outdoors, your head is the thing that most needs to be protected. Beulah, get one of Lloyd's rubber-ized hunting hats, one with a broad brim."

Beulah nodded and scurried away.

"Mrs. McHugh, let me make a deal with you. You wear the hat Beulah is bringing. I will keep your felt dry in a blanket. Before we get to the house, I will take it out and let you arrive at the lodge wearing it. None but the three of us will ever see you wearing the one Beulah brings."

Ever gracious, Mrs. McHugh kept her smile, softer now but still a smile. "Since you are my rescuer and you insist, I will accede to your demand. Now lead us to salvation from this un-godly storm."

The four went out on the porch. Sam stored their suitcases below the plank seats and then, stepping forward in the skiff, offered his hand to Mrs. McHugh, who set her foot slowly and cautiously across the gunnel of the skiff and stepped in. Once he had her seated, Sam led Beulah beside her and stepped to the rear, where he collected his pole.

"Milton, before you loose the bowline and push off, reach down into the bottom of the skiff. You'll find a hickory pole there. I'll need all the help I can get."

Twelve-year-old Milt McHugh beamed as he took his pole, loosened the bowline, and stepped into the skiff.

An hour later Sam poled from the road onto his parkway, relieved to find Larry's skiff tied to a tree.

"Milt, hop out and tie us to the same tree the other skiff's tied to."

As soon as they were secure, Sam jumped out the back of the skiff and, landing in knee-deep water, splashed to the middle of the skiff, offered Louise McHugh a hand, and supported her as she walked to the bow. Once there, he reached for her, put one arm under her knees, and lifted her from the boat to the ground. *My God, there is nothing left of her. She has the weight of a child.*

After a look that, in the dark, seemed to him the smile of a young woman swept off her feet, Louise commanded, "My hat, Sam."

He reached into the skiff, unwrapped the blanket in the bow, and removed her hat, handed it to her, and stood smiling as she swept the ugly rain gear off with one hand and lifted the wide-brimmed felt onto her head with the other.

I'll bet five raindrops didn't land on her head while she was doing that.

"Sam?" It was a question in her voice. "Your night is not complete, is it?"

He stood in the rain, peering in the dark at the small, firm face of Louise McHugh, trying to read her meaning. He could not.

"Sam, the founder of this house. You don't intend to leave her to a cold fate, do you?"

* * * *

"Why, Mr. Clark, what a pleasant surprise. But I don't believe I got your note asking if we were receiving this evening."

Sam wasn't certain whether Vivienne was teasing. "If you had a phone, I'd have called."

"Yes. Telephone. I've never quite understood the point. If someone wants to talk, we should do it tête-à-tête. If they want to know whether I'm available, they should send a note."

As was often the case with her, Sam didn't know quite how to respond.

"Goodness, my manners. Don't stand in that awful puddle. Please, do come in." Vivienne stood back and pulled the door open wide.

Sam stepped in and stood dripping on the floor. "Miss de Villiere, I'm here to collect you and Nancy. It's time to go."

"And wherever is it you expect to take us?"

"Mrs. McHugh is hosting a small reception at the lod . . . at Le Salon. She has asked me to extend her invitation and to collect you. Your carriage awaits at the front door."

"Doesn't she think the weather a bit inclement for a soiree?" The thin, pale, and wrinkled skin of her face folded into a gentle smile. She was enjoying this.

"Yes, she considered that but selected this moment because the weather, inhospitable as it is, is getting worse. In fact, the water on your porch is rising half an inch every hour. Within an hour it will be over your sill, and by morning this floor will be uninhabitable, and you and Nancy will be confined to the second floor."

Her sweet smile stayed in place. "Then perhaps, inclement as the weather is, and even with the short notice of her invitation, we should accept. Let me change into proper attire. I have a lovely black riding habit that might be appropriate, and we will be off." She turned toward the bedroom and then stopped. "And don't you stand there making a puddle on my floor. Take off that dripping wet slicker and sit down. We'll only be a moment." She turned again and spoke loudly, "Nancy!" And the frail angel moved across the floor.

Ten minutes later, she and Nancy were back. Vivienne was dressed in a solid black gown buttoned from the knees to the throat and draping down to the floor, sleeves fitted tightly to the arms were buttoned at the cuff. A white silk scarf was wrapped around her neck and tucked into the dress collar. The outfit was topped with a short-brimmed and flat-topped beaver hat. Nancy's choice reflected the frontier girl that the old woman always had been and still was despite her life spent in elegance. She had on a pair of heavy canvas pants and brown pull-on rubber boots. An over-large rubber slicker covered all. A wide-brimmed rubberized hat covered her head.

Sam quickly wiped the shock from his face and replaced it with his most winning smile. "Lovely, Miss de Villiere. Just lovely. But I fear the weather will ruin your gown."

"Oh, Mr. Clark, don't think me a fool. I have a long heavy flannel cape here in the coat closet." She nodded to Nancy, who opened the coat closet door and swung a wide cape off one of the hangers. She handed it to Vivienne, who swirled it around her shoulders with a gesture fit for a cavalry officer. "Shall we proceed?"

Sam looked sober now. "Miss de Villiere, I had this same conversation with Mrs. McHugh earlier in the evening. We will be an hour in an uncovered boat. That cape will be soaked in half that time, and by the time we get there, you will be soaked to the skin. And the hat will offer no protection at all. I must insist that you take the rubberized coat and hat I've brought for you, lest you catch your death."

Vivienne looked up at him, her jaw clamped tight, the purple lines of the veins running across her temples bulging. The smile was now forced. "Mr. Clark, it is not for you to insist on anything. Over sixty years ago I crawled out of a clay cave covered in nothing but rags. And I swore that to the day I died, I would never do that again. And I won't. If Death catches me, then I will meet him in style. Shall we go?" Her control and her smile had returned.

* * * *

The sun was shining outside, and the birds were singing their songs of praise for its presence. But the heavy curtains let in none of the light and only the faintest hint of the songs. Louise McHugh sat in a small chair pulled up beside Vivienne de Villiere's large canopied bed. Vivienne was raised up on large overstuffed pillows covered in white shams fringed in lace. Louise had one hand behind the frail white head, the other holding a cup of warm tea infused with honey, lemon, and bourbon and allowing it in small sips between her friend's almost white lips.

"No more, my dear. No more. It's all I can take."

Louise lowered the feeble head onto the pillows and placed the cup into its matching china saucer on the bedside table. She took a towel from the silver ice bucket beside it, wrung out the excess water, and put the cold compress to Vivienne's face. She held it first to her forehead, brushing back the silver hair as she went, and then stroked her cheeks gently, the always-high bones even more so now, the flesh melting from them, and finally stroked the thin long nose.

"It does feel good. Thank you for caring for me, Louise."

"Vivienne, you cared for me when no one else could or would. You, as much as my own mother, have given me the life I have lived. And it has been a good life you have given me. How could I not care for you when finally given the opportunity?"

Vivienne's thin, pale lips gave a small smile. "It is good I should die in this place, in this bed."

"You are not dying, Vivienne. I won't let you."

The frail head turned toward her; the grey eyes, seeming her only feature not ravished by time and still looking like a winter morning's sky, peered at her; and then the once-full red lips, now thin and almost colorless, formed into a sad smile. "I am, Louise, and there is nothing you or anyone else can do about it. But please, dear, when you think of me after, remember not my death, but my life. I have lived the only life I would have wanted to live. Do you know why, Louise?"

Louise used her silk hankie to dab a small tear forming at

the edge of one eye. She seemed unable to swallow the lump in her throat and so speechlessly shook her head.

"Because I created it, Louise. I was the mother of my own life. I made the life I wanted. How could I want another? There is only one more thing I need from you. Would you send Sam up to me while I'm still awake? I need to talk to him."

* * * *

Sam had done as Louise had instructed. He'd changed into his finest suit, the one he'd worn when he'd married Lilly. The one he had that was most appropriate for calling on a lady. He knocked softly and opened the door slowly. Vivienne was lying motionless, her head propped slightly on one pillow. He walked softly across the room and sat himself in the bedside chair. She didn't open her eyes, but her hand slowly moved across the top of the quilt and toward him. He laid his on top of it. They both sat quietly for several minutes.

Vivienne finally spoke. "Mr. Clark, thank you for caring for my home and bringing me back to it to end here."

Sam sat just holding her hand.

"This house was, is, my life. It is right that it should end here."

Silence came back to them.

"I have made a will. Lloyd McHugh has it and knows what's in it. I want you to know one part as well. Help me sit up just a bit."

Sam put his hands under her head and raised it enough to add a pillow.

She smiled now. "Sam. Yes, it's the time and place for me to be familiar. You were the only person who should have had this house. You were the only person who had a vision to use it as a place of joy and civility for more than a single family. I hope it has worked for you, because knowing what you were doing with it gave me joy."

"Your home has brought great joy to many people. It has been my pleasure to see that it has remained so, and I will do my best to see it continues to remain so, Vivienne."

She smiled. "Nothing lasts forever. But you have done well on your watch."

There was silence again and her eyes closed. Again, he took her hand. Even her hand was hot.

Momentarily, Vivienne opened her eyes again. "Sam, it came to me that the house you sold me was not yours. You were really just the custodian of a bequest from Larry's mother. Larry is twelve now. Have you made enough money to pay him back when he turns twenty-one?"

"No, but I will. Times are good, Vivienne."

"I think hard times will follow the good ones we are in now—they always do, Sam. My will solves the problem. The house is coming back to you."

Sam's face was startled. "Thank you, Vivienne," was all he knew to say.

"But it comes with a price. Two things I ask of you."

"If I can, Vivienne."

"Oh, you can. First, care for Nancy. Let her stay in the house. She is over eighty now. She'll be gone before it is Larry's time."

Sam nodded. "And the other?"

"Bury me here. This place is my heart and always has been. Let my bones keep me attached."

* * * *

"Father, accept the soul of this good woman. We commend her to your eternal care. Amen."

And the small chorus repeated Reverend Berlin's final words and stood in silence, absorbing the finality of her passing.

"I think you all know," Berlin's baritone boomed as though he were trying to project his words down the grassy hillside, past the magnificent structure that was her legacy, across the road, and into the beauty of the cotton grass blooming at the edge of the slough, "that Lilly has prepared a luncheon for Vivienne's friends and family." He paused. "So, please, come to the house and join in a small celebration of the wonder this woman created in our town."

As they all strode to the house, Sam walked up behind the minister, put his arm around the black-cloaked shoulders, and said, "Reverend, that was very good of you."

The shoulders seemed too old to carry the head and were stooped from its weight, but the preacher forced his back up straight and turned to Sam. "Good of me to do what, Sam?"

"Come perform the service for her. She wasn't even a member of your congregation."

The aging preacher smiled. "Not a member you say. I believe she was a Catholic, but I don't recall ever hearing of her going to Mass."

"Perhaps she felt she wasn't welcome, Reverend."

"Sam, it's funny what we do to ourselves. Was not Mary Magdalene with Christ when he died? And did this woman, Vivienne de Villiere, not do more to support my St. John's than anyone?"

Sam looked surprised.

The minister's face took on a knowing look. "Do you think I don't know who built our school? And gave us our teacher? She was ever welcome in my church, and if some members of the congregation would have been self-righteous in her presence, that's something they would have had to take up with St. Peter when their day came. But not with me.

"I think, Sam, the good Lord would have been very disappointed in me had I not welcomed her. And I am quite certain that St. Peter has.

"Now go mingle with your other guests. I know where you store the Canadian rye behind that bar."

Sam patted the preacher on the back and lengthened his stride on down the hill to catch up with his other guests. He found Lloyd McHugh waiting for him.

"I've not thanked you yet," McHugh greeted him.

"For what?" Sam was genuinely perplexed.

"Taking care of my family while I was gone."

"Lloyd, you were in Springfield taking care of us all. You knew I'd do that."

"Well, yes, I did. Truth is I never really worried as I got the news of the rising water. I knew you would. But I still want to offer my thanks."

"You're welcome. And how's your house?"

McHugh smiled. "Had to chase a couple of snakes out of the basement. Left that work to Milton. He liked it. It will take months to dry and clean the basement. Only damage in the rest of the house was to the carpets and floors on the ground floor. Probably have to replace both. Could have been much worse, Sam. Much worse.

"You know, Sam, this is a funny town. Know how many homes or stores were burglarized when they were evacuated?" Lloyd asked.

"How many?" Sam asked.

"None, Sam. None. Not one. Whole town evacuated for over a week. Nothing. Nothing stolen."

"That surprises you?" Sam asked.

Lloyd stopped walking and looked at the beauty of the slough unfolding below him. "No one in Beardstown, you and me included, pays a lot of attention to the law. My job is not so much to enforce the law strictly, to punish lawbreakers. My job really is to decide who is worthy of punishment. Who is more trouble than they're worth? I learned that from my father. My father said that by quoting some seventeenth- or eighteenth-century French philosopher, 'Laws are like the statues of certain divinities that, on some occasions, must be veiled.' I've always remembered that. It has served me well, and I think it has served the citizens of Beardstown well, too.

"Sam, our people have a moral code that is strong. They do not need law to give that to them. They need law to give them a structure for their voice in public affairs. Virtue they get from the likes of Reverend Berlin, not me.

"Now come on. Let's get to the house, and you can pour me a glass of the best illegal whiskey in the State of Illinois."

PART II

THE BLIND

In Tartary I freed the Cham,
Last June, from his huge swarm of gnats;
I eased in Asia the Nizam
Of a monstrous brood of vampyre-bats:
And as for what your brain bewilders—
If I can rid your town of rats
Will you give me a thousand guilders?
"One? Fifty thousand!" was the exclamation
Of the astonished Mayor and Corporation.

—From "The Pied Piper of Hamelin"
by Robert Browning

CHAPTER 19

July 4, 1933
Beardstown, Illinois

Milt and Larry stood on the outside rail of the high bridge over the river, each wearing only swimming trunks and each hanging onto a steel I beam with one hand and leaning out over the water, watching the big grain barge slide downriver fifty feet below them, churning a three-foot-tall wake behind.

"If we catch it, we'll surf it down one hundred yards before we swim into the marina. But if either of us misses it, we swim in here," Milt commanded. "Got it?"

Larry looked at Milt, his face aglow with excitement, didn't say a word, and jumped. He landed five feet in front of the barge's ever-expanding wake and swam like hell to get speed enough to catch it. He did and was elated to be picked up and pulled downriver. He turned his head as far to the side as he could. It was far enough to see Milt on the wave behind him and a bit closer to shore.

"Now!" Milt screamed from behind, and both boys peeled off the wave and paddled toward the marina.

Milt was the first to arrive and had pulled himself up onto the floating dock by the time Larry arrived. Larry pulled himself up onto the dock behind him. Both boys were laughing the laugh only ever made or known by young men who have done something very risky and been rewarded with the cheap thrill of defying death. They collapsed on their backs, forming one large pool of water at the dock's end, and lay staring up into the summer sun, letting it warm them. Their lives were perfect and they knew it.

Without turning his head from the sun, Larry asked, "What now?"

"Now," responded Milt, "we have to suffer walking back to the bridge barefoot to collect our shoes and shirts."

Larry rolled onto his side, propped his head up on his elbow, and said, "I didn't mean that, Milt. I meant, what happens to our lives now? Now that we are out of school? Now that we have to be men or pretend to?"

Milt rolled toward him and propped himself into the same posture as his friend and faced him. He seemed to study Larry's wide face and light-brown eyes. "I think, Lorenz, this is the most serious expression that's ever crossed your face."

"Maybe," Larry answered, but the expression didn't change.

"You're right, of course. This will be the last summer we spend together for a long time. You know I'm leaving for Yale in two weeks. I'll be gone."

"Why Yale?" Larry's expression didn't change.

"My great-grandfather—or someone back there—went to law school at Yale. Dad seems to think I should, too, and I got in, so I'm going. Who knows what after that? Law school, I suppose."

"Yep. McHugh's been state's attorney in Cass County as long as anyone I know remembers. Your turn will come eventually."

"Don't kill my dad off just yet. I kinda like him."

"Yeah, me, too. He's a good guy, your dad."

"How about you, Larry? You decided yet?"

"I 'spect you know the lodge is not doing well. Damn depression just seems to go on and on. Fewer and fewer guests, hunters, every year. Dad says we're losing money. I'll stay there, at least during the season. Not sure there's money enough to replace me."

"Dad says the Twenty-First Amendment will be ratified by enough states soon. Prohibition will be over. Think that will help?"

"Dad doesn't think so. Says all that will happen then is guys won't have to come to us to get expensive whiskey. They'll be able to buy it anywhere. And we won't be able to sell it for as much as we do now. Naw, don't think that will help. At least not much."

"So, you keep working at the lodge during duck season. What about the off season?" Milt asked.

"You think I'd make a good salesman, Milt?"

"How long you been selling ducks?"

"Since I was fourteen."

"Did OK at that, didn't you? What you gonna sell now?"

"Power company had an ad in the paper for guys to sell electric appliances."

"CIPS? Thought they just sold power." Milt seemed perplexed.

"Dad says they're trying to sell power by getting people to use electric home appliances—irons, vacuum cleaners, and things like that."

"Well, you can't leave here, your dad, the lodge, hell, my dad; they all need you. And jobs are darn hard to come by. You tell them you carried suitcases full of ducks to Chicago and walked down alleys calling on hotel and restaurant kitchens to sell them. They'll hire you, Larry."

Larry pulled his legs under him and stood up. "Hope so,

Milt. Because I'm a Beardstown river rat. I'll make my life here. OK, time to see how much gravel and twigs my feet can take without my mouth complaining."

He reached a hand down to Milt and pulled him to standing. "You be home for Christmas?"

"Don't think so. Long train ride. See you next summer, I suppose."

CHAPTER 20

September 3, 1933
New Haven, Connecticut

The only place Milton McHugh had ever seen any man dressed like the one before him was in *Gentlemen's Quarterly*. The young man was his age but taller and thinner. He was dressed in white linen slacks, double pleated and tailored to fall to the heels over his two-toned, wing-tipped spectators. His jacket was powder blue and, to Milt's eye, appeared to be unwoven silk. A light-yellow necktie was precisely knotted at the neck of his Sea Island cotton shirt. The entire ensemble was topped with a straw boater wrapped in a black hat band with a red stripe. He held a martini glass between the middle and index finger of his left hand.

"So, Milton, you are from Illinois? Do your parents live in a log cabin?" The words came out in a condescending lisp. He seemed to punctuate the insult by tilting his head over his shoulder and winking at the boy beside him. He and the other two companions seemed to enjoy the look on Milt's face.

"Well, from the look of you, you must live in the back room of a men's clothing store," Milt shot back.

"The term you're seeking, my good man, is haberdashery. Perhaps that word has not yet arrived at the frontier," his new classmate lisped back.

And again, all his friends seemed to enjoy it immensely.

"There is a term that has drifted to the hinterlands that I think applies here. In fact, I think it applies to you," Milt said.

"And what is that?" he asked, adjusting his tie with an affectation of complete indifference.

"Asshole," Milt responded lightly, his whole face beaming a smile of pleasure.

"Well, isn't our new frontiersman displaying his savagery? It's cute . . . in a primitive sort of way."

His friend growled agreement and moved up closer to Milt and a small arch.

"Let's try this for cute. How about you and I leave this reception and step outside?" Milt offered calmly. "And bring your friends if you'd like. After I've kicked your ass, they can each have a turn as well."

* * * *

The gold lettering on the frosted-glass panel in the door read, "Arthur Ambrose, Dean of Men." It was 2:55 p.m. His appointment was at 3:00 p.m. Milt exhaled, opened the door, and stepped inside. What he entered was a reception area, a single desk against one wall, a leather sofa with accompanying chairs along two others, and a door, apparently to an inner office along the fourth. The receptionist was a middle-aged woman with just-beginning-to-grey hair pulled up on top of her head, the wire frames of her glasses wrapped behind each ear.

She looked up, unwound the glasses, her face expressionless.

She didn't speak, so Milt did. "My name is McHugh, Milton McHugh. Dean Ambrose had a note sent to my dorm room saying he wanted to see me at three o'clock."

Her expressionless silence remained.

"I'm here," Milt added.

"Have a seat, Mr. McHugh. I'll tell him you're here at three o'clock."

Milt sat on one of the chairs, somewhat intimidated. He looked up at the school clock on the wall: 2:58 p.m.

At precisely 3:00 p.m. she rose from her desk and, without a word, walked to the door to the inner office and knocked softly.

"Come!" came the muffled bass from inside.

She opened the door, walked through, and shut it behind her. Two minutes later she returned, looked at Milt, and said, "The dean will see you now." She stood, holding the door.

Milt rose, took four steps across the office, and entered the open door. It shut behind him.

Arthur Ambrose was looking at him, taking every bit of him in, just appraising his charge. Without rising to introduce himself, he commanded, "Sit down, Mr. McHugh."

Milt did. He tried to cover his intimidation and simply appraise the dean as he was being appraised. He hoped he managed but somehow thought the dean got the better of the exchange.

"I presume you know why I've invited you here?"

"I believe I do," Milt responded.

"And tell me what you think that is."

"There was an . . ." Milt searched for the right word. "Incident," he finally said. "At the freshman reception Saturday afternoon."

The dean gave a small smile. "I guessed right about you. I did not expect you to be coy or even self-protective. We're off to a good start, Mr. McHugh. I'd be interested in your version."

"Do you have Brookings's version?"

"I've not spoken with Mr. Brookings. Not certain it will be necessary. Why do you ask, Mr. McHugh?"

"My father is a state's attorney. That makes him a prosecuting attorney in Illinois. I've heard enough stories of inquisitions to know it's best to know where I stand."

"Is that what you think this is, Mr. McHugh, an inquisition?"

"Isn't it? I presume I've violated some school code of conduct and Brookings has come whining, so here I am."

Ambrose smiled again. "You are very direct, aren't you, Mr. McHugh? And courageous, as well, it appears."

"I will plead to direct, Dean Ambrose, but I don't know what it is you think I've done to suggest the latter."

"Mr. McHugh, in the course of my career, I may have had a thousand conversations similar to this, but I've never had a student so lacking any sense of circumspection. Now tell me what happened, if you will."

"Sure, don't know what I did to offend Brookings. Maybe he just saw a new guy without the trappings of local society and wanted to amuse himself and his friends tormenting someone he saw as vulnerable. But he introduced himself and asked where I was from. When I said Illinois, he started with a bunch of 'country bumpkin' sorts of condescending insults. It deteriorated from there. I invited him outside to discuss it further."

Ambrose nodded and sat still for a moment. "That's all, Mr. McHugh? I heard about it from the staff. They said you threw a drink in Mr. Brookings's face."

For the first time Milt let an expression of contrition cross his face. "I may have been out of line there."

Ambrose nodded and stayed silent for a moment, his hands propped on the vest covering his ample belly. "Yes, Mr. McHugh, you were out of line there. But I've not invited you here to punish you or even chastise you. I've invited you here to try to share some wisdom."

Milt exhaled deeply. "I think I could use some wisdom from you, sir. I have the feeling it's not going to be easy here."

"It will be if you let it, Mr. McHugh. I want you to try to

listen to what I'm about to say," Dean Ambrose continued. "I may make this overlong, but it's my way. The issue here is one of culture. You come from a world where men are used to handling their own lives and problems. Men fashion their destiny and don't ask for much help. Do you agree?"

Milt thought for a moment. "Aren't all men like that, Dean Ambrose? Isn't that what a man is? Or at least should be?"

Dean Ambrose smiled again. "Good. I thought you'd agree with that. What I want you to hear, Mr. McHugh, is that Mr. Brookings doesn't see the world that way. None of the people around Mr. Brookings do. They see a man as one who dominates his circumstances, but not alone."

Milton sat straight and leaned forward in his chair.

"What you will learn here at Yale is that as societies mature, the space for individual action narrows. Men, to live together, in large, sometimes very large, groups must develop civic institutions that are two things. First, strong enough to protect their members so men do not handle their problems individually, as you did. And second, trusted enough by the members of the society that they expect everyone to use the institutional answers for their problems. That is why you so shocked Brookings. He just presumed you would rely on some institutional response. Perhaps complain to some authority. A dorm monitor. Perhaps even me."

"Some institution he could control. Is that right?" Milt asked.

Ambrose smiled deeply. "Perhaps, Mr. McHugh. Perhaps. But is his reliance on his strengths any different than your reliance on yours? What you will learn here is why such institutions are necessary and perhaps, just perhaps, how you can achieve the same, or even more, power with them than you can with your fists. And, Mr. McHugh, I hope you learn some of that quickly so I'm not required at some point to throw you out of this institution, even though you are in the right."

Dean Ambrose rose and extended his hand across his desk. "That's all, Mr. McHugh."

Milt rose, leaned forward, and accepted it. "Dean Ambrose, when I came in here, I thought you were going to do just that, throw me out. I'm glad you didn't. It would have broken my father's heart." He let go the hand and turned to leave.

"And what about your heart, Mr. McHugh?"

Milt stopped and turned back to the fat man staring at him. "I'm not certain, Dean. I'm not certain."

CHAPTER 21

March 18, 1936
Beardstown, Illinois

Fred Lenz drove slowly down the darkened block of Monroe Street, peering over the wheel and looking for 436. Just last week he'd spent the day walking this block of Monroe Street, knocking on every door and trying to get "the lady of the house" to agree to an appointment later in the evening when "the man of the house was home" to display and demonstrate the Electrolux vacuums he was paid to sell—paid on commission, no sale, no pay. When no one was home, he left a small postcard showing a very happy and well-dressed housewife vacuuming her fine Persian carpet with an Electrolux, a large toothy smile on her pretty, young face. The other side of the card offered his services to display the product and blank spaces to fill in "time most convenient to see this marvelous, modern, time-saving device displayed."

No one had been home at 436. He'd left the card that had been mailed back requesting a demonstration at eight o'clock this evening. At 7:55 p.m., he pulled up to the curb and, the threadbare collar of his greatcoat pulled up, sat huddled, wishing the heater in this damn Studebaker would work. Since Studebaker had gone into receivership and the local dealership had closed, there was no way to service it even if he had the money. He was also miserable because he wanted to be home. Patricia would put Julie to bed by 8:45, and if he weren't back by then, he wouldn't be able to kiss his darling baby to sleep. But it was a job. And since Kleinschmidt's Hardware had laid him off in October, it was the only one he'd found.

At 7:58 p.m. he stepped into the street, opened the back door, yanked out the vacuum, and started to the door. He rang. The porch light came on, and the door was opened by a tall young man in his early twenties, a head full of curls falling down into his eyes. The young face presented a problem for Fred and stunned him for a moment. He had to decide. "Is your mother in?"

"Nope. You're the Electrolux guy, right? Come on in out of the cold."

Fred stepped across the threshold and shut the door behind him, glad for the warmth.

"Here, let me take that coat."

Fred set down his demonstration model, shrugged the coat off, and gave it to his host, who quickly hung it in the coat closet. Fred looked around waiting for a woman—mother, maybe wife—to come into the room. None did.

"If not your mother, is it your wife who's expecting me?" Fred asked, hesitant now.

"No. I'm the one who sent the card. This is my house."

"Yours? So young."

Larry laughed. "Perhaps. It was my mom's. She died a long time ago. Now it's mine."

"I'm so sorry, Mr. . . ."

"Clark," Larry offered and extended his hand.

Fred took it, his best sad expression in place. "I'm so sorry for your loss, Mr. Clark."

Larry gave a small laugh. "It's all right. I don't even remember her really. Now tell me your name. I don't remember it from the card I sent in."

"Fred Lenz, Mr. Clark."

"It's Larry. Now have a seat and tell me what you drink. It's late and it's cold. I'm sure you need something."

"Bourbon. Sour mash if you have it."

"Sit on the sofa, Fred. I'll be right back."

Fred set the Electrolux in the middle of the room. *Keep his eye on it.* And sat down.

Larry returned, handed him a crystal tumbler of Kentucky bourbon, and sat down in the armed chair at the end of the sofa.

Fred took a sip and then another. It was very good. "Tell me what it is you do, Larry."

Larry took a drink of his own, peered intently at Fred, a small smile showing at the corners of his eyes and mouth, and then leaned forward even closer to him. "Same thing as you, Fred."

Fred Lenz's mind registered warning, as his widening eyes and his back pushing hard into the sofa cushion revealed. "Same as me? What does that mean?"

"I spend my day walking the streets of Beardstown, setting up appointments for evening demonstrations."

"Of what?" The two words came out slowly.

Without saying a word, Larry stood up, walked to the coat closet, opened it, pulled something up off the floor, and set a brand-new Kirby vacuum right beside the Electrolux. "I'm your competition," Larry said. The tone was very friendly. "I thought we should meet." He walked back to his chair and sat down, a very satisfied look on his face.

"Why?" That Fred Lenz was totally confused could not have been more obvious.

Larry sipped at his whiskey before he answered. "I think it would be to our mutual benefit."

Fred seemed a bit less frightened now, his control returning. "How?"

"Fred, I get one, maybe two appointments set up every day. Nobody wants to see me on Friday, Saturday, or Sunday night. So I have four to eight demonstrations each week. About the same with you?"

Fred started to nod, stopped himself, and said, "Go on."

"I get a sale in about one of four demos. So that's one on a bad week and two on a good one." And again, he asked, "That about the same for you?"

Fred sipped and didn't answer.

"Fair enough. No reason to tell. But whatever it is, I think you could double it." Larry's eyes grew excited. "And so could I. Want to hear how?"

Fred nodded, still untrusting and unwilling to offer anything.

"Know how I sell against you, Fred?" Larry stood and walked to the middle of the room, unwrapped the cord from his Kirby, and plugged it into the wall socket. "Plug your machine in." Larry paused then said very politely, "If you would."

Fred stepped to his vacuum and then did as Larry had.

"Fred, my machine sucks harder than yours. A lot harder." Larry reached in his pocket, took out two marbles, and laid them on the floor. He turned on his Kirby and sucked one up. "Now you."

Fred did and with a satisfied smile watched the marble disappear down the throat of his Electrolux.

Larry reached back into his pocket and took out two more marbles, larger than the first two. Again, he turned on the Kirby and sucked one up and then nodded to Fred.

Fred turned on his Electrolux and approached the larger

marble. It came to his machine but very slowly, it seeming a great effort for the vacuum to swallow it.

"But marbles aren't what I use, Fred. I use these." Larry reached into this pocket a third time and laid two small steel ball bearings on the floor. A ball bearing rattled down the throat of the Kirby and disappeared. Larry turned off his machine and nodded to Fred.

Fred turned on the Electrolux and approached the remaining steel ball. It didn't move. He held the throat right next to it, and it slowly disappeared but did not rattle. Larry reached over to the wall and unplugged Fred's vacuum. The steel ball rolled slowly back onto the carpet.

"Not as much suck, Fred. Now tell me, how do you sell against me?"

Fred stood flat-footed in the middle of the room as though contemplating the risk-reward ratio of Larry's challenge.

"OK, OK," Larry said, "you don't have to tell me. I know. Your bag is bigger. Way bigger. Isn't it?"

Fred's fear seemed to dissolve. He broke into a big smile and nodded. "Take my coat out of the closet and hand it to me."

Larry did as instructed. Fred reached into a side pocket and pulled out a sack that seemed to expand when removed from the constriction of the pocket.

Fred opened the bag and shook it fully open. He looked at Larry with an almost evil smile.

"Go ahead, Fred. I know what you're going to do."

Fred held the open mouth of the bag near to Larry's carpet and shook out a mighty cloud of dust and debris. "Plug my machine back in."

Larry did, and Fred immediately proceeded to suck up the huge pile of dust. Every speck of it. When he was done, he turned off his machine, opened it, took out the bag and shook it all over the floor. "You try."

Larry knew his competitor. He knew his Kirby, which

didn't have as large a bag, wouldn't collect it all. But he got what he could. When his carpet was a bit more than half cleaned, no more would go up the throat. The bag was full.

Larry, looked at Fred. "Would you be so kind as to suck up the rest?"

Fred did as Larry unplugged his machine and put it back in the closet. As Fred finished, Larry walked to the next room, returned with the bottle, and refilled both glasses.

"Your point in all this is exactly what, Larry?"

Larry nodded again to the sofa, inviting Fred to sit and continue the discussion. Larry sat and started talking. "Fred, CIPS doesn't really care if you sell appliances or I do. This vacuum sales thing is pretty much break even for us. What CIPS wants is to sell power. To do that they need people to buy power. Both machines accomplish that for them. But I care. I care 'cause I'm on commission just like you. No sale, no money. And my boss cares 'cause he gets paid to make certain I do sell them. But you and I both need the same thing to succeed."

"And that is?" Fred asked.

"A higher percentage of sales from our demos. We double the close rate, we double the income. And here's how we do it. We eliminate the competition."

"And how do we do that?"

"We take away the clients' concern that they are making the right decision. We assure them the product they pick is the best. No question."

"And how do we do that?"

"Every time I get a demo, I'm going to invite you. My client will be shocked, but I'll assure them I've invited you because I know, absolutely know, my product is better. You act cocky, 'Yeah, sure shot' kinda talk. And then we each demo our machines. And when I set up an appointment, it's a 'suck-power test.' We use the ball bearings. When you set up, the competition is a 'volume test.' We use bags of dust.

"Fred, I know you've been skeptical since you walked in. So, I'll go first. I have an appointment arranged tomorrow night at 731 Madison at seven thirty. You willing to meet me there?"

Fred held up his glass, and the smiling competitors clinked tumblers and drained their glasses.

CHAPTER 22

June 17, 1936
Beardstown, Illinois

There was no shade anywhere, so Milt just sat down on the top of the levee he and the work crew were extending, opened his lunch pail, took out a sandwich, and chewed his first bite, looking north across the river at the black dirt of Schuyler County.

"Join you?" the strange voice standing over him asked.

Milt looked up at the thin, angular face and the sober brown eyes looking down at him.

"Grateful for the company," Milt responded.

The figure folded gracefully down beside him and immediately extended his hand. "Wilbur Briney is mine."

"Pleased to meet you, Wilbur. I'm Milt McHugh."

"McHugh?" It came out a question. "Of the Beardstown McHughs?"

"Yep," Milt responded and reached to the extended hand.

"Related to Lloyd?"

"He's my dad."

"Funny, I didn't think you were from around here."

"Why's that?" Milt asked.

"Well, for one thing, the guys on this WPA crew are from all over the country. And second, I've been watching you work. You're a bit of an odd mix for a river rat."

Milt studied Wilbur Briney's face—high cheekbones, thin nose, a mop of thick brown hair and deep-set eyes. The features were all patrician, but the ropy, muscular arms, the worn T-shirt and jeans, and the speech were all farm boy.

"And what odd mix is that?" Milt was more curious than upset by the description.

"You got a strong back, but a brand-new T-shirt. You're handy, but your hands are soft. You're rubbing them or spitting on them half the time I look toward you."

Milton laughed. "I grew up on this water"—he pointed to the river—"and handled all sorts of boats all my life." He smiled then. "And had the calluses to prove it. But the last two years I've been away at school. About all I've asked these hands to do is write." He held them up, staring at the blisters forming on them. "They'll harden up soon enough. Where you from, Wilbur?"

The boy stuck a long, muscular arm out to a spot across the river. "How good are your eyes?"

"I can see a goose coming in before most other hunters."

Briney smiled. "Then look into that river flat, and about two miles out you see the dot of one lone house in the middle of it. That's where I'm from."

"So, you went to school in Frederick and then Rushville. That's why we never met."

"Yep."

"Guess I didn't know anyone actually lived out there. Thought all the farmers lived up the bluff and came down to farm those years it didn't flood."

"My great-great-grandpa—guy named Nathan Briney— took that as his bounty land after the War of 1812. Story is people tried to talk him out of it. Said, 'Some years, maybe most, it's gonna flood. You'll not only get flooded out; you'll get poor not being able to count on crops.' Seems he understood that but said, 'This is the richest land on earth. Someday, some Dutchman who knows how will build a dike and keep the floods back, making me or my descendants the richest farmers in the state. Maybe the world.'"

Milt snorted. "That's funny."

Wilbur's sober eyes showed a hint of anger at the edges.

"Wilbur, no insult to you or your ancestor intended. In fact, it looks like he was right. I just laughed at how right he actually got it. About a Dutchman building a dyke."

Now Wilbur looked confused. "What about it?"

"Roosevelt," Milt said and smiled.

"What about him?"

"Roosevelt is a Dutch name. We're building this dam because of him."

"I'll be damned." Wilbur smiled now. "And he's right about the getting rich part, too. That soil is so rich, you hold it up to the sunlight and sprinkle it through your fingers and it's still black. From now on the Briney family is gonna get rich."

Both men chewed their sandwiches in silence. Wilbur took a drink from his thermos, turned to Milt, and asked, "Why you workin' here, Milt?"

"School's out for summer, and Dad won't have me living in his house and not contributing. I admit I'd hoped to work in his law office or at a newspaper. Someplace that didn't give me blisters." He held up his hands to examine them again. "But there's not a job in town I could find. Even Dad didn't have anything. This WPA digging thing was all I could get. How about you?"

"Pretty much the same. Depression has made life rough for us"—he pointed again to the speck of a house in the distance—"for the last five years. Seems like too much crop and rules supposed to keep us from planting. And then there's no other work. Been bad since I was a kid. My dad and brother took care of the farmwork. My job was to come up with some hard cash. Like you, this was all I could get."

After a moment of silence Briney added, "Where you going to school, Milt? Champaign?"

"Nope, I'm in Connecticut."

"It different there?"

"Yeah, most folks there are not like you and me. They're rich, Wilbur. Makes them different."

Wilbur pulled the hair back out of his eyes and studied Milt. "Your family is the richest I ever heard of. They that different from you?"

Milt threw his head back and laughed. "Way different. Way different. It's true, my family lives just fine and my daddy drinks 'call whiskey.' But these people are 'yacht in the New York harbor' rich. Nothing like anyone you or I know."

Wilbur looked perplexed. "Even in this depression?"

"Oh, I've heard stories of some of them losing it all. Even know a couple of kids who had family friends commit suicide. So, some have had it hard. But some have made it just fine. They're still around, Wilbur."

"How'd they do it, Milt?"

"Wilbur, all of us out here, you, me, pretty much all of us, have ancestors, people like your great-great-granddad and my great-great-granddad, all came here to scratch our own lives out of this river. And mostly we did it on our own. Oh, neighbors pitched in and helped, but it was all individual.

"I guess that's how they started, too, but for them that start was a long, long time ago. Now it seems all those rich families are in charge of something. They make wealth not from scratching but from other men scratching. And it seems to work for damn near all of them."

Wilbur's deep-set eyes stared intently. "How?"

Milt pondered the question for a moment. "OK, let's look at you and what you're doing here. That piece of land over there"—Milt pointed across the river—"has been worked by you and your family for four generations. The Brineys have sacrificed for four generations to create something—if nothing else, wealth for yourselves. And you've all been willing to devote your lives to it. Right?"

"Right." The black hair fell into his eyes again as he nodded.

"And many of those years it's been more heartache than gain. But now look what we're doing. Look what the US government is doing. Thousands of men, and a few women, are devoting themselves to building a levee so high that even the flood of '27 wouldn't get over or by it. Hell, they are even engineering a concrete retaining wall at the foot of State Street to ensure Beardstown won't flood again. On top of that, millions of tax dollars, other people's money, are being spent to build it. To make the Briney family dream come true. Right?"

"Yes, it seems so," Wilbur agreed.

"So, let me ask you a question. How much of the profit from that should you give to them, and how much should you get to keep?"

"We'll pay our taxes. Might not like it, but we will."

"And if the government helps you do this, should you be able to do whatever you want on your farm? And how closely should you follow their rules? After all, they made you rich."

"I don't get it. The labor and farm are mine. The rules are mine."

"But you said earlier the government had already imposed rules designed to stop the depression that told you how much you could plant. And the rules say what you'll sell it for as well. Haven't they?"

"Yes. They have."

"See, these rich guys manage to set up systems where lots of rules govern lots of people, and yet somehow they stay rich."

"And what do you think of that, Milt?"

"I'm not sure yet, Wilbur."

Wilbur took another bite of his sandwich, seeming to ponder what he'd just heard. Finally, he spoke again. "Tell me something else, Milt. What are the girls like, these rich girls?"

Milt laughed loudly. "They are different, too."

"Like how?"

"Lots of ways."

"You got one?"

Milt nodded and smiled.

"Tell me about her."

"At Rushville High, what did you read in English class?" Milt asked.

Wilbur Briney thought for a moment. "I remember reading *Huck Finn*."

"Just a book, right? Read it, liked it or not, and forgot it. Right?"

"Pretty much."

"Well, I go out with this girl. Rich girl." Milt looked up to the sun and smiled. "Her name's Barbara. She's an English literature major. She's read pretty much every story ever written in English. Even fairy tales. *Grimm's Fairy Tales*. It's a book, Wilbur. I swear. And do you know what it means?"

Wilbur just shook his head.

"It means she takes this stuff seriously. She probes it for meaning. Meaning in stories. And she expects me to as well."

"What's this Barbara look like?" Wilbur asked.

Milt tilted his head until he was looking directly into Wilbur's face. "Like a dream, Wilbur. Like a dream."

"But what does she look like?"

"Tall, five foot seven, curly brown hair that she always wears pulled up on her head. Her neck is long, and I always want to kiss it."

"Do you?"

"Wilbur," Milt said, his tone teasing, "there are some things a gentleman doesn't say."

Briney's smile was almost wicked. "One thing you left out."

"What's that?"

"She got big tits?"

"Wilbur, I told you there are some things . . ."

CHAPTER 23

July 7, 1936
Poughkeepsie, New York

Cavanaugh Proctor was an imposing man in almost any circumstance, but today it was hard for Milt not to laugh. Standing at the top of the gangplank, as he was, made him appear even more imposing than his six foot four inches of height normally granted. The crease in his white linen slacks seemed even sharper than the bow of his yacht. The pants ended in a pair of white buck shoes made even whiter than the trousers by someone's, certainly not Cavanaugh Proctor's, generous application of talcum powder. The blazer was a deep blue, double-breasted burlap held closed with brass buttons. The regimental striped necktie beneath it a pattern of alternating blue and white stripes. But the thing that made it all seem absurd was the white barracks cover with the black bill polished to reflect sunlight. Proctor's perfectly trimmed grey curls showing under the black hat brim and the smoke puffing from his long-stemmed pipe made it impossible for Milt not to stand on the gangplank, salute sharply, and bark, "Request permission to come aboard, sir."

"Milt." Barbara's voice was part hiss and part tease. "Don't torment Daddy so."

He turned, looking over his shoulder toward the beautiful young woman dressed in a fitted white skirt hemmed at the calves and with white stockings showing the rest of the way down her legs to short white pumps. Her blouse was light silk, also white, open at the neck, with sleeves cut off at the elbows. Her brown curls were pulled tight behind her neck, and her head was covered with a short-brimmed white straw hat pulled to one side at a rakish angle.

"Can't help myself," he whispered just as his host bellowed, "Young man, you know you are welcome on my yacht or my daughter would not have extended her invitation."

"Good start, Milt. And you promised to be nice," she whispered in his ear. But there was affection in her tone.

Milt stood aside to let Barbara rise up the gangplank before him. Her father threw his arms around her and craned his head down to kiss her cheek. "Hello, baby."

"Hello yourself, Daddy. I'm looking forward to this day with you."

She stepped back and allowed the two men the ritual handshake. As soon as the greetings were complete, Proctor turned to his ship's captain and ordered, "OK, John, bring in the gangplank and head downriver. I want to be there in time to get anchorage just the other side of the bridge and as close to the rowing lanes as possible. It will be crowded today."

"Aye, aye, Skipper," the man responded, and turned to give instruction to his crew of two.

"Babs, honey, show Milt up to the deck in front of the pilot house. I'll get us drinks and be right behind you," Proctor instructed.

By the time Proctor arrived, Milt and Barbara were leaning on the top rail, the wind gently blowing at their hair and the motor-sailor steaming down the Hudson. Proctor handed a champagne flute to his daughter and a tumbler of iced bourbon to Milt. "The usual for both of you, I presumed."

"Yes, sir," Milt said.

"Milt, I believe you're used to river traffic, aren't you?"

"Yes, sir. Grew up on one. I can oar or pilot most any watercraft. At least I thought so until I walked up your gangplank. I've never been on or near anything like this."

Proctor smiled with more than a hint of pride. "From neither what you've said to me in the past nor what Babs has said about you do I believe you to have ever seen an eight-man shell, an 'eight' we call them. Have you?"

"An 'eight,' sir?"

"The boats we're here to see race. They have eight oarsmen and a cox. Coxswain."

"Aren't they sculls?" Milt asked.

The tall man laughed. "You are about to see something very exciting, Milt. You may enjoy it. Hope you do. And no, a scull is a boat where the rower has two oars. In an 'eight,' each oarsman has just one."

"It was Daddy's sport in college, Milt," his daughter bragged. "He was stroke on Columbia's number one boat his senior year."

"Stroke?" Milt did not understand the word used that way.

"The stroke is the man immediately in front of the cox," Proctor explained. "The cox calls pace, strokes per minute. It's up to the stroke to translate that instruction into oar speed. The other seven key off him. Stroke screws up, they all screw up."

"The captain?" Milt suggested.

"Not quite," Proctor corrected. "The cox is definitely the one making the decisions. But you're right in the sense that the stroke leads the work. Milt, the race will start here by that boathouse." Proctor pointed to the large floating shed at the river's edge. "We're now motoring four miles to the finish. That's the length of the race."

"How long will it take?"

"More than twenty minutes, less than twenty-five. And they will be the hardest minutes an athlete can endure," Proctor responded.

Barbara Proctor looked up at her father, her pride in her father's past glory clearly evident.

"And your Columbia team is in today's race, I believe? And if the *New York Times* is to be believed, among the favorites to win."

Proctor smiled. "Yes, to both, Milt. One of these eight teams will call themselves the 1936 collegiate champions by the end of the day. And that will make them the favorite to win the Olympic trials in two weeks. Though this is four miles, a long haul, and Olympics are only two thousand meters, a sprint really. So maybe not."

"Mr. Proctor, as you said, I've not only never seen this race; I've never even seen one of these boats, but I've been reading. You willing to bet your Columbia boat will win?"

"I wouldn't bet any other way."

"Would you be offended if I offered you a small wager? Very small," Milt added.

Proctor looked down at him, turned his head to his daughter, who nodded approval, and looked back. "What did you have in mind?"

"I'm embarrassed to offer, but I'm also on a tight budget. How about $5?"

"Who's your team?"

"Washington, sir."

"Now, Milt, what is it you read that makes you pick them?" the patrician asked.

"They are my kind of men, sir. They are Westerners, frontiersmen a generation or two removed."

"Now what's that got to do with it?" Cavanaugh Proctor seemed genuinely interested.

"I don't know everything about them, but I know a little. They are not patricians, not refined or well educated. They are from mining camps and logging camps in the Northwest. They have no family connections. They are men who have gotten where they are relying on no one but themselves. One of them was left entirely alone when the family farm failed. His parents had too many mouths to feed when they left, and he was the oldest, the most able to survive on his own, so they left him. One of them had a mother who died in a mining camp. His father brought in a new woman who kicked him out. He was nine years old."

"Very romantic story, Milt. I like it. But you admit you know nothing about rowing. The best single quote I know to explain rowing is from a guy named George Pocock. He's famous with all us race fans." Proctor swung his arm in an arch taking in all the yachts lining the race course. "His lesson is, and I quote exactly and from memory, 'It isn't enough for the muscles of a crew to work in unison. Their hearts and minds must also be as one.'"

Milt smiled, looking up at the taller man. "Doesn't sound like something a Westerner would say."

"The man lives in Seattle, Milt. If you still want that wager, here's my hand."

Cavanaugh Proctor extended his hand and Milt McHugh took it.

"Milt," came the sweet voice beside them. "Would you go to the galley and get me another glass of champagne?"

"Of course, Barbara." Milt accepted her empty glass and stepped into the pilot shack and down the stairs.

"Daddy!" she scolded the moment Milt was out of sight. "You weren't exactly being fair, were you?"

"What did I do now, Babs?" The tone was teasing.

"I've been around you and your crew stories all my life. I know who George Yeoman Pocock is. He's a Brit."

Proctor smiled the smile of a Cheshire cat. "He is a Brit who makes the best eights in the world and does it in Seattle."

She looked hard at him.

"I was just trying to save your impoverished 'charity case' some money."

* * * *

The eights were less than half a mile away when they came out of the fog and could be picked up in the field glasses all three of them kept pulled tight to their eyes. The first to come were California and Columbia, too close to tell who led at that distance.

"They're each pulling about thirty-seven," Proctor announced. "I don't think they can keep that up all the way. Someone will quit."

Washington came out of the fog hard behind.

"My boys have a chance!" Milt suddenly shouted.

"Milt, they are three lengths behind. They'll never make that up in less than half a mile," Proctor advised in a tone of knowing wisdom. "Hope you've got that $5 bill handy."

"What happens if neither of us wins?" Milt asked without putting his glasses down. "'Cause the Cal boat seems to be passing a very tired Columbia crew." He had to shout to be heard over the roar coming from the boats anchored gunnel to gunnel on both sides of the last half mile.

"Oh God, no!" Proctor lost his composure as Cal slid by an exhausted Columbia crew no longer able to keep up the thirty-seven pace. "Jesus. Jesus Christ!" Proctor shouted now. "Washington's doing maybe forty and went by my blue-and-white like it was parked."

Then he pulled his glasses down and looked sadly at Milton. "But they won't keep up the forty and they won't catch Cal."

Milt had stayed eye sockets held tight into the binoculars. "Maybe look again, Mr. Proctor."

The roar had become impossibly loud, a roar across the water. With two hundred yards to go, Washington moved past a Cal shell that seemed not to have seen them until they were neck and neck. The Cal cox screamed something into his megaphone, and the Cal stroke tried to pick up the pace. The other oars were not able to follow, and suddenly the Cal boat was no longer gracefully smooth as oars went into the water flat and came out upright.

The Washington boat flew with the grace of an arrow across the line, half its oarsmen across before the tip of Cal's bow hit the tape.

* * * *

The Cadillac V16 Fleetwood pulled up to the curb in front of Penn Station.

"Barbara, do you mind staying in the car with Taggert? I'd like to walk your young man to the train if you'll let me."

Her look was wondering, but she nodded agreement. Milt looked more disappointed than questioning. Both men stepped out. She rolled down the window and screamed after. Milt turned to look, and she beckoned him back. When he'd lowered to the open window, she kissed his cheek.

"He likes you. It will be fine. See you in English lit class Monday morning."

Milt turned to see Cavanaugh Proctor smiling at the scene.

As they entered the station, Proctor said, almost with warmth, "Babs tells me you're planning on law school."

"That's my plan, Mr. Proctor."

"Have you decided where yet?"

"I'll have to do that this fall. Right now, no real plans. Probably stay on the East Coast. Law schools are generally better here, certainly more prestigious. But Northwestern is close to home and very good." Milt looked down at the marbled floor for a moment. "Why do you ask, Mr. Proctor?"

"Have you thought about Columbia?"

"One of the best schools there is. Not sure I can get in, but yes, of course I have."

"If you need a recommendation, I just want you to know I'll write one for you."

Milt stopped and stood listening to a thousand footfalls on the marble floor. He looked over at the wooden benches and saw one vacant. He swallowed. "Mr. Proctor, I've a few minutes before my train. Would you sit with me?"

When the men were seated, Milton McHugh looked at Proctor, studied his face for a moment. "Mr. Proctor, I'm very grateful. Very, very grateful. But I'm not sure that's such a good idea."

It was the second time today he'd seen shock on Proctor's face. "Why?" It came out more a command than a question.

"Mr. Proctor, I'm very fond of your daughter. At the risk of impertinence, I think it's fair to say I love her. But I have obligations to a small town in the Midwest. What you'd probably call 'the middle of nowhere' if I were not around. Three generations of McHughs have served that town as prosecutor. We were a booming railroad town, but the railroad may be going. I'm needed there, Mr. Proctor. I'm not needed here; I'm needed in Beardstown, Illinois. I have to go home. I'd thought law school would be a good opportunity for Barbara . . ." He stopped and swallowed hard. "I thought it would be an opportunity for her to . . . make other arrangements."

Cavanaugh Proctor continued to study the young face before him. Milt was the one who finally looked down. "Milt, I'm not sure you know my daughter as well as you think you do. She is an awfully stubborn woman."

Proctor rose and Milt behind him. Proctor reached in his pocket, pulled out a bill, and put it in Milt's hand. "Here's the $5 your knowledge of human nature has won for you. And my offer is, and always will be, good." He turned and walked back through Penn Station, Milt watching him as he went.

CHAPTER 24

January 11, 1940
New York City, New York

Milton McHugh sat quietly across the desk from Young Berryman Smith, dean of Columbia Law School. He had dressed his very best for this visit including the finishing touch of a regimental necktie of Columbia blue-and-white stripes. He had presented the final draft of this year's law school review and sat quietly as the dean reviewed the work, or as quietly as he could. He knew that absolute stillness represented confidence in the work he and his committee had prepared. But knowing and doing were two different things. The trickle of sweat running slowly down his spine wanted to be scratched or patted or attended to in some way. But he didn't. He tried to distract himself by intensive study of the eighteen-inch-tall miniature bronze replica of Gieng's blind Justice on the credenza behind the dean.

Mostly he'd sat here without moving for almost twenty minutes now, enduring not one question, not one comment or even change of expression from the dean.

Finally, the austere man picked his head up, rolled his neck in a circle, gave a small, very small, smile, handed the paper back, and said simply, "Submit it."

Milton was overjoyed. Editor of Columbia's *Law Review* and the work were well received. He tried to stay all business and not let the huge smile in his heart move to his face. But he failed and he knew it.

"Thank you, sir. Thank you very much. The committee will be thrilled to know their work meets your approval."

"As am I, Mr. McHugh. As am I." Even this sober academic's voice showed his pleasure now. "Is there anything more you need of me, Mr. McHugh?"

"No, sir. . . ." And then he paused. This was the moment. "Well yes, sir. There is one other thing if it's not too presumptuous."

"You'll have to ask, Mr. McHugh, before we know whether it's presumptuous. Go ahead."

"Would you write a letter of recommendation for me?"

"To whom, Mr. McHugh?"

"Sir, I'd hoped upon leaving you to get a job clerking at a Circuit Court."

"That, Mr. McHugh, I am pleased to do. It is a job for which you are eminently qualified. And I happen to know almost all the justices on the Second Circuit."

"Oh, sir, it's not the Second Circuit that interests me. It's the Seventh."

"Mr. McHugh, why would anyone prefer Chicago to New York?" Before Milt could respond, the dean's face lightened. "Now I remember. Your father is an Illinois state's attorney in one of the downstate counties."

"Cass County, sir. That's right."

"Mr. McHugh, forgive my being personal, but are you not engaged to Cavanaugh Proctor's daughter?"

"Barbara Proctor. Yes, sir." Milton was surprised that Dean Smith knew this.

"Forgive me, but I have to ask. Does Miss Proctor know you will go to Chicago when you have a chance to stay in New York?"

"Miss Proctor and I started dating as undergraduates. When we became close enough to discuss these things, I made clear that my father and his grandfather before him had served Beardstown, my hometown, and I felt it was my obligation to do the same. So yes, she knows my path."

"And her father?" The dean seemed unwilling to give up the line of inquiry.

"Again, sir, yes."

"Then I will write the letter, Mr. McHugh. And I will be delighted."

As he rose from his chair to leave, Milton pointed at the statue behind the dean. "My father has a similar statue in his office but not of the famous Gieng. I don't know the artist of which his is a copy."

"She's very old, you know. Some say she originated with the Greek goddess Themis, but there are Egyptian works of a goddess named Maat who is also blindfolded," Smith offered.

Milton smiled broadly. "My father always questioned the blindfold. He always asked, 'If Justice is blind, how can she see which way the scales are weighted?'"

CHAPTER 25

February 3, 1940
Beardstown, Illinois

The two men stood looking out the window of George Grainger's second-story office at the roundhouse yard below covered in snow and littered with the bodies of those too injured to walk or crawl away. All three ambulances from Schmitt Memorial Hospital had arrived, the flashes of their rotating roof lights making the snow-covered ground look even bloodier than it was. Aside from the hospital medics racing frantically to aid those they could on the spot and get those who needed more serious treatment to the hospital, the only man standing was Talbot, who stared defiantly up at the authority of the CB&Q. Despite the cold, Talbot had nothing on over his coveralls and only a T-shirt below them. Blood dripped down from his forehead, and steam rose up from his uncovered head. He held an ax handle, one end of which he used to beat a slow steady tattoo on the asphalt-covered ground. It was the same rhythm with which he and three hundred other strikers had greeted the scabs C.C. Cunningham had brought in on two freight cars just an hour earlier. In addition to the freight cars full of temporary workers willing to break the union picket line, the train had included two cars of tough Pinkerton agents paid to intimidate or beat their way through. But the three hundred members of the several rail brotherhoods had met them ready for combat. And they had won. The temporary workers and the Pinkertons were gone, their train pulling slowly out of the yard, back to Springfield. The victorious strikers were all gone for a joyous early-morning celebration. All save Talbot, who would stand and beat his defiant tattoo as long as he had an audience.

C.C. Cunningham looked down at the man beating defiance to him. "That is a very hard-assed man, George." As he spoke, he reached over to the corner of the window and pulled the cord, lowering the blinds.

"Hard-assed. That's an understatement," Grainger responded. "Shove a lump of coal up his butt and in a week, he'll shit a diamond."

Cunningham smiled a wane smile. "Pour me a drink, George." He dropped himself into the chair, looking more exhausted than angry. His very thin grey hair hung in wisps off his forehead and behind his ears. He pulled the wire frame of his glasses from his face, pulled the silk pocket square, and wiped them. Big George Grainger, old as he was, was still a bull of a man. He towered over Cunningham when both were standing. Now, as he poured, he was as a giant next to an old man seemingly wilting below him.

Cunningham sipped the whiskey and nodded to the chair beside him. "Sit, George, and pour yourself one as well."

The big man did as instructed.

"You know how old I am now, George?"

Grainger swallowed his entire tumbler of whiskey and shook his head.

"I'm eighty-two, George. And I've been at this railroad thing for over sixty years. I'm tired, George." He sipped again and set the glass down. "This is almost the end for me, George. Almost."

"What's left, C.C.?"

"I'll move this operation to Galesburg."

George Grainger's face showed no expression. "Will that make it better? We have trouble there as well."

C.C. didn't look up. He rose, pulled back the curtain, and looked again at the mess below him. As he spoke, he continued to look out. "Yes, there's trouble in Galesburg. There is trouble all over America. Railroad men, these men"—he pointed below—"and their families have struggled for ten years. Roosevelt's government goes from one bad idea to the next, and nothing he does helps. It always makes things worse. Hard to blame them, George."

Cunningham dropped the curtain, turned back to the chair, poured himself another drink, and then poured for Grainger as well. "But Beardstown is the worst."

He sat back down and looked at Grainger for the first time since he'd started to talk. "No, Chicago is the worst. But we have to be in Chicago. It is the rail center of America. We really have no choice there. Here"—he pointed at the closed curtain behind him—"here, we have a choice. This is the most pro-union town in the CB&Q operation. Here the union even runs the city. I've been fighting with this city for over twenty-five years. I'm tired, George. Very tired. They have won today, but they'll find it was a Pyrrhic victory. This place will die when we leave."

George Grainger rocked forward, put his hands on his knees, his broad forehead sloping down to bushy grey eyebrows pushed closer to Cunningham. "Yes, it will die. You're right. And we'll be killing it."

"Yes. But it won't be murder. It will be self-defense."

Both men sat silent, each trapped in the thoughts of his own head. Cunningham finally spoke.

"There's one thing I need you to do, George. One thing about cleaning this up."

Grainger's deep voice rumbled, "What's that?"

"The state's attorney here. McHugh. That his name?"

Grainger nodded.

"Do I remember he's a lodge mate of yours?"

Grainger nodded again.

"Find out what he plans to do about this. He's the one Republican in this Democratic hellhole of a city. Maybe he has a solution."

* * * *

George Grainger sat waiting at the bar in the Masonic Lodge. There was no urgency in his wait. Everything that was about to unfold would do so in its own way and in its own time. The forces driving it were far stronger than any skill of words he might muster. He was just here to gather information and to pass it on. And he knew it. He felt a hand land on his shoulder and turned to face Lloyd McHugh.

Grainger could see McHugh was trying to look nonchalant, but his tenor voice gave away a touch of anxiety.

"Lloyd, I don't see you enough. In fact, last time I saw you, the hair that always hangs in your eyes was brown not grey."

Lloyd slid onto the bar stool. "As long as you don't tell me my pointed chin has become a double pointed chin or the blue in my eyes has faded away."

Both men chuckled.

"Not to be abrupt, George, but I presume the reason you wanted to talk to me was yesterday's little fracas in your rail yard. Am I right?"

George nodded.

"Gonna cost you a drink. Or maybe two."

"Delighted to and have been ever since our state's attorney allowed me to buy it again."

"Somehow, George, I don't think my work ever stopped

you." Lloyd stepped behind the bar for his bottle, poured two tumblers full of good scotch, set them on the bar, and walked around to take his stool.

Grainger held up his glass. "To honest conversation among friends."

McHugh's face lifted into a wry smile, and he repeated the phrase as they clinked glasses.

"So, what are you going to do about it, Lloyd?"

McHugh responded with a question of his own. "What do you want me to do about it, George?"

"Put every man who had a club in his hand in jail for aggravated assault," Grainger said, his base voice lowered almost to a whisper.

"Would you also have me include those with brass knuckles and saps? I hear that was what your boys were carrying."

"My boys, as you call them, were only there to escort a bunch of local and out-of-work lads to a paying job."

McHugh turned the tumbler in his hand, looking into it as though hoping magic words would float to the surface. "George, do you know how many conversations I've had with men who want me to arrest you, Cunningham, and every man who got off that train? And if I do as either of you ask, do you know what will happen? There will be a trial, and at the trial every man accused will have a dozen witnesses who saw somebody else start it. Even if we move a trial to some faraway county, the result, whichever way, will tear this town apart. So no, George, I won't be doing as you ask. And I won't be doing as they ask. I will be exercising what the law refers to as prosecutorial discretion. I will let sleeping dogs lie and hope the memory of their bad dreams goes away soon."

Lloyd McHugh looked up at the big man beside him. Now that he was no longer trying to seem nonchalant, his deep-set brilliant-blue eyes showed no upset, no defense, only wisdom.

Grainger studied them intently for a moment and then

exhaled. It was an exhale that seemed to drain him of any previous emotion. "Lloyd, you know I understand. I hope you know I had to ask."

McHugh nodded.

"Do you know what's going to happen now, Lloyd?"

Suddenly McHugh's face showed great interest. "What?"

"The CB&Q will move the roundhouse and shops to Galesburg. Only a few people to operate the station and supply passenger and freight services locally will remain."

Lloyd McHugh's expression of great interest left him, replaced by a look of great sadness.

Grainger looked down into his glass. "Lloyd, I take no joy in this. There is no victory here for me or the CB&Q. It's just a business decision."

McHugh's sadness turned to anger. "George, Beardstown is a river port. It's a place of businessmen. Entrepreneurs. Men who would strike out on their own at great risk to themselves and their families. We are river rats and proud of it. This is a place whose citizens floated $150,000 in bonds eighty-five years ago to pay for a railroad bridge across the river to get something here to replace river traffic when it went away. You can't just leave!"

Grainger took long composing himself and his words. He wanted to say this just right. "That city, Lloyd, the one you just described, the CB&Q would not abandon. But that city no longer exists. It is now a city of groups, not individuals. It is a city that attempts to muscle the men you just described and wring from them money that they could not figure out how to create on their own. When we leave, the only hope for this place is that you do everything you can to encourage those brave men of vision who may still be among you and let them create new visions of wealth for themselves and this place.

"Thanks for the drink, Lloyd." Grainger raised his aging body off the stool and left.

* * * *

Lilly was busy in the kitchen cleaning up from dinner, and Sam was shuttling back and forth between the bar and the library with drinks for the billiard and card players. He was standing behind the bar when he heard the front door open and so was looking up when the door between the cloakroom and the front room opened to let in the large frame of George Grainger.

"George, you old son of a gun, I was half expecting you."

"Why?" George rumbled as he crossed the floor.

"You've had a rough couple of days. Thought you might find this lodge more relaxing than your other lodge for the moment."

Grainger smiled a knowing smile and pulled up a stool. "The usual."

Sam opened a bottle of Crown Royal and poured a few fingers neat. "Here you go. Lilly's still got some pie from dinner. Want a slice?"

"Thanks, Sam, but no. I really came to talk to you. Can I keep you away from your guests for a few minutes?"

Sam wiped his hands on the bar towel as he walked from behind the bar to the kitchen door. "Lilly, honey, would you keep an eye on the library for a bit? George Grainger is here and wants to talk."

He came back and took a stool next to Grainger. "What's up? You need me to come back to work early?"

Grainger smiled. "I'd not ask you to cross the picket line, Sam. I hope you know that."

Sam just smiled and nodded.

"In fact, what I want is just the opposite of that."

Sam's face became puzzled.

"You been driving trains for me for over thirty years. Right?"

Sam's face became a bit suspicious. "Yeah." He arched his

head to one side and looked at his boss from under his brow. "So what?"

"So you now have a nice pension coming, for the rest of your life."

"Yeah . . ." Sam's suspicion now showed in his voice.

"I want you to take it." Grainger's words rumbled out even more than usual.

"Don't think so, George. I like the work, and I'm not sure I can make this lodge pay with no other income. At least until this damn depression is over."

Grainger rolled the rye around in his glass. "Then you get to move to Galesburg."

"Galesburg? Why?"

"'Cause that's where the roundhouse is going."

Sam set his glass down on the bar and turned his stool to face Grainger eye to eye but said nothing.

"Sam, your annual sabbatical is up at the end of next month. Strike won't be over then, so you either cross the line or you're on strike. We're going to try to fire every striker, and whether we manage that or not, we'll be moving the whole operation to Galesburg. So, you come back to work, and all the money you'll get for it is a little daily strike benefit from the brotherhood and you may be moved to Galesburg. Just quit now and you get a nice, honorable retirement and a regular monthly check until you die."

Sam sat silent for a long time. Reached over the bar for a bottle of bourbon and poured himself a refill. Realizing George's was empty, he reached again for the bottle of Crown Royal and poured him a refill as well.

"Tell me one thing, George. How is moving to Galesburg going to make anything better for the CB&Q? You got trouble with the union there as well."

George sipped on his drink as Sam asked the question. He set it down and answered. "Wherever we go, we got union problems. But here, here in Beardstown, it never goes away. Never. Most of downstate Illinois votes Republican. They're all independent cusses and vote that way. Chicago is the exception. They all want to cling to a group to get the result they want. Hell, this town is so Democratic, it not only has a full slate of elected Democrats running the place; it didn't even vote for Lincoln. Not even in '64 for God's sake. We have more trouble here than anywhere south of Chicago and don't see that changing. We'll move."

"And you want me to retire?"

"Yep!"

"One more question, George."

"Shoot."

"You're older than I am and have more time in than I do. You gonna retire?"

George Grainger took a long drink and emptied his tumbler. He turned the stool, rose, and walked across the floor to the coatroom entrance. He stepped inside, and when he reappeared, he had on his big overcoat and hat. "Sam, do as I say, not as I do."

CHAPTER 26

December 25, 1941
Beardstown, Illinois

"You want to drive or shall I, Dad?" Larry asked.

"It's my car; I'll drive," Sam responded as the three stepped out of Larry's front door and onto the porch.

"Larry"—Lilly turned to him as she pulled the black sable collar up onto her neck—"since when did you start shoveling the snow off your steps and sidewalk?"

Larry pushed his black wavy hair off his forehead with one hand and pulled the fedora onto his head with the other. "Only when my beautiful stepmother is coming to visit."

They stepped into the softly falling snow and toward the big black Buick parked at the curb.

Lilly smiled, turning her head back toward him. She'd always liked her husband's charming, if somewhat irresponsible, son. "New hat, Larry?"

"Christmas present to myself. Stetson, 5X Beaver," he responded.

Her eyes twinkled up at him. "Now what on earth is a 5X Beaver?"

Sam, beside her and holding her elbow, responded. "It means two things, Lilly. It means it's more beaver than wool felt, and it means my son is, typically, spending more money than he's got."

Larry scurried past, crushing dark footprints into the snow that now covered the lawn, ran in front of the Buick and into the street, opened the front passenger-side door, and stood holding it for Lilly. She slid in, and he closed it behind her and then opened the rear door, put a foot on the running board, and stepped in just as his father closed the driver's door. Larry laid his forearms on the back of the front seat and put his chin on top of his hands. She turned to him, and he focused his light-brown eyes on hers.

"Christmas present to myself, Lilly. Last expensive thing I'll have for a while."

His father, pulling away from the curb, the tires making a crisp, low crushing sound as they rolled over the new fallen snow, snorted. "That I doubt."

Larry's voice was all teasing cheer. "It's true, Dad. I won't be spending much because I won't have much to spend."

"Why, you quit work?" His father's voice borrowed the teasing tone.

"Matter of fact, I did, Dad."

Sam hit the brakes hard. The rear wheels locked, and the sedan slid sideways. He held his foot on the brake pedal and turned to lock his light-brown eyes on his son's matching ones. Sam's molars held very tight made his jaw even more pronounced than usual.

"You what? And why?" he demanded.

"Joined the navy."

Lilly snapped her head around, and he was caught between them, unable to look at both. Larry maintained eye contact with his father.

"Aren't you a little old for this? Twenty-six. Twenty-seven in a few weeks."

"Dad, stop. You don't mean that. It's what I should do, and we both know it."

Sam's jaw loosened and he nodded. "Why the navy?"

"Because of you."

"Me." Sam's nostrils flared. "What have I got to do with it?"

"All my life I've heard about California and the navy yard. I was so young, I don't remember a bit of it. I want to see it again."

Lilly put her gloved hand on top of his. "I doubt they'll send you to California. A couple of ladies at church have sons who've gone, and they're all in Atlantic ports."

Larry smiled his mischievous, boyish smile. "I told them I was a really good shot and would join the army and do what I'm good at unless they guaranteed the Pacific. I've got orders right here." Sam patted the breast pocket of his overcoat. "Naval Training Station, San Diego. I'm due in two weeks."

Sam started to drive again, straightening the car before he picked up any speed. "So, what did you tell them you're good at besides shooting?"

"Said I could handle any small craft in any water. They liked that."

*   *   *   *

Beulah McHugh opened the front door and threw her arms around her sister, Lilly, as she pulled her away from the threshold. "You two stomp the snow off your shoes and your hats before you come in," she directed, looking at the two men behind her sister.

Sam and Larry both stomped their feet on the porch, took off their hats, and shook them and their coats as well.

"Now come in here and shut the door before we all chill."

Immediately behind her stood Lloyd McHugh, beaming goodwill at his friends. "Merry Christmas, all."

Beulah hung up the coats and tucked the hats onto the top shelf of the coat closet, and all shook hands and exchanged greetings. But the interest turned as quickly as civility would allow to the couple standing in the middle of the room. Barbara McHugh stood tall, her tailored skirt tapered down to three-inch pumps. Her erect posture made her seem taller than her father-in-law. Her brown curls were pulled up to reveal every inch of her long neck, which emphasized her height and made her appear nearly as tall as any man in the room.

Each of the Clarks took her in. The posture, the height, the chiseled nose and facial structure, showing her patrician to the core. But their eyes didn't linger. They flew almost instantly to the man standing beside her. It was not the Milton McHugh they knew, or thought they knew. This Milton McHugh was dressed from spit-polished brown brogans to brown khaki shirt and tie in the uniform of a lieutenant in the army of the United States of America.

The Clarks all stood in dumb silence, not knowing what to say first or to whom. And then the room burst into bedlam with a clatter of exclamations and greetings, handshakes, hugs, well-wishes, and questions. It was a moment when visions for a future world and each person's part in it were revealed.

Dinner was, of course, goose. The table was heaped with yams and cranberries and dressing and potatoes and rolls and all the other things with which they planned to stuff themselves and have this one last feast before life and war took them to the edges of the globe.

"Milton." It was Sam who raised his voice over the hubbub to get the attention of all to his question. "You might as well tell us all at once or you'll have to tell many times." He paused. "The uniform? What? Why?"

The talking stopped. Some knew the answers, some did not, but all wanted to hear.

"Mr. Clark, it truly is not complicated. The world is at war. I don't care about that so very much, but my nation is at war. I, like Larry, will do my part."

"And what will your part be, Milt?" Sam spoke again.

"I requested the court release me from my job as clerk of the Seventh District Court in Chicago. They have agreed. I have been commissioned as the lowest-level officer, a second lieutenant, and will be assigned to the Office of the Judge Advocate General."

"Milton, may I ask what that is?" Lilly asked.

"The army has its own laws," Milton answered. "They are written in a document called *The Uniform Code of Military Justice*. I am to learn that code and then help administer it."

"Where will you be stationed, Milt?" This time it was Larry's voice.

Barbara looked at Larry and then stared intently at her husband, but she did not speak.

"My orders are to report to the Pentagon in Washington, DC, on January tenth. I'll be there for training, but then I don't honestly know where they'll send me." He looked at his wife beside him.

The two continued to stare at each other, their eyes giving away nothing and everything.

"Barbara, if I may be so forward," Lilly asked, "what do you think of all this?"

"Mrs. Clark . . ."

"Please, Barbara, call me Lilly."

Barbara smiled softly. "Lilly, you can imagine how much Milt and I have talked about it. These choices do not come easy. And Milt and I do come from different worlds. Oh, all American but certainly we are a country with different segments of society. We grew up in very different ways, Milt and I. But there is no other man I've ever met that I'd want to spend my life with." She looked away from the table and directly at Milt again. "He is my man." She stared at him without a breath being taken at the table. "And I am proud of him."

There was not a sound in the room. No jiggling of silver or tinkling of glasses. Barbara looked down at her plate, cut a bite of goose, put it in her mouth, and chewed. "Ouch!" she suddenly exclaimed, put her fingers to her lips and pulled out a small lead pellet. When she put it on her plate, the shot made a light, almost tinkling sound as it rolled across the china. Everyone laughed as the tension was released. Everyone but Barbara, who clearly did not understand.

"Forgive us, dear Barbara." Beulah's tone was loving. "We are all used to this. The goose was shot"—she nodded toward Sam—"by Sam, I believe."

Sam nodded agreement.

"And we have a custom. Anyone who finds a pellet in the goose gets to kiss whoever at the table they wish. That privilege is now yours."

Barbara's chiseled face broke into a huge smile that brought life to her full, kissable lips. She turned sideways in her chair, put her hands on her husband's face, and kissed him full on the lips, not letting go. The table's roar of approval gave way to applause as the kiss continued.

The ladies had cleared the table and brought out dessert, which consisted of apple pie with cheddar cheese slices or pecan pie with ice cream. Coffee was served as well, and the ladies sat back down to join, just a bit more, in the indulgence of overeating that was part of a holiday feast. As others ate, Barbara rose and walked slowly to the kitchen. She returned momentarily, carrying a tray with seven snifters, each filled to the bulge in the middle. She placed the tray on a hand-carved oak sideboard and, making several trips, placed one in front of each diner. She returned to her chair, a snifter in her hand, and after seating herself, spoke.

"I don't know if all like cognac, but this is my father's favorite, so I grew up with it used for special toasts. And I'd like to propose one. But before I do, there is a comment I'd like to make to all of you. My beloved Milton"—she put a hand on the back of his neck and rubbed it—"tried very hard to talk me out of marrying him. In fact, he even tried to talk my father into talking me out of it once." She took her hand away and smiled gently at him. "Didn't you, dear?"

The table laughed gently.

"His main point being that I would not like his world. That a girl who grew up in East Coast society would find his world unrefined. 'Frontier' was a word he used frequently. But what I have found"—she looked at him again with the same gentle smile—"are loving, well-educated, interesting people. I have found"—she picked up her dessert fork—"Gorham silver." Barbara brought it to her eye admiringly. "My mother always prized King Edward." She gave a complimentary look at Beulah, who smiled in recognition. "I have found china I can see through." She took her coffee cup off the saucer and held the saucer to the light. "I have found the finest of handstitched Chinese linen and a family of the greatest refinement. Having said all that, perhaps just to prove even Milton is wrong sometimes."

The table gave another gentle laugh.

"Let me resort to my English literature degree and borrow the finest Christmas toast ever. Charles Dickens put it in the mouth of Tiny Tim: 'God bless us every one!'"

* * * *

Larry and Milt walked, feet crunching the freshly fallen snow on the sidewalk, each wrapped tightly in a greatcoat and muffler, Larry's head covered in his new fedora. Each puffed on after-dinner cigars, alternately exhaling vapor of breath and smoke of cigar into the air.

"Milt, what will you do after the army, the Army Judge what?"

"Judge Advocate General's Corps."

"What will you do when it's over? Will you go back to Chicago and clerk again?"

"No, Larry, I've put in my time there. It's on my résumé; I've made the connections in the court and power structure of Illinois. Clerking has given me what I need. I'll come home when the war is over."

"And join your dad's law firm?"

"And join my dad's law firm."

"Why not stay in Chicago and get rich? You've studied for a long time to do just that. Why not use it?"

"Funny, Larry, Barbara's dad asked me the same question." Milt exhaled a huge cloud of smoke and gave vent to an almost wicked smile. "I'll tell you what I told him. Beardstown is my home. It's not just that I'm comfortable here. Hell, after eight years on the East Coast, I'm comfortable there, too. Very comfortable." He stopped and turned his head to look directly at his friend. "I love New York City. It is a wonderful place with much to offer." The wicked grin returned. "You're a hustler, Larry. You might like it, too." Sobriety returned to his face. "But I'll stay because Beardstown needs me. Someone here has to deal with the mess all you river rats create. It's been a McHugh responsibility for a very long time, and I think that burden will fall to me."

"Burden!" Larry's tone was shocked and surprised. "Seems to me the McHughs have all lived a pretty good life carrying this burden."

"Oh, you're right about that, Larry. I won't starve, and Barbara will have a life of grace. But I won't have the forty-foot yacht here I'd have in New York. But that sacrifice is not the burden. The burden is making the choices a man must make to decide how a society, his town, lives best. What is the balance between creative and cutthroat, between freedom and order? You've not seen it, Larry, but I have. I've lived every day watching my father make those choices. It's not as easy as he makes it seem. It is his burden. It was his grandfather's, too, and someday it will be mine."

They walked in silence, puffing and pondering. Milt finally broke it.

"What of you, Larry, what will you do after the war?"

"Well, I know I'll come home. This is my home and the home I want. Like you, it's not just that I'm comfortable here. You will tease me for what I'm about to say because neither you, nor anyone else, really knows what I think, beyond the goodwill and irreverence I boom out constantly. But, like you, I have watched men—your father, my father—all my life. And I have come to understand that this pool in which we swim is a very unique place. It is a live-and-let-live place. We are very stubborn and self-sufficient, and we reach for what we want, with our own hands, and don't care so very much about what the rules are that control what we reach for and how we do it. I am Beardstown's son. It raised me and it will nurture me. I'll come home."

CHAPTER 27

May 17, 1943
London, England

Milt bounced high enough that the top of his barracks cover was thrown against the roof of the jeep. "Sorry, Leftenant, 'ard to miss all these bomb craters."

"Slow just a bit, Sergeant, and it will be easier," McHugh barked as he rubbed the back of his neck. "Sergeant, these apartment buildings don't look so much bombed as burned out."

"'Tis true, sir. They are burnt out. Toward the end of the Blitz, Jerry got downright nasty. Started dropping incendiary bombs. Burnt some two hundred and fifty thousand Londoners out of their 'omes. Killed maybe thirty thousand more. Lord knows how many injured.

"Been two years now, and we still 'aven't 'ad time to replace them. Seems we've 'ad more urgent projects. Your bachelor officer quarters are just two blocks. Fear you won't find them much, but you've got a roof and I 'ear warm water as well."

The jeep pulled up to the curb in front of a three-story

brick apartment building. It was the first one standing after the long row of bombed and burned buildings. The driver hit the tinny-sounding horn of the jeep twice, and an older man in the uniform of a corporal came out of the building. He hobbled on one good leg as he approached the jeep. The driver jumped out, pulled McHugh's bag from the rear seat, and carrying it, strode briskly around to the left side door and held it open as First Lieutenant Milton McHugh stepped to the curb. The driver shut McHugh's door behind him, dropped the bag to the sidewalk, and saluted palm forward, the backs of his fingers touching his forehead. Milton returned the salute, palm down, index finger to his eyebrow.

As both men released their salutes, the driver said, "Leftenant, this is Corporal 'iggins. He'll get your bags to your room and see you in." The driver turned to go but stopped as he stepped off the curb. "Glad to see you here, Yank. Your boys been comin' for a year now. Few more of you and we'll be ready to kick the Huns' arse."

Milt smiled and watched him go. He turned to the hobbling corporal, who stood rigidly at attention, his hand held in the same comical salute the driver had used. Milt returned it, managing not to smile. "Welcome, Leftenant. I'm 'iggins, as your driver said. I'll be taking care of you while you're with us." Higgins reached for the flight bag.

"No, Corporal Higgins, I'll get it."

The British soldier stood bolt upright. "No, sir. I'll not 'ear of it. This is a task for me."

Milt was taken aback by the formality of it all. "Of course, Corporal Higgins, and thank you."

McHugh followed Higgins up two flights of stairs and then down a hallway to a door marked "306—Flight Lieutenant Richard T. Sutton." "Sir, I believe Flight Leftenant Sutton is in. Let me announce you." Higgins knocked sharply, twice.

His knock was greeted with a single word. "Come!"

Higgins opened the door, set the flight bag he was carrying on the floor, and then straightened himself to his full height. "Sir, First Lieutenant Milton McHugh of the US Army is here. I believe you have been informed he is to share quarters."

"Thank you, 'iggins. I have been so informed. Please, show the leftenant in."

With that, Higgins stepped fully into the room, pulling the door open as he did so and making room for McHugh to enter behind him.

Milt stepped into the room. His first view of this man, with whom he would share quarters for the foreseeable future, was of a man sitting in a small wingback chair, a book in his lap. His face was heavily backlit by the window behind him, but despite this, Milton could see his features were very refined with a mass of black hair combed straight back and an equally black pencil-thin mustache above thin, almost hard lips. His face was open, his eyes very dark brown, almost black, backlit as they were, set below thin black brows.

Sutton had evidently been reading, as he took a thick volume off his lap and set it on the table before him. In doing so, he freed his right hand, which he used to grasp the knob-shaped brass head of a walking stick, a stick that he placed firmly onto the floor to assist him in rising. The man was tall, at least six foot three, and almost as thin as his mustache. His uniform was blue. The pants were royal blue and sharply creased. His shirt was a lighter, almost robin's-egg blue, and his tightly knotted necktie appeared black, but Milt knew it would show as navy in better light.

Sutton transferred the stick into his left hand, took a step forward using the cane to brace what was obviously a bad right leg.

Milt hurried to cover the three steps between them to save Sutton the labor. Both men extended their right hands and shook firmly.

"My pleasure to meet you, Sutton. And my apologies for disturbing your reading."

"My pleasure as well, McHugh. And I'll be glad for some company. How shall I call you?"

"May we agree to Christian names right off? Mine is Milton, but my friends call me Milt. I'd like it if you would as well."

Sutton gave a warm smile. "That would be my honor. And my name is Richard."

From behind him, McHugh heard the cockney brogue of Corporal Higgins calling. "Sir, I'll take the liberty of hanging your clothes in your armoire in the next room, if I may."

Milt turned and merely nodded his approval. Higgins, flight bag in hand, disappeared into the adjoining bedroom.

"Milt, sit. Please."

Milt took the chair on the other side of the window.

"Milt, I know we British are supposed to be reserved, but let me shock you by being direct." It was said with a smile.

"Why is it that I have the privilege of an American officer as roommate in a British BOQ? Why aren't you with the tens of thousands of Eisenhower's other men in tents and Quonset huts somewhere north of here?"

"Just luck, I suppose," Milt responded, and the two men indulged in the first of many laughs together. "The real answer is that I'm an attorney. I'm with the US Army's Judge Advocate General's Corps. Same as your Adjutant General's Corps. I've been assigned as liaison from our legal department to yours."

"So, when your blokes and our blokes smash one another's noses over the affections of some tavern wench, you and someone with our Army Legal Services decide whose rules apply and who will apply them?"

"And hopefully, between now and the time Hitler yells uncle, it never comes to more than that." Milt offered the response with a smile.

"Sir," Higgins called from behind. "You're unpacked, sir. I presume the rest of your things will follow. As soon as they arrive, I'll bring them." He stepped across their front room and to the door. As he opened it, he commented, "Leftenant McHugh, by tomorrow this time, I'll have your name on the door."

"Thank you, Corporal Higgins," McHugh answered.

The corporal nodded and stepped out the door. "Leftenant McHugh, one last thing."

Both men looked around. "May I second the sentiments of your driver? We're damn glad you and all the Yanks are here. Thanks for coming, sir." Higgins walked out and shut the door behind him.

"Milt, the fading light tells me it's time for dinner. Don't know if they told you, but this may be the only BOQ in the British army that does not have a mess hall. I presume your army will give your pay a ration allowance. Mine does. Not too many places to eat nearby, but allow me the honor of treating you to your first dinner in London."

* * * *

The two officers walked slowly down the bombed-out street together. McHugh was wearing his brown uniform with barracks cover, a raincoat thrown over as protection from the constant drizzle. Sutton had pulled a leather bomber jacket on and pulled the wool collar up around his neck, his garrison cap shoved onto his head. They walked at a pace set by Sutton, his walking stick making a thump with each step.

"You willing to tell me about that leg?" Milt asked.

"Oh, nothing much really. My part in the Battle of Britain was far easier than most. I'm from a port along the south coast. Southampton. Grew up there, enlisted there, and after flight training, got stationed there. My squadron did not fight over London. Our job was to protect Atlantic shipping. And we could do it for maybe three hundred miles from the coast. We only had a six-hundred-mile range, so three hundred was the point of no return. But for three hundred miles we could keep U-boats away. We were more spotters than anything, but Jerry feared us and kept away. One fine winter's day I was cruising and saw a German sub. Usually, we just saw silhouettes underwater. The clearer the water, the deeper we could see, but if they were underwater, we could do nothing to them but radio for a destroyer. If there was a destroyer close enough, maybe we'd get one. Mostly it was the threat of us that kept them at bay. But in January, I was out about 250 miles and saw a U-boat on the surface. They sometimes came up for air or to take a look through their periscopes for better hunting. But this one seemed to stay on the surface. Don't know if it didn't see me or had troubles of some kind, but it didn't dive. So, I radioed a destroyer and stuck around to keep watch."

Sutton paused for a moment then continued. "As I was watching, it occurred to me that the Royal Air Force had put four twenty-millimeter cannons on this Hawker Hurricane for a specific purpose, and I should use them for such. And so I did. Swung well out before Jerry, got right down on the water, and took a nice long strafing run. Saw at least one Kraut fall back down the conning tower. I had a little petrol left, so I took a loop and got in front of him again. I presumed he'd dive, but the bastard fooled me. He came up higher and brought his bow out well above the waterline. And on that bow was planted a fifty-caliber machine gun. I got the gun crew and they missed me. Or so I thought until I noticed my fuel gauge going down alarmingly fast. I couldn't decide whether I should slow to preserve fuel or speed up, knowing it was flowing out a hole somewhere. I decided the latter and pushed it to 200 mph. Made it to land but not to a landing strip. Made it almost to somewhere near Penzance before the engine coughed and sputtered its last. I was out of gas so hoped I wouldn't explode. Found me a lovely flat sheep's meadow and would have made a perfect landing were it not for a small ditch in the middle. Little ditch pitched me sideways hard enough to catch a wing tip in the dirt. It all went topsy-turvy from there. Engine didn't break loose to crush me, but somehow my right femur got warped around the stick and the stick won. Once they set it, they let me convalesce at home, but now I'm back and able as I'll get. Can't fly anymore, but I can act as a liaison, a 'go-fer' I believe you Yanks call it. It's not doing much for old Britain, but it's better than staying home and watching my father-in-law spend the last of his family's patrimony."

"My God, Richard. That's one hell of a tale. I've heard what heroes you RAF types are. Now I know."

"Well, I have carried on long enough. But we're here now in any case. That little door there on the left. You'll see it's quite large inside, but with the windows blacked, you can't tell from here."

Richard Sutton stepped in front of Milt to grab the door handle and held it open. They stepped out of the drizzle to warmth of both a fire and the laughter of many human beings. A fat man wearing a large white apron saw Sutton and nodded, as to an old friend, pointing to a large booth in the far corner. The room seemed full of festivity and mirth. Richard threaded his way through the crowd, who seemed to give him no real notice, but all managed to make his passage clear.

The two men slid into the booth. "What'll ya 'ave, loves?" came almost as soon as they'd eased in.

Milt looked up into eyes as blue as twinkling topaz. Her blond hair was piled up on top of her head. She wore a patterned skirt that flared wide from her waist. The top was a linen blouse pulled down off her shoulders to expose collarbones and the tops of full, rising breasts.

"I'll have a beer, miss," Milt answered, trying hard to keep his eyes on hers.

"A Yank. That's why the odd uniform. I love Yanks. Anything else you want, love?" Her wide red lips broke into a mischievous grin.

"Milly, our new Yank has just arrived. Be gentle on him for a day or two."

"Why, Leftenant, I'm always gentle." The smile grew even wider.

"Well, while you're being gentle, Milly, bring me a pint as well and each of us a Cornish pasty."

"What's a Cornish pasty?" Milt asked as Milly pirouetted toward the kitchen.

"Local and filling. But the beer makes up for it," Richard responded. "Milt, I've talked way too much. Tell a bit about you." His voice was insistent.

"OK. You got my background in law. From a little town in the middle of the country. Not much more to tell."

"Looks like I'm going to have to pry this out of you. You married?"

"Yep. Married to my college love. She's a New Yorker. We married in '41."

"Kids? I think that's what you Americans call your children, don't you?"

"Yes, to both. Boy and a girl. Boy's name is Cavanaugh after her father. Girl is Beulah after my mother."

"Cavanaugh? And from New York. They Irish?"

Milton laughed. "Not that I know of. Last name is Proctor. Funny, as long as I've known Barbara, that's my wife, she's never mentioned her family stock by ethnicity."

Milly slapped two mugs overflowing with foam onto the table and bent especially low toward Milton as she did so. "Shout when you want more?" The smile was unchanged as she walked away.

"She does like a uniform, that girl." Milt grinned.

"No, Milly is usually no nonsense. Has too many single

soldiers to put up with and won't. I think she meant it. She likes Yanks. Your wife staying with your parents while you're away?"

"No, she preferred to go back to New York. She's a city girl. More comfortable there. How about you, Richard. You married?" Milt asked.

"Yes. Normally men like you and me would not be in BOQ. But these are not normal times. Your wife can't even get here, and mine needs not to be in a place that's being bombed. We're not the only married men in bachelor officer quarters."

"Children?"

"Yes, two boys. Older is named for me. Younger is Robert."

"And are your wife and sons with your family in . . . was it Southampton?"

"It was, but no they're not. Bini is like your wife. She preferred to stay where she grew up, West Sussex."

"Bini? Bini Sutton? Interesting name."

Richard's thin lips turned into a smile big enough to show crooked white teeth. "Lavinia Guinevere Winifred Arundel. Story is when she was little, they took to calling her 'Vini.' She couldn't pronounce her *v*'s, and when she said it, it came out Bini. Seems that stuck."

Milt tilted his head to one side and looked at Richard slightly askance.

Milly slapped a large crockery bowl in front of Milt. It landed with a harsh thud. Both men looked up just in time to see a second bowl slapped in front of Richard. Milly smiled down at Milt. "Hope you like the pasty. I see you're low. Care for another pint?"

"Bring two." It was Richard who commanded.

Milly gave him a slightly condescending smile and left.

"Milt, break open that crust and let it cool for a bit before you bite in. It will be hot." Richard followed his own advice and used his fork to break open the crust of his Cornish pasty in a long, wide gash. He seemed to watch as the steam rose.

"And Arundel doesn't sound English. More French maybe?" Milton inquired as he mimicked Richard and broke the crust of his dinner.

"Shooting at that sub got a few Germans and got me 'married fairly well.'"

Milt nodded as he took his first bite of dinner. He chewed rapidly and swallowed easily.

Richard swallowed, drank the last of his beer, exhaled, and finally spoke. "I was in the hospital in Southampton after the crash. There are a lot of women in the South of England. The Blitz chased them out of London and other cities, and a lot came back to their ancestral homes. Some to wait out the war, some to learn to be widows. Bini was one of them. Like many of them she wanted to do her bit and took to visiting the wounded in military hospitals. She came to me one day. Sweet, kind, pretty, caring. And then she came again and a week later and then almost daily. When they took my cast off, I was allowed limited liberty as long as there was someone to push my wheelchair. Bini offered to take me home for the weekend. Assured the staff she had plenty of help. And she did."

Richard took another bite of pie. "Bini is an Arundel. You guessed French. That's close. It's Norman. Some ancestor came over in 1066 with William of Normandy, the Conqueror, we call him. Her father is the last surviving of the line, Count 'Enree Arundel."

"Jesus!" exclaimed Milt. "Sounds like you didn't marry fairly well. Sounds like you married very well."

"Loves, here's your pints. I'm here all night when you want more," Milly said as she set down two new mugs and collected the old.

Richard scowled up at her, "Thanks, Milly, but we're talking about wives right now."

She looked away from Richard and toward Milt. "When

you bore of that, love, I'm here." And again, she pirouetted away, this time giving a coquettish smile over her shoulder.

"I didn't marry Bini for her title. True, my older boy will be Count Sutton, but it no longer matters here. I love her. And besides, my family has more money than hers."

"Really?" Milt looked surprised.

"The Suttons are very prosperous confectioners from Southampton. For several hundreds of years, the Arundels controlled the entire valley. The last hundred years it has all gone the other way. All they own now is the land where their old Georgian house sits. A house on which they can afford neither the taxes nor the upkeep. What little money is left, the old count is spending on fast horses and faster women. Bini and I will have to make our way the same as everyone else when this is over.

"Now eat before the food gets cold and the beer gets warm."

CHAPTER 28

December 6, 1943
Honolulu, Hawaii

Larry had selected the picture postcard very carefully. It was a photo taken from a thousand feet in the air showing much of the south shore of O'ahu Island from Pearl Harbor to the volcano that is Diamond Head. He'd have enjoyed sending one of a beach scene with some native Hawaiian girl in a grass skirt, nothing but a grass skirt. But Mom wouldn't like that at all. He had searched several tourist shops in Honolulu until he found one with five-by-seven format cards. He wanted to be certain he had enough space to write his folks the nice letter they had been expecting.

He wrote cautiously and slowly, making certain he wrote in small but clear letters.

Dear Mom & Dad,

As you can see, the navy is treating me well. Hawaii really is beautiful and every day sunny and warm. The humidity is like home in

August, but here they have what are called "the trade winds." They blow constantly at about two knots—slow and gentle. You only feel the humidity on the rare days they don't blow.

But as beautiful as Hawaii is, it would never be a place for me. Maybe it's just all the military, but they sure have a lot of rules and they sure enforce them. There seem to be MPs (that's military police) everywhere. A guy can't sit on a lawn or have a beer too many without getting busted. I'll take Beardstown over this. And, Dad, that's what I plan to do. Soon as I'm out, I'll come home. You keep the lodge afloat until this war is over, and then I'll be there, shoulder to shoulder with you. Together, Dad, and by hook or by crook, we'll make it work.

I love you both,

Lorenz

P.S. Heard Bing Crosby's new song, "I'll Be Home for Christmas"? That's me, folks. I'll be with you in my dreams.

CHAPTER 29

May 31, 1944
London, England

"Richard, this set of mess dress whites is not US Army issue. It's regulation but not issue. Barbara bought it for me. We've got to get a picture before the night's over so she'll know her money was not wasted," Milt offered as he struggled with the bow tie.

"Milton, my friend, you are getting it all wrong. First, you've got the bow tie confused with a Christmas ribbon. Second, every picture taken of you tonight will be with some stunningly dressed woman on your arm. That your wife will not thank you for showing her."

"I thought we were invited as 'stags'? The invitation was quite specific."

"Oh, you colonials." Richard rolled his eyes. "Here, let me retie that thing starting from scratch. And let me explain to you, you frontiersman," Richard said, his tone appropriately haughty, "what it is a 'stag' does at a formal military ball. Your job is to ensure that, at no time, is any woman at the ball unattended. You will exude charm, insofar as that is possible for you. You will light cigarettes; you will manage champagne flutes and cocktail glasses; and you will dance. You can dance, can't you?"

"The Virginia Reel," Milt said, a smug look on his face.

"Whatever that is, don't do it here. There, your tie is sufficiently straight. Your white waistcoat falls just below your belt; you are showing an eighth of an inch of shirt cuff below your jacket sleeves; your shoulder boards are straight and your new captain's bars duly polished. It is as good as I can make you."

* * * *

"Drive very slowly," Sutton instructed the chauffeur. "All these dark sedans without headlights, someone is going to hit someone, and your job is to ensure we are neither the hitter nor the hittee."

"Yes, sir," the driver agreed.

Thirty minutes later, they reached their destination and moved forward in the line of sedans to their exit at the curb. The triple-sized British lions rising above the steps on either side appeared ready to roar in the moonlight. And the moon was all the light there was, save a periodic burst as the door at the top of the steps was opened for each entering guest.

As the two officers rose toward the entrance, Milton asked, "Why it is that in a time when all windows are covered to prevent this building becoming a bombing target, the British army is hosting a ball?"

"Well, first, our host is not the army. Our host, hostess really, is Princess Elizabeth of York. And she is hosting this ball for two reasons. The first, and most obvious being that we Britons are proud, terribly proud, of our sense of indifference to troubles. 'A stiff upper lip' is the term we use. And no inconsequential German führer will disrupt our lives enough to preclude our honoring of tradition. So if our eighteen-year-old heir apparent wants to throw a ball, she will damn well throw a ball."

"And the second reason?" Milton asked.

"We're about to invade Europe. The last time we fought a world-changing battle in Europe was in 1815 near a quaint little village in Belgium named Waterloo. The night before the battle, the Duchess of Richmond threw the largest ball in the history of that little country. Doing so keeps things in perspective, you see.

"We are almost there, Milton, so let me warn you."

"Of what?" Milton's skeptical smile showed in the moonlight.

"Widows. There will be many here and perhaps some who fear they soon will be. They will all be perfectly quaffed and as beautiful as they are able. Their dresses will be long, closely fitted, and some low-cut. They will be drinking, and you, my Yank friend, will be viewed as a conquering hero before the battle even starts. I am aware that neither Milly, nor any other woman as far as I know, has been able to tempt you from your precious Barbara. Tonight will be a challenge."

They arrived at the door, which opened immediately and briefly. The doorman closed the door behind them, examined their invitation, and gave it to the herald, who struck the floor with his staff and announced, "Flight Leftenant Richard Sutton, Royal Air Force, and Captain Milton McHugh, United States Army."

No one gave much attention aside from a casual look by a few closest to the door. The hall was huge and lit with crystal chandeliers suspended from thirty feet above. The wooden floor was empty in the middle, but hundreds were gathered at the edges, being served champagne and cocktails from one of the many bars or from tuxedoed waiters carrying trays of drinks. The men were dressed in a cacophony, almost riot, of colorful, perhaps gaudy uniforms. And Sutton was correct about the women. The women all looked as though war and its depravation were simply not part of life. Most of their gowns hung to the floor and were formfitting much of the way. All had shoulders squared off in long pads, and many were cut deep in the front, the back, or up from the floor. It was a celebration of life unfettered by the knowledge that for many, death would come before their next ball.

Richard led away from the door, around the edge of the dance floor, to a bar at the far side of the room. He waded into the forest of uniforms getting drinks and returned with a tumbler of amber-colored liquid for Milt and a flute of champagne for himself. "Bourbon was hard to find, but I insisted."

"Thanks, Richard. I may need many more of these before the night's over."

"Ladies. Gentlemen." The voice at the mic got their attention. "My I present our hostess, the Princess Elizabeth of York and her father, His Royal Majesty King George the Sixth." The polite applause grew from a ripple into a roar as the beautiful teenage princess, on the arm of her stately uniformed father, strolled to the middle of the floor. The bandmaster dropped his baton, and an orchestra from above opened the slow strains of a waltz. As her father turned her, the long train behind her swirled with the slow grace of a kite riding a storm not of its own making.

"She dances like Ginger Rogers." The voice spoke with the sound of an angel.

Milt turned to see the voice beside him. Her gown caught his attention before he could even look up. It was black, solid black satin. The shoulder pads extended well beyond her shoulders and fell to sleeves loose at the top, tightening as they went until fitted to her skin from her forearms to her wrists. The dress was cinched tight at the waist and then gathered so the satin fell in folds to her ankles. The top of the dress was open almost to the bottom of her breast but cut tight so they were not exposed.

A long string of pearls kept his eyes in place. The bottom of the dress was slit from the hem to her knees. The dress was a creation of mystery. It promised nothing; it suggested a great deal.

Milton finally forced his eyes up to her face. She was older than he, a bit, perhaps more. It was an unlined face, but a face that had seen much and knew much. It was a face framed in soft honey-blond curls that hung down to the shoulders.

She didn't smile at him; she just looked. Like the dress, the look was of mystery. It promised nothing.

"She does, doesn't she?" The black angel spoke again. "Make you think of Ginger Rogers when she dances?"

Milton snapped back into control and turned to look onto the dance floor. Others had joined the royal couple, but he could still see them clearly. "In America we see Ginger Rogers but not royal couples. There is magic in that. We don't want ones of our own, but yours are lovely to admire."

She now studied him seriously, and for the first time the look gave some reflection of her thoughts. "And you have come to save that which you admire." It was not a question.

Milton studied the eyes for a moment. They were back to just looking. "Perhaps but I think not."

"Then why do you come?" she asked.

"To destroy what we fear."

The eyes twinkled now, and for the first time he saw that they were blue. Azure-blue gems framed by honey-blond hair.

"You can tell," Milt offered, "that I'm an American."

She nodded. "Your accent would have given you away even if your uniform had not."

"I'm not used to this sort of society. Never been to such an event. My invitation said I was to be a stag. I didn't know what that meant, but a British officer told me it meant I was to see that no woman, at any time, was unattended. I was to light cigarettes, fetch drinks, and offer to dance. Are any of those services of interest to you?"

* * * *

The princess and the king were long gone. The orchestra still played and the bars were still serving, but the hundreds of couples were down to mere dozens. Milton and Anne Palmer sat in the main lounge area. Both appeared content and perhaps weary. He was sitting well into the back of the overstuffed sofa, his legs crossed and one hand lying on the armrest. She had also given her body into the comfort of the padding and had one hand on his shoulder.

"I've been looking for you, Milt. Knew time would bring you to the bar."

Milt sat up, momentarily struggling with the grip of comfort. But he rose and offered Anne his hand. She accepted it and rose with a grace that belied the hour.

"Flight Lieutenant Richard Sutton, let me introduce Anne Palmer . . . correction, Marquess Palmer." He looked at Anne and added, "I don't understand the system here, but if one becomes a count by marriage, then my friend is properly Count Richard Sutton."

Both seemed slightly embarrassed for Milton's ignorance of custom and manners as they extended their hellos without the clumsy American gesture of handshakes.

"Marquess, may I call you Anne, as we seem to have friends . . . well, *a* friend, in common?" Richard asked with a charm that relieved any tension.

"You may indeed, if the intimacy is also offered to me, Richard." She turned and looked to Milton. "And no, dear, in our own eccentric way, we English offer titles to the female spouses of nobility, which is how I got mine, but not the male spouses."

Richard smiled and fell into the subject. "But I, Lady Palmer, will die knowing that my son will have such honor."

There was momentary silence.

"The witching hour is upon us, isn't it?" She looked at Milton and added, "I've not wished for a ball to continue forever in ages. But this one I have. It is not often in this world that a widow gets the company of two charming and handsome young officers, but I would so enjoy it if you gentlemen would escort me to collect my wrap and then to my car."

"The privilege is ours, Anne," Richard offered immediately.

Ten minutes later, bathed in the light of the low half-moon, they stood outside waiting with Lady Palmer for her car. Most were already gone, and there was no traffic at the curb. A black Rolls-Royce Phantom slowly appeared out of the dark and pulled up to the curb before them. It was unspoken and no gesture made, but Milton and Richard both knew. Richard said his good nights and stayed on the curb as Milton walked in front of the car and led Anne to the rear door, which he opened.

She stood, beautiful and almost vulnerable, in the moonlight, looking at Milton as he held the door. "May I offer you a lift home, Milton?"

The moonlight gave both warmth and mystery to her azure-blue eyes.

Richard had been right. The night had been a challenge and was getting more challenging by the minute. "Thank you, Anne. Thank you very much, but Richard and I have a car."

She studied him again. She didn't smile; she just looked. Like his first thought of her dress, it was a look that suggested a great deal. Lady Anne Palmer rocked slightly forward and pushed up on her toes. As she kissed his cheek, she slipped something into his hand. Then she stepped into the dark abyss of the Rolls-Royce.

Milt shut the door and watched her disappear slowly, softly, gently into the night.

CHAPTER 30

June 15, 1944
Saipan, Mariana Islands
Western Pacific

"Lieutenant, welcome to my boat. As soon as you get your platoon in here, we're off."

"I can't read navy insignia. What's all that stuff on your blouse mean?" the young marine officer asked.

"It means, Lieutenant, that I'm a petty officer third class and that you outrank me by a bunch of pay grades. It also means I'm the coxswain and this is my ship. I command it. Minute I drop that front ramp, you're in charge again. But between here and the beach, you do what I damn well tell you and I'll get you and your men there alive."

The fresh-faced marine didn't give Larry any shit. "Aye, aye, Cox. And I gotta tell you getting in here is a whole lot easier than climbing down a Jacob's ladder hung over the side, leading down to something pitching and in the sea."

"Get 'em in, Lieutenant. And tell your tough guys to hang on. When I drive this little 'amtrac' off this ramp, your platoon is going to think it's a submarine. I'll get it back up and onto the surface, and we'll have a pleasant cruise to that nice warm beach in front of us. Just don't let 'em panic that first moment."

The lieutenant barked instructions to his marines as the bow ramp of their mother ship opened and Larry put the amphibious Landing Vehicle Tracked into gear and ran the eighteen tons of steel into the ocean. It fell as though diving straight to the bottom until water flowed over the high sides and into its open top. A few of the marines swore, but all hung onto their balance straps and none panicked. The boat bobbed up like a cork and started forward immediately.

"Lieutenant, your ear for a moment," Larry called, and the marine, in wet fatigues and wearing a full combat pack, tilted back his helmet and nodded. "Since you practiced in the old Higgins boats, there are a couple of things you should know about these new ones. This is the first they've been used. Unlike the Higgins, they're steel with a quarter inch of armor plate on the sides and a half inch on that front ramp. Japs think their bullets can kill, but even their heavy machine guns won't penetrate. If your guys don't know that, I suspect they'd like to. We've got two fifties in the bow, and my crew might manage to kill a few Japs before your guys do. They could sink us with their big guns, but they can't get off too many rounds from those in the time it takes us to get to the beach. The biggest threat is their mortars when we get close. You don't need me to tell you we got no cover above. They get lucky and lob one of those into the middle of this boat, we won't feel a thing. All be dead in an instant. Other thing is I can track this thing up on the beach. I'm not here to play tank for you today. My orders are to get up on the beach and then go back for more. But when we get to the beach, if a few extra yards keep a few of your boys alive, let me know and I'll do it. Got it?"

"Thanks, Cox. I'll keep my head down until we get close.

I may take you up on it." He turned to walk through his men with instructions.

"Oh, Skipper!" Larry shouted behind him.

The young lieutenant turned back toward him.

"The only crew I got is those two guys on the fifties mounted on front. They are sitting above the armored sides. Until I open that ramp, they're the Japs' target if they're smart. If one of them goes down, feel free to have one of your marines man the gun."

Larry sat high, higher even than the gunners. But he had a half inch of steel in front of him. He'd be fine unless an extremely lucky shot came through the eye opening. That or a mortar round dropped straight down on him. Or one hell of a big wave.

Bullets started to pound on their sides, and the marine lieutenant again shouted instructions to get down.

Larry screamed into the twenty-five feet of air separating him from his gunners. "They can hit us; you can hit them. Get those damn fifties working."

Both gunners jumped to their stations and started the steady kawump, kawump, kawump that was a fifty-caliber machine gun. Suddenly the LVT hit something and momentarily lost forward momentum. Larry grabbed the gear lever and kicked the track lower, and the boat started forward slowly, eating coral as it went. And then they were across the lagoon and less than one hundred yards from the beach. The hits they were taking were frequent now as the range shortened. The waves were lower, but the reef hadn't stopped them entirely. As the bottom rose, the waves were forced up, and the back of the boat rose with them and rolled high with each one.

And then the mortars started.

"Cox, that one was only ten yards in front of us!" the lieutenant screamed up at him.

Larry paid no attention. He could hear the next mortar

screaming down at him. He didn't look up. It exploded behind him but close enough that the splash washed over his uniform.

"Cox, the Japs have zeroed in on us. The next one is going to be in our belly unless you do something."

"I told you it's my ship, Lieutenant!" Larry screamed back.

The aft of his boat rose on the next wave. He kicked the rudder, which jammed the boat broadside to the wave instead of across it. The wave turned the whole boat sideways and tipped the starboard side low to the waterline, moving the entire boat in a direction lateral to the beach. The mortar landed starboard and five feet in front of them. Larry whipped the rudder to forward, the track catching the sand and pulling them up on the beach.

"Lieutenant, you want this taxi pulled to the curb here or up a block?"

The lieutenant stood behind one of the gunners, surveying the beach. "Take me up to the bottom of the dune twenty feet more. It will give us cover as we dismount."

Larry straightened the track and pushed it into high gear. The mortar went off beside them and threw sand into the boat. He dropped the ramp and listened as the lieutenant screamed. "Now. Go! Go, go, go."

Larry watched, and as the last marine cleared the ramp, he raised it, turning the LVT 180 degrees to cross the beach and run back out.

He heard the scream of the mortar coming down. Neither he nor either of his gunners heard the explosion that killed them.

CHAPTER 31

April 30, 1945
West Sussex, England

They had left London with the dawn and headed due south to Brighton, where the English Channel opened up before them in the morning sun, then west along the channel, the road weaving in and out along the coastal inlets. Sometimes the road would open up views of the widening channel and even periodically a beach, the surf breaking into high, rolling waves peaking with white froth as they crashed against the rocks. Sometimes it twisted back inland and up a hill to reveal pastures green with new spring grass, separated by a periodic copse of massive oaks, their spring leaf cover allowing fireworks of light to burst into their dark shadows.

Richard drove, his ever-improving leg seeming not to rebel against the constant pressure of the gas pedal. He never spoke, but he smiled often and every now and again pointed, without comment, at some item he especially admired in the passing English countryside, wishing to share his admiration with his foreign companion. Milton had never seen anything like this and wanted no conversation. Having the same effect as it did on Richard, the beauty of Southern England seemed to keep him transfixed. The road eventually ran up the approach span of a steel bridge crossing a river that even after the spring rains, seemed to meander, rather than rush, to the sea.

"It's the Arun!" Richard also shouted to be heard over the rattles of the US Army jeep, a vehicle designed more to offer transportation over terrain without roads than to cruise at fifty miles an hour along asphalt highways. "We're in the county of West Sussex now. Shortly after we cross, we'll head upcountry for a few miles to the old Arundel place."

Milt turned to look upriver, but Sutton's head and the jeep's canvas cover blocked most of his view. But from what he could see, the Arun didn't seem a river navigable enough for trade. He shivered slightly in the spring chill. Sutton seemed to have noticed.

"I told you to bring a heavy jacket. You did, didn't you?"

"Yep," Milt barked back into the wind. "But it's spring; the day will be warm enough."

"It's not the day." Richard laughed. "It will be the nights."

Milt looked puzzled.

Richard slowed and made a right turn onto a gravel road seemingly shaded as far as he could see with overarching oaks. He'd never adjusted to the fact that a right turn here was like a left at home. The jeep had to swing out across the gravel road to the far side. *The wrong side.*

The jeep threw a little gravel from its rear wheels as they slid and then straightened.

"I told you," Richard said. "The Arundel place is an old Georgian. That means it's two hundred years old. Heat was from fireplaces, if at all, when it was built. By the time furnace heat came into vogue, the Arundels' fortunes were apparently already in decline. They never managed the retrofit. Place is still beautiful, but it's big, stone and brick, and very cold at night. After dinner we will gather around some fireplace large enough to sit inside of and pretend it's charming, which it is. Charming and cold."

Twenty minutes later they turned left through tall arched stone columns onto a graveled rut, no more than a path. Richard downshifted and worked his way slowly up some two hundred yards of rising hill. As they crested, before them, and across an open lawn, stood a magnificent two-story stone-and-brick house. The front was decorated with a series of ionic columns between each of which were two large windows on both floors. Mullions separated each window into eighteen sections, six high and three wide. The roof was grey slate with smaller dormer windows above each set of windows below. Chimneys appeared out of the roof at each end of the structure as well as one in the middle. The gravel road ended in a circulation some fifty feet in front of the ten marble steps rising to a portico-covered ten-foot-tall double-wide front door. The walkway between the end of the circulation and the front door was trimmed on both sides with a three-foot-tall hedge. The hedge was blooming in small purple flowers.

Sutton sped up the last hundred yards of the path and, braking sharply, threw the wheel hard to the right and slid the jeep neatly to a stop, Milt's door centered exactly at the walkway.

The front door burst open, and a young woman of middle height, dressed in a bright-yellow, flowing cotton frock, ran down the steps two at a time. Richard, despite the impediment of his right leg, jumped out his door, ran around the front of the car, and planted himself, arms akimbo, in the middle of the walkway. The running girl, when she was two steps from him, leaped and threw herself at him. Richard caught her, one arm behind her back, his other scooped below her knees, picked her up fully to his chest, and twirled the two of them in full circles. Their lips were pressed to each other's the whole time.

Milton was delighted at the sight but felt as though he were prying. He took one step back and two sideways to put the hedge between him and the public passion on display. To avert his eyes, he looked up. Standing on the porch was a man old enough to have the thinness, not of youth, but of loss of muscle mass. His full grey beard confirmed what his body suggested: that he was able to hold himself rigidly erect, only when assisted by a black walking stick with what, even from this distance, appeared to be a silver head. He wore tweed trousers and a baggy, dirty-white wool sweater, the neck of which was folded double under his chin.

The old man seemed to examine the scene before him with a cool eye. The hand not holding his stick was braced on the shoulder of a boy of about three, whose thin body and rich black hair marked him as his father's child. The boy wore tweed knickers and an open white shirt. The figure of an even smaller boy clung between his older brother and his grandfather. Those small eyes seemed to share his grandfather's expressionless gaze.

"Milton, Milton. Stop hiding behind the hedge and come over here. Let me introduce my wife."

Milt stepped toward the couple, their arms still wrapped around one another but now both standing.

"Captain Milton McHugh, allow me the pleasure of introducing my wife, Lavinia Guinevere Winifred Arundel Sutton. Captain McHugh, my love, has, as you know from my posts, been my roommate and friend these last two years."

She unwound herself from her husband's arms and took a half step toward him. "Captain McHugh, would you just call me Bini, please? That will make this of becoming friends much easier." Her smile was warm and welcoming.

"If you'll call me Milt, I'll be delighted."

"Of course. Now come and meet my father and my husband's sons."

As they rose up the steps, the old man's expressionless gaze lay upon the three of them. Richard moved, a step in front of his wife and friend, to greet his father-in-law. "Count," Richard addressed the old man, "my thanks."

"For what, Richard?" the old man's voice came out with the roughness of a wood rasp.

"Why, sir, for taking care of my family while I'm unable."

For the first time the old man smiled. It was a look of deep understanding. "Richard, they may be your family, but they are my heirs." He tightened his grip on the shoulder of the young man beside him. "After a thousand years, I must do all I can to ensure my line continues."

No one spoke for a moment until Richard added, "And for allowing me to invite my friend into your home for a few days. Now let me introduce him. Count 'Enree Arundel, allow me to introduce my friend and the US Army's legal liaison to His Majesty's Adjutant General's Corps, Captain Milton McHugh."

"It is my pleasure to host any liaison to His Majesty. Now come in. The day grows late, and you will want to wash up before dinner. Charles will show you to your rooms."

A man so old Milt was surprised he could still be of service appeared in the open doorway even as the old count spoke. "If you'll follow me, sir, I will show you the way."

* * * *

Milt came down the stairs an hour later, dressed in the uniform of his office. When he reached the bottom of the stairs, he could hear voices to his right and followed them. A short corridor opened into what appeared to be a dining hall. At the far end of the room, he saw a fireplace that looked more than six feet tall and perhaps ten feet wide. The fire it contained was quite modest, and the light it threw off was just enough for Milt to see the walls of the room covered with plate armor and heraldic symbols and paraphernalia. Mounted over the high fireplace was the head of the most enormous deer Milt had ever seen. Above that neither the modest light from the fire nor the dimming light from the windows allowed him to see. Between him and the fireplace was a dining table that looked capable of seating twenty or more. Now it was set for just four at one end. The voices came from the space between the table and the hearth.

Milton's footfalls announced him as he walked across the stone pavers. When he rounded the table, he saw a couch, chairs, and a small table. The other three were there. "Count, that head mounted above you is without doubt the largest beast I have ever seen."

The old man sat in an overstuffed leather chair closest to the fire. He was still wearing tweed trousers but had changed his wool sweater for a cotton turtleneck and donned a dark blazer festooned with two rows of brass buttons down the front. "Our red deer are larger than your elk, I believe. This one was my grandfather's prize. Family lore says it was nine feet tall, but I've observed that sometimes beasts grow larger in death than in life."

Milton chuckled. "Still and all a twelve-point buck is a big animal by anyone's count."

"Richard, pour our friend a drink, if you would," the count commanded and then, looking up at Milton, said, "Please, do sit and join us."

Milton sat on the sofa, the other end of which was occupied by Richard, also in uniform. Bini sat in a chair matching her father's and across from him. Richard handed him a crystal tumbler of neat whiskey. Milt swirled it and gave a long sniff. It had a beautifully rich peaty smell. *I'll like this.*

"I presume, Captain McHugh, that you are from the eastern portion of your country," the count observed.

"Really, the Midwest, sir."

"But not the Rockies or West."

"Correct. But how, may I ask, did you come to that?"

The old count gave a hint of a smile. "In the West of your country, that deer above you would be only six points, I believe."

Milt took his tumbler away from his lips and looked very quizzically at the old count. "That's correct, Count. In the West they only count the tines on one side of the rack. East of the Great Plains we count them all."

"And I presume, Captain, that you are a hunter, given your observation."

"Correct again, Count. I grew up on the best hunting grounds on the Mississippi flyway. My father owned a minor piece of what is perhaps the most famous hunting lodge along that portion of the water."

"Do you ride as well, Captain?"

"My father's generation were all horsemen. My generation is better with things driven by motor. But I have some skill with a horse. Not much, but some. Why do you ask, sir?"

"Oh, I'm sure Lavinia and Richard have things to attend to tomorrow. I thought perhaps I could entertain you with a hunt."

"In April, sir. I'm sure I'd enjoy the day, but this is nesting season for the birds at home, and I presume here as well," Milt responded.

"Oh, not birds, Captain. No, no, no, we wouldn't hunt those now. Or deer or any other game. It's time for all of them to raise their young now. No, I was thinking of hunting pests."

"Pests, Count?" Milton was genuinely confused.

"You've not been out of London or you'd know. England is sheep country. Nothing foxes like more than lamb chops. Nothing we English like more than keeping them from it."

"Count Arundel, Lieutenant and Mrs. Sutton, Captain McHugh, dinner is ready." It was the croaking voice of Charles calling them.

The four were seated, the count at the head of the table, his daughter on one side of him, and Milt on the other. Richard was seated next to his wife. Candles, at shoulder height, in stands behind each of them lit the end of the table. But the length of the long table, wood blackened from hundreds of years of smoke, seemed to disappear into the darkness of the unlit hall.

Charles, the only servant Milt had seen, was assisted in bringing the food into the dining room by a pimply-faced teenage boy who laid the platters on a sideboard somewhere in the dark behind them. Charles served.

"Milton, if I remember properly from Richard's letters, you are married." It was Bini who spoke.

Milton's sudden smile showed even in the candlelight. "Yes, Barbara is her name. She was my college love. Married after I got out of law school. That will be five years next month."

"And I believe Richard told me you have children," Bini continued.

Milton's smile grew. "Like you, I have two. But I have one of each. My son, Cavanaugh, is about the age of your elder. Maybe a few months more. And Beulah was born just before I was transferred to London."

"Do you miss them?"

"Very much. More than I can say really."

"Captain." It was the count's voice. "How do you find English women?"

"I've met few, Count, save at work. There are female officers in the office of Army Legal Services and a few clerks. All I meet are kind, polite, efficient."

"You know none socially?" The count was almost probing now.

Milton smiled. "Well, there is your daughter, Count. And she is all I said before as well as beautiful and charming."

"Milton is not telling the entire truth. Milly, at the pub where we eat, has done everything but slip him her key."

"So much for British reserve," the count laughed. It was the first laugh Milton had heard from him.

"Richard, before you get me in trouble and ruin my reputation with your wife, you might add how that's worked out for Milly." Milt made light of it all.

Richard looked at his wife with a false sense of severity. "Milt is right. Poor Milly has been at him for two years now, and he not only doesn't respond; he doesn't even flirt back."

"Perhaps serving wenches are not to the captain's taste." It was the old count's gravelly voice.

"Count, you may be right," Richard said. "Did you ever know a Marquess Palmer?"

The old man seemed to ponder for a moment. "I believe the most recent one died in Dunkirk before they could get them all off the beach. Never knew him, but his father and I met a few times."

"Yes. That's the one. Well, Milt and I were invited as stags to the young princess's ball last year. The son's widow was there. She was so taken with our Yank that she slipped him her card, I believe."

"Richard, you've had too much to drink, I believe. You're beginning to make your friend look naughty."

Richard was holding the mirth back now. "Did I tell any lies, Milton?"

"Only by omission. Please, do finish the tale."

"He tossed it in the trash."

"Thank you, Richard. I don't want your family to think I'm an American rogue. It has been my firm observation over the last two years that you English are entirely proper. You seem a society of sin-free souls, and I'd like to maintain my reputation among such a class of people."

"Milt, Richard and I write almost daily," Bini commented.

Milt nodded. "Yes, I catch him at it almost every night."

"And he writes of you often. Often enough that I felt I knew you before we ever met. And I assure you that I, for one, understand that what I hear from him now is just the teasing that comes with affection. But I also think if you were here longer and came to know us better, you would find that we British are not the saints you seem to make us out to be."

* * * *

Milton walked out the front door of the mansion to face the sun just rising above the forest across the road. His eyes immediately snapped to a specter of vivid red. It was the long coat of Count Arundel blazing almost brighter than the rising sun behind him. The coat extended to his hips. Below it, chalk-white pants extended to his knees where they were tucked into tall black riding boots. He stood holding the reins of a very leggy dun-colored horse in one hand and a short-brimmed, black cap in the other. A second, slightly shorter mare stood tethered to an iron hitching post Milt had not noticed when they had arrived yesterday. Charles stood in the middle of the circulation, holding the leads on three very excited foxhounds.

As Milt walked up the path toward the small gathering, he zippered up the front of his leather flight jacket and pulled the wool collar up toward his ears. "Good morning, Count. Looks like your dogs are all ready to go."

"Good morning to you, Captain. Care for a nip of brandy to warm you before we start?"

Milt nodded and the count offered a silvered pocket flask. As Milt accepted it, the count said. "I see the US Army provides pretty good weather gear. Not exactly traditional for us, but it will serve."

"My apologies, Count. Had I known you were going to make this offer, I'd have tried to find proper dress in London. And I admit I didn't bring a weapon of any sort." He took a nip from the flask and handed it back. "But I do hope I'll not embarrass you, in my current state."

"Not at all, Captain. Not at all. It is only you and I today, so there is no cause for embarrassment on your part. And as for the weapon, I do have a small pistol, but the weapon is really there." The count pointed to the pack of dogs. "They take great joy in it and would be disappointed if we didn't let them finish what they start. Now mount up and we'll be off."

Milton walked to the horse hitched at the post. He looked first at her and, seeing no resistance, ran his hand along the dish of her face. She gave a whinny of acceptance. "Looks like we'll get along fine, girl, if I can adjust to this saddle." Milt raised his foot high, much higher than he expected, to reach the stirrup. He had to work the wide toe of his flight boots into the narrowness of it and, having done so, hoisted himself up. "Count, I've never ridden in a saddle this far forward. To that I'll adjust, but are the stirrups supposed to be this high?"

"However did you colonials corrupt your equipment so?" His smile was something between avuncular and patronizing. "When you sit properly forward over a horse's shoulders instead of trying to break the poor beast's back by putting the pressure of your weight in the middle, you'll find it all works better if you're able to rise up like a proper jockey when needed. Makes jumping one hell of a lot easier, I assure you."

"Jumping?" Milton's look was something between fear and inquisition.

"You've not jumped a horse before?"

"No, sir."

"I thought perhaps as much. Maggie, that's her name"—the count pointed at Milt's mare—"is gentle and a good jumper. A rare combination. When you approach the obstacle to be jumped square on, give Maggie her head. And for God's sake, and your own and hers, whatever you do, don't pull her up short. She'll do what she's supposed to. Your job will be nothing more than staying on. Charles, release the dogs."

The old man did, and the hounds started around to the rear of the house at a trot. The two hunters followed.

"Your Charles is a jack-of-all-trades, I see," Milt observed as the horses rounded the mansion and started down the slope of the meadow behind.

The count gave a small sigh. "Needs to be, I fear. He's really all I've got anymore. Oh, there's a cook, of course, and you may have seen the village boy who helped last night. But times are very hard, I fear. Taxes have become the highest ever. No complaint; it's to support the war effort. Necessary, you know. Honest truth is I'm not certain I'll be able to pass this place on to Bini. Life in England has become very difficult for all of us, but especially men of my class. We'll beat Jerry and win the war, but that won't save the England that has been my life."

In an instant the yipping of the hounds became a steady bay.

"They're on the scent, Captain. Keep up if you can." The old man kicked his horse. It bolted forward and moved from a trot to a gallop in one stride. "Tallyho!" he shouted over his shoulder, and went racing down the hill.

Maggie seemed to break into a gallop even as Milt touched her flanks with his heels. He wanted to reach for the saddle horn to steady himself, but there was nothing in the front of his saddle save Maggie's mane. Milt loosened his grip on the reins and rose up an inch in the stirrups, forcing his toes upward, his heels turned in. The count was no more than three lengths in front of him, the distance remaining constant. He could hear neither the baying of the dogs nor the pounding of Maggie's hooves, so loud was the pounding of his own pulse in his ears. And then he saw the count's red coat come down almost flat against the dun's neck as the horse rose high over a hedge.

Every fiber of Milt's fear commanded him to pull hard on

the reins and stop Maggie before she sent both of them sailing to their doom. *Keep your hands loose and your toes in those stirrups or you will die.*

Maggie rose with the grace of power and practice. Milt held his seat with nothing but willpower. Maggie landed and continued to race forward. It was the most exhilarating thing Milton had ever done. He was full of adrenaline and joy. Only he, Maggie, and maybe God heard his scream of "Whoopee!"

They were over two miles from the mansion when the fox came to bay. By the time Milt dropped down into the small glen bisected by a one-lane dirt road, Arundel was already off his horse and staring at two dogs growling and snarling, trying to force their snouts into a narrow culvert pipe. "McHugh, don't dismount. Cross up over the road. One of the dogs has the other end of the culvert. They seem to think the fox has gone to ground inside the pipe."

Milton touched Maggie's flanks and directed her up the two steps to the top of the road, across, and down the other side. As the count had predicted, one of the dogs was on its belly, its nose forced into the pipe and trying to wedge its shoulders in.

"He's here, Count," Milt called at Arundel's now-capless grey head showing above the road and ten feet away.

"McHugh, you're going to have to snap a leash on that dog to pull him off. I've got one. Step on over and I'll give it to you."

McHugh walked back over the road to Arundel, who already had leather leashes snapped to his dog's collars but was not pulling them off. He handed a leash to Milt.

"McHugh, you'll need to do a couple of things. In order, snap this on the dog's collar but don't pull it off. Find a branch small enough to fit in the culvert and long enough to push through. Get that up to the pipe, pull the dog off, and force the little red lamb killer to me. I'll pull the dogs back enough to give him room to run out. Then we'll see who gets him."

Milt nodded, took the leash from Arundel, and crossed back over the road. It took a few minutes among the trees along the edge of the road to find his long, thin branch. Once he had dragged it back to the end of the pipe, he snapped the leash on the dog and pulled him off with one hand and pushed in the branch with the other. "Here goes!" Milt shouted across the road.

Arundel pulled his two dogs back and waited for a red nose to appear. "He's not coming out, McHugh. Can you push that branch in farther?"

"That's all I've got, Count. And my arm's in up to my shoulder. Let me see if I can find something to push the branch a bit farther."

The roar of a pistol shot reverberated through the culvert pipe and exploded into Milt's ear.

"Got the little red bugger!" came the shout from across the road.

Milt stood up, stuck his palm against his ear, and pumped to stop the ringing. He dusted the twigs and grass off his flight jacket and, holding Maggie's reins in one hand and the dog's leash in the other, walked back across the road to the site of the old grey count holding up a dead fox by the tail in one hand and holding the dogs at bay with the other, a smile, wide enough to straighten his wrinkles, covering his face.

"McHugh, could you grab them? They're too excited to obey."

* * * *

The two men rode slowly across the ground they had covered so quickly less than an hour before, the dogs, who had led them with such vigor, trotting contently behind.

Count Arundel handed the silver flask to the McHugh, who sipped and handed it back. The count screwed the top back on and slid it into his coat pocket. "Captain McHugh, you said something at dinner last night I found interesting. I wonder if you could tell me more about your thoughts on the subject?"

"What was it I said that interested you?"

"You said something to the effect that you found us English 'entirely proper.' A 'society of sin-free souls' was, I believe, your phrase."

"Yes. Something like that," McHugh agreed.

"I'm curious what has led you to that?"

"Gambling and women, I suppose," McHugh said.

"More, dear Captain. Give me more."

"Perhaps I should tell you a bit about my home so you understand the difference I see," Milt offered. "I come from a place that's less than 130 years old. It was wilderness, inhabited only by savages when a man named Thomas Beard showed up in 1818. Before he died, it was not only a civilized place, but a place of wealth and some refinement. But also, a place of considerable freedom and not so many rules. So, vices, especially gambling and to some degree prostitution, were quite out in the open. They still are. Every bar in town has a poker game or two going. We even have slot machines in drugstores. And women—for the evening or even the hour—are not hard to find. Most of those bars with a card game will also have a barmaid or two who are available."

"I'm surprised to hear that prostitution is legal in America," the count replied.

"Oh, there are laws against these things, of course, but they are only enforced against social outcasts and miscreants. If a man is an upright citizen, and that's most of us, he simply isn't charged with acts of moral perfidy. The citizens and the law look the other way. Here in England, I simply don't see anything like that."

Count Arundel rode quietly for a minute before he responded. "You're wrong about us, Captain. As my daughter said to you last night, if you came to know us better, you would find we British are not the saints you make us out to be. You presume that because you do not see sin that it is not present."

McHugh looked into the count's face but said nothing.

"I will make of myself an example for your benefit," said the count after a beat. "You see in me an exemplar of British manners and refinement, I trust. At least I do my very best to present myself to that standard. But I am a man, who like many of my class and generation, has spent the last of dwindling patrimony on fast horses and faster women. Or perhaps it was fast women and slow horses; I'm never quite certain."

"You surprise me, sir," replied McHugh. "All of this gambling and sex, not visible to an outsider—where do you hide it?"

"Gambling is easy. There are bookies everywhere. Bookies in each class of society. Bookies to cater to the trade of their class. I can get a bet down on any horse anywhere with merely a telephone call. As for games of chance, there are, even during the Blitz, private gambling clubs all over London. Sex is perhaps a bit more veiled. Last night you were teased over dinner about both the barmaid, Milly, was that her name?"

"Yes."

"And the other was Lady Palmer. If I understood the teasing properly, you could have had either of them, or both, with very little effort. Or perhaps none at all."

"But they are not prostitutes," Milton objected.

"Do you know Kipling? Rudyard Kipling? He's rather a national poet of ours."

"*He Who Would Be King, The Jungle Book*—yes, I've read him. Lovely stories."

"'The Colonel's Lady and Judy O'Grady are sisters under the skin.' It's a line from one of his poems and perhaps more evocative of our system than yours. You see, had you accepted Milly's offer and ended up in her bed, she'd have not only been pleased to have you leave a shilling or two on her table; eventually she'd have demanded it."

"And Lady Palmer?" Milt asked.

"Lady Palmer, Captain, has much larger financial problems than Milly. She would not have wanted a shilling or two. And she'd not have asked, at least originally. After a few visits, gems would have been appropriate. And then perhaps a discussion of her taxes. Had you been unable to provide, she'd have toyed with you a bit and then moved on until she either found an appropriate companion or lost her position or drank herself to death. In England, Captain, these things happen, just not as publicly as you describe them. We British are entirely proper, but that is a far stretch from being free of sin."

The two men and the hounds rode in silence for a moment with Milton seeming deep in thought. Arundel let him ponder.

Milt finally spoke. "Count, if those behaviors were put on a ballot in an effort to legalize them, would you be in favor of them?"

"Oh, heavens no, McHugh. No, no, no."

Milt turned his head and looked quizzically at his host. "So you admit to indulging in those vices, and you accept that many, perhaps most, Englishmen do as well, but you object to them being public. Isn't that . . . ?" Milt struggled for a word that would not insult his host.

"Hypocritical?" It was Count Arundel who said it. "Of course it is, McHugh."

Now Milt looked stunned. "And you don't object to the hypocrisy?" His voice became shrill as he said it.

The old count chuckled as though being amused by a small child. "McHugh, hypocrisy is underrated. Very underrated."

Milton McHugh did not know if what he was hearing was stupidity, wisdom, or sophistry. The look he gave Arundel was one of stunned disbelief.

Again, the count laughed. This time there was more joy

in it. "Captain, think of all the things you hold dear. Pick one. Pick the most important one. Say perhaps your children. Have you never done something that was in your interest, not theirs? Say, perhaps, lost your temper with one. Maybe even slapped them because you were angry rather than because you wanted to teach them a lesson. I'm not asking if you have. I want no confession. I just want you to engage in a thought experiment. Now if you have ever done that, does it now preclude you from being an advocate for good, loving parenting? Of course, it does not."

McHugh winced, becoming noticeably uncomfortable. The count continued.

"That I have moral weaknesses—women and gambling—does not preclude me from knowing that they are weaknesses and advising my friends or society against them. If it did, then virtually no voice could speak publicly for virtue. It would certainly have eliminated St. Paul as well as St. Augustine and a lot of others. Truth is, if you used the standard you suggest, the only person who could speak to virtue would be he who was perfect. And he has been dead for getting on two thousand years."

CHAPTER 32

May 2, 1945
London, England

"Now we get to see how you do in traffic." Richard pointed through the windshield as the outskirts of London came into view on the horizon.

"So, you decided to wake, did you?" Milt inquired.

"I wasn't sleeping so much as hiding my eyes."

"Been driving since dawn and haven't managed to kill either of us or even dint the US Army's jeep. I'll be able to turn it back into the motor pool no worse for wear," Milt said.

"Well, if you've learned nothing else in England you do seem to have learned to drive on the proper side of the road," Richard continued to tease.

Milt didn't respond. His face took on an aspect of introspective gloom. "I may have learned something even more important than that during my stay. Not sure, though."

His friend sat upright and pulled his barracks cover with its "50 mission crush," straight. "What is that, my thoughtful friend?"

"Richard, while you've been sleeping, I've spent hours thinking about a conversation I had with your father-in-law yesterday."

"Tell," Richard said.

Milt thought for a moment. "I'd rather ask."

"Then ask away." By now Richard was sitting entirely upright and looking at the driver to his right.

"What do you think of your father-in-law?"

Richard lifted his legs up as far as his damaged right one would allow and pulled his back forward from the jeep seat. "He is a self-indulgent patrician of another age, living out his life and what's left of his family fortune in this one."

"Tell me something I don't know." As Milton said it, a small, conspiratorial smile crossed his lips. "Is he wise?"

"Wise? He is smart, Milt. I have to give him that. He does his best to hide it and pretend he is just a self-indulgent old count, but he understands the history and politics of his land. He does feel like England belongs to him. Him and a small coterie of thousand-year-old families. He thinks it's theirs. But I think he feels responsible for it as well. Charles, for instance. His family has lived in the village and worked for the Arundels for longer than anyone knows. He hasn't much left in him, old Charlie. But 'Count Henry' feels responsible for him. He'll let him live in that house and take care of him until one or both of them dies.

"Truth is, Milton, I think the reason the old count has become so self-indulgent is that his station has given him responsibilities but taken away the resources to fulfill them. He's just given up. And perhaps he feels a great guilt about doing so."

Milt stared at the road for a minute, the tallest of the buildings now rising before him. "So you think for all his moral failings, the old man has wisdom?"

"Milt, I asked you to tell me what was on your mind. You said you wanted to ask instead of tell. You asked and I responded as best I could. Now it's my turn to ask. Why this?"

"OK, I'll tell. After Arundel shot the fox, he and I ambled back to the house. And as we rode, a conversation of culture and morals came up. I live in a place where peoples' vices are open, pretty much for all to see. We don't hide that we do things that make us fall short of our own moral code. We publicly gamble and some even womanize. Very little of it is hidden. The count, for all his peccadilloes, makes that sound barbaric. He believes propriety is far better in a society even if that propriety is sheer hypocrisy."

"And why do you care what he thinks, Milton?"

"Maybe he's correct."

"So what?"

"Richard, my family's mandate is far smaller than that of English gentry. But small as it is, my father is truly the arbiter of morals among the ten thousand or so I grew up around. He is called 'state's attorney.' It means he has the power to indict and prosecute. That burden will eventually fall to me."

Richard laughed. "Yours is a far, far larger mandate than the old count's. Perhaps larger than any Arundel's ever was. But titles aren't hereditary in America; why do you think it will fall to you?"

Milton took his eyes off the road and looked over his left shoulder to his friend. "It is my lot. My fate."

"So, you think the Norns, the three Norse goddesses that spun the threads of fate, have spun yours and that is what your life will be?"

"Yes."

"And you are thinking about how you should fulfill your assigned task?"

"Yes."

"Pull over, Milt. I'm going to take you somewhere."

* * * *

Richard pulled into the parking lot at the Tower of London and directed the jeep into a vacant space before the lawn. As both men got out, ravens sitting on the lawn hopped toward them, like so many elegant beggars.

"Myth is that as long as the ravens remain at the Tower, England will stand. Nice thing Hitler didn't seem to know that. Place never took a hit." Richard spoke over his shoulder as he hurried to the gate. "We need to hustle. They'll close in half an hour."

Their military IDs got both through the gate. They entered the ground floor through the armory. Richard scurried through the room filled with racks of edged weapons and suits of hard plate armor standing behind them.

Milt stopped for a moment and let out a low whistle looking at the plate of what was obviously a big man. But it wasn't his size that caught Milt's eye, at least not the size of the man's body, but the size of the metal codpiece between the metal legs. "I think he's bragging."

Richard stopped and turned to look at what had caught Milt's attention. "Henry the Eighth. It may have been large but seemed not able to give him sons. Come on; that's not what we're here for."

At the back of the room, Richard turned up a wide staircase and made his way up two flights of stairs as rapidly as his still-weakened right leg would allow. At the third floor, he turned down one corridor and then another. He proceeded directly to a room, opened the door, and walked in. The room was perhaps twenty or twenty-five feet square. To the right of the door was a large canopied bed draped in heavy curtains. To the left was a fireplace with a limestone mantel. The exterior wall had two windows, which looked down on the courtyard below. The room was furnished with a sofa, several chairs, and a desk.

"What is this place?" Milt asked.

"It's a jail cell."

"If this is a jail cell, it's the most elegant I've ever seen."

"Milt, this particular jail cell was for enemies of the Crown, very rich enemies of the Crown. Its inhabitants would have considered these furnishing meager."

"And why are you showing it to me?"

Sutton nodded his head to the left. "Go look at the fireplace, Milt. The mantel especially."

Milton walked to the cold fireplace. "There is nothing on the mantel."

"Not on it, Milt. At it."

McHugh dropped his eyes and saw what he presumed he was being directed to. There was a gouge in the limestone perhaps three-eighths of an inch deep. It was a scroll of letters extending more than a foot across the face of the mantel. Milt took one step backward to obtain adequate distance to read it.

ARUNDEL. The letters were deeply etched in the mantel.

"Milt, he was here over a year. It appears that every morning he used a knife to carve his name into the place."

"Why?" Milt asked.

"Why did he do it, or why was he here?"

Milt nodded his head. "Yes to both. And add, who is 'he'?"

"He was Thomas Arundel. He was Henry's twelfth great-grandfather. The Arundels were Catholics—still are. Thomas was implicated in the Gunpowder Plot. The more famous conspirator was Guy Fawkes. They were going to blow up the House of Lords and kill James the First. Plot was uncovered and foiled. Fawkes and some of the others were executed—hung, drawn, and quartered. Awful death. Evidence against Arundel was much weaker. He was eventually freed and allowed to go home."

Milt studied the carving for a long time, then walked to the window, put his hands into the small of his back, and looked out. "Why?" he said eventually. "Why did he do . . . that?" Milt turned and pointed to the mantel.

"I presume, Milton, he did it to remind himself every day who he was. Not just his name but his position. What his responsibilities were. Who depended upon him."

Milt turned his eyes to look up at his taller friend. He studied him. "Why are you showing me this, Richard?"

"The Arundels have born great responsibility for a very long time. It takes great wisdom to make anything last a thousand years, Milton."

* * * *

Captain Milton McHugh was seldom called from the offices of His Majesty's Army Legal Services Branch, but the message he received the following day was urgent. He was summoned to the US Army Judge Advocate General's office. He'd grabbed a jeep from the motor pool and driven north immediately. Now he sat in the colonel's waiting room.

The phone on the desk of the duty sergeant next to the colonel's desk buzzed. The sergeant picked it up, said nothing for a moment, and then, "Yes, sir," and set the phone back down.

"He'll see you now, Captain."

Captain McHugh rose, crossed the room, and knocked sharply on the door frame. He received the expected, "Come!" and turned the knob to enter. The colonel stood as he entered, looking at him with a sober expression as he crossed the room. Before he could reach the desk, the colonel pointed at a couch by the window. "Sit, Milton. Please."

Milt redirected to the couch and took a seat as the small, thin colonel, his uniform perfect, walked around from behind his desk. Instead of coming toward him, the colonel turned to his bookcase, where he poured two short glasses of scotch from a decanter he kept there. Only then did he turn to Milton. He handed one glass to Milt and then sat himself into a chair facing the sofa. By now Milt was very curious as to what was about to happen here. What was about to happen to him.

"Captain, I don't know you well enough. Your service to me and Judge Advocate and your country has been away from me. And it has been quiet. Very little heard. And that means you're doing a good job. Calls between His Majesty's Army Legal Service and me are always about trouble. And there has not been sufficient trouble in any of your work, or cases, for me to have ever had the occasion to come to know you well. But this matter is personal. Personal enough I feel the need to attend to it myself. Take a sip of that, Captain."

More than anything else it was the command to drink that scared him. He nipped quickly and set the glass down.

"Milton, it is about your father. He's suffered a stroke. A severe stroke, we hear." The colonel gave his words a moment to sink in.

"My father . . . he's, he's only fifty-nine years old." Milt looked at his commanding officer and struggled to command himself. He said nothing. He knew there was more.

"You are needed at home more than you are needed here. There is a 7:00 p.m. flight to Greenland. You will be on it. From there you will connect to Boston and then Chicago. I understand your home is downstate. From Chicago you can catch a train home."

Milt struggled with his self-control. He picked up the glass and took another sip. "Sir, do you know more of his condition?"

"Only that it was severe and he is in the hospital. The attending physician could give no prognosis but strongly suggested we send you home if possible."

"How much leave am I allowed, sir?"

The colonel shook his head, making the light twinkle across the top of his slicked-back hair. "No leave, Captain. You will be discharged."

"Discharged!" Milt was stunned. "There is a war on, sir."

"Not for long, Captain. We all know that. Since Patton has pushed back the Germans' last attempt at the Bulge, it has been a race to Berlin between us and the Russians. We'll be there within weeks. Your nation has appreciated your service these last three years, but we can now get by without you. The sergeant will have your orders. Your discharge papers will follow as soon as we can get them completed."

"Sir, your kindness is greatly appreciated. There is one thing I would ask if I may."

"What's that, Captain?"

"Can your sergeant get me a line to New York? I'd like to tell my wife myself and arrange for her and my two children to meet me in Chicago."

PART III

THE DECOYS

When the reformers take over, the town dies. They are not the cause.

—David Mamet, *Recessional*

CHAPTER 33

May 1945
Oak Grove Cemetery
Beardstown, Illinois

The McHugh family plot was clearly delineated by low marble fitted stones that were more boundary markers than fence. Inside stood headstones and people, the headstones marking the entry and exit of three, now four, generations of McHughs. The newest, crisply chiseled and freshly polished, read, "LLOYD MCHUGH 1885–1945." The same six men who had carried the casket from the hearse to the freshly opened soil now managed the ropes that slowly lowered this McHugh into his final resting place. At his feet stood a minister, Bible tucked under one arm, his face raised to God and warm sunshine. At the other end of the open grave were a man in the uniform of the US Army and a woman, who appeared beautiful even through the black veil covering her face, holding the hand of a three-year-old boy on one side and an even smaller girl on the other. Beside them stood two older women of medium height, shoulders slumped with grief or age or perhaps both, and one older, but still large-shouldered gentleman, his white wavy hair, in stark contrast to his black suit, blowing gently in the breeze. Hundreds of others surrounded the open grave, some to offer comfort to the family surviving him, some, perhaps, to gloat, but all to pay him honor by their presence.

The minister spoke to God on behalf of the past and the present. After his final "Amen," the crowd started to drift away, first from the margins, as the six took shovels to cover Lloyd McHugh with his final blanket. Toward the center of the gathering a line seemed to form of those who wished to express condolences to those who grieved. The women all hugged the women and children and expressed grief as they could to the two men standing as stoics, holding themselves in check. With the men there were other themes. Many spoke brief stories of how the fallen had touched their lives.

Some, more self-serving if circumspectly so. "Milton, I'm so sorry for your father's untimely passing. He was a fine man, and he served this city well his entire life." And then a pause. "Milton, your father's passing leaves a vacancy in our hearts. It also leaves a vacancy as state's attorney. We'll need a new one. We trust McHughs in Beardstown. You'd serve us all if you'd replace him."

To which Milton nodded, shook their offered hands, and expressed gratitude for their support of his father and their trust in the family name.

Several added more emphasis. "Milton, if I can be of any help at that, just ask." And again, Milton nodded. One or two added a final gesture. Inside the handshake was a folded bill. Milton pulled his hand away without clinging to the paper.

CHAPTER 34

October 30, 1945
Cass County, Illinois

Milt pulled the old Chrysler to a stop in front of the farmhouse. He stepped out and onto the running board, stretched his neck and back, stepped down, and walked toward the screened porch as the big hound came running toward him. Milt bent down on one knee and held one hand forward. "Hello, big guy. Nice to be greeted with such enthusiasm." The dog slowed, sniffed at him, and then laid his muzzle under the outstretched palm. After Milt scratched his ears, the hound escorted him to the porch. By the time he got there, a tall, thin farmer stood in the open door. He was burned brown from the tip of his nose to the open neck of his shirt. Above his cheekbones, his skin was as white as the belly of a fish.

"Evening, sir," Milt offered as he extended his hand. The farmer stepped down to the dirt at the bottom of the two steps his floor was set above the ground, looked momentarily at Milt, and then cautiously accepted the hand.

"Evening yourself, stranger. What you selling?"

Milton chuckled. "Would you believe me if I said, 'Nothing'?"

Now the farmer looked even more skeptical. "Then what is it that brings you to the edge of the county? What do you want?"

"Now we're getting somewhere," Milt said. He reached down to the leggy hound still standing beside him and again scratched behind his ear. "I want three things."

"What are they?"

"I want to introduce myself. My name is Milton McHugh. That's one."

Suddenly the farmer's brown eyes twinkled brightly from behind their white sockets. "You're McHugh, are you? Knew your daddy. Met him a few times. Sorry to hear of your loss."

"Thank you for that, sir."

"Now, what are the other two things you want, McHugh?"

Milt smiled. "To tell you I'm running for state's attorney in Cass County."

"And?" the farmer asked.

"To ask for your vote."

"That's it?" It was the first smile the man had given him. "No pitch."

"No, sir. No pitch. Just to ask for your vote."

The two men watched one another for a moment before the farmer reacted. "Son, you're a McHugh. That's good enough for me and mine."

"I was hoping you'd say that, sir. Thank you. If I win, you know where I'll be anytime you want me. Just like my daddy was."

The two men nodded and shook hands again. Milt turned to walk to his car.

"McHugh," the farmer called, and Milt turned to look. "How many doors you knocking on?"

Milt cocked his head and pondered a moment. "All of them. I left home before the CB&Q moved out. We were about ten thousand people in Beardstown then. Maybe another five thousand in the county. County probably still that size but town is down to maybe seven thousand. Lots of vacant houses. So, let's say twelve thousand people. Maybe three thousand homes. I started in September and have until next Tuesday. I plan to make all of 'em."

"And what you said to me is what you say to all of them? 'My name's Milt McHugh. I'm running for state's attorney. I'd appreciate your vote.'"

"Yes, sir. That's it."

"You'll win."

* * * *

On the evening of Election Day, the three women in Barbara McHugh's kitchen worked with the efficiency that only practiced hands could effect. And while the Wright girls—Beulah and Lilly still thought of themselves as the Wright girls on occasion—had not said it, they were impressed, and a bit surprised, that "the rich girl Milt brought home from New York" was as easy and handy in a kitchen as they. Especially given that the kitchen was itself a work in progress.

"Barbara," Lilly asked, "whatever was it that possessed you and Milt to buy this old place? What a lot of work it will be."

Barbara rose up from the oven, pulling the roast beef out with towels protecting each hand from the heat of the pan. She laid the pan and the towels on the chopping block in the middle of the room and used one forearm to whisk a long strand of unruly brown curls off the side of her face. "Milt said he'd always admired the old Leonard home. Said it was Beardstown's first mansion. I said that makes it what, one hundred years old?" She smiled and the sisters giggled. "You know Milt. He just smiled at me. Daddy had never given us a wedding present, so he said he'd buy it. But he was very clear, 'I'll buy it as is; the rest is up to you two.'"

This time the sisters nodded knowingly.

"You're almost correct about the age, Barbara," Beulah added as she pulled her apron down over her stomach. "It was built in 1840. What do you plan to do to it?"

"Well, I like the floor plan. That won't change save we don't need that huge formal dining room. Not sure what we'll do there, maybe expand Milt's office and the living room. Or maybe a playroom for the kids. But the rest we'll leave alone. I like the tall ceilings both upstairs and down, and I will give Mr. Leonard and his architect that they liked light as much as I do. The windows are great." She picked up a filleting knife from the sideboard and probed deep into the roast. Holding it apart, she nodded to Lilly. "Done enough for you?"

Lilly peered into the open cut of beef at the pink edges and red center. "Perfect, honey. The men will like it. Tell us more about plans for the house."

"Outside will stay the same, save maybe a pergola over the sidewalk from the kitchen door to the garage. We'll repaint all the trim but no more than that. But the inside. Oh my! All new plumbing and fixtures, all new wallpaper, refinish some of the floors and add new carpets to the others. But, Lilly, you tell me about yours. I understand your entire married life you've lived in that huge Chandlerville Road house, and now you're my neighbor. I've gone from small apartment to big house while you've gone from mansion to bungalow. That must have been hard."

As Beulah opened the oven to poke her finger at the rolls, Lilly was ladling cranberry sauce into a large cut-crystal bowl. "Parts of it are much easier, Barbara." She said it without looking up from her work. "Taking care of that huge place was constant work. Not so much work to which I objected but still, work. And the honest truth is Sam and I have struggled from the beginning to keep the lodge open. First it was the depression, and then the railroad moved out. Those things affected the number of hunters who could afford us. It was fun, especially for Sam, but we always struggled to keep our heads above water. When Larry was killed, I think it took the heart out of Sam. Not having anyone to leave it to made the work dismal for him. When it turned out that Larry left us the house his mother left to him, it just seemed like it was meant to be."

Barbara stood, her full height giving all her attention to her mother-in-law's sister. "What will happen to it now, Lilly?"

"Sam sold it pretty cheap and just to the farmer who held the property next to us. He'll try to live there, but it may become cornfields for all we know."

The kitchen filled with the silence of sadness.

"You know what Sam misses most?" It was Lilly who chased the silence away. "You'd guess it was the dogs or the boisterous men who filled the place nights or even the poker games." Lilly stopped and held up her finger bejeweled with a two-carat stone. "Sam was always good at cards. Won this for me one night. A straight against three aces and a $200 dollar pot against this ring. Guy said it was a diamond. I've never told Sam, but I'm pretty certain it's white sapphire instead."

The women all laughed loudly.

"What is it, Lil? You didn't answer your own question."

"He misses the library. We kept what books we had room for, but over his life Sam has become a real reader. He sat most every night in that library with a brandy and a book. I think he may have read every book Vivienne de Villiere had. Well, not those in Greek, Latin, or German, but all the ones in English."

Barbara stood, eyes fixed on Lilly. "I had not heard about the library. I'd have loved to see it. I was an English literature major."

"You and Sam may have more to talk about than you would have thought," Beulah observed.

Barbara clutched the silver handles on the serving tray on which she'd put the roast. "If you are ready, ladies, I'm guessing we have two very hungry men and a couple of children waiting for us."

The women processed out the kitchen door and into the overlarge dining room and were greeted with cheers by all.

* * * *

Sam and Milt sat in Milt's study. The children were in bed, and the women were cleaning up after the feast. Sam sat admiring his brandy snifter, sipping periodically. Milt paced back and forth slowly across the red Bokhara rug on his office floor. And at every turn he looked at his phone.

"Milt, it won't ring tonight no matter how much you look at it. Everyone says you'll win this going away. And even though the polls are closed and the ballots are probably counted in the town, they're not in from the county yet and won't be until late. It will ring in the morning and give you the news you want."

"Promise?" Milt's brown eyes twinkled at him. It was a look that said, "I know that, but I'll worry anyway."

"Promise. But I do have a question."

"Fire away," Milton allowed.

Sam sipped his brandy, studying over the rim the man he had known from a boy. "You promised nothing in your campaign. Just asked people for their vote. Right?"

"Right."

"But there is talk, Milt."

"Talk of what?"

"Of what you will do that you did not promise."

"What's that?" Milt asked, the edges of his mouth turned into a small grin.

"That you plan to stop any hint of vice in Beardstown."

Milt now laughed. "Sam, Uncle Sam, there is not a hint of vice in Beardstown. There is an epidemic of vice in Beardstown."

"So, it's true?"

"For the sake of discussion, let's presume I win. We'll know that tomorrow. Between then and the time I'm sworn in, I'll just be citizen Milton McHugh. Let's further presume for the sake of discussion that what you say, the talk you hear, is true. Do you suppose with a card game in every bar, no less than three gambling establishments in town with roulette, craps, and other games, and over four hundred slot machines in the county, there may be people who object?"

"I do."

"And do you suppose some of them may extend their objections beyond the length of the ballot box?"

"Probably."

"And do you think I might like to shelter my family from those objections as long as possible?"

"Of course."

Milt sat on the front of his desk facing his uncle. "Then I will speak candidly with you as I have with no one else on the understanding that our conversation does not go outside this room. Even to Lilly. Agreed?"

"Agreed. Now would you answer me?" Neither Sam's expression nor his tone of voice had changed since he first asked the question.

"Yes. The first thing I will do is issue notice that all laws of the State of Illinois will be enforced by blind justice across the county. That will start with emphasis on gambling."

Sam sat passively and stared into his brandy as though it were a magic pool. "Your father sometimes quoted a guy named Montesquieu. Something like 'Laws are like statues of certain divinities . . .'"

"'Which on some occasions must be veiled,'" Milt finished the quote for him.

"What's changed?" Sam asked.

Milton grabbed a straight-backed chair with one hand and placed it in front of Sam and then sat on it, looking down at a man he had admired his entire life. "The world has changed, Sam. We are no longer a small town on the edge of civilization able to make our own rules as we go." He paused momentarily and looked up into the darkness. "Well, that's not quite right. We can, I suppose, but we can no longer do it without anyone knowing it is so. We are seen by the world, the entire world, and they will think we are small and little and primitive and beneath them. There will be no way for them to honor us. And if they do not, then they will not come to us. We will stay isolated and become poor."

Sam looked into those intelligent and flaming eyes. He studied them and tried to peer behind them. But all he could see was conviction. He exhaled as though what he was about to say were useless, but he would say it anyhow. "Milt, you have seen much more of the world than I. You have seen and mingled with a wider variety of men than I. But I am not ignorant of men. I meet many men who have wealth and power far beyond what we see here. And that is thanks to Vivienne de Villiere—a whore!" Sam stopped talking to let that word not go by unnoticed. "I am a well-read man. A well-read man who knows his town. Knows it very well. This was the first place of wealth in this part of the frontier. Wealth and culture. And do you know what made it so, Milt?"

Milt said nothing by way of answer, just looked and waited.

Sam continued. "It was made so by liberty. Men who felt free to create the world they wanted and not bother overmuch about the rules of other men. First, they used the river and then they used the rail. But the river traffic dried up. Now the railroad has left. How long has it been since you left? Was it '39?"

Milt nodded.

"When I arrived at the beginning of the century, we were almost fifteen thousand here and with everything prosperity and culture could provide. When the river traffic died, we'd have collapsed but saved ourselves by bringing in the rail.

When you were a boy, we were something over ten thousand but still prosperous. The rail left after you did, in '40, and now we're seven thousand and going broke. If we don't create something new, we will die. Driving liberty out will squeeze out creativity, and there will be no one to come up with the next new thing, the thing that would have saved us. Beardstown may not be a proper place, but it is a free place, and freedom is both more important and valuable than propriety. Free trumps good."

There was a long silence between the men who loved and admired one another but saw the world so differently.

Sam finally dropped his eyes, his face cloaked in sadness. "Milton," he said, his eyes still fixed on the rug at his feet, "you will not, cannot, make the people who live here virtuous. You will merely drive their vices out of sight. You will make us not only wicked but hypocrites as well."

Milt sat staring at the top of a head of wavy white hair. "Uncle, it will not be easy for any of us. But from what I've seen of the world, hiding our vices from public view is the path to acceptance in this new world America has created.

"Uncle, you quoted the Montesquieu phrase my father so loved. Let me quote another Frenchman to you. Guy named La Rochefoucauld. 'Hypocrisy is the tribute vice pays to virtue.' I will lead us into this new world. It will be fine. I promise."

CHAPTER 35

Tuesday, December 11, 1945
Beardstown, Illinois

Sam stepped into the kitchen, his feet in slippers, his body covered in a long, quilted robe. "Morning, honey. Coffee smells good. What's a fellow need to do to get a cup?"

"A smile and a little kiss would be payment enough." Lilly smiled.

He gave her both and turned to the small table by the kitchen window.

Lilly followed right behind him, a cup of steaming coffee in hand. She put it in front of him as soon as he was seated. "The paper on the table. You're not going to like the headline."

Sam unfolded the paper with one hand as he picked up the cup with the other. He blew across the top of the steaming cup and read, "Gambling Ban on Through Cass County."

* * * *

Three stars were visible in the east. Milt saw them as he looked out his front room window. Milt dropped his eyes to the street in time to see a tall, white-haired man walking up State Street toward him, a dog at his heel and a shotgun in his hand. By the time the man turned up his walk, Milton McHugh recognized the figure of his uncle by marriage, Sam Clark, walking toward him. Milt walked to the front door, opened it, and stood framed in the doorway.

"Sam, what brings you out at this time of night?" Milt was doing his best to keep his voice calm.

Sam pointed down at the dog. "Teddy doesn't get as much exercise as he used to. Thought I'd take him for a walk."

Milt smiled. "Uncle, how many dogs named Teddy have you had?"

Sam returned the smile. "All of them."

"Come on in, Sam. Let me pour you a brandy."

"Good of you, Milt, but no thanks. There is something you could do for me, though."

"What's that?"

"Can't adjust to my new mattress so well, and Lilly keeps the house too damn hot. Felt like sleeping outside and on something hard. You willing to offer me a chair and a blanket?"

Milt looked at him without amusement. "You don't really think it's going to get that rough, do you?"

"River rats, Milton. You never can be certain of them. Part of their charm, I suppose."

There was silence.

"Might be best if I took the back door. Wouldn't want your voters to think you let people sleep on your front porch."

Milt remained silent and just looked at the old man. Finally, he nodded. "Walk Teddy around back. I'll meet you there."

Milt was at the kitchen door, his wife standing behind him, when Sam arrived. "Evening, Barbara" was all Sam had to say.

Barbara looked almost amused. "Evening yourself, Sam. Is the West really this wild?"

"Just felt like sleeping outdoors tonight. You'll indulge an old man, won't you?"

She continued to smile. "Only if he promises to stay for breakfast."

Within five minutes Sam was seated in a large wooden Adirondack chair, the blanket across his lap held in place by a 12-gauge pump, a dog curled up at his feet. Inside the house, two very calm adults talked.

"Milt, do you really think someone may try to shoot us?"

"I've told you there were threats. I don't think it will happen, but I do think Sam's right that showing we won't be easy targets may not be a bad idea. We've talked about this. I'll spend my night at the front door. You stay upstairs with the kids. I've seen you shoot. You're good with a shotgun. Keep the 20 gauge with you. If you hear anything down here, don't come down. Just lie down at the top of the stairs and kill whatever walks up. Unless, of course it's me or Uncle Sam." He said it with a smile.

She gave him a kiss, held his head in both her hands, turned, and walked up the stairs, the 20 gauge dangling at arm's length.

* * * *

It was still dark with just the faintest hint of grey against the eastern horizon when Teddy growled. It was a low growl. He didn't move, but his head came up from its curl into his body, and he craned his neck to get a better scent. Then he growled again a bit louder. Sam raised his head and shoved his fedora back farther onto his head. Teddy stood now, his nose pointed toward the sidewalk on Seventh Street. The growl become a low rumble.

"Easy, boy," came the soft command. Sam rocked forward just a touch in his chair, putting both hands on the shotgun, and watched in the direction Teddy pointed. He turned his eyes slightly to one side, knowing night vision was better out the sides of the eyes than front on. No shape appeared, but the value of darkness changed somewhat along the sidewalk as it cleared the neighbor's trees. Sam put a reassuring hand on Teddy's head and watched. The darker mass grew and started to form. And then the darker values became shapes, the shapes of three men and a dog, a very large dog. The shapes moved slowly, turning up the gravel driveway. Sam let them come some ten feet onto the property before he stood pumping one shell into the chamber as he stood. The shapes froze.

"Arresting sound, isn't it, gentlemen?" Sam asked into the darkness.

The light was changing as he watched. They were clear now. He could not make out the faces, but the outlines were clear and becoming defined as the dawn provided more light.

"Who's there?" a voice on the driveway asked. It was a voice that revealed a little fear.

Sam walked down the three steps from the porch, the shotgun held low at his belly but pointing forward.

One of the shapes turned slightly.

"I wouldn't do that if I were you," Sam said softly but loudly enough to be heard across the thirty feet that separated them. "In the dark I might mistake that gesture for a man trying to bring a gun around. Be a terrible mistake on my part, I'm sure, but even worse on yours. You can be certain of that, whoever you are."

Teddy's growl was louder now. The big dog in front of him made the same noise.

"I see you're pointing a gun at me." The voice was trying to show control. "That's all."

Sam walked a few feet closer. "There is a difference between me pointing a gun at you and you pointing one at me. Know what it is?"

There was no answer.

"Well, I'll tell you," Sam said. "You're on private property. My property. Three armed men, in the middle of the night and on private property. Why, if I made a mistake and shot one of you, I'm pretty sure even if the state's attorney wanted to prosecute, and somehow I don't think he would, I'm pretty sure a Cass County jury would understand my mistake."

"Sam, you all right?" The voice came from the lawn behind him.

"Fine, Milton. Just passing the time of day with some early-morning visitors."

Milt walked up beside him, shotgun in hand, and looked at the three men closely. The light was revealing enough now to make them out. "I don't seem to recognize any of you gentlemen. A bit early for a social call, isn't it?"

"We were just off hunting. Didn't mean to wander onto your place. Our mistake."

"Hunting is it?" Sam asked. "Don't think that big, muscular brown-and-black thing with you is a retriever. What is he?"

"Rottweiler" came the answer.

"Doesn't seem real happy, does he?" Sam asked.

"He likes to fight other dogs. He wants to get after yours." There was as much aggression in the answer as in the dog's throaty growl.

"So, you three are off hunting, are you?" Milt looked at the big man with the big dog. "Interesting gun, that pump of yours. I'd like to see it." Milt, holding his shotgun in his left hand, reached out and took it. Sam simply held his at waist height.

"Hey!" the big man shouted, surprised at the quickness of Milt's action.

Milt simply smiled and, propping his gun against his thigh, held the pump in his hands and started pumping. "One," he said as the round in the chamber came out. "Two," he said, and the next shell pumped out. Then again, "Three," and finally,

"Four." "So that's one in the chamber and three in the magazine. Now since Illinois state law says magazines have to be plugged if they are manufactured to hold more than three rounds, it would be a real shame if I pumped this again and another came out."

Milt stared at the big man's angry face and pumped again. "Five." And then he pumped again. "Six. That is a shame, Mr. . . ." Milt halted. "Sorry, I didn't get your name. What is it?"

The anger seething in the man showed all over his face. "Mitchell" was all he said.

"Well, Mr. Mitchell, it is a shame you forgot. Law calls for a loss of the gun, your license, and a fine. That is unless it's a mistake. An honest mistake. Was that what it was, Mr. Mitchell?"

Anger at this humiliation held Mitchell's jaw so tight, he seemed not to be able to open it to speak. Finally, he spat out, "Yes, a mistake."

"What kind of mistake, Mr. Mitchell?"

He seemed about to explode. "An honest mistake!" he finally growled.

Milt threw the empty shotgun straight at Mitchell's chest. He got his hands up before it hit him but barely. The force caused Mitchell to lose his balance and stagger a step backward.

"Well, Mr. Mitchell, get that plug in before you go hunting. And next time you come calling, make it at a decent hour," Milt barked.

The two men with him turned to go, but Mitchell stayed in place. He turned to look at Sam. "That dog of yours, a Chessie? Right?"

"Yep."

"I hear Chessies like to fight. That so?"

Sam just looked at Mitchell and said nothing.

"He's been growling at Bruno like he wants a piece of him. Care to let him try?"

"That would be up to Teddy," Sam responded. He reached down to scratch Teddy behind the ear and then took a half step back.

The two dogs growled and leaped at each other. There was a snarling and tearing as they ripped at one another's muzzles. Teddy suddenly yipped, pulled away, turned, and ran across the lawn, the Rottweiler two steps behind. Mitchell's laugh roared across the lawn. Sam just watched as the Rottweiler caught up with Teddy and leaped for his throat.

It was too quick to see if you didn't know it was coming, but Sam knew it was coming and saw it all. Teddy rolled tail over head in a somersault as though he'd stepped into a gopher hole. And as his head rolled up from the ground, he clamped his teeth onto the Rottweiler's forepaw and continued to roll, snapping the ankle as the bigger beast was thrown to the ground. In a second Bruno lay helpless and whimpering, belly up, Teddy growling at his throat.

"I think you should go get your dog. Seems to need help." Sam said it with the sweetest smile. Then he whistled and shouted, "Teddy, here, boy!"

The curly brown retriever came loping across the yard, responding to the call. Tongue lolling, he sat at Sam's feet, basking in his master's unspoken praise.

The porch door banged closed behind them. Sam and Milt turned, the pre-sunrise light revealing the figure of a tall woman, long, untidy brown curls hanging down the sides of her face. She wore a long bathrobe that appeared a soft blue in such light as was available. A 20-gauge shotgun dangled from the crook of her right arm.

"Gentlemen," Barbara said, her tone surprisingly soft and controlled given the drama of the moment, "you've had a long, and it appears exciting, night. If you'd care for steak and eggs and some strong coffee and you're willing to see a woman with unkempt hair, I can have it on in ten minutes."

The two men turned and without comment made their way up the few steps to the door as Barbara pulled the large Adirondack chair aside. She held the door open as the two men walked into the kitchen. The dog following curled up behind them on the porch in the exact place and posture in which he'd spent the night.

"You two go wash your faces and hands. Coffee will be on the dining room table by the time you get back."

Barbara turned on the gas on the stove and filled the percolator with water and ground coffee. She then opened the refrigerator and pulled out three steaks. Two she threw in a frying pan on the front burner. The third she held in her hand as she walked to the porch door. As she opened it with her free hand, the dog looked up at her with curious eyes. "You, Teddy, did a whole lot more than either of them. You deserve this as much as they." And with that she tossed the steak toward him. Her aim was good. Teddy didn't even have to rise to catch the steak in his jaws. She left him happily chewing as she closed the door.

Ten minutes later the two washed but unshaven men sat, seeming small and almost insignificant in the mass of the overlarge dining room. Barbara, still in her blue chenille robe and slippers, put large plates of steak, eggs, potatoes, and toast in front of each. "Give me just a moment to get my plate and I'll join you. You know I want to hear all."

She returned momentarily with her own plate, the same as the men's sans the steak, in one hand, a large enameled pot steaming the smell of fresh coffee out its spout.

As she sat down, Sam looked at her, his face a combination of sobriety and warmth. "So, tell me, Barbara, how does it feel to be the wife of the Pied Piper?"

Barbara's face broke into a knowing smile.

Milt looked puzzled. "Pied Piper, Sam? What's a Pied Piper and why is that me?"

Sam swallowed what he was chewing, took a long drink from his cup, and still looking at his plate, said, "Old myth, Milt. It's from the Middle Ages, time of the black plague, and about a German river town named . . ." He pondered for a moment.

"Hamelin," Barbara added for him.

"Yes, that's right. He was the Pied Piper of Hamelin. Thank you, Barbara. Town was plagued with rats. Lots of rats. They couldn't seem to get rid of them. So, this piper came along. Seems they called flutes pipes then. The guy was a flute player." Sam stopped and took another drink of his coffee. "Don't know why they called him 'Pied' but that was him. 'The Pied Piper.'

"Learned all this, Milt, by reading one of Vivienne's books. Written, maybe 'compiled' is a better word, by a couple German brothers named Grimm. Don't know who translated it.

"Anyhow, this Pied Piper guy came along and told the town he could get rid of all their rats, their river rats. So they hired him to do it. Offered him a thousand guilders, whatever those were, and he accepted. And then he did it. Cleaned out all the rats. Stood in the middle of the town square and started playing his pipe, and all the rats came to him. Like calling ducks, I guess. Anyhow, he led all the rats right into the river and drowned them all. Cleaned the town of rats, just like he said he would."

Milt had stopped eating and was staring at Sam, his face almost luminescent with joy. "I like that. That will be me. A Pied Piper." His smile grew even broader. "I'll be an American Pied Piper."

Neither Sam nor Barbara joined in his glee.

"Milt, before you get so fixed on that," Sam said, "that's not the end of the story. It didn't work out so well."

"What happened?" Milt was leaning forward now.

"Town refused to pay him," Sam said.

Milt chuckled. "Civil servant's lot, I guess, not to be

appreciated. Politicians are loved and voted in one day and kicked out and forgotten the next. I can live with that."

Sam looked at Barbara, holding up his cup. "May I have another? It's good."

She nodded and poured.

"That's still not the end of the story, Milt. It gets worse," Sam continued.

Milt seemed to finally absorb the sadness showing on their faces.

Sam looked at Barbara. "Barbara, you know the story. Tell our would-be American Pied Piper how this ends."

"When the town refused to pay him," she said slowly, "he went back to the town square and started to play his pipe again. This time the tune was different. All the children of the town came to him. He piped them to the river and, just like the rats, he drowned them all."

Any joy in the room disappeared.

"He cleaned up the town, but the cost was all its youth," Barbara finished.

"And without the children . . ." Sam spoke very slowly. "There was no creative vigor, and without that, the town had no future. Story doesn't say, but I suppose the town died eventually as well."

Sam continued. "You know I've disagreed with you on this. I've said as much and tried to persuade you to let Beardstown be what it is, a place of frontier spirit where the rules are not tight and maybe even ignored but a place that caters to minds that create their own futures and make the futures of others better.

"Milt, you and I have both resorted to quoting Frenchmen who seem to have opinions that support our differing positions. I think if you do this, there may be a French idiom for what you'll be doing to Beardstown. 'Coup de grâce.'"

CHAPTER 36

February 22, 1946
Beardstown, Illinois

"This place looks like a set from a Hopalong Cassidy movie, Paul."

Paul Jensen looked up from the papers he was reviewing to see Milton McHugh entering his jailhouse and approaching the desk he kept at the public entrance. "Milt, it's probably the model. It's what, a hundred and twenty years old now? Still serves to lock up local drunks and give the sheriff a small enough office to keep him humble. To what does that sheriff owe the privilege of this visit today from the state's attorney for Cass County?" Jensen's eyes and tone were cautious. He never liked visits from this young man with a salvation complex. He always wanted some knickknack rule enforced. Some rule that had been on the books forever and never enforced. Never enforced because the citizens of Cass County didn't want it enforced, and Paul Jensen didn't either. "I suppose it's because I haven't busted enough petty criminals this week?" He made no attempt to hide the growing contempt in his voice.

McHugh forced the smile he'd put on his face when

opening the door to stay on his face. He pointed to the wooden chair in front of the sheriff's desk. "Mind if I sit down for this conversation?"

"Suit yourself, Counsellor." Jensen said no more and left it for McHugh to speak.

"You've not done so bad as all that in the last two months, Paul. You seem to have closed all the public card games. I neither see nor hear of any remaining in local saloons. And from what I hear, or don't hear, every bordello that had a sign on the door has been closed. But we have more work to do. Much more work to do before Beardstown looks and acts like a twentieth-century town."

"I'm not sure who you think wants to live in a dry town with no cards or girls. Not the men who live and work here. Of that I'm damn certain."

McHugh kept the smile. "Paul, they voted for me."

"They voted for you because of your name, McHugh. A name that had stood for liberty and growth for two generations. But they didn't vote for your platform because you didn't bother to state one. You hoodwinked all of us."

"Perhaps, Sheriff, perhaps. And you'll get another election in four years, and we'll see what they say then."

The two merely stared at one another, the state's attorney with an insincere smile and the sheriff with an open frown of undisguised contempt.

McHugh finally spoke. "On the way over here, I needed a refill of a prescription. I shopped where I always do, Jensen's Pharmacy. And while they were filling my order, I heard the sound of a slot-machine lever being pulled. I turned and looked and, yep, it's still there. Get it down, Sheriff."

Paul Jensen sat quietly. His posture didn't change, but his expression did. The anger that left his face was replaced by the calm determination of a man who was not about to give in. "You know Tom is my cousin?"

"I know."

"Let me tell you what you don't know. As the population of Beardstown has fallen, so has Tom's business. No surprise there. His revenues had fallen to the point that he was no longer able to pay his son for working after school and then so much he wasn't making rent on the store. That was when he put in the slot machine. It's set to give him a ten percent return. And it brings him enough to keep the pharmacy open. Just enough."

"We agree, Sheriff, that Beardstown does not thrive like it did before the war. And I am not without sympathy to the plight of local merchants like your cousin. But the war changed the world, and my job is to see that Beardstown changes with it." The state's attorney stood up and walked the three steps to the door, where he turned and looked Paul Jensen in the eye. "Take it down, Sheriff."

"And if I won't?"

"Then I'll issue a warrant for your cousin's arrest. Good day, Sheriff." The state's attorney turned and walked out the door.

CHAPTER 37

June 6, 1955
Order of Elks Lodge
Beardstown, Illinois

Milt McHugh found himself facing a panel of five well-dressed, middle-aged men all sitting across a long oak table from him, each with the same stern mien. After a moment of settling into their respective seats and a few clearings of throats, the man in the center chair addressed him directly.

"Mr. McHugh, you are aware, I presume, that the Order of Elks is not a social or business club. We are rather a benevolent organization and as such are dedicated to the service of our community."

"I am. That is why I have asked that my name be considered in nomination for membership."

Again, the speaker cleared his throat. "And we, Mr. McHugh, the panel you see before you, are the membership committee of the Beardstown Chapter of the Order of Elks. As such, it is our function to consider your application. And so, I would ask you, Mr. McHugh, what you have done in the course of your career that would suggest to us that you are 'dedicated to the service of your community'?"

McHugh had known this meeting was for the committee to ask him a few questions before he'd be allowed to join the Elks but envisioned the meeting as a friendly chat. That he was startled at the formality of the occasion showed all over his face, and he knew it. But he was a prosecuting attorney and used to court procedures. He was comfortable on formal, even adversarial, ground and recovered quickly.

"Well, Mr. Chairman, in almost all of the ten years since I returned from the war, I've served this county as state's attorney, charged with enforcing the laws of the State of Illinois. I have served my community by helping to maintain its social and legal standards."

"And have you had success in that endeavor, Mr. McHugh? Have you made Beardstown a better place for all of us to live and prosper?"

"If by that you mean have the laws of the state been properly enforced, I certainly think so. I have firmly put a stop to gambling and other public vice."

"Yes, but have you served your community?"

McHugh was so startled at the suggestion his previous answer hadn't been satisfactory that he did not answer quickly.

"Let me be more specific, Mr. McHugh. Do you think your enforcement of the law has helped your community? Allow me an example. One member of our order was manager of the F.W. Woolworth, just down the street." He nodded toward the river. "My verb tense is intentional. As I'm sure you know there is no more F.W. Woolworth in Beardstown. Our member was not able to find suitable employment in Beardstown to replace his job. He and his entire family have been forced to move to Springfield in order to continue to thrive and prosper."

"Are you suggesting I was responsible for the closure of Woolworth's?"

Several panel members looked at one another, but none spoke. The chair finally replied.

"Mr. McHugh, in your ten years of adjudicating the law, the population of Beardstown has declined by over one thousand souls. It is not just Woolworth's. One of our largest employers, the flour mill and elevator company, Schultz, Baujan & Co., didn't close, but it sold to a Colorado firm that has reduced operations significantly. There are rumors that Wells Lamont Gloves may pull out and Delta Tank as well. It is not unreasonable for an organization whose mission is dedication to the community to ask one of the most powerful and leading figures of the community if he feels he bears any responsibility for the decline."

Milt's instincts were of the courtroom. He wanted to fight back. But not here. Here that was the wrong tactic, and he knew it. He exhaled, collected himself, and responded calmly. "All you say, Mr. Chairman, is of socioeconomic background, so allow me to return in kind your logic. You say there is rumor of Wells Lamont and Delta Tank leaving and taking their jobs with them. Fair enough. But there is also rumor that Oscar Mayer will open a slaughterhouse and bring over two thousand jobs with it. If my administration of justice in Cass County must take blame for firms leaving, then we must also get credit for those we attract." Milt almost let his smile show.

"Mr. Chairman, may I respond to that?" It was the committee member at the far end of the table who spoke.

"Of course," the chairman responded.

The speaker addressed himself to McHugh. "Mr. McHugh, I'm a hog man. Raised them all my life. Know pretty much everything about the industry. And my knowledge tells me that Oscar Mayer will come. This corn country of ours is perfect for raising hogs, and so perfect for slaughtering them. And it will be big. There will be two thousand jobs. And it will be good for me. But you know who it won't be good for, Mr. McHugh?"

The question was rhetorical and Milt knew it, so he didn't speak.

"It will do no good for the working men in Cass County. Oh, Oscar Mayer will hire a few hundred locals when they arrive, but they won't last. Slaughterhouses are miserable places to work. They are kept cold, very cold, because they have to be cold to maintain health standards. It is not only miserable work, Mr. McHugh; manual labor in the cold creates arthritis in the hands. Oscar Mayer knows that the men here don't want to work like that. So, the day they open that plant, or even before, they will have recruiters all over Mexico posting jobs. They will have hundreds, maybe thousands, of migrant workers within the year."

The hog man rose halfway up in his chair, thrust his forefinger and chin toward McHugh, and virtually shouted. "What will you do about that, Mr. McHugh? What will you do about all the creative vitality you ran out of town?"

Milton rose from his chair and deliberately and slowly pushed it back square to the table. "Gentlemen, it is clear I'm not wanted here, so I'll take my leave. And once you get down off your soapbox, maybe you'll realize that my lack of welcome has more to do with the fact that I closed down your penny-ante poker game ten years ago than anything that's happening here in Beardstown."

With that, the state's attorney of Cass County turned and walked out the door.

CHAPTER 38

February 16, 1959
Sangamon Slough, Illinois

The huge birds rose in a slow upward spiral, their long black necks and heads extended stiff as tree branches before their fat grey-brown bodies, the brilliant white triangle, formed from the back of their heads to the bottom of their necks, evoking the image of the chin strap below a palace guard's black beaver hat. But what it really was, was a perfect target. But before the flock leveled off into its elegant "V" flying formation and passed over his blind, Sam lost them. He could see a very vague outline, but it moved and shimmered like a mirage. It was not still enough or clear enough to define a target.

Sam pulled his gun down from his shoulder, broke it open, and used his fingernails to pry the brass of the shell away from the breach. He did it to both barrels and slid the shells back into his vest. "Teddy," he said to the clearly bewildered Chesapeake, "it looks like there will be no hunting today. Or perhaps any other day."

* * * *

Sam walked into the bank, slowly and with a pace that secured each front foot as he landed before he took faith enough in its landing to lift his rear foot and move forward. He knew the lobby and could see well enough to negotiate to the counter. He was unfamiliar with the young face before him and dropped the center of his vision to her name tag. He read and then raised his head and said, "Hello, Elizabeth. I've been coming to this window for over forty years, but I don't believe you and I have ever met. I'm Sam Clark."

"Hello, Mr. Clark. It is my pleasure to meet you. Please, call me Liz. Everyone does. You and I have not met because I'm brand new. Just started this week. How may I help you, Mr. Clark?"

Sam reached into his jacket pocket and fumbled with his fingers until he grasped the edges of the paper he'd shoved in there—a check. A check made to himself in the amount of $100. Handing it to Liz, he said, "You can help me, Liz, by cashing this check. And by telling me your last name so I'll know you next time."

"It's Sinclair, Mr. Clark, Liz Sinclair." She reached for the check he had laid before her, studied it for a moment, and then added with a somewhat impish smile, "'One Hundred Dollars' made out to yourself, Mr. Clark. Don't spend it all in one place."

She reached into her cash drawer and counted out five $20 bills, which she placed before him.

As he laid his palm upon them, Sam responded. "Going to the doctor this afternoon. They get expensive."

"One hundred dollars for a doctor visit in Beardstown. That's hard to believe."

Sam smiled as he scraped the money off the counter and put it in his pocket. "Not here, Liz. Springfield. A specialist. Calls himself an ophthalmologist. And he is expensive."

"Forgive my ignorance. What is an ophthalmologist, Mr. Clark?"

"Eye doctor, eye surgeon really. Saved my eyes once before. Cross your fingers he can do it again."

"Well, it's a nice straight road from here to there, but if you're having eye trouble, watch that intersection where Highway 78 crosses at Virginia."

"Now, Liz, how does a Beardstown girl know that road well enough to know that dangerous crossing in Virginia?"

"I drive it three days a week, Mr. Clark."

"Really, why so often?"

"I'm going to school at Sangamon State in Springfield."

"What do young women study in college today, Liz?"

She gave a short laugh. "Mr. Clark, I don't know about young women, but I'm getting a degree in finance."

"Finance!"

"If I'm going to make a career of banking, Mr. Clark, don't you think I should learn something about how it works?"

* * * *

Sam could hear the splashing of water in the sink behind him as the ophthalmologist washed his hands. He came back from the sink, stepped around his desk, and sat down.

"No reason to be other than direct, Sam. The cataracts have come back. The lenses of both eyes are clouding over again."

"Well, you whipped it last time, Doc. Same thing this time, I presume."

"It's different this time, Sam. You just spent too much time peeking under those goggles, with your head outside the engine compartment and your train roaring at seventy miles per hour, cinders flying up from the roadbed below. Your eyes are just responding now to the damage you did them back when you were working. Seems to happen to most of you railroad types—well, at least the engineers among you."

"That's what you told me last time. And all you did was put me under and scrape the clouded tissue off my lens. Why is this different?"

"Because there is damn near no lens left. If I scrape the cataract, I'll scrape what's left of the lens off as well. You'll come off the operating table stone-blind."

Sam's face was quizzical rather than angry or frightened. "And if you don't do it, how long before I'm stone-blind?"

"Hard to say, Sam. But I'd guess six months, maybe a year."

* * * *

"Honey, what can I get you? Care for another cup of coffee or a single malt?"

"I'll take the single malt."

She was back in two minutes. He could hear Lilly's every step but couldn't see her. In fact, he could not see anything, even the sunshine warming him in his rocker on the front porch. He felt her skirt brush across his knee as she stepped in front of him to set the tumbler of scotch on the table by his right hand.

"What else, my love?"

"Nothing. There is nothing I want now."

Lilly bent forward and kissed his forehead. "If you want anything, shout. If I don't hear from you, I'll be back when dinner comes out of the oven."

Sam merely nodded.

When she returned, Sam's head was still pointed straight forward. The only light in his eyes was from the setting sun. No longer did any come from inside the man.

CHAPTER 39

March 1994
Beardstown State Bank
Beardstown, Illinois

The front doors of the bank were locked and all the lights turned off in the lobby. Liz walked down the rear hall to the door marked "Nigel Hoskins—President" and knocked.

"Come on in, Liz," came the response in a pleasant if somewhat weary tone.

She entered, walked across the room, and took the seat in the chair to which her boss pointed.

"How's my trust officer doing this evening?" Nigel asked.

The question brought a smile. "Your head teller. I'm still not used to the sound of that, but I do like it," she responded.

"You may be the first female trust officer Beardstown State Bank has ever had, but I'm guessing you'll be the best. You've earned it. Worked here since you were a young girl and got a degree in finance along the way. You prepared. And you're not only the most famous employee this bank has ever had; you may be the most famous person in the town."

"Stop. You'll make me blush. One little appearance on the CBS *This Morning* show may make me a bit of a novelty but not famous."

"OK, if it doesn't make you famous, name one other investment club in America besides your Beardstown Business and Professional Women's Investment Club that's ever been on national television."

Liz Sinclair just smiled. "Your trust officer has reconciled all four cash drawers—they were each perfect to the penny. And she has locked all the money in the vault. So the day's work is done. But the president of the Beardstown Business and Professional Women's Investment Club has a favor to ask."

"Fire away."

"Did you listen to the CBS interview?"

"Of course. Everyone in town watched your interview."

"Well, off the air, they asked me a question to which I didn't know the answer."

"Something about average annual return, wasn't it?"

"Yes, average annual return on the club's investments since its founding ten years ago. I'd like to be able to answer that question, and NAIC has an easy way to do it."

"Who, or what, is NAIC?" Nigel asked.

"National Association of Investment Clubs. Our investment club is a member of that association. It's really their push that got us the CBS interview."

"OK, how do they make a very long and tedious series of calculations easy?"

"They have a piece of software that does the calculations. Just plug in the number and it pops out an answer."

"Wow, computers just make lives easier and easier, don't they?"

"One small problem, Nigel."

"What's that?"

"Neither I nor any other member of the club has a computer."

Nigel smiled knowingly. "But Beardstown State Bank does. You have the password and know how to use it, and you'd like to do so?"

Liz just nodded.

"Have at it. If I'm gone before you finish, you know how to lock up."

CHAPTER 40

December 15, 1994
Rockefeller Center
New York City, New York

Phil Donahue stood in the middle of the stage, his mass of white hair perfectly quaffed, his blue eyes simultaneously twinkling the command and charm that were his trademark. He leaned forward toward his audience with the intimacy with which a mere mortal might lean across a dining table to hold the concentration of a guest.

"Ladies and gentlemen, for this next segment we have a truly rare treat to share. We have with us thirteen women of whom you may have heard. They come from a small farm town in the Midwest where they formed an investment club, the Beardstown Business and Professional Women's Investment Club. They each pay twenty-five dollars per month in dues, which the club invests and has been since 1984. With what they describe as sound, common-sense wisdom, these ladies have, over the last ten years, earned a whopping average annual return of twenty-three-point-four percent."

Donahue's audience exploded into applause.

"To you, my audience, let me present 'the Beardstown Ladies'!"

Donahue turned to the wing and joined in the bellowing round of applause as thirteen very well-dressed grey- and white-haired ladies walked out from one wing of the stage, at first showing some sense of startle and perhaps just a bit of shock but seeming to pick up pace and confidence with every stride.

Donahue walked to greet them, shaking hands and pointing his guests to the sofa and chairs the staff had added to make room for so large a number. Donahue took the elbow of the first lady in line. She was of middle height and middle-age, stout, dressed in a navy-blue worsted suit, the fitted skirt of which was hemmed at her knees. The long, unbuttoned lapels of her suit coat revealed a white silk blouse, buttoned up the front and crowned with a strand of pearls at her neck. Her lapel was decorated with a gold, pearl-encrusted broach. Black, short, wide-heeled pumps finished the outfit.

"I've requested Liz Sinclair, president of the investment club, to sit beside me while I ask the questions, the answers to which I think we're all dying to know. Liz, let me start by asking about Beardstown. Tell us about it."

Liz Sinclair, her knees held primly together and turned slightly to face Donahue, sought to open with a tone that made her seem neither a "hayseed from flyover country" nor the cold, hard, bank trust officer that she was. The tone she sought was confident charm. "Well, Phil, first thanks for having us all, and while I know it's bad form to correct my host, I fear I must."

Donahue let his face fall into warm acceptance of the chiding. "How's that, Liz?"

"Well, in your introduction, you said Beardstown was a farm town. It's not; never has been."

"Really?" Now Donahue looked genuinely surprised.

"Phil, all your audience may not understand what I'm about to say, but you're from Ohio, so I think you will. Beardstown is, always has been, a river port. That's a very different thing from a farm town."

Donahue's face immediately registered understanding, and he nodded with a smile. "You're right, Liz. I do know the difference. So, forgive my error, but please explain for those not from the Midwest."

Liz now turned slightly to face more toward her audience. "There is a river bar at Beardstown that, during periods of low water, made the river too low for the old paddle wheelers to pass. So, Beardstown was the end of the line for river traffic in the mid-1800s. It meant we were the center of transportation for the middle of the State of Illinois. Beardstown got rich as a result. A prosperous city of over fifteen thousand before the Civil War." She had Donahue and the audience entranced.

"But you're only about six thousand now. So, what happened?" Donahue pursued.

Sinclair knew how to command a room, and it showed. "After the war, Civil War that is"—she smiled at the audience and got an appreciative giggle—"rail replaced river traffic. Beardstown adjusted to the times. The city funded a bridge construction and got the railroad to put in not only rail but a roundhouse and workshop. So, rail continued to supply great wealth when river traffic went away." She turned to smile charmingly at Donahue. "Phil, neither you nor anyone in this audience would ever guess it, but Beardstown still has the largest number of certified Victorian homes in the state."

Now Donahue looked truly surprised. "How is that possible?"

"Two things, I suppose," Liz continued. "First, when Victorians were all the rage at the end of the nineteenth century, all the rich grain traders in town vied with one another to see who could build the most beautiful one. That and the fact that the Chicago fire burned all their wood structures and they have used brick and stone ever since probably helped."

Again, she got an appreciative laugh from the audience.

"But now?" Donahue continued to query.

"Well, we're like every other small city in the Midwest, I suppose. Our manufacturers seem to have closed, one at a time, and moved away. Last things to go were a refrigeration plant and a glove manufacturer."

"So, what do people do in Beardstown now?" Donahue asked.

Liz smiled again. "It's funny, Phil, but we seem to be back where we started."

"Meaning?"

"One of the very first businesses in Beardstown was a hog-slaughtering plant. Lots of corn grown around us means lots of hogs raised around us. And that's what we've got now. Oscar Mayer had a plant until 1987. They closed then, and Cargill bought it almost immediately. They employ over twenty-two hundred men there."

Phil Donahue was quiet for a moment, almost as though calculating. "Liz, Beardstown is about six thousand souls. Right?"

"Fifty-nine hundred is what the sign outside of town says." She nodded.

"And you have twenty-two hundred employed. Seems like you should be bigger," Donahue observed.

Liz allowed a slow and sardonic smile to cross her face. "We may be, Phil. We may be."

"Now I need you to explain." Donahue looked momentarily like an overmatched host.

"Cargill hires a lot of migrant workers from Mexico. It may be they're living with us and not filling out a census form." She stopped and looked at Donahue, an expression of defiance on her face.

Donahue, back in command, let silence make a point. "And is Beardstown in hard times?"

Liz straightened herself in her chair, her charm and some pride returning. "Perhaps, Phil. We're tough. Still frontiersmen really. We always find a way. We always have."

"And that's what we really want to hear about. Tell us about the club. Its formation, how it works, and how it's doing."

"Let me have Alice answer that, Phil. She's really the one it started with." Liz turned and looked to the woman sitting to her right.

Alice Miner was in her late seventies and looked it. Her abundant white hair was piled on top of her head and pulled into a bun held in place by what may have been long oriental pins or porcupine quills. Her face had lost its battle with gravity, but her dark eyes peered out at the world with an expression that said, "Bring it on." Her voice had the deep rasp of a lifelong smoker.

"You started all this, Alice?" the host asked benignly.

"Yep, wanted to invest a little. Never been in the market." Her low rumble was almost a growl. "Called a couple of brokerage houses in Springfield and didn't hear back. Finally, on the third try, one of them answered. Said he hadn't called back on purpose. Said he'd checked and found out I was a retired med tech with no investments and presumed it wasn't worth his time to answer my questions and teach me to invest for a piddling hundred bucks or so. Pissed me off."

The audience roared.

"So, I called Liz. We went to church together, and she was a banker. I suggested we talk. We met in the basement of the church one Thursday evening. That was in 1983, and we've been meeting there the first Thursday of the month ever since."

The audience seemed to love the crabby, old, take-no-bullshit woman and applauded to prove it.

Donahue was all smiles. "You the oldest, Alice?"

She smiled now. "Naw, I'm a spring chicken. Connie and Meg are in their eighties. Which may be why they decided not to accept your invitation. But I'd never flown before and wasn't going to miss this for nuthin'."

Donahue and his audience laughed with glee and "the Ladies" joined in.

"So, how does it work, Alice?" Donahue asked when the laughter stopped.

"I think I'll let Melody answer that. She's our newest and youngest, so we make her do the work. Keep notes and such."

Donahue looked down the line. "Which one of you ladies is Melody?" he asked.

"I am," and a hand popped up halfway down the line of women.

Melody Brush was clearly the youngest. The youngest by perhaps twenty years, at least fifteen. And she looked the part. Like most of the others, she was dressed in a suit, but hers had pants. The shoes sticking out under them showed three-inch stiletto heels. Her hair was cut in a short "smart" bob, and merely sitting still she exuded an energy that made an observer think she would spring up at any moment. But she merely leaned forward, her hands on her knees and blue eyes sparking intensity at the host.

"Phil, while we were standing waiting to come in, I heard you say we collect twenty-five dollars per month for dues. That's correct. And for the sixteen of us, that gives us forty-eight hundred dollars a year to invest. As Alice said, we meet monthly. And all sixteen of us have an assigned task every month. For instance, we don't just sit on stocks we own. We monitor them. Each of us has a stock or two that is our personal responsibility, and each month we must recommend what the group do with it. To sell it; to hold it; or to buy more."

"And how do you decide that, Melody? Or even before that, decide what to buy?"

"Phil, you've given me a perfect opportunity." Melody seemed almost unable to keep her seat. "Earlier this year, Liz was interviewed. . . ." Melody came to a slow halt and looked at Donahue, a question on her face. "Phil, may I mention a competitive network on your show?"

Donahue laughed loudly. "If you're going to mention Liz's interview on CBS *This Morning,* go ahead. It's part of the story."

The tension eased from her face, and the energy came back. "Liz was interviewed on 'that other show.'" She smiled conspiratorially. "She seemed to be popular, so they called to invite her back. And when they did, they asked . . ." Again, she wound to a halt. "This is Liz's story. Maybe she should tell it."

Donahue looked at Liz Sinclair beside him. "So, tell, Liz," he commanded.

"The producer said they wanted to ask what the average annual return on our portfolio was. Truth was, I didn't know. We liked our returns but had never calculated them. So, I got hold of NAIC. That's National Association of Investment Clubs. We belong. They have helped us all along the way. And I asked their help in doing it. They said they had this software that does just that, but we'd have to buy it. Trouble was, none of us had a computer. So I asked the bank if I could borrow theirs. They agreed. We bought the software from NAIC, installed it in the bank's computer, plugged in the inputs from our books, and ran it."

"AND!" Donahue's sense of showmanship knew this was the moment his audience wanted.

"In the ten years since we started, we had averaged a twenty-three-point-four percent annual return."

The audience gasped.

Donahue looked appropriately impressed. "You're beating the market. Substantially."

"It appears." Liz Sinclair and the ladies were all smiles.

"But there is more to the story. Right, Liz?"

"Yes. A bit overwhelming but yes. After that second interview on CBS, I got a call from the Disney Company."

"And what did they want, Liz?" Donahue's smile was huge.

"They wanted us to write a book telling all that you asked Melody to tell. We were flattered and, of course, agreed."

Again, huge applause from the audience.

"When does it come out, Liz?" That Donahue knew the answer showed on his face.

"Phil, your audience is the first to hear this. And I'm pleased and proud to tell them, and you, that *The Beardstown Ladies' Common-Sense Investment Guide* will be out right after Christmas. January 1995."

Donahue rose, looked at Liz Sinclair and the other ladies, and started to applaud. The whole audience stood and followed. The ladies sat in stunned silence.

When the applause finally stopped and something approaching silence came back to the room, Liz Sinclair put her hands on the arms of her chair and rose. All, including Donahue, watched in silent anticipation of what she was about to do or say.

When she finally had her feet firmly under her, Liz looked at Donahue and said, "Phil, there is one more thing I'd like to say."

Donahue merely nodded.

Liz Sinclair turned away from her host and toward her audience. "We wrote this book to show people you don't have to have a master's degree from Harvard to invest wisely."

The audience and the host rose again in loud applause.

CHAPTER 41

Thursday, February 2, 1995
First Evangelical Lutheran Church Basement
Beardstown, Illinois

Liz Sinclair stood behind the podium, addressing the public audience as much as the club members. "In summary of tonight's meeting, Donna Matthews, who follows Home Depot for the club, has recommended we continue to hold our position. Nancy Wallace, who follows Wal-Mart for the club, has recommended we increase our position, and Kim Smith, who follows Wendy's for the club, has recommended we sell our position. Those recommendations have been agreed upon unanimously by all sixteen members, and the decisions will be implemented.

"To those of you who are not members of the club but are here to observe, we welcome you and hope you have found our meeting and our work productive." A huge, full-toothed smile formed on Liz's face before she added, "And those of you who are here to have your copy of *The Beardstown Ladies' Common-Sense Investment Guide* autographed, just bring it on up, and all or any will be more than delighted to do so.

"This monthly meeting of the Beardstown Business and Professional Women's Investment Club is adjourned."

She struck her gavel soundly to the applause of all in attendance. The friends, family, onlookers from Beardstown and afar rose from the folding chairs and made their way to a long front table where the members smiled, giggled, shook hands, and offered a few kisses to their joy and the enthusiasm of the large crowd of attendees. They also signed a lot of books.

* * * *

Liz Sinclair folded the last of the chairs and put it on the rolling rack with the others as Melody Brush finished rinsing out the large coffeepot.

"You all done, Melody? If not, I'll help you finish. If you are, we can lock up and walk out together."

Melody Brush turned to look at Liz. An expression of sobriety replaced her usual buoyant manner. "I intentionally worked late with you, Liz, so we could talk alone—without the others around."

"Why, Melody, whatever is it?"

"Can we sit for a moment?"

Liz pulled two folding chairs off the rack and flipped them open, facing one another. "Sit, sweetie. Whatever it is, let's talk."

The two women sat almost knee to knee.

"Liz, I know I'm a new member and have not been around since the beginning, so maybe that's it, but something's bothering me. Seems not right."

"What, Melody?"

The younger woman picked up her purse from the floor, reached into it, and pulled out a copy of their national bestseller. She held the cover facing Liz and pointed to the bottom. "Liz, look at what it says all in bold type."

Liz looked at the indicated line on the cover: **23.4% Annual Return**.

"Yeah." It came out very slowly.

"You sure?"

Liz seemed to ponder for a moment as she ran her fingers through her hair. "I think so, Melody. I ran all our books through the software program we purchased from the National Association of Investment Clubs, and that's how it came out. Why?"

"Liz, I've only been a member a few years, not all ten. Maybe there were huge gains in the beginning I wasn't part of. Maybe I don't understand our undistributed gains in the stock we hold. But just going by what I receive from the club, my returns aren't half of that. So, I just wanted to check."

"You may have it in what you've said, Melody. We did have some huge years in the late eighties, and what stocks we're holding are worth more than we paid for them. That could be it."

"Could be?"

Liz's smile became maternal. "Melody, I don't want to leave you with any unanswered questions about the club or the way it's managed. Tell you what. Just to make you feel better, I'll go back into the bank computer and recheck my numbers. I don't want you, or any members, to have doubts. In fact, I'll tell you what. I'm not doing anything this evening and it's still early. I'll go back to the bank and do the work now. Took me hours the first time, but now that I've learned the program, it should be easy."

"Oh, Liz. I don't mean to put you out."

"Don't be silly, Melody. It's my job with the club. I'll do it."

* * * *

At seven thirty the next morning, the two women sat in the corner booth at the Star Café, as far from the entrance as possible.

Liz had picked the spot because the high back of the booth hid their faces from all but the closest passersby. Liz's expression was one of not just composure, but forced composure.

Liz set her mug of black coffee down on the Formica tabletop. She stared intently as though fascinated by the steam rising from it. She picked up her napkin and wiped the water ring below her glass. Then she looked up, her head rising slowly, very slowly.

"I'm sorry I got you out so early, Melody." The words came out studied, almost as though rehearsed.

"Liz, what did you find? Last night I was the worried one. From your tone on the phone and the look on your face, I've managed to transfer all my worries to you."

"In my entire life, nothing has ever pained me so much to say, Melody, but you were right."

"I was right?" Melody said, sounding dismayed. "What did you find?"

"Our twenty-three-point-four percent average annual return—it's wrong. There is no, never was a twenty-three-point-four percent average annual return. It's only about nine percent."

"Liz, I think I'll sip my coffee and let you talk for a while."

Liz looked back down. The steam had stopped rising from her mug. The surface of her coffee was still and smooth. She stared into it as though seeking a glimpse into the future. "After we left the church last night, I went back to the bank and booted up the computer. I brought up the file that held the NAIC software, opened it, and started checking all my inputs number by number. There was a mistake. A very fundamental mistake. It took me hours to find it, but when I did, it was glaring."

She looked up into Melody's big blue eyes. They were focused on nothing but her. Melody didn't speak, so she continued.

"There is an input labeled, 'Income.' It is the place for inputting income from our portfolio. And I'd put quarterly earnings and stock gains there. But I'd also put in all of our monthly dues, seeing them as income to the club. And they may have been that, but it certainly was not income to our portfolio. In other words, I'd effectively entered as income to the club not only our earnings but the dues we used to buy the stock. I've double counted, Melody." The older woman dropped her head into her arms folded onto the table.

Melody remained calm, watching the older woman softly sobbing. She reached into her purse, pulled out a cotton hankie, and holding it in her right hand, reached across the table and lifted Liz's chin with her left. Liz did not resist in any way. Melody dabbed the tears from the corners of her friend's eyes. Then she rose, stepped out of the booth, and slid in beside Liz, wrapping her arms around her as she did. She waited until she could feel her friend's breathing become normal before she spoke. "Liz, you've made a mistake, but it's an honest one. There was no intent to cheat anyone. You've done nothing wrong."

Liz seemed to be jarred back to normal by the younger woman's words. "Perhaps not wrong, Melody, but not the kind of mistake for which a bank trust officer can be forgiven. I've worked very hard to make banking my career. When this comes out, I will no longer be deemed reliable. Perhaps the bank will keep me on, perhaps not, but either way I'll be a laughingstock. My career is finished."

"When this comes out? Wrong conjunction, Liz!"

Liz unwound herself from Melody's arms, straightened her back against the booth, and turned her head to look directly at the younger woman. "What do you mean, 'wrong conjunction'?"

"The word you seek, Liz is 'if.' As in 'if' it comes out."

"Of course it will come out."

"Why? Who on earth has been hurt enough to pursue this? To even think about it? The club members? I don't think so."

Liz shook her head as though clearing cobwebs from her mind. "Melody, that book is a bestseller. Disney says maybe as many as a million copies will be sold. The buyers have been hurt."

"Really? How's that? Have you read that book? Of course you have. You, as much as any of us, wrote it. It's full of very sound advice, even wisdom."

"But it's false advertising, Melody. They've been buying it because they think we beat the market. That's why they're willing to spend $10.95."

"So? Don't think false advertising is a crime in the State of Illinois or America for that matter."

Liz's eyes showed her emotions no longer had control. "How about everyone in Beardstown. We'll be thought of as a bunch of hicks. I've sullied the town, all of us."

"Forgive my profanity in advance, Liz, but bullshit! You've made us look clever. Even if the truth ever comes out, you've made us river rats. Beardstown river rats look like real hustlers again. We've outfoxed the whole New York City financial market. Stop it, Liz!" It came out as a command.

Liz was clearly now seeing her friend with entirely new and respectful eyes. "So, what do we do, Melody?"

"We pay the check, Liz. We walk out of the Star Café, get in our cars, go to work, and act like nothing has happened. But there is one thing, Liz, we don't do. No matter what, we don't say a word of this to anyone. Most especially other club members. If you just have to tell, become a Catholic and tell a priest. But no one besides you and me hears a word of this. They don't need to, and you, despite any desire you may have to tell anyone besides me, do not need to share the burden. When more than two people know a thing, everybody will eventually know it." Melody's face broke into a very large smile. "Coffee's on you this morning, Liz."

CHAPTER 42

May 14, 1997
Approaching Beardstown, Illinois

The Cadillac DeVille rolled south along Highway 67 with a hypnotic smoothness. The afternoon sun beaming into her window had lulled Liz Sinclair almost into a trancelike state as her limo rose up the high bridge across the Illinois River just south of town. The spring beauty of her downstream view, the slowly flowing river trimmed in dense semiaquatic greenery, and all wrapped in the seemingly endless acres of rising corn made her smile big enough that she noticed her reflection in the glass.

"From this view, Beardstown along the river and the railroad bridge in the distance look so beautiful and peaceful." Even Alice Miner's raspy voice sounded contented as she said it. "Driver, at the bottom of the bridge, you'll be able to turn left onto Sixth Street. Take it." This time the voice had its usual commanding quality.

"Yes, ma'am," the driver rumbled back.

The limo slowed and turned from the asphalt highway to the light rhythm of Beardstown's signature brick streets.

The pulsation seemed to shake Liz from her trance. "Driver, continue on Sixth until you get to State, and then turn left."

This time the response was a mere nod of his bald black head. It was enough.

"Not the way to your house or mine, Liz. Where are you taking us?" Alice asked.

"Indulge me, Alice."

The old woman nodded, the turkey waddle below her chin exaggerating the gesture. "Want to be seen, do you!"

Liz looked across the deep black upholstery, a gentle smile on her face. "No, I want to see."

"See what?"

"I was drifting as we rode, and that led to a thought or two. I want to look at Beardstown. I want you to look at it with me."

"Honey, I know every pothole, cracked sidewalk, and broken window in this place."

"You know the trees. Look at the forest with me."

After the driver turned left onto State Street, the homes changed from old single-story, brick structures, some with cars up on blocks in the front yard, to even older, but still-elegant two-story homes with balconies, window alcoves, and covered entries whose grace, marred by the ubiquitous window air-conditioning units, untrimmed shrubbery, and basketball hoops nailed over garage doors, remained.

"Turn right again on Third Street. Follow it all the way out of town past the park."

Liz's instruction was affirmed with another nod.

They passed commercial buildings, a third of which were vacant, with sun-bleached "For Rent" signs tacked to doors or taped to windows. As they continued east, the character of the neighborhood changed again to residential, cheap residential, a double-wide trailer parked on a concrete pad upon which a brick cottage once rested. The street curved as it ran through the large municipal park whose far boundary was the thirty-foot slope of a dirt levee holding back the Illinois River.

"Driver, slow a bit. At the curve just in front of you, you'll see a small asphalt ramp leading up to the levee. It's a very hard left. Take it."

As instructed, the driver slowed enough to make a left of about 120 degrees and rolled gently up the embankment. Once they were atop the levee, the asphalt strip continued. The paving had been painted long ago with large white arrows pointing in their direction. The arrows were faded now, but their point was still made: "This levee road isn't wide enough to pass. The shoulders are too steep to move to one side, so the traffic must be in just one direction."

To the right and below them lay the spring beauty of the Sangamon Slough opening slowly out onto the Illinois River's main channel. But between here and there, cattails danced five feet high in a soft breeze with the colorful markings of red-winged blackbirds darting among them. To the left, the levee was high enough for them to secure a view across the park and into the city, become a hamlet, which this river had made.

"The levee road will run about a mile and then ramp back down. Stop at the top of the ramp. Between here and there, go slow."

"Ma'am, I will. This view is far too beautiful to pass quickly."

"Depends on which way you look, I suppose." It was the first thing approaching conversation she'd had with the man in the four hours since he'd picked them up, right on time, at O'Hare Airport.

In less than ten minutes the road turned sharply to the left and back down to street level. The driver stopped at the top of the curve.

"Did you see any of the forest, Alice?"

The older woman turned to face her younger companion,

a look of sobriety, if not sadness, on her face. "Maybe I did, honey."

"Tell me what you saw."

"You had him stop here on purpose. The symbol of the rise and fall of Beardstown right in front of me. Those massive grain elevators coming out of the ground below us and rising to tower over this levee and the town. And they are by the water because it was by the water that our grain flowed to St. Louis and New Orleans and the world. And after that by rail. And when I look closely, I can see the rail running between the elevators. Rusted rail with not a car on it. All four elevators not only abandoned but their rooves and sections of their walls caved in. And worst of all, nobody even has the money to tear them down. We've just put a cyclone fence around them to keep young boys from playing in there and getting hurt. 'Attractive nuisance' is, I believe, what suit-happy attorneys call it."

"Anything else, Alice? Tell me more of what you saw."

"Well, every house in town, big or small, is run-down. And so many shops closed. That's about it, Liz. Is that the decaying forest you wanted me to see?"

Liz nodded her head. "But you didn't mention the part that makes me saddest. Even more than these abandoned grain elevators." She pointed out the window at the decaying hulks before them.

"What's that, honey?" Alice asked.

"The grass. Grass grows between the bricks in our streets. We don't even have enough traffic in our streets to keep the grass away."

Both women became silent. Just pondering.

"Why, Alice? Why?" Liz asked. "You and I are rich. Rich. In the last five years, we've been interviewed by ABC, NBC, and CBS. We've published a book every year. We've got the best-selling DVD in the history of America in *Cooking Up Profits on Wall Street*; we've been interviewed by the *New York Times*,

US News and World Report, Kiplinger's Personal Finance, Modern Maturity, Working Women. You name it, they wanted to talk to us. And with every conversation, we sold more stuff. It wasn't that hard. It wasn't that goddamn hard. What the hell is wrong with this place?"

Alice Miner looked at the woman beside her, who was truly distraught and unable to answer her own question. "Oh, honey, it's not us. People, young men, go to places where there is opportunity. And they take their young women with them. Industry moves to big cities; finance moves to big cities. Beardstown just has no opportunities for them, so they go. They leave, and they take their youth and their vigor with them. There's just nothing here for them."

Liz Sinclair shook her head. Shook it violently, her grey hair coming loose and flying around her face. "No! I don't believe it. We have all sorts of opportunities here. First, we have what we've always had. We have the river. Sure, there's no commercial traffic, but it's the best hunting and fishing in the state. This"—she pointed out the window to the river—"is still the best flyway in the state. Maybe on the whole Mississippi drainage. And the sheer beauty of it. America is rich, filthy rich, and Americans spend more money on sport and travel than ever. But not to go to little shitholes. Look at our marina—a dump— and our historic Park Hotel has become a biker bar. And history. My God, we have the only courtroom where Abe Lincoln was the attorney in a famous criminal trial. What do we use it for? To pay parking tickets. Fucking parking tickets."

"The answer to your 'why' question, ma'am . . ." The unexpected intrusion came from the driver.

Both women's heads snapped forward like a piece of furniture had spoken.

"The answer, ma'am, is 'animal spirit,'" the furniture spoke again.

He was a man who was so black his skin glimmered purple

in the sunlight pouring through his windshield. His skin color made the white of his teeth gleam as though lit by a pencil spotlight.

"What?" Liz seemed totally distraught. "What are you talking about?"

"Animal spirit is the term an economist, a Brit named Keynes, used to explain the force that drives men to take risks, especially in business. You two ladies have it." He turned and pointed out the window. "This town does not."

Both women looked at him like he was an alien.

Liz recovered herself first. "Sir, may I ask how you came to know about John Maynard Keynes?"

"Ma'am, I don't work for someone else. I own this limousine. It's my business. I paid $40,000 for it. Black men driving cabs don't have a lot of credit with Cadillac dealers or banks. Took me a number of years to save enough. But I knew when I did, I could make it. Disney called me and asked me to collect you two when you came in from LA. They use me a lot. I know about risk. I know about animal spirit."

Both women now looked at him with newfound respect.

"But you didn't answer my question," Liz said. "How did you come to know about Keynes?"

The driver's face became one large smile of pride. "The reason it took so long to save the money is I—my wife and I really—had to save for our son's education first. The University of Chicago isn't cheap even with a little scholarship help and him living at home. From what he tells me, the university talks a lot about Keynes. He says they don't much agree with the man, but his name keeps getting into the conversation."

"You know, sir, I think you may be onto something." It was Alice's deep, gravelly voice that responded. "I was born here. Promise not to tell, but that was 1918." Alice managed to look coquettish as she said it. "When I was a girl, this town was wide open. Truth is it was a little wicked, naughty at least. Oh, we all acted with great propriety, but people pretty much did as they wanted. 'A free place,' my father called it. Ministers often preached for public morals, still do, but their sermons aside, much was allowed. Sometime after the war, that all changed. I was in my later thirties when Beardstown had a great rush of embarrassment about our history. We got pretty good after that. Good but poor."

Liz looked across the limo seat at her friend. "Are we good, Alice? Am I still good?"

CHAPTER 43

February 8, 1998
Beardstown, Illinois

"Bull Marketing: Debunking the Myth of the Beardstown Ladies and Their Spectacular Stock Market Gains" by Shane Tritsch, *Chicago*.

Milt folded the Sunday supplement of the *Chicago Tribune* and laid it on the reading table, took off his wire-framed glasses, and set them on top of the paper, shut off the lamp, rubbed his eyes, and sat in stillness for a moment. He spoke quietly to himself. "So that's how they did it. I'll be damned."

CHAPTER 44

May 14, 1998
First Evangelical Lutheran Church Basement
Beardstown, Illinois

"Melody, now that we're all here, would you please lock the door?"

Melody Brush, who had seated herself by the door, rose immediately, stepped to it, and threw the bolt.

"Ladies, I'd sent each of you a note saying that tonight's meeting of the Beardstown Business and Professional Women's Investment Club would be members only. I also appreciate your coming an hour before the regular scheduled meeting time, but I could not think of any other way to ensure we had no guests here who might be difficult to remove—like the press. Melody has hung a sign outside saying, 'No BB&PWIC meeting tonight,' but we may still get some who try to enter, which is why I've asked her to lock the door."

Liz Sinclair did not look her usual professional self tonight. She wore a cotton dress with a full skirt and a top closed at the neck with a wide collar with lace along the edges. She was also wearing a printed apron with frills along the hem and straps. Her grey hair was pulled into a bun at the top of her head.

"We're having a rough year. Not from our investments or with our royalties from Disney on books and DVDs. We're having a very rough year in the press. We've tried to counter. As you know, I wrote an open letter of apology and said we were truly sorry."

"Melody"—she nodded to the youngest member of the group standing in the back of the room dressed in jeans, flat-bottom work boots, and what appeared to be one of her husband's denim shirts—"also had a nice way of saying it. Said we were naïve old ladies."

The group gave an appreciative giggle, given that among them, Melody was clearly not an old lady. Melody made a mock curtsy. That the members of the beleaguered club still had humor was made abundantly clear.

"Some papers had harsh things to say," Liz continued. "Several said we were frauds, and one even said we should be jailed."

"But here's the one I suspect you've not heard and which is why I ask that we don't let our usual crowd of listeners in. There is a New York group that is trying to put together a suit."

It drew a gasp but no other comment.

"I think this brings us to a point where we all need to talk seriously about the future. I've talked to counsel, and it looks like the suit will be against Disney. We, ladies, are not worth the time and effort for a group of rich tort lawyers to blow to hell. Disney is. So, they'll point the big guns at Disney—I think. But as you all know, Disney has dropped 'the Beardstown Ladies' as a client. If they do point those big New York guns at us, we may have to be ready to defend ourselves.

"One other thing that hurts me to bring up but I think needs to be said. Over the last five years, each of us has made a lot of money. But it's been off publishing revenues and speaking fees. Our investment returns have continued, but they are insignificant as compared to the other. For some of us, this income has been life-changing. But I think, if any of you have plans that include future cash flows like we've had since our first book came out, you have to reconsider them. We're now about as rich as we're ever going to get."

CHAPTER 45

April 1999
Cass County Courthouse
Virginia, Illinois

The old man wore a tweed three-piece suit, the half–Windsor knot of his paisley necktie kept neatly in place with the aid of a gold pin holding the collar of his white broadcloth shirt tightly against it. His pace was slow, his very erect posture assisted with the use of a black-lacquered walking stick, its silver handle held in his still-firm grip. The lack of grey in his unruly brown hair seemed to belie the message sent by the face of a man in his mideighties. He took the broad steps rising to the courthouse with measured dignity. Upon entering, he looked both ways along the marbled hallways leading from the small rotunda, decided on the one to his right, continued until he saw the door labeled "John Dahlem, State's Attorney," and entered.

The receptionist, a middle-aged woman with a face bereft of any truly distinguishing features, greeted him with the same professional smile that she'd used a hundred times yesterday and would use a hundred times today and each day into her future as far as it was given her to see. "May I help you, sir?"

"Would you tell Mr. Dahlem that Milton McHugh is here to see him? I have a ten-o'clock appointment."

"Of course, Mr. McHugh. If you'll take a seat"—she pointed to a row of wooden chairs with cane bottoms and backs placed against the far wall—"I'll tell him you're here. He's usually quite punctual."

The receptionist let herself into the only other door off the reception area without knocking and returned in less than a minute. "He'll see you now, Mr. McHugh."

Milton rose slowly, took a moment to balance on the balls of his feet, placed his walking stick before him, raised his back to its full height, and stepped through the door that she held open.

McHugh was met by a portly man in his midfifties, thinning hair combed straight back, jowly cheeks almost aglow as he stepped around his desk and extended a pudgy hand, the palm of which was as white and soft as cold cream.

McHugh took the hand. "It is very nice of you to make time for me in what I know is a busy schedule, Mr. Dahlem."

"Mr. McHugh, it is indeed my delight to meet you. Your reputation precedes you, you know. Merely meeting you fills a hole in my professional career. Please, have a seat." Dahlem pointed to a red-leather-clad wingback chair in front of his desk.

McHugh lowered himself into it as Dahlem walked back around his big desk and sat in his overstuffed high-backed chair. "Mr. McHugh, I started my practice in Springfield in 1960 and didn't move it to Cass County until the early seventies. By then you were no longer in politics or even regular practice. So, it has never been my pleasure, until this moment, to meet perhaps the most distinguished man to ever occupy this chair." Dahlem half rose and pointed to the seat below him.

McHugh offered a reserved smile. "I'm not certain it's the same chair, and I'm absolutely certain I'm not that distinguished."

Dahlem chuckled. "Let's agree to disagree on that part." When McHugh offered no reply, Dahlem cleared his throat. "How may I serve you, Mr. McHugh?"

"I'm here to see what you will tell me about the intentions of this office toward a group of women in Beardstown who have come to be known as, perhaps reviled as, 'the Beardstown Ladies.'"

Dahlem looked startled for a moment, and when he recovered, his expression of bonhomie was replaced by one of professional coolness. "That is a very interesting subject. And I will answer you, but before I do, may I ask the nature of your interest?"

"I should like to know if you intend to indict them on any criminal charge."

The state's attorney appeared shocked at the directness of McHugh's answer.

"In honor of your stature in the community, I will be as direct in my answer as you were in your question." McHugh nodded and the state's attorney continued. "As you know, a group of tort attorneys in New York has formed a class action law suit against Disney, alleging false advertising."

McHugh nodded again. "The class is suing the publisher, not the ladies. And a New York court has dismissed the suit."

"And San Francisco Superior Court has picked it up and allowed it to proceed," Dahlem countered.

McHugh smiled for the first time in their discussion. "California courts will accept any suit no matter how flimsy," he jollied. "And false advertising is not a crime."

"But fraud is," Dahlem almost barked. He stopped, collected and composed himself, and then studied McHugh closely, sliding a pen up and down between the fingers of one hand the whole time. It was as though he were suddenly seeing

McHugh in a completely new light. "Counsellor, are you representing the Beardstown Ladies?"

"No," McHugh responded. "They do not even know I'm here. But I don't wish to fly false colors. If it becomes necessary for them to seek counsel, and if I am asked, I will."

Dahlem's look was still cautious. He nodded finally, his expression showing he had decided to continue. "Let's explore this together for a moment, Mr. McHugh." Dahlem opened one of the side drawers of his desk and pulled out a small device perhaps three inches wide and five long and less than half an inch deep that he slid from its black plastic case. "You familiar with these, Mr. McHugh?" He held the device up. It displayed rows and lines of keys with various symbols on each and a small display window at the top.

McHugh leaned forward, studied what he was being shown, and finally shook his head. "Can't say I am."

"This tiny little thing, Mr. McHugh, is a financial calculator. Texas Instruments came up with them just a couple of years ago. Do in the palm of my hand financial calculations that used to take a desktop computer to do. All I have to do is put in some numbers. Say, forty-eight hundred dollars invested—that would be what sixteen ladies contributing twenty-five dollars per month for twelve months would have to invest each year."

Dahlem tapped several buttons on the calculator.

"Now suppose we do that for ten years."

He made a few more taps.

"And suppose we plug in twenty-three-point-four percent earned."

He tapped yet again.

"And then we query for what that's all worth in ten years. Know what the answer is?"

McHugh just looked at him placidly.

"That stream of investment at that return per year over

that time comes out to be worth $186,000. Now let me change one little thing in that calculation. Let's suppose they only got a nine-point-one percent return. That's what the Price Waterhouse audit being used in the suit says the actual return was."

Dahlem tapped a few more keys.

"The new answer is $84,743. These women sold almost eight hundred thousand books touting themselves as financial gurus. You suppose a jury will believe they didn't know $186,000 from $85,000?"

McHugh looked very calm. "As long as we're supposing, let's suppose some more, Counsellor. Let's suppose that you are looking at a Cass County jury box and they are looking at sixteen old women in the dock. Women who are dressed in print dresses, aprons, and their grey and white hair up in buns. And suppose one of them goes on the stand and says something like, 'None of us owned a computer. Knew nothing about them. We bought this software to answer a question that we'd been asked to prepare for in an interview. I borrowed a computer at work and loaded it with the software and the information from our books, and that's the answer it gave. I'm terribly sorry if it was wrong, but I assure you I knew no better.'

"And then maybe she even looks at the jury, a most sincere expression and her grey hair falling in wisps along her cheeks, and says, 'I don't know how many of you have computers or have ever loaded software, but doing it right isn't easy. I and all the ladies,' she says, pointing to the row of blue-hairs sitting beside her, 'we are terribly sorry for any of you we've hurt.'"

By now Dahlem was smiling. "I had heard you were very good, Mr. McHugh. You are. Very good, Mr. McHugh, very good. I see now why you did so well. But let's look at another set of facts. That $186,000 return the ladies made included their investment. So, what they really made from their investments was about $138,000. You divide that by sixteen, and each of them made something like $8,600 over ten years. That on the club's investments. But you know what they made on books and DVDs?"

Again, a very calm Milton McHugh just shook his head.

"I'm not certain either, Mr. McHugh, but I can come close on one of the five books. They sold 770,000 copies of their first book. It sold for $10.95 a copy. That's a bit more than $8,400,000 gross. I've checked with a publisher friend of mine, and while I don't have their contract, industry standard for an unknown would be something like fifteen percent of the gross—originally. As they sold more, it might rise to twenty percent. But let's stay at fifteen percent. That means the club's share, from just that one book, would be about $1,260,000 or maybe $80,000 each. That's serious fraud, Mr. McHugh."

McHugh smiled. "We're supposing a lot here, Mr. Dahlem, but let me suppose just a little more. First, assuming it is a fraud, tell me how many people in Cass County were frauded? How many here bought that book? I know a few, and not one of them will give it away. Most went to a club meeting and had it autographed. More after the *Chicago* article than before.

"Let me keep supposing. Cass County has been on the decline since after the war, some fifty years now. We have lost tremendous wealth and what prestige we may have had. We're now 'Flyover County.' It's been a long time since we've had a win, since anyone has made it big, since anyone has put Beardstown, Illinois, in the news. Do you suppose that jury sees these Beardstown Ladies as John Dillinger or Robin Hood?

"And my very last suppose. Yours is an elective office. My last question applies not just to some hypothetical jury but to your very real voters. What do you suppose they would think of such a prosecution? And the prosecutor who brought it?"

Dahlem pushed back into his large chair and stared up at

the ceiling. He did nothing but that for a long time. Eventually, he looked back down and sat far enough forward in his chair that his back was no longer against it. "Mr. McHugh, I've heard a story about you. I wonder if you can tell me the truth of it."

For the first time in their meeting, Milton McHugh had to work to control his bland expression. But he did. "Ask and we'll see."

"I've heard that for your entire professional life you have wanted membership in the Beardstown Lodge of the Order of Elks. And that never in the last fifty years have they been willing to invite you in. Is that true?"

McHugh did his best not to let it show that he was both surprised and just a little hurt by the opening of a very old wound. "It is" was all he said.

"Why is that, Mr. McHugh? Why won't they let you in? Is it because, in 1948, you closed down their penny-ante poker game? That's how the story is told."

"If that's how the story is told, then it's told correctly."

Again, Dahlem pondered, but this time he stared into Milton McHugh's eyes the whole time as though attempting to discover some deep truth buried in the man. "Mr. McHugh, you are a legend in Cass County. You are the one who came home after saving the world of democracy to save your hometown from vice. You cleaned out all the river rats. Oh, there was a price to pay—stories say your life was threatened as well as those of your wife and children. One version says you and your uncle sat up nights at the front and back doors with shotguns to make certain that didn't happen. Many in Beardstown hated you for it. Hated the change and never forgave you for it. You sacrificed what most of us hold most dear, friends and fellowship, to drag your city, kicking and screaming, into goodness and virtue. You sacrificed all that, and now fifty years later, you change your mind and want to defend an entire cult of fraud. Why? Why would you do that?"

McHugh placed his walking stick firmly between his legs, pushed against it, his weight resting on the stick, his chin thrust forward, and his eyes burning back at the state's attorney.

"Because . . ." McHugh halted for a moment and swallowed. "I was wrong!"

HISTORICAL NOTES

1. In October 1999, the class action suit against Hyperion/ Buena Vista/Disney was settled. The settlement called for each one of the 770,000 purchasers of *The Beardstown Ladies' Common-Sense Investment Guide* to receive any book in the Hyperion catalog for free. In addition, Hyperion paid $1,400,000 in legal fees—presumably most of it to attorneys. "The Ladies" admitted to no wrongdoing.
2. "The Ladies" were never criminally prosecuted.

ABOUT THE AUTHOR

Foster lives and writes overlooking R.A.T. Beach in Torrance, California. He is the author of the five-star reviewed *Alpha Male*, the Pushcart Prize–nominated *Non Semper Fidelis*, and the first two books in the American Trilogy series, *A Panther Crosses Over* and *Beardstown*.